MARRIAGE MIRACLE IN SWALLOWBROOK

BY

ABIGAIL GORDON

For Stephen and Judith who generously gave me their time and their hospitality while showing me Lakeland

First published in Great Britain 2012
by Mills & Boon, an imprint of Harlequin (UK) Limited.
Harlequin (UK) Limited, Eton House, 18-24 Paradise Road,
Richmond, Surrey TW9 1SR

ISBN: 978 0 263 89789 0

Harlequin (UK) policy is to use papers that are natural, renewable and recyclable products and made from wood grown in sustainable forests. The logging and manufacturing process conform to the legal environmental regulations of the country of origin.

Printed and bound in Spain
by Blackprint CPI, Barcelona

*

MARRIAGE MIRACLE IN SWALLOWBROOK

BY

ABIGAIL GORDON

CELEBRITY IN BRAXTON FALLS

BY

JUDY CAMPBELL

MILLS & BOON

Recent titles by Abigail Gordon:

SPRING PROPOSAL IN SWALLOWBROOK**
SWALLOWBROOK'S WINTER BRIDE**
SUMMER SEASIDE WEDDING†
VILLIAGE NURSE'S HAPPY-EVER-AFTER†
WEDDING BELLS FOR THE VILLAGE NURSE†
CHRISTMAS IN BLUEBELL COVE†

***The Doctors of Swallowbrook Farm*
†*Bluebell Cove*

Recent titles by Judy Campbell:

REUNITED: A MIRACLE MARRIAGE
FROM SINGLE MUM TO LADY
HIRED: GP AND WIFE
THE GP'S MARRIAGE WISH

Dear Reader

Once again we meet between the pages of one of my books. This time it is the third story out of four about *The Doctors of Swallowbrook Farm*, and here we meet Gabriel, a doctor who has a great sense of dedication towards his profession, and Laura, his wife, who throws their lives into chaos quite unintentionally.

Their story is about the love and loyalty that binds them together at a time of great unrest in their lives, and how the strength of it finally brings back the happiness that they thought they had lost. I do hope that you will enjoy meeting them.

With very best regards

Abigail Gordon

Abigail Gordon loves to write about the fascinating combination of medicine and romance from her home in a Cheshire village. She is active in local affairs, and is even called upon to write the script for the annual village pantomime! Her eldest son is a hospital manager, and helps with all her medical research. As part of a close-knit family, she treasures having two of her sons living close by, and the third one not too far away. This also gives her the added pleasure of being able to watch her delightful grandchildren growing up.

CHAPTER ONE

A SUMMER sun was shining when Laura Armitage drew back the curtains in the master bedroom of the house that her uncle had given her. Its mellow golden rays were spreading far and wide from the ripening corn in distant fields to the shores of the tree-lined lakeside nearby, but to the woman at the window the brightness of the morning was blotted out by dark uncertainties about the future.

A month ago she and her children had moved into a spacious old house that she'd had renovated in the beautiful lakeland village of Swallowbrook. She'd been offered the position of practice manager at the medical centre in the village and, desperate to leave London, she'd accepted the opportunity to take up where her uncle, who had held the position before her, had left off. He had gone to spend his retirement in Spain and as a parting gift had given her his house.

The children, eight-year-old Sophie and six-year-old Josh, loved the place after the noise and bustle of London. The lake, beautiful in all weathers, was encircled by a bracelet of rugged fells that attracted walkers and climbers from far and wide all the year round, especially at this time, while down below them an assortment of craft of all types and sizes sailed the lake's clear waters.

The children's favourite pastime was when the three of them sailed to its far reaches on one of the pleasure launches that went to and fro all the time during the hours of daylight. But wherever they went, whatever they did, there was always the same question coming from Sophie, 'Mummy, when is Daddy coming home?'

'Soon,' she would tell her gently. 'He is just so busy looking after the sick people.'

As she gazed unseeingly out of the window Laura thought that she would love Swallowbrook as much as they did if only Gabriel was there with them. Without him life had no meaning. But a horrendous turn of events had taken him from them and until he surfaced again she had no idea if the light of a marriage that had already begun to fade had been extinguished completely.

He knew that she'd taken her uncle up on his offer of the house called Swallows Barn, and that she was now employed at the practice from nine o'clock in the morning to when the children came out of the village school in the afternoon.

When she'd told him about her uncle's generosity he'd been less than enthusiastic, 'Fine, if that's what you want, Laura, but when I get out of here I intend to go straight to the town house.' And with a bleak smile he'd added, 'I take it that it's still there? That it hasn't been repossessed?'

'No. of course not!' she'd said steadily, holding back the tears that she had never shed in front of him on the nightmarish visiting days when they'd sat across from each other at a small table without touching and behaving like strangers.

She'd never wept in front of the children either, determined that nothing should spoil their youthful innocence. Her tears were shed in the long hours of the night in the big double bed that was bereft of the presence of the husband she'd adored.

'I've taken the job in Swallowbrook to help pay the bills while you're not around,' she'd told him that day. 'The gift of my uncle's house clinched it with regard to moving there, but from what you've just said it would seem that you aren't intending to join us. I thought you were desperate to see the children, Gabriel, knowing how much it must have cost you to refuse to let me bring them with me on days like today.'

'I *am* desperate,' he'd said grimly, 'but first I want to get a decent haircut, and to be able to turn up looking the same as when they last saw me. Yet it doesn't mean that every day I'm without them isn't hell on earth.'

'And what is every day without *me* like?' she'd asked, stung by the lack of any mention of herself.

'An exercise in accepting that I was never there when you needed me, and in the end for a fleeting moment I mistakenly thought you'd turned to someone else,' he'd said in the same flat tone.

'Yes, and when you came home early for once and found me in another man's arms, you felt entitled to become judge and jury without providing the opportunity for any explanation, *and* nearly killed someone who *did* want my company,' she'd parried, without raising her voice in the crowded visitors' area.

They'd gone over the same ground countless times while they'd been waiting for the court hearing, and it was only the fact that he had resuscitated and brought back to life the man he had attacked when he'd found him holding her close that had saved Gabriel from a longer sentence than the one he was serving now.

He had dragged her free of his hold and with one fierce blow had sent Jeremy Saunders reeling backwards and his head had hit the big marble fireplace behind him with an ominous crack. When they'd bent over him they'd discovered that his heart had stopped beating and it had been then that Gabriel had come to his senses and his medical training had kicked in.

She turned away from the window and slowly made her way downstairs, the hurt of that conversation as raw as ever, and saw that it was time to look forward instead of back if the children were to get to school on time.

They had settled into life in the country as to the manner born, with Sophie her usual caring self where her small brother was concerned. She was like Gabriel in both looks and personality, dark hair, hazel eyes, quick thinking and determined when it came to life choices, even at such an early age.

Josh was more like her, or rather how she used to be. She was no longer steadfast and tranquil, wrapped around with the contentment of the joys that life had brought her in the form of a husband she adored and who adored her in return, and a small son and daughter to cherish.

They'd lived in one of London's tree-lined squares, not far from where Gabriel had practised as a consultant oncologist working entirely within the NHS and very much in demand, so much so that over the last few years she had begun to feel like a one-parent family because he was never there.

Both of his parents had died of cancer when he'd been in his teens and on choosing medicine as a career he had decided to specialise in oncology. Every life he was instrumental in saving from the dreadful disease helped to make up a little for the loss of those he had loved.

She had always known and accepted that was the reason for his dedication to his calling, but as time had gone by the ritual of him arriving home totally exhausted in the early hours of the morning and being asleep within seconds of slumping down beside her on the bed that was so often empty of his presence had begun to tell.

Then it would be back to the hospital again almost before it was daylight and their physical relationship had become almost non-existent as it had seemed that his obsession with his career was going to drive them apart if he didn't ease off a little to give them some time to be a family.

It had been of all things a swelling in her armpit that had brought everything to a climax. Gabriel had already left the house and been on his way to the hospital one morning when she'd been drying herself after coming out of the shower and had felt something under her arm that hadn't been there before.

Immediately concerned, she'd phoned him to tell him about it and on the point of performing a major operation on a cancer patient he'd said, 'Pop along to the surgery and get them to have a look at it, Laura. I'm just about to go into Theatre.'

She'd put the phone down slowly. No woman on earth would want to find a lump in the place she'd described, but she was the lucky one, or so she'd thought. Her husband was one of the top names in cancer treatment, so it was to be expected that anything of that nature with regard to his wife would have his full attention, *but instead he'd told her to see her GP who, knowing who her husband was, had observed her in some surprise.*

He had tactfully made no comment and after examining the swelling had told her, 'It could be anything, Mrs Armitage, but we doctors never take any chances with this sort of thing, so I will make you an appointment to see an oncologist. Have you any preferences?'

'Er, yes, my husband,' she'd told him, and his surprise had increased, but it hadn't prevented the appointment being made for the following day.

* * *

When she'd arrived at the hospital Laura had seated herself in the waiting room with the rest of those waiting to be seen and when a nurse had appeared and called her name she had followed her into the room where Gabriel was seeing his patients.

He'd been seated at the desk with head bent, having been about to read the notes that he'd just taken from the top of the pile to acquaint himself with the medical history of his next patient. When he'd looked up she'd watched his jaw go slack and dark brows begin to rise as he'd asked, 'What are *you* doing here, Laura? Can't you see that I'm busy?'

'I need to see you,' she'd said implacably.

'Whatever it is, surely this is not the right place to discuss it,' he'd protested. 'Can't you wait until I come home?'

'No, I can't, that's why I'm here, Gabriel. You're never there, and it isn't anything domestic I want to discuss. I'm here as a patient.'

'What!' he'd exclaimed. 'Why? What's wrong with…?' His voice had trailed into silence as for once his quicksilver mind hadn't been working at top speed, and then realisation had come. 'The swelling in your armpit? You've been to see the GP?'

'Yes,' she'd told him woodenly. 'He managed to conceal his surprise at me consulting him when I'm married to one of the country's leading oncologists and made me an appointment. I'm surprised that my name didn't register with your secretary, but she wouldn't be expecting me here as a patient, I suppose.'

'Let me see it,' he'd said as remorse washed over him in shock waves, and as he'd felt around the swelling they were both acutely aware that it was the first time he'd touched her in months and it had to be for something like this.

'It's difficult to say,' he'd announced as she'd replaced the top that she'd taken off. 'It could be hormonal, or muscular strain, even a benign tumour, so don't let's jump to any conclusions until we've done the necessary tests, which I'll set up for tomorrow. Okay?'

'Yes,' she'd said, and without further comment was about to depart.

'If you will hang on for a few moments, I'll run you home,' he'd offered contritely, but she'd shaken her head.

'No, thanks. I'll be fine.' And before he could protest, she'd gone.

Amongst the uncertainties of her life, the position that Laura had taken up in the medical practice at Swallowbrook was like a calm oasis in spite of the pressures of a busy surgery and enough paperwork to keep her fully occupied.

There were four doctors in the practice, husband and wife Nathan and Libby Gallagher, and Hugo Lawrence, newly married to Ruby Hollister, who had joined them some months previously as a junior doctor. But soon they would be down to three again as Libby was pregnant and about to become a full-time mother to her new baby and Toby, their six-year-old adopted son. Laura had been working in hospital administration when she'd met Gabriel Armitage and the attraction between the clever oncologist who had a dark attractiveness that made him stand out amongst other men, and the serene golden haired vision behind a desk in the office had been an instant thing.

It had been at the hospital's Christmas ball they'd met and the romance had progressed from there with wedding bells not long after, and until Gabriel had become one of the area's leading experts on cancer and in huge demand, they had been a united happy family with their two children.

But the end of that had come on the day when he had arrived home early for once and along with his anguished regret for letting a situation develop where his wife had been forced to make an appointment to see him, he'd brought flowers, a huge bouquet made up of all the blooms she loved the most.

But no one on the staff at the surgery knew much about her, and for the moment she was happy to keep things that way. As far as they were concerned, she had taken up the job on Gordon Jessup's recommendation.

Though she'd carefully kept details of her private life to herself it seemed as if her new colleagues assumed that her marriage had suffered a split, and it was altogether easier to let them continue to think this, at least until she had some idea herself of where things were going with Gabriel.

Still, her new workmates had been very welcoming. The two Gallagher doctors had invited Laura and the children round for afternoon tea one Sunday as a welcoming gesture and Toby and Josh, of a similar age, had hit it off immediately, while Sophie, who was the proud owner of a pink mobile phone, had received a call and chatted non-stop to the caller on a bench in the garden while the boys kicked a ball around close by.

'That was Daddy,' she'd said with cheeks flushed and eyes sparkling as they'd walked home, unaware of her mother's heartache because Gabriel hadn't had anything to say to her. How could they ever hope to mend their marriage if Gabriel wasn't even prepared to talk to her? Or for him was it simply too late? Did he want out of the marriage once he got out of prison?

They'd gone in the ambulance to A and E on that dreadful day, with Gabriel and paramedics watching over Jeremy Saunders, and she huddled beside them in a state of shock brought on by what had happened to him and the knowledge that Gabriel, who had been her joy and her life no matter how much he was absent from it, had thought her capable of infidelity.

If he'd arrived just a few seconds later he would have seen her pushing the other man away and sending him packing, but after what had happened earlier in the day he'd been in no state for coherent thought after his wife had come to see him as a patient who might or might not have cancer *because she hadn't been able to get his attention any other way.*

The police had been waiting at the hospital when

they'd got there, having been notified by the ambulance crew of the circumstances of the emergency they were bringing in, and while the injured man was being treated Gabriel had been arrested on suspicion of grievous bodily harm.

She would have gone to the police station with him but he had insisted that she stay with their neighbour, who lived alone and as far as they knew had no close relatives, and there had also been the matter of their children due out of school soon.

'Phone the school, Laura,' he'd instructed, as, still in shock, she had stood by white faced and trembling. 'Ask them to keep the children there until you can pick them up.' As he'd been led away she'd nodded mutely and done as he'd said.

In the early evening, with Gabriel still at the police station, his secretary had phoned to say that his solicitor had been on the phone with a message from his client to say that her husband was insisting that she keep the appointments that had been made for her the following day and that he would be back as soon as possible.

'Whatever is wrong, Mrs Armitage?' Jenny Carstairs had asked, mystified at the unusual turn of events.

'It is something that we got involved in this afternoon, Jenny,' she'd told her, 'and knowing how Gabriel likes to have all ends neatly tied he's sending me a reminder about the scans, that's all.'

As soon as the secretary had gone off the line she'd rung the hospital to check on Jeremy's condition, knowing that if it had been someone other than Gabriel who had struck him he might not have survived the terrific blow to the head on the marble fireplace.

Jeremy was responding to treatment, she'd been told, there was no bleeding inside the head but he had sustained a skull fracture that was being dealt with, and his heart was being monitored all the time.

So it had seemed that Gabriel's quick response to what he'd been responsible for had probably saved the other man's life and she'd had to be satisfied with that, knowing that her husband was in police custody because of his angry reaction at finding her in the arms of another man.

Jeremy had seen her arrive home in tears and had been quick to step in to offer the comfort of his arms to his attractive neighbour in her moment of weakness. He'd been holding her close and stroking her hair, and at the moment that Gabriel had arrived he had been taking advantage of the situation and kissing her, and Gabriel had misunderstood what was happening.

As he put his key in the lock of the London house, the feeling of unreality that had been there all the time he'd been serving his sentence didn't lift. He was free of the punishment he'd received for loving his wife too much, he thought grimly, but what now? He looked around a hall that smelt musty from the lack of fresh air, and as he opened a window wondered if maybe that was how he smelt, *for the same reason.*

Would Laura ever forgive him for doubting her? She'd visited him dutifully while he'd been in that place but every time he'd seen her he'd known that the bonds that had always held them together had been broken and it had been due to his neglect.

After her appointment as a patient on that never-to-be-forgotten day almost a year ago, he'd sat staring into space as the reality of what was happening to their marriage had hit him. The woman he loved had been reduced to consulting him as a member of the general public. They'd lived in the same house, slept in the same bed, yet that was what she'd had to do to bring his attention to something that could have been serious.

Laura hadn't known at that moment that he'd passed all his appointments for the day to his second in command when she'd left and in the early afternoon had gone home with the intention of telling her that in future his dedication to the sick and suffering wasn't going to take over his life as much as it had been doing, that they were going to be a proper family again.

With that in mind he had arrived to find her being kissed and cuddled by the guy who lived next door, who was the laziest devil he'd ever come across and considered himself to be irresistible to women. Of independent means, he spent his days socialising with the city 'jet set' while he, Gabriel, was often operating for twenty-four hours non-stop, and in those first few seconds of rage it had seemed to him as if the sloth from next door had turned his attentions to Laura.

When his case had come up in court he'd been sentenced to nine months in prison for grievous bodily harm and been told it would have been twelve if it hadn't been for the fact that as well as endangering the other man's life he had also saved it in those first few moments of realising the horror of what he'd done, otherwise he might have been facing a charge of manslaughter. The marble fireplace had played its part, but he had been the one who'd struck the blow and his life and Laura's had never been the same since.

In the weeks prior to his case coming up they had slept in separate rooms, discussed only household matters and the children's welfare, and though he was no weakling mentally or physically the thought of being shut away from her and the children for any length of time had been agony. The only bright spot had been that Laura's test results had come back negative for cancer. The swelling was benign.

The first thing he did in the silent house was strip off and wash away the smell of where he'd been, and then got dressed in some of his own casual clothes that had hung unworn over the months.

When he opened the fridge it was well stocked and he wondered when Laura had found time to drive up to London to do that. He had the answer when a few seconds later the phone rang and Jenny, his secretary, was on the line, welcoming him home and asking if the food she'd bought him was all right.

'Laura rang and asked me to do a shop for you,' she explained.

'It is fine, Jenny,' he told her, 'and many thanks for taking the trouble'

'It was no trouble. I'm just glad to know you're home,' she said awkwardly. 'Everyone on the unit wants to know when you're coming back.'

'It might be if rather than when,' he replied. 'I've got some thinking to do, Jenny, but I'll be around to see you all soon.'

He finished his conversation with Jenny, but almost immediately the phone rang again. This time it was Laura.

'Gabriel! You're home! Thank goodness! How does it feel?'

'Quiet, peaceful,' he replied. 'Jenny has done what you asked so I'm going to have a snack lunch and then maybe a walk in the park. I see that next door is up for sale. Did you know?'

'Er, yes. Jeremy phoned to tell me.'

'Why would he do that, then?'

'I don't know. I wasn't interested and told him so,' she said levelly, and into the silence that followed added, 'When are you coming to see the children?'

'Soon,' he replied. 'One day during the week maybe.'

'I see,' she replied, and she did. She saw that Gabriel had no intention of taking up where they'd left off on that dreadful afternoon. They'd lived like strangers in the same house after the event while waiting for the case to come up, and she was no more eager than he was to go back to that kind of life.

The move to Swallowbrook hadn't just been because of her uncle's generous gift of the house. She'd harboured a secret hope that it might be a new beginning with Gabriel away from the happenings of the past in a beautiful place, but it seemed that he had other ideas and when they'd finished the call she wept for all that they'd lost.

Laura had chaired a meeting of the doctors the night before to discuss a project that was already under way—the building of a clinic for cancer patients that Nathan Gallagher was keen to see take place on the same plot of land as the surgery.

The relevant authorities in the area had approved it and work had already started. The practice building had once been a farmhouse where Libby, his wife, had been brought up, and there was land to spare all around it.

The intention was that the clinic should be an offshoot of the local hospital's oncology department, which was always extremely busy, and if plans went ahead it would be somewhere for local people to see a consultant without a longer wait than was necessary.

Libby hadn't been at the meeting. She was retiring from the practice very soon and had suggested that Laura take Sophie and Josh round to their place to play with Toby until it was over.

When she'd dropped them off Libby had thought that the new practice manager looked tired and stressed but hadn't said anything, as on getting to know her better she was realising that Laura Armitage was a very private person.

The other woman in the practice, Hugo Lawrence's delightful new wife Ruby, who had joined them as a junior doctor some time ago, had similar feelings about the new practice manager and was doing her best to make her feel at home. She felt that Laura was under pressure of some kind and it was noticeable that there was never any mention of the children's father in any conversation with her.

Though not so with her young daughter, Sophie was obviously in touch with her father, even if her mother wasn't, if the number of times she mentioned him was anything to go by.

After speaking to Gabriel on Friday morning, Laura decided that if life had felt unreal ever since he'd come charging in and found the opportunist from next door using her distress to get to know her better, the stilted conversation they'd just had on the phone took unreality into a new dimension.

He still believed she'd been about to cheat on him, she thought. That she'd turned to Jeremy Saunders of all people because of his own neglect of her, and that maybe it hadn't been the first time. Never having been prepared to discuss it with her since, now he was making it clear that there wasn't going to be any loving reunion, not as far as he was concerned anyway.

Sleep was long in coming when she went to bed. As she lay wide-eyed beneath the eaves of Swallows Barn, Laura heard Sophie call out his name on a sob and couldn't believe that Gabriel could stay away from the children now that he was free. If he didn't want to be with her, fine, but he adored Sophie and Josh, and if he didn't appear for them soon she would… What? *File for divorce and have to live without him for evermore?*

CHAPTER TWO

ON THE Sunday after Gabriel's release from prison, Laura set off with the children for a picnic on an island in the middle of the lake. It was a quiet and peaceful place, uninhabited except for just one property—an attractive house built from lakeland stone and appropriately named Greystone House.

They had told her at the surgery that it belonged to Libby and Nathan Gallagher, that he had bought it for her as a wedding present, and she'd thought how romantic that was. It seemed that the two of them and their small son spent every weekend there.

This Sunday the two doctors were going to the wedding of a friend who lived down south and so there would be no one but her and the children on the island today.

Sophie and Josh were keen to explore everywhere and as it was small enough for her to keep them in view all the time, she was happy to let them wander where they wanted as long as they didn't trespass on land belonging to the house.

Once they were happily occupied she set out the picnic for when they would be ready to eat, and then opening up the folding chair that she had brought with her settled herself on it and let her thoughts take over.

It hurt that Gabriel hadn't rushed straight up here to see the children at least, though he obviously had no interest in rebuilding their marriage.

She often thought that if she hadn't gone to the hospital as his patient that day, he wouldn't have come home so early, and when Jeremy had taken advantage of her distress, she would have sent him packing without Gabriel knowing anything about it and it would have been the end of the incident.

But Gabriel's timing had been all wrong and so had Jeremy's for that matter. They had all paid a high price for what had happened in the moment when his self-control had snapped. She could hear the engines of another passenger launch approaching and she sighed. It had stopped, and the peace she craved would be gone if others had the same thought in mind that she'd had.

Calling Sophie and Josh to her, she began to pour the cold drinks that she'd brought and almost dropped the flask when a shadow fell across her and the children came to a halt as if they'd seen a ghost.

She turned slowly with a tingling down her spine and when she looked up Gabriel was there, observing her gravely, and it was as if the four of them had been turned to stone, until Sophie broke the silence by crying 'Daddy!' and began running towards him, with Josh not far behind. As he scooped them up into his arms Laura saw the wetness of tears on his cheeks and thought achingly that this was a moment that none of them should ever have had to endure, but it had been thrust upon them. Where did they go from here?

Desperate to get away from the place where her life had been shattered, she'd spent the time that Gabriel had been away from her and the children picking up the pieces by moving to a new home in a beautiful Lakeland paradise, and although it had only been half a life without him there, she'd coped and would continue to do so whatever the outcome of his coming back to them.

When the children had calmed down after lots of hugs and kisses and were tucking into the food, she asked in a low voice, 'How did you know where to find us?'

'I didn't. I was parking the car by the lakeside when I saw the three of you in the distance boarding one of the launches, but it had sailed by the time I got there. I asked the girl in the ticket office if she knew where you were bound for. She said the island, so I caught the next boat.'

'I see. So you decided to come earlier?'

'Yes, but I'm not staying.'

'Oh, fine!' she said coolly. 'The children won't like *that*! Don't you think they've waited long enough to be with you?'

'Yes, I do, but, Laura, my life has been on hold for long enough. I have things to sort out at the hospital, matters that have accumulated while I've been in prison. I want the way ahead to be clear with regard to my career, so that I know my position, what I'm doing.'

The hurt inside her was beyond bearing as she listened to what he was saying and it came forth in anger as she said tightly, 'So nothing changes Gabriel? It's still career first and family second.' She glanced at the children, who were out of earshot. 'Well, don't let us stop you. Do dash off to wherever it is you prefer to be.'

'Would it be all right to stay the night?' he asked, with no answer forthcoming to her protest.

'You shouldn't need to ask!'

The vestige of a smile was tugging at the corners of the mouth that had kissed her a thousand times in what seemed like another life.

'All right, then,' he said, adding with grim humour, 'Just as long as the sheets are of Egyptian cotton. My bedding of recent months has hardly been luxurious, and if the house has a spare room, that will do fine'

She turned away. How could he joke about something like that and at the same time make it clear that he didn't want to sleep with her? With a change of subject she pointed to the food and said stiffly, 'There is plenty to eat. What would you like to drink?'

As he squatted down on the grass, with the children chattering one on either side, it seemed so normal that she could hardly believe that for what had seemed like for ever the only man she had ever loved had been serving a custodial sentence for grievous bodily harm because of what had been the worst day of her life.

'I hope you'll like the house,' she said uncomfortably when they arrived at Swallows Barn with the children still on a high, having been driven home in Gabriel's car.

'If *you* are happy with it, that is all that matters,' he said levelly.

Sophie urged, 'Come and see my room, Daddy!'

'And mine!' Josh said, and as the three of them went upstairs together Laura thought that Gabriel could tell the children that he wasn't staying. She wasn't going to be responsible for causing them any upset.

When they were asleep after receiving a promise from their father that he would take them to school the next morning, an awkward silence fell upon the house until it was broken by Gabriel asking casually, 'So what is the medical centre like in this place, Laura?'

Was that all he could talk about, health care? But she answered civilly enough, explaining who was who and outlining her responsibilities.

They'd passed the practice on the way home and he'd noticed that a new building was being erected on the large plot of land next to it and had wanted to know what it was going to be.

'It is going to be a clinic that will be an offshoot of the main oncology unit at the local hospital,' she told him. 'All the staff at the surgery are very excited about it.'

'Hmm, impressive forward thinking,' he commented. 'When is it due to open?'

'Some time in the autumn if all goes according to plan.'

But she had questions of her own to ask and they weren't about health care. It was the first time she'd had the opportunity to ask him what it had been like being shut away from his life's work at the hospital and his family, and was hoping that his reply would give her some degree of understanding of the stranger that he had become.

'So what was it like in there?' she asked gently, and watched his face close up.

'It was a piece of cake.'

'I'm not asking for mockery,' she told him. 'I want the truth.'

It had been hell on earth being away from them, but he had brought it on himself. He must have been insane to think that Laura would have anything to do with the low life from next door, but seeing that creep with his arms around her had ignited a fury like he'd never known. Perhaps in hindsight his uncharacteristic behaviour had been amplified by his feelings of guilt over neglecting Laura.

He'd flung himself at the man like a coiled spring and since that moment life had been totally unreal, but Laura was waiting for an answer and so, referring to the lighter side of his sentence, he said, 'I worked in the prison hospital for most of the time, which provided some degree of job satisfaction, and had a constant stream of inmates queuing up outside my cell for advice regarding their health problems, true or imaginary, but the nights were long.'

How long he couldn't bear to tell her, with visions of her coping with the children on her own, and in the middle of it all moving house, which showed clearly that by the time he was released she wanted to have made a new life for herself.

There *had* been indications that Laura wanted him to join her and the children in their new home, but he didn't want to rush into anything. Things had been going wrong between them even before that terrible incident. There was no way he could sidle back into her life without having something to offer in the form of trust and understanding, and the reason for him returning to London the following day was connected with that.

'And the rest of it?' she persisted.

'Not good in parts, but I had a debt to repay, didn't I, Laura? And now I can get on with my life knowing that ghastly episode is over, that Saunders is fully recovered, and that you and the children are all right.'

'And that is it?'

No, it isn't, he wanted to tell her. *When you came to see me as a patient I had to accept that I wasn't being fair to you. That I was guilty of gross neglect, and shortly afterwards I found myself believing that you were betraying me with that guy of all people, that you'd turned to him for comfort. I should have known better, of course, but I wasn't thinking straight at the time.*

Instead he said, 'For the present, yes. I'll keep in touch of course and if you need me for anything don't be afraid to ask.' He looked around him. 'Though you seem to be managing very well without me.

'I sussed out the spare room while I was upstairs, so

will get my case out of the car and settle down for the night if that's all right with you.'

'Don't you want a meal first?' she asked woodenly, bringing her mind back to basics, and when he shook his head a deadly calm began to settle upon her as the impact of his 'don't be afraid to ask' comment took hold.

In a measured tone she said, 'Just a moment before you go. You said if there is anything I need from you I have only to ask?'

He was observing her questioningly. 'Yes, I did. So is there something?'

'Yes. I want a divorce.'

She watched his jaw drop and amazement darken the hazel eyes looking into hers, and then he said in a grating voice that was nothing like his usual upbeat tone, 'So I was wrong. Am I still going to be paying for what I did?'

'And you think *I'm* not?' she said, doing her best to keep all emotion out of her voice. She could be just as coldly analytical as Gabriel if that was how he wanted things. 'I wanted you home, but not on the terms you're laying down in such a patronising manner. I've been living for the day when you were free of that place. But it seems that while you've had time on your hands you've been making plans that don't include me, which makes me think that you still aren't sure about how you found me in somebody else's arms, so, yes, Gabriel, I want a divorce!'

The strong lines of his face were set like granite as he turned and went out to the car without any further comment and when he came back inside she said, 'Breakfast will be ready at eight o'clock and if you still intend taking the children to school, they have to be there for quarter to nine.'

'Of course I'm going to take them,' he said levelly. 'I've never let *them* down!' *Like I have you,* the voice of conscience said.

Gabriel couldn't sleep. Twice he padded quietly to where the children were sleeping and gazed down on them tenderly, but the door of the master bedroom across the landing remained firmly shut. He had made everything worse between Laura and himself by not telling her what was in his mind. But first he had to speak to his friend James Lockyer, chairman of the board of governors at the hospital where he'd worked.

Jenny kept phoning to say how much they were all looking forward to his return, but she had no say in the matter, neither had those who had worked alongside him, and *nor had he.* So he wanted to get from James the full picture of what came next to put in front of Laura when he returned to the house where he'd felt like a visitor.

It had been at his suggestion that he'd slept in the spare room, not hers. Had she wanted him back in her bed?

But, no, how could she? Only hours before she'd asked him for a divorce. He'd been totally stunned at her request and was praying that it had been a spur-of-the-moment thing that she would change her mind about.

* * *

Breakfast was a stilted affair with only the children's chatter to liven it up and when the three of them were ready for the short walk to the village school Laura told him, 'I'll be ready to go to the practice soon. What time do you intend leaving?'

'As soon as I've seen the children safely inside I'll be back for the car. I need to be in London before three o'clock.'

'I'll hang on, then, so that I can lock up once you've gone,' she told him

'Whatever,' he agreed absently as his glance took in the vision she presented in a smart navy suit and white blouse with matching navy footwear, and the fair swathe of her hair swept back into a neat coil. She was so fantastic, he thought achingly. How could he have been so careless with the love they'd had for each other?

The children were tugging at him, with Sophie anxious to show off her father to her friends, and dressed in their neat school uniforms of gold and green and each carrying a small satchel they placed themselves one on either side of him and the trio disappeared in the direction of the village school.

When Gabriel came striding back half an hour later she was standing at the gate, waiting for him, and it felt like a dream. She'd imagined this moment so often, him walking towards her in sunshine, back where he belonged, and now that the time had come it was like groping through fog.

'Have you got everything?' she asked weakly as the shock waves of his nearness washed over her.

He nodded, and after locking up she waited to see what he would do next. Would he just drive off with a brief goodbye after her announcement of the previous night, she wondered, or give her a formal peck on the cheek?

As he bent towards her it seemed as if that was what it was going to be, but not so. His arms reached out to encircle her, his mouth was on hers and he kissed her long and lingeringly before letting her go, then without a word having passed between them he got into the car and drove off in the direction of the motorway that ran past the village.

She put her hand to her mouth. It was the first time he had touched her in any shape or form since that awful day, and she thought despairingly that she'd had to mention divorce for him to show any signs of still wanting her.

Yet he had gone for reasons best known to himself without any mention of when he would see her again. How was she supposed to feel? For now she chose to put her hurt and anger to one side and she set off for another day at the Swallowbrook Medical Practice.

On arriving, she went straight to her office on the lower ground floor and so didn't see Nathan arrive dumbstruck after taking Toby to school.

'I've just seen some guy seeing Laura's children into school,' he told Libby. 'It would seem that the missing father has turned up!'

'Really!' she exclaimed. 'What was he like?'

'That's just it!' he told her with amazement unabated. 'What are they called?'

'Er, Sophie and Joshua?'

'No! I mean their surname. It's Armitage, isn't it?'

'Yes. Why?'

'It was Gabriel Armitage, the cancer specialist, with Sophie and Josh. I've seen his face often enough in medical journals to recognise him. I had no idea that they were connected.'

With her amazement on a level with his she said, 'I recall he hit the headlines a few months back but can't remember what it was about, but it's good to know that Laura has a husband in her life to help her with the children, *and cherish her like you do me*,' she said softly, with the memory of long years of loving the man by her side without any signs from him, until one wonderful day he had returned to Swallowbrook and swept her off her feet.

'I don't think we should say anything to Laura,' she advised. 'Let her tell us about the man in her life in her own time.'

'Sure,' Nathan agreed, with his mind already switched on to the busy day ahead.

As Gabriel approached the hospital that he hadn't seen for many long months, James Lockyer, head of the board of governors, was pacing the boardroom. He was one of the oncologist's closest friends and had been devastated when Gabriel had been sent to prison for the last thing he would have expected him to be guilty of, but he had known the number of hours his friend had put in on the cancer unit with dedicated zeal and it would seem that he'd finally cracked.

When he'd phoned to ask to see him that afternoon James had thought that the hour of reckoning was going to come for Gabriel a second time, but from a different source—the hospital—which meant that his career could be in jeopardy, even though what had happened on that never-to-be-forgotten day had only been connected with his work from a stress point of view.

During all the time Gabriel had been head of oncology there had never been even a second when his expertise and judgement had been questioned, and now because of a split second of anger James was going to have to set the wheels turning that would bring his friend before the hospital board, who would decide whether he should be allowed to continue practising there.

The incident with his next-door neighbour would most likely have passed without notice if the other guy hadn't cracked his head on the fireplace with disastrous results as he'd fallen backwards, and from that had come the court's decision to award a prison sentence.

As the two men shook hands James was aware of the change in his friend. Gabriel had always been a man with a strong sense of purpose. Being shut away hadn't altered that, but there was a grimness about him that had never been there before and as they discussed his future the reason for it became apparent.

'You know that we want you back here as soon as

possible, don't you Gabriel?' James said, 'But the wheels of hospital protocol turn slowly and I will have to instigate the usual procedures with regard to the hierarchy coming up with a decision as to whether you should be allowed to continue working here.

'I know how much your work means to you and will move heaven and earth to get you back with us, but I will be only one voice amongst others when the meeting takes place.'

'I understand all of that,' Gabriel told him, 'and will face the music when summoned, but, James, whatever the result it won't make all that much difference to my future plans. I'm giving up medicine and moving to the countryside to be with Laura and the children.

'While I've been away she has moved to a charming lakeside village and I intend to move there to be with my family. It was my neglect of her, due to the job, that started it all, and there is not going to be any more of *that*. Let me know when the "firing squad" wants me up before them and I will be there, otherwise I shall be involved in rural life.'

'I can't believe what you're saying!' James exclaimed. 'You are the best we've ever had and we won't be able to exist without your work.'

'I don't know about that,' he told him, 'but one thing I do know. I can't exist without Laura…and she's just told me that she wants a divorce.'

'Ah, now I understand.' James nodded sombrely. 'But do let the wheels turn with regard to you being allowed to return to medicine one day. You might change your mind at some time in the future when you've put things right with her.'

'I doubt that will happen. It could be the same thing all over again if I do.' Gabriel rose from his chair. 'I'll leave you my phone number so that you can get in touch when I'm needed to face the board. And, James, it's been great to see you.

'I'm going to have a quick word with my team before I go. Jenny, my secretary, and no doubt the rest of them think I'm going to be able to take up where I left off here just like that, so I owe it to them to explain and say goodbye.'

'Yes,' James agreed, 'but it will be a sad day for this place.'

'No one is indispensable. There will be others to come with the same skills as mine. For all I know, they might have already appeared,' he told him, and went to carry out the next painful thing that he had to do, say hello and goodbye to those he'd worked with.

When he arrived back at the town house in the smart London square Gabriel sat staring into space. If someone had told him a year ago that he would calmly give up practising medicine with no other kind of job prospects in view, he would have laughed in their face.

But the fact of it was that he'd had to make a choice, his career or his family, in particular his wife, and he knew that he could just about exist without the one, but not without the other.

He was going to phone Laura, as he'd promised, but

later when the children were in bed and when she knew what he'd said to James, maybe she would change her mind about wanting a divorce.

The children were asleep and the house was still around her as Laura thought about the day that had started with Gabriel actually being around to take the children to school, then going back to London as swiftly as he had come.

He was always happiest there for the very good reason that it was where the hospital was, the huge, red-brick magnet that could always attract him away from her and the children and would soon be casting its spell over him again if he was allowed to continue practising there after what had happened.

Where was Gabriel now, she wondered, celebrating his freedom somewhere with James, or in a bar with the members of his team? She wouldn't blame him for doing either of those things. He'd been shut away from reality and needed to get back to it.

Though wasn't his idea of reality to see a patient cured, or at the least provide more time for them to enjoy what quality of life he was able to give them?

When the phone rang she was there in an instant, heart beating faster, nerves stretching, but it was Nathan's voice coming over the line to say that the doctors would like to get together with her to discuss some refurbishment of the surgery premises and would she arrange a meeting to that effect?

It rang again shortly afterwards, once again breaking into the silence of the house, and this time it was the voice she wanted to hear.

'I've been to see James to find out what happens now with regard to my position at the hospital.' Gabriel said, bypassing small talk in order to get to the news he hoped Laura wanted to hear. 'He says there will be a meeting shortly to discuss it, and that in view of my stay in HMP he won't be able to guarantee them agreeing to me taking up where I left off.

'All of which is no surprise, and until I hear more about it from him I will be returning to Swallowbrook some time tomorrow if that is all right with you.'

'Yes, of course,' she told him unsteadily, after trying to take in what he'd been saying. They'd both known that the sentence Gabriel had served could affect his career, but he was in much demand medically, and James would not want to lose him as one of the hospital's top consultants.

When he'd rung off she spent the rest of the evening in a state of acute anxiety. His career was Gabriel's life, she thought desperately.

If he couldn't treat the sick he would be devastated, yet he'd sounded calm enough at the prospect. *But she wasn't.* His job might cost them their marriage if he was allowed to go back to it, yet she couldn't bear the thought of him being separated from it. And what did he mean by announcing his intention to join her and the children here? It was as if their earlier conversation had never happened; he still hadn't responded to her request for a divorce.

The night that followed was not one of peaceful sleep. She tossed and turned and eventually went into the kitchen to make a drink at four o'clock as a midsummer dawn was beginning to lighten the sky, and as she gazed unseeingly to where the lake shimmered on the skyline the thought came that if Gabriel was given the chance to go back to his life's work, a divorce might be the only answer. It would leave him free to follow his calling without his responsibilities to her and the children weighing him down.

She'd told him it was what she wanted in the middle of a hurtful moment, not really meaning it, but maybe in the long run it would be the best thing for all of them if she could endure the agony of a permanent separation. The one that she'd just lived through, if living was the right word to describe it, had been hard enough to cope with, and that had been only for a matter of months.

CHAPTER THREE

When Laura arrived home the following afternoon after collecting the children from school, there was no sign of Gabriel's car on the drive, but he arrived shortly afterwards and relief washed over her. He was back where she could see him, touch him, not shut away like a common criminal.

She'd spent most of the day trying to imagine his conversation with James and her spirits had been at a low ebb, but now that he was back again the dark thoughts were receding, His friend wouldn't let the world of medicine be deprived of Gabriel's contribution to it, she decided.

'I'm so glad you're back,' she told him. Sophie and Josh came running out. 'And so are the children.'

'I told them I would be,' he said with a tight smile. 'If the traffic hadn't been so bad I would have been in time to pick them up from school. The last thing I want is to upset them by doing another disappearing act.'

They were on the drive where she'd gone out to greet him when she'd seen the car pull up outside and he said,

'Maybe we should go inside to talk rather than discussing our affairs out here. I'll get my stuff in later.'

Once they had closed the door behind them she said sombrely, 'It is awful that you have to justify yourself to these people who can decide your future with just a few words.'

'They won't be doing that, Laura, it's sorted,' Gabriel said, wishing he didn't have to tell her in one way, yet in another he needed to see her reaction when he told her that he was giving up oncology and anything else medical.

He wanted her to know how much he regretted his past fixation with his career and wanted to put things right between them, but before he could explain she was saying joyfully, 'You mean it's all right? You don't have to face any meeting of the board? Your job is safe?'

'Not exactly,' he said slowly, with a sinking feeling inside. 'At this moment I have joined the ranks of the unemployed. I've just told James that I'm quitting.'

'What?' she asked in a strangled whisper. 'It was your life, Gabriel! You can't just walk away from it.'

'Yes, I can,' he told her. 'Before I became a workaholic you and the children were my life, we had a good marriage, were a happy family, but always there was in my mind the longing to try to save others from the same fate as my parents and I let it govern me.

'But not any more. I intend to make up for my neglect of you by being here when you need me, and also when you don't. This place you have moved us to is paradise and I intend to make every moment count.'

'What about your staff?' she asked urgently. 'Your team worship you. What will they say?'

'They know. After I'd told James I went to see them.'

'And how did they react?' she croaked.

'They weren't happy, but I explained that I wouldn't have been able to take up where I'd left off with them for some weeks or even months if I'd intended staying, as it would have depended on the powers that be whether I would still be able to practise, so there you are.'

Yes, there I am, she thought. *Obviously the days are gone when we made life-changing decisions together.*

The nightmare she'd created that day at the hospital was still there, assuming larger proportions all the time, and now there was this awful news that Gabriel was ready to cast his life's work aside because of it.

All it had needed had been a little adjustment in their lives, a little more time spent with her and the children, but it had turned into a monster that was eating up their happiness, *what was left of it*.

'And what are we going to do about the town house?' she asked, as if she cared after what she'd just been told.

'Nothing for the moment,' was the reply. 'It is too early to start making any decisions about that.'

'Yes, whatever,' she agreed wearily, and moving towards the kitchen turned her attention to something less shattering, the preparation of the evening meal.

Dismayed at her reaction to his news, he followed her and framed in the doorway said softly, 'Laura, please don't be like this. Life can only get better without the weight of my job in our lives.' But she carried on peeling and slicing vegetables with her head turned away from him as her hopes for their lives getting back to normal were disappearing with the news of the extreme measures he'd gone to for her sake.

She'd never wanted anything from him except a little more of his time, but Gabriel had given her all of it in one magnificent gesture, and instead of being overjoyed she was horrified.

The atmosphere during the evening was not lively. The meal had been mediocre due to the state of mind of the cook, and Sophie was developing some sort of a virus infection, was hot and fretful, and was for once happy to go to bed.

With nothing they wanted to say to each other after the painful moments in the kitchen earlier, they went up to bed themselves not long after the children, and once again Gabriel headed for the spare room after he'd checked that Sophie was no worse and was sleeping peacefully. Tonight Laura was relieved that she wasn't going to be sharing a bed with her husband.

The next morning when she went downstairs after a night that had been a mixture of dozing and sleeplessness and checking on Sophie, Laura heard voices and found Gabriel giving the children their breakfast amidst lots of laughter, with his daughter looking better after a good night's sleep.

'What can I get you?' he asked, taking note that she was pale and puffy-eyed. He felt like kicking himself for unloading the news that he was jobless of his own choice the moment they had been together again.

'Just a cup of tea,' she said, and perched down beside the children, who had almost finished eating. She could feel Gabriel's dark gaze on her and turned away. She was in no mood for any further discussion at such an hour and when she'd finished the drink went upstairs to get ready for whatever was waiting for her at the practice.

How he was going to spend his day she didn't know and wasn't going to ask. If he intended staying here with them at Swallows Barn, as he had said he would, their roles were going to be reversed, and it wasn't an unhappy thought to know that she was going to be the one who came and went jobwise, while he took over the role that had been hers in the form of seeing the children to school, shopping, cooking and keeping the house in order.

It hadn't been like that when they had first been married, they'd shared the chores because they'd both had jobs. But when the children had come along and Gabriel's workload had assumed huge proportions, she had fallen into the role of the domestic 'goddess', and although accepting that it was a necessary procedure she had sometimes been reminded of how her mother had been kept tied to household chores by her domineering father, and how she, Laura, had vowed that she was never going to be the same.

But with a husband who was never there the mantle of it had fallen onto her shoulders and now maybe there was going to be a change of plan regarding who did what, and if she read Gabriel's mind right, he wouldn't bat an eyelid.

She was still in a state of shock from his news of the night before, but was adjusting to it, and foremost was the thought that if anyone was due for a fallow period in their lives, he was.

'I'm taking Sophie and Josh to school again and will pick them up this afternoon,' he informed her. 'I have so much lost time to make up with them.'

'Yes, I do know that,' she replied. 'Why not take them for a sail after school? They love being on the lake.'

'What about you?'

She shook her head. 'I have a practice meeting about the refurbishment of the premises this afternoon and can't get away. I won't be home until half past five at the earliest.'

'And what would you have done with the children if I hadn't been here?' he wanted to know.

'There is an arrangement at the school for those children whose parents can't be there to collect them at the normal home time. Games and refreshments are available to keep them occupied until they arrive.'

'I see.'

He was groaning inwardly, feeling even more surplus than he did already. But Laura had been in a position where she'd had to cope without him while he had been serving his sentence. She'd had to be on the top of things with regard to Sophie and Josh, moving house and going back to administration after being out of it ever since the children had been born.

No doubt her capabilities came from already having been thrust into the role of single parent while he'd been working almost round the clock. Maybe that was the reason why she'd mentioned divorce, the knowledge that she'd already done all the things that it would ask of her.

Sophie and Josh came downstairs at that moment ready to go and their stilted conversation drifted into silence.

They could have all gone for a sail in the evening if Laura couldn't be with them in the afternoon, he thought as the three of them walked to the school. But he'd been able to tell that she was relieved to be otherwise occupied and would no doubt have had a reason why she couldn't go with them later in the day if he'd suggested it.

The barriers were up. He'd done the wrong thing as far as she was concerned in deciding to give up medicine, even if he *was* given the possible opportunity to take up where he'd left off. He was trying to atone for his neglect but she hadn't seen it that way. She'd obviously thought him reckless and uncaring to unburden himself of his career in such a manner. Never in her darkest moments would she have asked him to do that.

He'd taken the children for a sail on the lake, as Laura had suggested, and as on the other occasions when he'd been with them on his own since arriving in

Swallowbrook had enjoyed every moment of the time spent with them.

Was getting to know Sophie and Josh better going to be the silver lining of the dark cloud that had hung over him during past months? he wondered. He'd always been a loving father but because of the job it had been on a limited scale and now there was all the time in the world.

It was half past five and the three of them were walking towards the surgery, eating ice cream cornets. It seemed as if the meeting might be over as the only staff to be seen were Laura and a tall guy chatting on the forecourt.

She was laughing at something he'd said and he realised it was a long time since *he* had made her laugh. Cry, yes, he could do that all right.

When she saw them approaching he watched the colour rise in her cheeks, yet she was in control of the situation and on the point of introducing him to the stranger but she was forestalled by Sophie and Josh crying 'Dr Hugo!' and running up to him as if they knew him well.

'Hello, you two,' he said ruffling Josh's fair mop, while casting a curious glance at the man standing silently just a few feet away.

'Hugo may I introduce my husband, Gabriel Armitage?' Laura said at that moment, and her companion observed him in astonishment.

'Not *the* Gabriel Armitage, the oncologist!' Hugo said, and when he received a nod of acknowledgement went on, 'I am delighted to meet you.'

'My daddy is famous,' Sophie chipped in at that moment, and as the two men shook hands Gabriel thought that 'infamous' would be a better description, but maybe this nice guy hadn't heard about his criminal activities.

'I must go,' Hugo said at that point, as if he felt he had to explain his presence to the silent stranger. 'My wife has gone on ahead to get our evening meal under way. Laura and I were just comparing notes about the meeting that has just taken place.'

Turning to her, he said, 'Do bring Gabriel round for dinner one evening, Laura. We'd love to have you both if you can find a childminder, or otherwise bring the children with you.' And off he went to Lakes Rise, his house not far away, where his new wife, who he adored, would be waiting for him.

'He seems a decent sort,' Gabriel said as the four of them made their way home.

'Yes, he is,' Laura agreed. 'Hugo made me welcome from the word go when I came here, and helped me to get settled in Swallows Barn. He was married just a short time ago to Ruby, our junior doctor who came from Tyneside to join the practice. She'd lived in Swallowbrook when she was young and had always wanted to be part of the medical team here. With regard to the two of them I think it was love at first sight.'

So Hugo Lawrence *was* a decent sort, as he'd imagined him to be, Gabriel thought, but *he* was the one who should have been there to look after Laura's needs at such a time. Would he ever be free of the feeling of having let her down *over and over again*?

When the four of them had eaten, the children went into the garden to play until it was their bedtime, and noting that her listlessness at breakfast time was still there he said, 'I'll clear away, Laura, while you relax, and maybe when Sophie and Josh are asleep you might feel like continuing our discussion about the future from last night.'

'I won't have time,' she said immediately. 'I need to write up the minutes from today's meeting before I begin getting in touch with contractors and others that we are going to employ to carry out the refurbishment of the practice.'

'Fair enough,' he said evenly. 'In that case, I might go down to the pub when the children are asleep. I can't remember when last I sat behind a glass of beer.'

'Yes, whatever,' she agreed.

He paused in the kitchen doorway on his way to join Sophie and Josh at their play and when she looked up he was frowning. 'I hope that bringing work home from the practice isn't a regular thing. It is a bit much for them to expect that of you.'

'It is my own choice,' she told him. 'Something I do before starting on any chores that need to be done once the children are in bed.'

'I see. In other words, you've got it all sorted and don't need me around. Is that why you want a divorce?'

She didn't reply. Had something happened to Gabriel's keen perception while he had been shut away from them? She needed him with every beat of her heart, with every breath she took.

What had happened to them had taken the last of the glow from a marriage that had already been fading and she ached for it to be as it used to be, but not at the cost of him giving up medicine, never that!

Gabriel had done what he'd said he might do and had gone to The Mallard where the conversation would be light amongst the visitors and residents who packed the place on summer evenings. There would be noise, laughter and good temper, all a far cry from the home he had just left and the wife who had nothing to say to him.

The children were asleep and it was so quiet Laura felt she would be able to hear a pin drop. The notes she'd made that afternoon were in front of her and with little enthusiasm she began to arrange them into a semblance of order, but not for long. The phone rang and it was James at the other end of the line.

'Laura!' he said at the sound of her voice. 'How are you?'

'Surviving, James… Just about,' she told him wearily. 'If you want Gabriel, he has gone to the pub to find some light relief from my company.'

'I did want to talk to him,' was the reply, 'but it can wait. You and I haven't spoken since he was released, have we, and I've been anxious to know how things are between you. Has Gabriel told you that he's giving up medicine? Leaving the hospital whether they want him to stay or not?'

'Yes, he told me last night and I was devastated for

two reasons amongst many, James. First of all because fighting cancer is his life, he will shrivel and die without it, and secondly because he has made a decision of such importance without consulting me!'

'That may be so, Laura,' he told her soberly, 'but it was you that he was thinking of when he did that, not himself. I'm just as upset as you are.

'I feel for both of you, but I also have the cancer unit to concern myself about. The patients and staff here need him, or someone like him.'

'What were his chances of being able to carry on if he had wanted to?' she asked.

'I'm hopeful. I will be pointing out that it wasn't the force of the blow that was struck that nearly killed the other guy. It was the misfortune that the marble fireplace was behind him as he fell backwards, and I will also be reminding the board that Gabriel immediately cast off the mantle of the betrayed husband and stepped back into the role of the lifesaver that he has always been.'

She had to ask. 'Does he still think he was the "betrayed husband"?'

'He has never mentioned it since. I would very much doubt it, but he hasn't said anything to me either, I'm afraid, except that he is filled with remorse about everything that has happened.'

'I have never, ever looked at another man since the moment I met him,' she told him.

'That I can well believe.' And she could tell that James was smiling at the other end of the line. 'He has it all—the looks, the charisma, the beautiful wife and the high-flying career.'

'That is in the past,' she reminded him. *'He hasn't got a career now!'*

She heard the front door click open and with a rapid change of subject said, 'Gabriel is here now, James.' Passing her husband the phone, she picked up the paperwork that she'd been sorting and went to spend another miserable night alone under the covers.

When Laura went down to breakfast the following morning it was the same as the day before, with Gabriel in charge again. Though he had only been back with her and the children a couple of days, already the four of them were slipping into a routine, with him as the house husband and her with the position of practice manager to go to each day. It was ironic that she was now the one involved in health care instead of him.

But she daren't dwell too long on that. Just the thought of him idling the days away when he could be treating the sick made her want to weep, but of course there was the small matter of whether he would be given the chance to do that even if he wanted to.

Yet James had been reassuring and she couldn't resist asking Gabriel if he'd said the same to him as he'd said to her...that he was hopeful for a clean slate for Gabriel as far as the hospital was concerned, because the blow that he'd given their neighbour wouldn't have been enough to cause serious injury on its own, and that the fireplace had been a contributory factor.

He was engaged in pouring milk onto the children's cereal and didn't look up until he'd finished what he was doing. When he did and their glances locked he said, 'Yes, he told me all of that, and a few more things as well, such as I was crazy wanting to leave medicine. But as I pointed out, *he* hasn't got a wife who wants a divorce.'

Now was the moment to tell him she wished she hadn't said that, even though she'd meant it during the few seconds that the words had fallen from her lips, but almost immediately had regretted them. How could she face a life without Gabriel?

He was turning away to take bread out of the toaster and they were alone, Sophie and Josh had gone into the sitting room to watch TV so the opportunity was there to tell Gabriel that the last thing she wanted was a divorce.

But he'd just been commenting on his proposed departure from the London oncology scene and might think that her change of mind was connected with coaxing him back into cancer care, when all she had ever wanted had been a lighter workload where she and the children saw more of him, where their life was how it used to be, with him holding her close in the night and sharing the occasional meal with them.

With Sophie and Joshua a continual joy, they had planned to have another child, but that idea had been put to one side because Gabriel had always been too tired, and as she had been beginning to feel more and more like a single mother, the thought had lost its appeal.

* * *

Hugo's wife, Ruby, sought Laura out in the middle of the morning at the surgery and said laughingly, 'You are a dark horse, a husband who is a London consultant, and Gabriel Armitage of all people.'

Laura smiled back at her. She liked the slender young doctor with the short, chestnut-coloured hair and ivory skin. It was plain to see that she was much cherished by her new husband, but sometimes she picked up on melancholy in Ruby, though it always disappeared when Hugo came into view.

The two of them, husband and wife, did the weekly antenatal clinic at the surgery and once when someone had asked Ruby jokingly how she would feel when she was pregnant and was doctor and patient at the same time, Laura had seen her turn away as if she hadn't heard the question.

'I just stopped by to remind you that it's Swallowbrook's Summer Fayre on Saturday,' Ruby said. 'Weather permitting, it will be on the village green, otherwise in the church hall. Everyone turns out for it, and as you and your family are newly resident here I thought I would make sure that you knew about it.'

'Thanks for that,' Laura told her. 'We will certainly be there. Sophie and Josh will love it.' *Whether Gabriel would want to go she didn't know, but that was up to him.*

Saturday dawned bright and clear with a summer sun high in the sky, and Laura's spirits lifted. When she'd told Gabriel about the coming event after her chat with

Ruby he had shown more interest than she'd expected, commenting that there was something to be said for country life, especially when a beautiful lake was part of the package.

Having always been a city dweller and recently having spent some time in exceptionally depressing surroundings, he was realising just how much he had needed a change of scene from the pressures of what had been his life before this. But always there was the knowledge that he was paying a high price for it and so was Laura. Even relinquishing the career that had been so fulfilling and worthwhile hadn't brought her back into his arms.

He wanted to talk it through with her, clear away the cobwebs and start afresh, but it would seem that the void between them had grown too wide for that. He wanted to talk but she didn't, and the spectre of divorce hung over him like a black cloud.

Yet no one seeing the four of them amongst village folk and visitors on the village green would have guessed that all was not well between the two parents.

Laura's light mood persisted as they wandered amongst carousels and ducking stools, watched Morris dancers, and browsed around stalls selling food and goods made by local people.

Libby and Nathan were there with Toby and when introductions had been made the two young boys stayed together as their parents strolled along, but Sophie didn't leave Gabriel's side, clinging onto his hand tightly. Laura thought that never again must their children be separated from their father, no matter how flat and lifeless their marriage had become.

Meals were being served in the village hall by members of Swallowbrook's Community Association with the vicar's wife in charge, while her husband wandered amongst his parishioners from table to table, chatting and smiling benignly upon them.

When he stopped to have a word beside where they were sitting Laura saw that Gabriel was listening to him intently, and when the vicar had moved on he said, 'Is his voice always so hoarse, Laura?'

'Having only just got to know him I haven't spoken to him very often,' she replied, 'but when I have, yes, it has been like that.'

He was rising from his seat. 'Maybe I should have a word with him,' he murmured, and followed the other man, who, having welcomed all those present, had found himself a quiet spot to have some refreshment of his own.

'My name is Gabriel Armitage,' Gabriel said when he drew level. 'I am an oncologist and would suggest that you make an appointment to see someone about your voice box, just to be on the safe side.' As the vicar observed him in surprise, he added, 'I hope that I'm mistaken, but there could be a problem with the larynx that is making your voice so hoarse. How long has it been like that?'

'Er, quite a while,' came the reply, 'but I have put it down to my doing so much talking. It goes with the job, I'm afraid. Please accept my thanks for your concern. I will most certainly do what you have suggested. There will be a clinic opening soon here in the village that will be treating that sort of thing. Maybe I could see someone there when it is functioning.'

Gabriel shook his head. 'Don't wait. See someone now.' And leaving the vicar looking stunned, he went back to join Laura and the children.

'What did you tell him?' she asked.

'Just that it would be wise to have the hoarseness checked and to do it now. The vicar suggested waiting until the new clinic opens, so he had tuned in to what I was hinting at, although neither of us mentioned the "C" word.

'But I've heard that kind of hoarseness before. In many cases that is what it has been, and everyone knows that early diagnosis can save lives.'

As they looked across to where the vicar's wife was listening open-mouthed to what her husband had to say, she knew that it wasn't likely that Gabriel would be wrong.

For the rest of the afternoon the four of them strolled amongst the crowds and stopped from time to time while the children went on the various rides and gazed at the sideshows, and Laura thought this was what they'd all been short of, family outings, time together.

But the cost for this to come about had been high for all of them, and they had paid dearly for it. She had asked for just a little of his time and now was getting all of it.

Walking beside her, Gabriel was aware of her every

mood swing, every smile, every frown, and asked, 'What is wrong? Do you want to go home?'

'No, I'm fine,' she assured him quickly, and observing Sophie and Josh, who were consuming toffee apples with great relish, she said, 'And I don't think the children are ready to go yet.'

'Not even if we go down to the lake and have our evening meal at one of the restaurants there?'

'Well, maybe if we go for a sail first. Why don't we ask them?'

'Yes,' the two of them chorused when the boat trip was mentioned, so shortly afterwards, with farewells to the surgery crowd, they left the village green and made their way to the lake.

As they boarded the *Swallow*, one of the larger passenger launches, Gabriel observed the fells that encircled the lake, bleak in winter, but on a bright summer day displaying a rugged sort of magnificence that would account for the many who were walking and climbing on their steep slopes and high ledges.

'They are something else, aren't they?' he said. 'A challenge that lots of people won't be able to resist, whether they are experienced enough to go up there or not.'

'Yes,' she agreed. 'Both Nathan and Hugo are involved as doctors with the mountain rescue team when it is called out.' Having mentioned them, she chose the moment to ask, 'Do you think they know about what happened to us? No one has said anything.'

'That doesn't mean that they aren't thinking a lot,'

he said dryly. 'But I don't mind people knowing I've been in prison. It's in the past, Laura. When are you and I going to talk about the future?'

The children broke into her thoughts at that moment, pointing to the island where they'd had the picnic, and for the rest of the sail and during the meal at the hotel on the lakeside, the happy family charade continued until they were back at Swallows Barn and the children were in bed.

When she came downstairs after their bathtime Gabriel had taken drinks out into the garden and was waiting for her on the patio. As she lowered herself onto a chair opposite him he said, 'We can't go on like this, with you clamming up every time I want to talk.

'I know that our thought processes are not exactly in harmony at the present time, but never discussing our problems isn't going to make them go away. Surely you understand that.'

'The workings of *your* mind seem to have become very shallow since you've been away from me,' she said soberly. 'You say that we never talk, but what has happened to us making decisions together about the important things in our lives? That is how it has always been until recently.

'So did you come out of medicine to show me how much you love me, or to teach me a lesson? That you had your priorities right when I had to make an appointment to see you, and I hadn't?'

'I can't believe you could think that,' he told her, 'but I suppose I've asked for it, like everything else.'

He had risen from his chair and was looking down at her, and as she raised her eyes to his he asked, 'Do you still want a divorce?'

She shook her head. 'No. It might be the best thing for us, Gabriel, but it wouldn't be for the children, Sophie especially. I watched her holding your hand ever so tightly at the Summer Fayre and can't count the number of times she asked for you while you were shut away from us. They need you in their lives all the time, not as a part-time father with visiting rights.'

'But not you? *You* don't need me in *your* life any more?'

'I think we've just about exhausted that topic of conversation,' she told him, standing to face him. 'It has run its course.'

'Maybe,' he agreed, 'but *this* hasn't.' And the next moment he was holding her close, pressing the soft curves of her against the hardness of his chest, and with his hand under her chin he raised her mouth to his and kissed her with a hunger that came from long nights without her in a prison cell and the heavy, reproachful burden of regret that weighed him down.

Laura's legs had gone weak at the sudden onslaught of his passion upon her own yearnings. Any thoughts of resisting were disappearing. It was only when reality with its calm common sense took hold of the moment that she found the will to push him away and tell him breathlessly, 'We're not going to resolve our problems this way, Gabriel.'

As his arms fell away she turned and went back

into the house and when he followed without speaking she wished him a frail goodnight and disappeared once more into the room that was beginning to feel like a cloistered cell, knowing that the only man she would ever love would be sleeping just across the landing, and if her passion was at a low level, it would seem that his wasn't.

CHAPTER FOUR

SUNDAY brought with it showers and sunny spells so Laura was content to spend the day indoors with her family. Apart from the weather there were chores to be done and preparations for the coming week to deal with for her and the children.

What Gabriel's plans were for the days ahead in the limbo he had created job-wise, Laura didn't know. He hadn't mentioned looking for any other kind of employment and remembering his comments about the attractions of Swallowbrook, maybe he intended to spend what to him would be a summer idyll in the place. And if he did that, couldn't she be less critical of the decision he'd made about his work with cancer? He'd had little enough opportunity to unwind in the past.

The children loved having him around and his help with the domestic side of things was a relief from having to juggle the position of practice manager with all the other responsibilities that had been hers while he hadn't been with them. It made the job so much more enjoyable and fulfilling.

Whether Gabriel was achieving the same amount of

pleasure from his switch from well-known oncologist to stay-at-home husband she didn't know, but he seemed happy enough with the present circumstances in spite of having given up the job she would have thought he would have wanted to do for ever.

If they had been communicating the way they used to in the early days of their marriage she would have been aware of what it was costing him to be shut off from his life's work, but that sort of closeness was missing, and sleeping in separate beds in separate rooms wasn't going to bring it back.

There had been no news from James over recent days and her experience of hospital administration at that level had taught her that committees and that sort of gathering often did what they had to do at snail's pace.

But didn't Gabriel realise that by giving up his consultancy she was being made to feel that she was to blame for all that had happened to them? She would be seen as shallow and selfish, the wife who had felt she should come before his work, when that had not been the case.

When she looked out into the garden he was seated on the patio, reading the Sunday papers in the very same spot where he'd wanted to make love to her the night before, and she felt the sting of tears. That part of their lives had been wonderful once, but not any more, because it had gradually disappeared.

Now there was all the time in the world to make up for it, but on what basis when the foundation of their marriage was crumbling? No way could she face the thought of what had been a magical coming together of tenderness and desire being replaced by lust.

As if he sensed her watching him, Gabriel looked up and the children, who were playing near him, waved. She waved back, and through the open window called to him, 'I'm going to go for a stroll.'

'Do you want us to come with you?' he asked.

'No,' she told him with a smile to take away the sting of the refusal. 'I need some time on my own for a change. Ever since the children and I moved to Swallowbrook it is something that has been in short supply, what with caring for them, starting a new job, the renovating of this place, and so forth.'

'Yes, I can imagine,' he said bleakly, with the agonising memory of long nights when he'd imagined her alone with the children and no one to protect her, should the need arise. Yet he hadn't exactly been around that much before then, had he?

Sometimes the night had been almost over before he'd wearily climbed the stairs with sleep the only thing on his mind. So Laura must feel that a vacant place in the bed here in Swallowbrook wasn't all that different from how it had been before.

She was waiting for anything else he had to say before she went for the stroll she'd mentioned and he didn't disappoint her. 'Being alone is the last thing I would crave,' he told her. 'I've spent enough time under those conditions to last a lifetime.'

'Yes. I know,' she told him wretchedly.

What he had endured because of her would be engraved upon her heart for ever, and instead of leaving Gabriel and the children for a while with a light step, her feet felt heavy and leaden as she left the house.

When the lake came into view she walked alongside it until she was away from the bustle of the boat terminal, and perching on a dry stone wall that separated the lakeside from one of the many farms in the area she let the quiet of the place wash over her. Maybe here with no one to make any demands of her, or to confuse her further, she would be able to get a clearer perspective of the future, she decided, but it didn't happen. She just sat gazing blankly into space, letting time drift by.

Back at the house Gabriel was doing the opposite, watching the clock. Laura was taking some stroll, he was thinking. The amount of time she'd been gone indicated a much longer exercise than that. He'd given the children their evening meal and they would soon be ready for bed, but not before their mother came back. If she didn't come soon, he would go and look for her and it would mean him having to take them with him.

When the doorbell rang he wasn't expecting it to be her, she would have a key, and neither was he prepared to see Ruby and Hugo Lawrence standing in the porch.

'Hello, Gabriel,' Hugo said. 'We just stopped by to ask if Laura is here with you. We've just been for a sail on one of the passenger launches and we thought we saw her sitting by the lakeside as we passed. It is so rarely that she is alone when out and about, so we thought that if we found her at home with you we were mistaken.'

'Come in,' he said, and they stepped into the hallway. 'No, she isn't here. Laura went for a stroll ages ago, saying she wanted some breathing space, some time to herself, and hasn't returned, so I was just about to go in search of her. If you could describe exactly where you saw her I'll go and bring her back. It could be that she's walked too far, or maybe hurt her foot or something, and she hasn't got her phone with her. She left it on the kitchen table.'

The children had heard Hugo's voice and were coming running at the sound of it, and Ruby said, 'You go, Dr Armitage. We'll stay with Sophie and Josh until you get back.'

'Thanks, I appreciate the offer,' he told her, and was behind the driving seat of the car in seconds, praying that he would find Laura where they'd said, or even nearer home if possible.

She'd been pushed too far, he thought grimly as the lake came into view, and he was to blame. He'd thought that by giving her *all* of his time she would understand how much he regretted what had happened to them, but again he'd miscalculated her love for him, and the sacrifice he'd made felt hollow when memories of the satisfaction that came from his kind of work came back to haunt him.

When he turned the car on to the last few yards of road that led to the lake she was there, walking slowly towards the home that she'd made for them, and his heart leapt with thankfulness.

She looked pale and heavy-eyed but she was safe

and as she got into the car the first thing she asked was, 'Where are the children? You haven't left them alone, have you, Gabriel?'

He smiled and felt as if his face would crack with the effort as he commented wryly, 'You should know me better than that. Your friends Ruby and Hugo Lawrence are with them. I asked them to sit with the children while I came to find you. You've been gone for ages, I was getting worried.

'Why did you stay out so long? I've been going crazy, wondering where you were. I thought maybe I'd pushed you too far, or at the least you were in no hurry to get back to me.'

'It was so quiet and peaceful where I was,' she explained, 'and instead of doing some uninterrupted thinking, which was what I'd intended, I fell into the best sleep I've had in days.'

When the car pulled up on the drive the door opened and the children were there with Hugo and Ruby smiling their relief to see Laura safely back where she belonged.

They didn't know the exact circumstances of Gabriel Armitage's sudden appearance in Swallowbrook, but remembered from way back that there had once been a court case that he'd been involved in.

But now, having met the man himself, they could not believe that it had been anything too disastrous because his manner and appearance spoke of integrity, and in the medical world his name was revered by all who'd had cause to seek him out for help. That he loved his family was also plain to see. He doted on his children and his anxiety with regard to Laura's non-appearance after her walk was proof of how much he cared for his wife.

Her smile of greeting for her friends was apologetic. 'I am so sorry you've been troubled on my account,' she told Hugo and Ruby. 'I'd gone for a walk and when I stopped to rest by the lake I fell asleep and didn't wake up for ages.'

'We didn't mind keeping an eye on Sophie and Josh,' Ruby said gently. 'Gabriel was so concerned that you hadn't come back, but all is well now, isn't it?'

I wish, Laura thought, but her reply was reassuring enough to put Ruby and Hugo's concerns to rest. 'Yes. It's fine. So can I make you a cup of tea or coffee, or get you a cold drink?'

'No, thanks,' Hugo said. 'Sophie has done the honours. We've all had an iced lolly out of the fridge and enjoyed it immensely, so we'll be off and leave you folks to enjoy what is left of the weekend. We'll see you in the morning, Laura.'

'Yes, you will,' she assured him confidently, the job being in a different compartment of her life, where all was uncomplicated and rewarding.

When they'd gone she made a meal for Gabriel and herself while he saw to bedtime for the children.

When he came downstairs afterwards he said levelly, 'James called whilst you were out. The board won't be meeting for some time because it's midsummer and holiday time. Some of them disappear for weeks on end, so it isn't going to be yet that your concerns will be answered one way or another.'

Laura put down her knife and fork slowly and looking directly at him asked, 'What about *your* concerns, Gabriel? Don't *you* have any?'

Oh, yes! He had them all right but wasn't going to voice them. Every time he thought about giving up medicine, especially in the form that he excelled in, it was like a knife in his heart, but his neglect of his family had an even greater effect.

As he met Laura's cool, questioning glance, his thoughts went back to the time when there had been no clouds in their sky, when the beautiful eyes that now were cold had melted with her love for him.

It had been a time that when night came and the children were asleep that they'd made love, and afterwards she'd slept safe and secure in his arms.

Now she went in and closed her bedroom door on him and he felt that he hadn't the right to protest.

'Yes, I have concerns, Laura, but they're coming from a different direction from yours and they won't go away until I see the way ahead clearly.'

After that Laura felt there was nothing left to say and they finished the meal in a silence that lasted until the summer dusk closed in on them.

The next morning there was little time for talking, with dinner money for the children to be sorted and school uniforms to be found.

When Sophie and Josh were ready for Gabriel to

walk them to school once more, he paused in the doorway and said, 'Will you still be here when I get back?'

'Possibly,' she informed him, 'but it will only be for a matter of minutes. I have a pharmaceutical rep due at ten o'clock. She's from one of the big companies and calls quite frequently, which is something that might be going to change, as the general feeling at the surgery is that the attraction was Hugo Lawrence, and now that he has got his heart's desire in Ruby we may not see so much of her.'

The children were waiting for him at the gate and he said, 'I just want a quick word, that's all.'

'Yes, all right, then,' she agreed, and thought it was more than she did. She hadn't slept a wink for thinking about their exchange of words from the night before.

When he came back, striding along the road where Swallows Barn stood amongst green lawns and a background of trees that were heavy with the bright green leaves of summer, Laura was hovering at the gate, ready to leave for work. But not in so much of a hurry that she didn't have time to dwell for a moment on the attractions of the husband who had become an unpredictable stranger during their months apart.

He was tall and trim, with hair dark and thickly curling, and hazel eyes that used to light up when he saw her, but were now guarded and unreadable.

When he stopped beside her Gabriel said, 'Sorry to keep you waiting. I met the vicar as I was coming away from the school. He was on his way to the surgery to see Nathan Gallagher with regard to what I said to him on

Saturday and wanted to chat for a moment. I do hope that I am wrong about the hoarseness.'

'But you don't think you are?'

'No, unfortunately, but you need to be on your way and all I wanted to say was that I regret burdening you with the news from James after the stress of yesterday evening. It could have waited as nothing is going to be happening soon.'

She loved him in that moment, loved his consideration for her feelings when the greater pain at the delay must surely be his.

Reaching out, she took his hand in hers and squeezed it gently, and with all the complexities of their lives put to one side told him, 'Regret is an awful word, Gabriel, and we've both had cause to think it and say it. Can we come to an agreement not to use it any more?' As his eyes widened she gave his hand one more squeeze and set off for the practice with a lighter heart than before.

Gabriel planned to go shopping that morning, something else that he'd had little time for before. Their wedding anniversary was only a few weeks away and he was hoping that the occasion might be as special now as it used to be, that it might be a time for new beginnings, and with that thought in mind he drove into the nearby town to buy an eternity ring.

He chose a circlet of diamonds on a gold band and he asked the jeweller for an engraving on the inside. He left the shop satisfied with his purchase and hoped that Laura would feel the same when he presented the ring to her.

He'd never forgotten their anniversary in spite of the glow fading from their marriage, but sometimes flowers, or a night at the theatre, had been arranged by his secretary, and he'd hoped on those occasions that if Laura had guessed, she hadn't felt that he loved her any less.

This occasion was going to be different. He had time to arrange something special, time for lots of things, but it always seemed that she hadn't, and aware that the tables had turned he wondered how she felt about being the career person while he spent his time with Sophie and Josh and kept the household running in an orderly fashion.

Laura had seemed to soften when they'd spoken briefly before she'd left for the practice that morning. Was it the beginning of the end of the cold war and now both of the girls in his life were going to be happy?

Whilst he had no worries about Josh, Sophie was very different. Intelligent, quick to pick up an atmosphere, and lost until he had come back into her life.

He would never forget her expression when he'd appeared on the island, the moment of blank uncertainty before she'd called his name and flung herself into his arms as if she'd thought she would never see him again.

They'd kept her young mind free of the truth about his time in prison, but maybe it would have been better if she'd known where he was and had understood that was why he wasn't with them.

But she was fine now, happy and content that he was back with them, and he intended that that was how she was going to stay. He'd given up his career not just for Laura but for the children's sakes too, and he could just about exist without it as long as the three of them were happy.

But with regard to his wife there might be a long way to go before that happened. She'd seemed loving towards him earlier on, but had it been because she was sorry for him?

In her basement office where the computers and patients' records were kept, Laura's busy day was under way and she was grateful for it, as for a few hours it would keep other thoughts at bay.

In a few weeks' time a heavily pregnant Libby would be leaving the practice after spending all her working life there, and as practice manager Laura was in the process of arranging a farewell party for the contented mother-to-be on the Saturday night after her last Friday at work.

At the same time discussions were taking place about finding Libby's replacement.

Also the refurbishment of the surgery was due to start during the coming week and unless organised properly would cause chaos for staff and patients alike. She had arranged that most of the work would be done in the evenings and at the weekends when the place was closed and that way hoped to bring confusion down to a minimum, but it was still going to be a big undertaking.

The pharmaceutical rep had been and with Hugo so obviously enchanted with his new wife hadn't stayed long, but had managed to get in a comment to the effect that she wouldn't have thought that a pale-faced beanpole would have been his type.

Back at the house Gabriel had received a phone call from Nathan. 'Well spotted with the vicar's hoarseness,' he said. 'We could do with you around permanently, Gabriel. Have you heard about the clinic that will be opening shortly at the side of the surgery?'

'Yes, I have,' he told him, 'but my life is rather complicated at the moment. I've just finished a prison sentence for GBH. It was a man who was taking advantage of Laura and I accidentally injured him quite seriously.'

'I knew there was something,' Nathan said, 'and I have to say that I would probably have done the same if it had been someone coming on to Libby. I'll keep my fingers crossed for you, Gabriel. It would be a shame for your abilities to be put on hold for any length of time.'

When they'd finished the call Gabriel stood gazing into space.

What would Nathan have thought if he'd told him that he had already *prevented himself* from practising and it was raw agony?

The thought of it was unbearable. It was his life, the fount of his existence, but so were his family and his past neglect of them had been unpardonable, so much so that he was determined that Laura was going to get back her confidence in him no matter what.

He spent the early afternoon tidying up the garden and before he went to collect the children went up to have a shower in the en suite in the master bedroom.

A robe that Laura was using hung behind the door and he held it against his cheek for a moment. It smelt of the bath essence she used and his throat closed up. Apart from the two occasions when he'd kissed her, unable to hold back even though he'd sensed resistance in her, there had been no other physical contact between them. Losing his career was bad, but losing Laura was much much worse.

When he arrived at the school he was told that Sophie's teacher wanted a word with him, and leaving Josh chatting to Toby in the playground where he was waiting to be picked up by either Libby or Nathan, he went into the empty classroom where she was waiting and observed her questioningly.

'We had a little upset this afternoon with Sophie,' she explained, 'so I thought I'd better have a word, Dr Armitage. We tried to contact you, but you weren't around at the time.'

'What was it?' he asked. 'My daughter is very happy here and so is Josh.'

'Yes. I know,' she told him, 'and we are pleased about that.'

He was frowning. 'So?

'Sophie fell in the schoolyard during playtime this afternoon and was quite shaken with the impact. She kept asking for you but we couldn't get hold of you, and she became distraught.'

'So didn't you try her mother? Laura works at the surgery.'

'Yes. She came immediately and offered comfort and Sophie gradually calmed down.'

'And was she hurt?' he asked anxiously.

'No. It was just shock, we think. When her mother left she took her back to the surgery with her, and when you've collected Josh you will find Sophie waiting for you there.'

He nodded. 'Thank you for looking after my daughter,' he told her, and went to seek out Josh with the feeling that he'd been congratulating himself too soon with regard to Sophie's need of him. It was still there in her young mind, the fear that he might disappear again. If that wasn't enough to tell him that here in Swallowbrook was where he needed to be, he didn't know what was.

'Why didn't you come when Sophie wanted you?' Josh asked as they made their way to the surgery.

The school must have phoned while he'd been cutting the grass. The noise of the lawnmower was enough to drown all normal sounds, or maybe it had been while he'd been under the shower.

Whatever the reason, Laura had been brought in to deal with Sophie's upset and must be wondering why he hadn't been around.

When they arrived at the surgery his tension slackened. They found Sophie in Reception, chatting to one of the nurses, who told him smilingly that his daughter had been telling her that she wanted to be a doctor like him.

Not if I can help it, he thought grimly as the three of them went down to where Laura was working in the basement.

'I am so sorry about that,' he told her in a low voice. 'I was cutting the grass. The mower drowns out all noise and I never heard the phone.

'I thought that Sophie's fears had been put to rest but it seems I was mistaken.'

'It was the shock of the fall that triggered it,' she told him evenly, 'and when you didn't appear to offer comfort, her confidence in you being around took a backward step, but she's fine now. I wouldn't mention it if I were you. I've checked her over and there doesn't appear to be any sign of injury so you can relax.'

'Yes, but can *you*?' he said stiffly. 'I know you're busy at the moment with all sorts of projects, and having to chase round to the school won't have helped things along with regard to that.'

'The fact that I enjoy the challenge of working here doesn't mean that I've forgotten where my priorities lie,' she said chidingly, and when the phone rang at that moment he didn't get the chance to ask what *his* rating was amongst them.

Gathering the children to him, he pointed the three of them in the direction of Swallows Barn and home, and took Laura's advice with regard to Sophie's upset by not mentioning it as she seemed to have forgotten all about it.

But he hadn't. It didn't alter the fact that the distress caused by his long absence previously hadn't entirely disappeared, and if Laura's calm handling of the incident had overtones of it all being part of a day in her life, was it surprising?

Added to that was Josh wanting to know why he hadn't been there when Sophie needed him, as if he, Gabriel, at that moment, was outside the safe circle that Laura had created for the three of them.

When she arrived home at the end of her working day he expected that the first thing she would do was check on Sophie, who was on her swing in the garden, but to his surprise she came straight to where he was and said in a low voice, 'Have you recovered from Sophie's upset?' She glanced at their daughter. 'It would seem that *she* has. I did feel for you, Gabriel,' adding with a smile that took the sting out of her next comment, 'But that's the price of popularity, I'm afraid.'

He sighed. 'The main thing is that she wasn't hurt. That was all I was concerned about at the time, but it does mean that she still has some feeling of insecurity where I'm concerned and I can't bear that any more than I was able to bear being shut away from the three of you.'

'So why don't we see if Ruby and Hugo will sit in for us for an hour when we've eaten?' she suggested. 'Sophie likes Hugo so she won't be fretting about where you are. The two of us could go for a sail or a stroll by the lake and still be back before their bedtime.'

He was observing her in surprise. 'That would be great if they can manage it, but it's very short notice, Laura. Are you feeling sorry for me because I can't put a foot right with any of my family and are prepared to give me some of your time? Even Josh wanted to know why I hadn't been there when Sophie needed me.'

'Yes, I do want us to have a brief time on our own,' she told him, 'and, no, it isn't because I feel sorry for you. You're far too capable to invite sympathy, but you've had a bad day.'

'I won't argue about that,' he replied. 'So, are you going to ring Ruby?'

'Yes, I'll do it now.' And seconds later she told him, 'They will be round in an hour, which will give the four of us time to have our meal and clear away before they come. Ruby said we needn't rush back as Hugo is the tops when it comes to reading bedtime stories.'

CHAPTER FIVE

THERE were no tears or protests when they left the children with Ruby and Hugo later that evening. The young ones knew them well enough, especially Hugo, to be happy in their care, and as Laura and Gabriel left the house with instructions from their childminders not to rush back, it had been such a long time since there had just been the two of them that for a few moments they were lost for words, until Laura spoke.

'There is an open-air band concert tonight at the far end of the lake. You like that kind of thing, don't you?'

'Yes,' he replied, 'but not tonight. We've too much catching up to do. It's like being on a first date but with baggage in the form of my stay at Her Majesty's pleasure and a marriage that is floundering.'

'I didn't suggest we spend some time together going over old wounds,' she said flatly. 'I was hoping we could put them all behind us for a while.' She pointed to woods, scented and silent at the bottom of one of the fells that swept down to the lake.

The evening sun was still warm and as they lounged on grass beneath the trees Laura was happy to have him to herself for a little while, and she lay back and smiled up at him. It was a mistake. The dark hazel eyes looking into hers were warming as he said softly, 'Laura, when I said it was like a first date I wasn't expecting this sort of thing to be on the agenda.'

He had rolled over and was looking down on to her and she said, 'If you mean what I think you mean, Gabriel, it wasn't, isn't, because it would be just sex. For us it was never like that. I brought you here where we would be quiet and undisturbed to have a short time of peace in our lives, and if by me lying on the grass I gave out the wrong signals, I'm sorry.'

'Don't be,' he said levelly. 'I've never forced myself on you and am not going to start now. But I rather think we've exploded the peace and quiet that you had in mind, and my determination is that we should discuss our problems, so let's go, shall we?'

Knowing that he was right, she got slowly to her feet and they travelled back the way they'd come in a silence that was only broken when they arrived back at the house, where Ruby and Hugo were waiting to inform them that after lots of fun in the garden their children had been successfully put to bed.

As they thanked them for their efforts neither Hugo nor Ruby was aware that the evening had been yet another hiccup on the way to peace between them.

The next morning the sun was still out to charm them and as soon as the children had eaten they were out in the garden, while their parents dined at a slower pace.

It was Saturday and would seem like an eternity if they didn't find something interesting to do, Laura thought, but after the misunderstandings of the night before there wasn't a lot she could think of that would lighten the atmosphere, and in no time at all Sophie and Josh were tired of the garden and wanting to go somewhere else.

'Libby and Nathan are spending the weekend on the island,' she told Gabriel. 'They have invited us to call if ever we are sailing in that direction and I'm sure the children would like that.'

She wouldn't. It would bring back the memory of his return to their world, unexpected and unannounced while they had been having their picnic, but there was no need for him to know that.

He had been quiet and remote ever since Sophie's upset. She had soon forgotten it, but Gabriel hadn't. It had been a reminder that past insecurities hadn't entirely been forgotten where his daughter was concerned, and Laura's hurts were something he lived with on a daily basis.

Only Josh, happy in his new life with his new friend, seemed to have come out of the painful past without hurt. Laura's suggestion the night before that they ask Ruby and Hugo to child-sit had lifted his spirits, but after it had turned out to be a non-event the remoteness was back.

Aware of it, Laura wasn't sure what his reply would be to the suggestion and was surprised when he said, 'Yes, why not? Why don't we take one of the passenger launches and stop off at the island for a while? Then pick up another of the boats at the landing stage there and sail to the marina for an early dinner.'

'That would be lovely,' she agreed, with spirits lifting, and he smiled a brittle smile.

She rang Libby and Nathan to ask if it was convenient for them to call and was assured that they would be most welcome, so with Josh running on ahead, eager to be with Toby again, and Sophie skipping along between her parents, they set off for the family outing that would occupy most of the day.

While the children played with Toby, and the two women talked babies, Nathan took Gabriel to one side and told him a bit more about the cancer care clinic that was being built.

'Where it stands and the land all around it used to belong to Libby's parents, who had it as a farm. The practice premises were the farmhouse and the land was where the animals were kept.

'When her mother died her father lost interest in the place. He let it gradually fall into a very poor state and had to sell it, and as the previous practice building was becoming too small for the ever-increasing number of patients, my father, who was in charge at that time, bought the farmhouse and the land to provide a new medical centre in the village, so it is seen as the ideal place to build the clinic, right on our doorstep, which couldn't be better as far as we are concerned.'

'I think it's a terrific project, quite cutting edge in its own way,' Gabriel told him.

'I know you have the hearing hanging over your head, but we could really use a man with your expertise. There won't be any decisions made with regard to staffing the new clinic until the late autumn,' Nathan told him, 'though, of course, they will have to start interviewing soon, but I'll keep you informed.'

'I would appreciate that,' said Gabriel. 'They are dragging their feet at the London end, which doesn't maker life any easier as I have Laura and the children to consider and whatever I decide it has to be right for them.'

Libby announced that lunch was ready at that moment so any further discussion had to be put on hold, and when the two families had eaten and the children had gone back to their play it was inevitable that the conversation turned to the practice, with three of the adults present working there.

Nathan informed Gabriel, 'The vicar has had the necessary tests done on his throat and there is cancer of the larynx, so he's being treated with radiotherapy as a first option. There has been no mention of surgery so far, but time will tell, as it always does.

'I imagine that he wants to thank you for your quick diagnosis and said he intends calling on you in the near future. He is fervently hoping that he won't lose his voice.' As Laura listened to what he was saying, the thing that was eating away at her was back. When it came to intensive treatment or surgery Gabriel would be missing from the ranks of oncology if he didn't change his mind about giving it up, *if those who decided such things from a practising point of view didn't do it for him.*

She would not have asked that sort of sacrifice from him, never had, never would. All she had wanted that day at the hospital had been that he should not forget that she was part of his life just as much as his patients, that she loved him and was willing to share him with them, would endure anything, except being ignored.

They stayed on the island with Libby and Nathan for a couple of hours then, feeling that they'd butted into their weekend long enough, picked up the next passing launch and sailed to the marina.

To anyone observing them they were an attractive family with the mother golden haired, blue eyed, and the boy by her side with a similar colouring. While the father, darkly attractive, was holding the hand of a girl child who was unmistakably his.

There was the choice of a fast-food eating place at the moorings or a smart restaurant that Gabriel was observing approvingly, and almost as if they were back to the old days for a moment Laura said laughingly, 'I think that our two young ones would go for chicken nuggets and chips with a can of fizzy drink, in preference to the kind of dishes that were our favourites...if you remember.'

His gaze was holding hers. Of course he remembered. His imprisonment hadn't been that long.

* * *

That evening they sat in silence on the patio after the children were asleep, watching the sun set over the lake and the outlines of the surrounding fells darken as the light began to fade. It was the kind of moment that once would have brought Laura into his arms, but the memory of the night before and all the other painful moments that had gone before it was still heavy upon her, and leaving Gabriel sitting in the summer dusk she went hopefully to let sleep blot out the uncertainties of the present.

The morning of their wedding anniversary dawned with grey skies above and when Laura drew back the curtains and saw the weather she sighed. The day wasn't going to be like times in the past when there had been flowers and presents, going out for a meal, and magical lovemaking, but it would have helped if the sun had been shining and lightened it a little.

Over the last few years the occasion had become less memorable because of Gabriel's workload, but he'd never actually forgotten it, even if he had been pushed to the limit and his secretary had been brought in to see to the arrangements.

Laura hadn't minded that too much, had understood the pressures he had been under. Until the unsatisfactory lives they had been living domestically had caught up with them.

She had something to give him to celebrate the occasion and was hoping he wouldn't read anything into it that wasn't there. Other than it was a large studio photograph of her and the children in a beautiful silver frame.

When she'd had it done she'd thought that he could read into it what he liked, that it was a reminder of their presence in his life, or a memory of a certain stage in the growth of their children to look back on in later years, or even as a flashback to when she'd made the totally preposterous demand for a divorce.

She gave it to him as soon as they met up in the kitchen before Sophie and Josh appeared for breakfast and as he gazed at it for a split second she saw the raw hurt in him, but it was gone in a flash and he said, 'When did you have this taken?'

'It was taken while you were away from us.'

'Ah, yes, I remember,' he said, with his voice softening. 'And I told you not to bring it for me to look at as it would have hurt too much, seeing the three of you so near in the photograph but so far away in reality.'

Without any further comment he began to start the preparations for breakfast. Feeling even less celebratory after that little chat, which hadn't included any signs of what Gabriel had thought fitted the occasion as a gift for her, she went up to wake the children on what was their last day of the summer term.

As Laura walked to the practice some time later the thought was there that the situation between her and Gabriel wasn't being helped by the stress of what was happening workwise.

The refurbishment was under way and not going well, *far from it.*

She was uneasy about the expertise of the small local firm chosen by the doctors to do the work. New to the area, she had gone along with their suggestion and was now wishing she hadn't.

Although the builder in charge and his two assistants were a likeable trio, she felt that there were too many tea breaks, too much chatting amongst them, and knew that irrespective of who had given them the contract it was she as practice manager who in the end was responsible for satisfactory completion of the work.

When she'd exchanged chaste kisses with Gabriel before she'd given him the photograph, she'd been determined that the evening ahead would have some lightness to it, even though it might lack the magic of earlier years, and as the day progressed had managed to get to the hair salon in the village in the lunch hour and fit in a manicure at the same time.

If Gabriel wanted her in his bed tonight she would be there for him, she vowed, and would forget for a few hours her hurts and yearnings.

She was the last one to leave the surgery at the end of the day. It had been a quiet afternoon for once, the contractors had left and so had the surgery staff. It was only when she was about to lock the door that she became conscious of water beneath her feet.

'Oh, no!' she groaned. 'Not tonight of all nights!' Even as she said it she was reaching for the nearest phone to get the builder back, and received no immediate answer.

When at last his voice came over the line and she explained what was happening, he seemed to have no immediate sense of urgency and merely said, 'Turn the stop tap off, Mrs Armitage, and I'll check the water pipes in the morning.'

'You will look at them *now*!' she told him with deadly calm, 'or you will be sacked!'

That got through to him and shortly after that the three of them turned up and announced that they'd been renewing pipework that afternoon and might have made a wrong connection.

'So put it right, then!' she told them. 'And then maybe I can go home to my family.'

They did as she'd asked but it was not to be a rapid repair and when she rang Gabriel with the hands of the surgery clock on half past seven to tell him that she would be at least another hour, she was hoping that he hadn't set too much store on this special day in their lives and so wouldn't be too disappointed at the delay in her homecoming.

It was hard to tell how he actually did feel when he answered her call. He just said flatly, 'So how long have the repairs been going on and why aren't Nathan and Hugo there to see to it? Have you told them what's happening?'

'I can't get hold of either of them,' she told him. 'It's a lovely evening, they're probably making the most of it somewhere, *and I am the practice manager, Gabriel.*

I can't leave the building until I'm sure that there will be no more leakage.'

'Yes, sure,' he agreed. 'So I'll see you about eight-thirty, then.'

'Hopefully, yes,' she replied, and rang off.

The children were asleep. The table was set with the best china and cutlery, candles were glowing in the centre of it, and it was almost nine o'clock.

No mean cook, Gabriel had made chicken parfait for the first course. It was one of their favourite dishes, and for dessert he intended to produce brandy-snap baskets filled with strawberries and topped with clotted cream.

What was missing was Laura sitting opposite him, sharing the meal, with the ring he had chosen for such an occasion on her finger, *but it wasn't happening like that*.

Their lives had turned full circle, he thought wryly. *He* was waiting for *her* to come home from whatever was keeping her job-wise. *She* was the one delayed by necessity, not as serious by far as the things that had prolonged his working day, but the change of circumstances was there, not to be ignored.

How many times must she have gone through this scenario and ended up leaving a note to say that his meal was in the oven, and then gone to sleep beside the empty space where he should have been?

When she came dashing up the drive a few seconds later, mortified to think that their wedding anniversary had ended up as much of a non-event as everything else in their lives at the present time, he met her at the door and as she stood panting in the hallway told her, 'It's all right, Laura. These things happen. The food I've prepared will be past its best, but the wine is still chilled and the flowers haven't yet started to droop.'

'No, I'm the one who's drooping,' she said wearily, 'drooping with fatigue brought on by the carelessness of others.'

He knew immediately that it wasn't the right moment to give her the ring. She'd had a catastrophic evening and was exhausted. Cries of delight would not be on the menu, so the jeweller's box stayed out of sight.

He had flowers and chocolates waiting for her, so she would know he hadn't forgotten, but the chance to show her how he really felt had been knocked sideways, as had the food, and the atmosphere he'd tried to create.

When she went into the dining room and viewed the effort he'd made to celebrate the occasion Laura was gripped by a sick feeling of dismay.

'Are you going to dish out the food?' she asked softly as tears pricked.

'Just help yourself,' was the reply. 'I'll see you at breakfast' As her mortification increased, he left her to it, and seconds later she heard the front door close behind him.

Once outside Gabriel walked towards where the lake slapped peacefully against age-old stone, and stood looking out across it as darkness fell, bringing with it moon and stars, and into the midst of his tangled thoughts came the memory of the place that had been his second home back there in London, the operating theatre.

The smell of it was in his nostrils, he could almost taste the tension that was always present, and every part of him needed to be there again, but tonight's fiasco brought about by Laura being late home had been the climax of all his recent observations about what life must have been like for her before their roles had been reversed.

Turning, he went swiftly back the way he had come, praying that she might still be up so that he could tell her there would be another night, another moment to share, when they might begin to find the way back to where they had once been.

When he arrived back at the house the routine was in place. There was no sign of her and her bedroom door was shut. But one thing was different: there were two notes on the kitchen worktop.

The first one said that she was so sorry that her job at the practice had spoiled the occasion, that she had enjoyed the food immensely, it had been delicious, and it would have been even more enjoyable if he'd been there. *And had he ever thought of becoming a chef?*

It had been a light-hearted comment with an undertone of having accepted that he wasn't going back to medicine, and he smiled a grim smile.

The second missive was to explain that she intended going early to the surgery in the morning to check that all was in order with regard to the building work before the day began, so she wouldn't be joining them for breakfast. Disappointed that the day had ended so badly after a shaky start, Gabriel turned out the lights and headed off upstairs himself to spend his anniversary alone.

Laura had kept to her decision of the night before and was nowhere to be seen when he went downstairs the following morning. But when he drew back the curtains he caught a glimpse of her striding purposefully down the road, looking neat and trim in one of the smart suits she wore for the job, and his thoughts of the night before by the lake came back. Now it was *her* turn to be gone for the day before *h*e was awake.

When she arrived at the surgery all was in order, with the workmen already on the job, and it seemed that there had been no further leaks during the night.

'I called back to check at two o'clock in the morning just to be on the safe side,' the boss said, 'and everything was okay.' As if aware that their lack of speed, carelessness and long lunch breaks might lose them the contract, he followed it with, 'We're going to forge ahead with it today and hope to be finished soon by working over the weekend like you asked us to.'

'Good,' she said absently, with her thoughts on Gabriel, Sophie, and Josh breakfasting without her. She had looked in on the children before leaving the house. Both of them had been sleeping peacefully, and she'd paused for a moment outside the door of Gabriel's room, but that was all it had been, just a fragment of time filled with longing before she'd set off for the day ahead.

A short meeting with the doctors to explain the trauma of the previous night before the day got under way had Nathan all for sacking the workforce on the spot, but Hugo said with his usual calm reasoning that as the refurbishments were almost completed they should allow them to finish but keep a close eye on the amiable trio, and once it was done have all the work checked over by their insurers before settling the account.

After that had been agreed upon, Laura carried on with the duties of the day and tried not to think about how Gabriel must have felt about his wasted efforts of the night before.

She'd sat gazing at the untouched food for ages after he'd gone and then, not wanting to cause him any further hurt, had eaten her fill of it and left a note to say how much she had enjoyed it.

When she arrived home that evening at the correct time he asked, 'So no more leaks or other hiccups?'

She managed a smile. 'No, none. The timing was all wrong, wasn't it?'

'Just a bit,' he agreed, 'but that was yesterday. Today I have had major heart surgery.'

'What?' she gasped.

Unbuttoning his shirt, he displayed a long white strip of material wrapped tightly around him and spattered with tomato ketchup.

As she laughed at the spectacle Sophie appeared with Josh close behind. 'We've been playing at doctors and nurses,' she announced with matron-like precision, and as he gave a theatrical groan she went on, 'Daddy was the patient.'

'That makes a change, then,' Laura commented. 'What was the problem?'

'His heart,' Josh said.

'Really!' she exclaimed with appropriate concern. 'And what was it that had caused that?'

'It was broken,' the young nurse in charge said, observing them with a look that was old beyond her years.

'We've had to mend it with sticky tape,' Josh explained.

'Incredible!' she breathed.

'Like father, like children,' Gabriel said, smiling at her above their heads, 'You see before you an amazing recovery.' Laura felt as if she was on solid ground for once.

For a moment they were back how they used to be, together, laughing at the antics of their offspring with all the cobwebs of the past scattering on the wind. If Gabriel had been a father not around much before, he was making up for it now and she loved him for it.

When the four of them were seated around the table for their evening meal it was still there, the tranquillity that came with minds in tune, brief though it might turn out to be.

It *was* brief, as it happened. They were watching the children have a last romp before bedtime when the vicar appeared at the side of the hedge that surrounded the garden and called across in the husky voice that had attracted Gabriel's attention, 'May I disturb you good people for a moment?'

'Yes, of course,' Laura told him, and went to greet him with a welcoming smile.

'It is actually your husband that I have come to see,' he said.

'I thought it might be,' she told him with the smile still in place, and when Gabriel joined them she left the two men together and went back to her seat on the patio to avoid being reminded on a tranquil summer night of the uncertainty of Gabriel's future in cancer care.

'I have come to express my gratitude for your concern on my behalf, Dr Armitage,' the vicar said as the two men shook hands. 'It was almost as if you were heaven sent. It seems I do have some cancer of the throat and am being given radiotherapy to see if it will clear up the problem.

'Thanks to you, it has been caught in its early stages and the outlook is good so I am very much indebted to you. Do I take it that you are having a sabbatical from your work here in our lovely village?'

'Er, yes, something like that,' Gabriel told him.

'So where is it that you practise?'

From her seat in the garden Laura couldn't hear the question being asked in the other man's hoarse voice, but she could tell what it was by Gabriel's reply, and it was as if their moments of togetherness earlier had never been as he said, 'I'm not involved with cancer care at the moment. I suppose you could say I'm at a crossroads, undecided which one to travel along in the future.'

'Ah, yes, I see,' the vicar said, and changed the subject as Laura decided it was time that she joined them. 'There is a barn supper in the village hall on Friday night,' he informed them. 'Do come along if you get the chance.'

'Yes, we will,' she told him, and off he went, back to the vicarage and an anxious wife.

'So what is a barn supper?' Gabriel asked when he'd gone

'It is a Country and Western type evening with dancing and a supper that everyone contributes to,' she told him. 'They were talking about it at the practice otherwise I wouldn't be so well informed.'

'I see, and now that you've explained that, Laura, perhaps you can tell me why the shutters are down again between us? Is it what I said to the vicar about the job?'

'It could be,' she told him. 'It sounded so lightweight the way you explained it.'

Lightweight, he thought grimly. It was the first time he'd ever heard a nightmare described as such.

Most of the refurbishment of the surgery had been completed. The building work had been passed by insurers and an outside company connected with the local council, to put Laura's mind and everyone else's at rest, and now it was carpet-fitting time with new seating ready and waiting to be put in position. As the final stages of the project unfolded before her, she wished her life would untangle itself so pleasantly.

There was much progress also taking place on the clinic next to the practice and Libby had once said when the two of them were taking their lunch break together that her father, when next he came to Swallowbrook from his home in Somerset, would be pleased to know that the farm he had neglected all those years ago was bearing fruit of a different sort from what he had grown, in the form of a centre of hope for the sick and suffering.

CHAPTER SIX

IT WOULD be Libby's last day soon and all the staff had been invited to a farewell party that Laura had been asked to arrange on behalf of the practice.

Previous similar occasions had been held at the hotel on the lakeside. John Gallagher, Nathan's father, and one-time head of the practice, had chosen to have his retirement party there, and so had Laura's uncle, Gordon Jessup, who had preceded her as practice manager.

But Libby's choice was one of the launches that sailed the lake with restaurant and bar facilities, and everyone was looking forward to the new venue.

Gabriel had been invited, along with other partners of surgery staff. Josh and Sophie were also on the guest list at Toby's request, and there had been a suggestion that Sophie bring a school friend for company if she wanted to.

With that event to take place shortly, the other three doctors were turning their thoughts to a replacement for Libby, and along with her other duties Laura was arranging interviews to find a suitable candidate.

Her working days seemed to fly past as summer

wended its way towards autumn. Having Gabriel there for Sophie and Josh during the long summer holiday from school was solving what could have been a problem otherwise, though not an insurmountable one with holiday clubs available for children with working parents.

But being with their father, who always had something interesting planned for the three of them, was what they liked best, and until they were asleep in the evening after the day's activities everything was fine.

After that, with Gabriel doing jobs in the garden and Laura drawn to what was left of the sun, the feeling of living separate lives was still there.

The four of them went to the barn supper as Laura had told the vicar they would, and it felt good, Gabriel thought when they arrived, as if they were no longer newcomers to Swallowbrook but belonged there.

As the children went to seek out their friends he took Laura's hand and as they joined the dancers already in Country and Western mood he smiled across at her.

Laura smiled back and it was there again, one of the brief moments of togetherness that came suddenly and went as quickly, but not this time, he hoped. When the caller cried, 'Swing your partner,' he swung her into his arms and held her close, and the longing they had for each other was there, vibrant, demanding, and never brought out into the open since the day that Gabriel had told her he was giving up medicine.

When the dance was over, still holding her hand,

he led her onto the deserted village green and in the shadow of an old oak tree that looked as if it had been there for centuries he said, 'When we arrived everyone smiled and waved and I had a fantastic feeling of belonging. It was like coming home, as if this place had always been waiting for me. Do you have that kind of feeling about Swallowbrook, Laura?'

'I didn't at first because you weren't there,' she said. 'I saw the house that my uncle gave us as just a means to an end with a job thrown in, and it still feels like that sometimes because we've lost something special along the way.'

She saw him flinch. 'But, yes, I do love living here, the children are so happy away from the big-city atmosphere and I enjoy working at the practice. But there are bigger issues at stake, aren't there, Gabriel?'

Watching his face darken, she knew that it would have been better if she'd let the matter of his career stay in the background of their lives, as she'd promised herself she would, because she'd just spoilt the moment that had been theirs when they'd left the dancing and come out into the scented night to be alone.

'I'm sorry,' she said contritely.

'For what?' he wanted to know. 'Sorry for what you knew was going to happen the moment we were out here alone, or sorry for mentioning the unmentionable—my lack of employment?'

'No, I'm sorry for breaking into the feeling of togetherness that comes so rarely in our lives these days,' she told him. 'I do understand how much you are hurting, but ever since you came back to me from that unmentionable place I've felt that you are shutting me out.'

'That's because I feel so guilty about everything.'

'Yes, I know,' she said gently, and reaching across she held his head between her hands and brushed her lips against his fleetingly, and the moment, delayed by her earlier comment, came surging back, this time with it feeling so right to be in Gabriel's arms with her mouth tender beneath his kisses and her body language telling its own story.

But they weren't exactly in the master bedroom of the house. Any moment someone might come along, and the children were only feet away inside the village hall, so at last he said reluctantly, 'We need to go back inside. Sophie and Josh will be wondering where we are.'

She nodded, and when she held out her hand he encircled it with his and they joined the dancers once more, as if they'd never been absent.

When it was time for the buffet that everyone had contributed to the vicar was there, looking less than his usual cherubic self after his first radiotherapy treatment but smiling and chatting as best he could to some of those present, and as he watched him Gabriel was overwhelmed by a feeling of uselessness.

Was that all he had to his credit over recent weeks and the months out of circulation? he wondered. His only role to provide a warning to the unsuspecting that there might be cause for alarm? He ought to be doing more than that, much, much more. If he wasn't carrying the burden of guilt that had made him tell Laura that his work with cancer patients was over, he would be back in the thick of it by now…*if those in authority would let him.*

The vicar's wife was approaching and knowing that the role of bystander could sometimes be almost as painful as that of the patient, he waited to see what it was that she wanted of him and was not surprised when she said, 'Am I right to be concerned that my husband is doing so much talking after the treatment, Dr Armitage? He is so used to chatting to everyone and thinks he can carry on like that, but…'

'He should be resting his voice as much as possible at the moment,' he told her. 'It will be painful for him to talk. I suggest that you persuade him to go home where he will not feel the need to chat.' He smiled reassuringly for the anxious woman. 'Tell the vicar that is what I advise him to do.'

There was silence as the four of them walked the short distance home after the barn supper. Sophie and Josh were tired after the late night and their parents were thinking their own thoughts.

Laura was remembering Gabriel's conversation with the vicar's wife and thinking he must surely be aware of how little he had to do with oncology in their present situation. For his part, Gabriel's feeling of inadequacy had returned to haunt him.

But the most memorable moments of the evening had been those they'd spent in the shadow of the old oak tree. For a precious short time they'd been moulded into one, like they used to be, and he wondered if she would come to him when the children were asleep to carry on where they'd left off.

Laura had showered and perfumed herself once Sophie and Josh had drifted into dreamland and it was as she was crossing the landing to Gabriel's room that she heard Sophie cry out in pain.

He'd heard it too as the door swung open immediately, and after one startled look in her direction he rushed to where Sophie's cries were becoming louder. Grabbing a robe hung behind the door to cover her scanty nightwear, she followed him at the same speed, with everything else forgotten except their daughter's need of them.

She was crying out in pain, flushed, had a temperature, and her cheeks were wet with tears as Gabriel asked gently, 'What's wrong, Sophie? Where does it hurt, sweetheart?'

'It's my tummy,' she cried, and as he pulled down the covers Laura saw that her small abdomen was swollen. Gabriel was feeling it gently and when he touched the lower part of it on the right side she cried out and started to sob more loudly.

'Could be appendicitis,' he told Laura, taking her to one side, 'but it is very rare in young children. We need to get Sophie to hospital. Will you go and get Josh up? The three of us need to get dressed fast, but first I'm going to call an ambulance and Josh will have to come with us. There is no one we can disturb at this hour to come and stay with him.'

'She is so young to have something like that,' Laura breathed as she helped a sleepy Josh back into the clothes that he'd only taken off a short time ago. 'Please don't let it be appendicitis.'

Gabriel thought, Please don't let it be anything worse, and if it is the appendix let us get there before the pain disappears, which means it's going to burst and she might develop peritonitis.

They were waiting for them in A and E and the doctor they saw was of the same opinion as Gabriel, that it might be appendicitis, but before tests were commenced he asked, 'Has your daughter had a cough or cold in the last few days, or raised lymph glands in the neck?'

'We haven't had cause to think her lymph glands were swollen,' Laura told him, 'but she had a virus sort of thing a week ago.'

'Why do you ask?' Gabriel wanted to know. 'Are you thinking that it might not be appendicitis, that it could be connected with some kind of mesenteric inflammation?'

'It could be,' the doctor replied. 'Do I take it that you are in the medical profession yourself?'

'Yes, I'm an oncologist, so this kind of thing isn't my forte, but I know that mesenteric adenitis is more likely to affect a child than appendicitis and can easily be mistaken for it.'

'Wow! Good for you!' the other man complimented

him. 'So let us hope that we are both right, for your little girl's sake, and now we shall do some tests.'

Laura had only been able to take in part of what they were saying as she was comforting Sophie and wiping away Josh's tears, which had been flowing ever since she'd had to wake him with the news that his sister was sick. The only time they had dried up for a few moments had been when he'd been enjoying the novelty of the ride in the ambulance.

She felt like weeping herself. Their beautiful daughter, who she sometimes thought was old beyond her years, was ill with something that could be very serious for a child of her age, and she was just as frightened and vulnerable as any eight-year-old would be in such circumstances.

'What is this thing that it might be?' she asked anxiously of Gabriel as they watched over her while tests were being done.

It was a blessed relief to have him there at such a time and the thought was present that in their lives before Swallowbrook he might have still been operating at that time of night.

'It is an acute disorder caused by lymph nodes in the membrane that keeps the stomach organs attached to the abdominal wall,' he explained. 'It usually occurs in children rather than adults after a throat or chest infection. The pain that comes with it is low on the right side of the abdomen, the same as in appendicitis, so care has to be taken not to confuse the two.'

'And which is the most serious?' she asked frantically.

'Appendicitis. The other usually clears up over a short time with analgesics to relieve the pain, so let's hope that is what it is. We should soon know.'

He took her hand in his. 'Laura, darling, I'm not going to let anything happen to our beautiful daughter, you can trust me on that. If there has to be an operation to remove the appendix I will request that I'm there while it is taking place. But let us not cross our bridges too soon.' He turned to Josh, who was looking tired and woebegone, and said gently, 'Are you watching what the doctors and nurses are doing for when we play that game again?'

'Yes, but it isn't pretend, is it?' Josh said. 'And I don't like it when it isn't.'

Neither do we, Laura thought raggedly, but the doctor in A and E was smiling when the test results came through and he told them, 'It is lymphmesenteric adenitis, to give it its full name. It should quieten down in a few hours with pain relief and rest.

'We want to keep her here for observation for a couple of days just to be on the safe side, but she should be all right after that. It is one of those things that flare up out of nowhere for a child and can be pretty painful at the onset. We are going to transfer Sophie to the children's ward and you can stay with her as long as you like.'

Laura felt that the relief was like healing balm on raw nerve endings as they walked beside the hospital trolley with Sophie on it, now drowsy as the illness began to subside after her being given pain control medication, and as her glance met Gabriel's she couldn't believe that in what seemed like another life she had told him she wanted a divorce. Whether near or far away, he was the centre of her world and always would be.

This was what their life together could be like if she would let it, Laura thought as she sat watching over Sophie at one side of the bed in the children's ward, with Gabriel sitting opposite and Josh asleep beside her on a visitor's chair.

She could have the relief of always having her husband there when she needed him if he kept to his resolve to give up on the stresses and never-ending demands of an oncologist consultant.

He was holding Sophie's hand and talking to her softly as the pain continued to ease, and she thought that with a nine-to-five position somewhere local he would still be around to walk the children to school, and if home first he could start preparations for the evening meal, and in times like this would be in charge, strong and reliable.

Life could be so good. She loved Swallowbrook and her position at the practice. It had helped to fill the empty days while they had been away from each other, and had given her shattered life some sense of purpose.

But there was one thing that would always prevent the present state of affairs becoming an idyllic kind of life for them all. Gabriel would end up feeling a lesser person because he had turned his back on his patients *and she could not be a party to that!*

The paediatric consultant on his ward rounds in the middle of the morning pronounced Sophie well enough to go home as she was now pain free and sitting up and taking notice of what was going on.

'We would have kept your daughter in for another twenty-four hours if there had been any signs that the infection hadn't cleared,' he told them, 'but she has fought it off very well and hopefully seen the last of it. Obviously bring her back if there is any recurrence of the adenitis, but I'm inclined to think that it was just an isolated incident due to the viral infection she'd had the week before.'

The atmosphere in the house for the rest of the weekend was subdued, with Gabriel in sombre mood, Josh still sleepy after being wakened and transported to A and E in the middle of the night, and Laura speechless with relief to know that Sophie wasn't seriously ill.

The only one of them who seemed to have benefited from the worrying incident was the patient herself, who, having been in close contact with real doctors and nurses, was keen for Josh and herself to take on the roles again, but was disappointed to find that having seen them at close range her brother wasn't all that keen.

On Monday morning it was back to normality, with Sophie fully recovered, and Laura left the three excitedly planning how to fill their day

At the surgery Laura was making final arrangements with the caterers she had hired for Libby's farewell party and feeling more like taking a long walk to clear away the thoughts about Gabriel that had been going round and round in her head since Sophie had been taken ill.

When Ruby came to her office in the middle of the morning and asked if she'd had a good weekend she was greeted with a definite 'No!' and it was therapeutic to be able to tell the slender young doctor about Sophie's brief but frightening illness.

'I've never heard of that before,' Ruby said when Laura described it.

'Neither had I,' Laura told her, 'but Gabriel had, needless to say.' And when Ruby had gone back to her patients Laura allowed her thoughts to go back to the moment on the landing when she'd been going to Gabriel to make up for all the times they'd slept separately.

He would have known what she'd had in mind after seeing her outside his bedroom door, but hadn't mentioned it since then and neither had she. Sophie's illness had blotted out everything else with the frightening speed with which it had come on. Sophie had been their first priority, and the moment of the rekindling of their passion hadn't materialised.

Gabriel called in during the lunch hour, minus the children, who were on play dates, to check that she was all right after the upsets of the weekend, and with the memory clear of him finding her outside his bedroom door her colour began to rise, yet why, for goodness' sake? He'd seen her like that often enough before the day that had put a dividing line between them that had proved to be so hard to cross.

She wasn't to know that his thoughts had been running along the same lines. He was totally relieved to have been there for Sophie when she'd needed his love and his medical expertise, but for the rest of it he couldn't believe that Laura had been coming to him for the first time in months at the very second that they'd heard her cry out.

So where did they go from here? Certainly not jumping into bed as if there wasn't a moment to spare, that was for certain. He had waited a long time for Laura to come to him and could wait longer if he had to.

A replacement for Libby had been found and was due to join the practice in a few weeks' time. Aaron Somerton, in his late thirties, was an acquaintance of Nathan's from when he had worked in a hospital in Africa for three years before coming back to Swallowbrook and discovering that his life belonged here with Libby.

Aaron occasionally rang for a chat and when he'd phoned one night to say that he was coming back to the UK and was looking for a less stressful life for a while, Nathan had mentioned the upcoming vacancy in the practice and Aaron had been immediately interested.

Having experience of the other man's worth from the time they'd worked together previously, Nathan had suggested that, subject to the agreement of the other doctors, he should join the practice for a trial period, and arrangements were now moving in that direction.

Aaron was unmarried and Laura at his request was in the process of finding him somewhere to live.

A couple of choices were available and she was on her way to view them one afternoon the following week when she met Gabriel with a line and rod that her uncle had left behind when he'd gone to live in Spain.

The children had been invited to the birthday party of one of their school friends and he was taking the opportunity to spend a peaceful afternoon on the bank of a nearby river.

'Hi. Where are you off to?' he enquired.

'I'm house-hunting,' she told him.

'Really! Who for?'

'The new doctor, Libby's replacement,' she explained, feeling suddenly irritated. At one time she would have been delighted to find him relaxing on a summer afternoon, but not now. It was as if he was going from one extreme to the other, that the role of overworked oncologist was being replaced by that of the local layabout, and when he flashed her a smile, not having immediately tuned in to her cooling-off, she said, without considering the effect it might have on him, 'How can you idle the time away like this, Gabriel, like some sort of layabout, when there are so many who need you?'

The smile disappeared. 'It would seem that we are at cross-purposes once again,' he said levelly. 'I've been trying to make up for past mistakes but I'm still not getting it right, am I? What exactly is it that you want of me, Laura?'

She was about to tell him that she wanted it to be the same as before, with him treating the sick with the degree of fulfilment that it had always brought but with a smaller workload, *not giving up medicine altogether!*

But the word *layabout* hung on the air like judgement from above.

How could she have been so cruel as to say such a thing? She wanted to tell him how sorry she was, but he wasn't giving her the chance. Gabriel was striding off towards the river as if there was nothing more to be said, and moving off in the opposite direction she began the task of finding a place to live for the stranger who would soon be in their midst.

After viewing the two properties that she'd narrowed the choice down to Laura decided on a spacious cottage up for rental with views of the lake and fells, and once back in her office emailed the details to Aaron Somerton and awaited his comments.

When she arrived home at the end of what had been a miserable day there was the smell of fish cooking and she wondered if it was Gabriel's reply to the way she'd described him. He'd caught a salmon, she discovered when she bent to peep inside the oven, and it looked delicious.

As she was straightening up, his voice came from behind, and as if their earlier exchange of words had been without rancour he said easily, 'Not bad for a layabout, eh, Laura?' and went on to explain, 'I met John Gallagher, Nathan's father, while I was down there. He lives in one of those delightful pine lodges by the river, and as I wasn't aware that I needed a permit to fish there he said that if questioned I could use his, which explains our colourful friend in the oven.'

'You never cease to amaze me,' she said laughingly.

'And disappoint you equally?' he questioned.

'No, never that,' she protested. 'All I ever want for you is the best out of life, Gabriel.

'I've got it. You and the children are that.'

'Maybe we are to some extent, but you deserve more, and I won't go into the details of that as you are already aware of them and must be weary of my frequent reminders.'

As the smell of the salmon strengthened and vegetables on the hotplate came to the boil she said in a lighter tone, 'So, are you going to open a bottle of wine to celebrate your first catch?'

'Yes, why not?' he agreed. 'And there are plenty of cold drinks for the children.'

'So I'll go up and get changed,' she said, the day's pressures lifting. 'I don't want my surgery clothes to smell of a fisherman's catch.'

'Some fisherman, though!' he said, with eyes warming, and he swung her into his arms and danced her up the stairs to where the children were playing in their bedrooms, and when they came out onto the landing to see what all the noise was about and found her laughing up at him, she said, 'We never get the timing right, do we?'

'No, but we will,' he promised, and she so wanted to believe him.

Where had all Gabriel's good humour come from though? Only that afternoon there had been coolness between them when she'd referred to him as a layabout. Surely catching the salmon wasn't the reason for his light-heartedness?

Yet it seemed as if it might be as while they were eating it he said, 'Nathan's father reckoned the salmon was one of the biggest catches for months down on the river, a*nd from an amateur*.'

He didn't explain that his good humour came from knowing that.

James had phoned to say that the hearing before the hospital board in London had been given a date, and much as he, Gabriel, wouldn't be looking forward to it, he saw it as one of two things—a new beginning or an ending. Once that had been decided he could sort out his working life. It was to take place in a month's time and he would be marking off the days to it.

He was going to break the news to Laura when the children were in bed and knew it would blow away the happiness of the day, but she had to know and would not take kindly to any delay in the telling of it.

'So it has come at last,' she said when he'd told her about the phone call, and she'd thought that the timing wasn't good, today of all days when they were so happy, but when would be a good moment to pass on that sort of news?

She understood Gabriel's relief to have heard something definite from the London end, but felt sick inside at the thought what it might mean.

'I'll go with you when the time comes,' she told him, but he shook his head.

'No way,' he told her. 'I caused the situation and I will sort it one way or the other, and until then, Laura, let's put it out of our minds and carry on enjoying life in Swallowbrook.'

'Do you think we can?' she whispered

'I'm sure we can,' he told her, 'and if we can hang on long enough, let's save that special moment that keeps eluding us until I come back from the hearing, If the news is good it will be a celebration and if it's bad it will be a sign of our strength. Yes?'

'Yes,' she agreed, and had never loved him more than she did then.

CHAPTER SEVEN

WHEN Laura arrived at the practice there was a message from Aaron Somerton to say that the cottage looked delightful, and asking her to put a hold on it for him. The message went on to say that he would be joining them in late September, would not expect to be met, and would make his way to Swallowbrook straight from the airport, as he did have some knowledge of the area.

So much for that, she thought. He was obviously someone who liked to have his finger on the pulse in more ways than one.

When Gabriel had told her about the phone call from James the night before she'd been amazed that he was so happy and cheerful knowing that the ordeal he had to face would soon be upon him.

'It would suit me if it was tomorrow,' he'd told her. 'I want to get it over with. It has been hanging over me like a black cloud and whatever the outcome at least I will know then what choices I have.'

He would be going back to be judged in the place where he'd saved so many lives and prolonged others, but not in recent months, he'd thought as he and the children had waved Laura off that morning with an arrangement that they would meet her for lunch.

He carried a burden of blame for having been absent from those who needed him, and without saying it out loud, if it hadn't been that he'd let someone else down too, he would have been pushing to get back in there long ago.

He knew Laura wouldn't have slept much after discovering that a day had been set for the hearing and had thought that a meal at the nearest of the restaurants would be better than a quick sandwich, so when she came out of the practice building the three of them were waiting for her, one on either side of him, holding his hand, and she turned away so that he wouldn't see tears on her lashes.

Gabriel's only crime had been caring too much about the sick who came to him, always being there for them, giving them the benefit of every ounce of his expertise, and he was still paying for it, she thought sadly.

Since he'd been back with her and the children he'd done everything in his power to make things right between them, even offering to cut himself off from his work if it would make her happier, with never a complaint about being shut away because a moment of righteous anger had turned into something else.

She knew he was tuning in to her thoughts as he watched her fight back the tears, but he made no comment. Instead he said, 'Let's go, Laura, or your lunch hour will be over before you've had time to eat.' And the four of them began to move in the direction of the nearest restaurant on the lakeside.

There was a garden at the back with tables and chairs and for a precious short time Laura felt at peace with herself as the four of them sat in a leafy arbour enjoying their lunch.

Until Sophie said, out of the blue, 'I don't want to live in our other house again. I want to stay here for always, but if we sell it, where will Daddy sleep when he goes back to work in London?'

As Laura waited to see what the reply to that would be he said, 'On a park bench, I suppose. Or I could stay with Uncle James maybe.'

No mention of him not going back to work in London, she noted, so what was that supposed to mean? That Gabriel had changed his mind about giving up medicine, but wasn't going to admit it in case he wasn't allowed to go back? Was it another decision that she wasn't going to be consulted about?

As the days passed Libby's farewell party was something special to look forward to and with that thought in mind Laura took Sophie shopping for dresses on the Saturday after the phone call from James with the date of the hearing.

'What colour shall I wear?' she asked Gabriel before they set off.

'You always look stunning in black,' was his reply.

'And me?' Sophie wanted to know.

'How about yellow or blue for my beautiful daughter?' he said, and Laura thought if he'd suggested all the colours of the rainbow Sophie would have been happy if they'd been her father's choice.

It was lovely to see them together. She had been so unhappy while he'd been away from them, unable to understand why he hadn't been there, and no way had she been going to tell her where he was as Sophie would have been bewildered and upset.

They shopped for her first, and at Gabriel's suggestion chose a pretty party dress in pale yellow that was perfect to go with her dark hair and eyes. Then it was her own turn to find something and she settled on a black cocktail dress because she needed to be told she looked stunning, that she wasn't the miserable drab that she felt most of the time, and Gabriel was the only one she wanted to hear it from.

But before she was to hear those words from her husband there was a surprising announcement from Ruby and Hugo. Laura had invited them round for supper one night and when the children were in bed and the four of them were sitting in the garden Hugo said to his new wife, 'Are we going to tell Laura and Gabriel our good news, Ruby?'

They are going to announce that Ruby is pregnant, Laura thought. These two delightful people are going to cement their marriage with a child.

But as Ruby explained with heightened colour exactly what their good news was, she realised that though a child was involved it wouldn't be theirs. They had been accepted on to the waiting list of adoptive parents and some time in the future would be given the chance to adopt.

Before arriving that evening they had discussed sharing their problem with Laura and Gabriel in confidence, knowing that they could rely on them not to spread around the reason why they couldn't have children of their own.

Taking Ruby's hand in his, Hugo explained, 'We could have children of our own, lots of them if we wanted, but they could be born with the same gene that Ruby carries, that of haemophilia, which could give any boy children we might have the blood-clotting problem and any girls the burden of being a carrier.

'Neither of us would want to wish that on to any child of ours, so we will either foster or adopt when we are ready, and would ask that you keep this matter to yourselves, if you don't mind.'

'Of course,' Gabriel said, and Laura, holding Ruby close like she would a younger sister, wiped a tear from her eye as she thought that sometimes the troubles of others helped to bring one's own nightmares into perspective.

When they'd gone Gabriel said, 'Those two are something special, aren't they?'

'Yes, they really are,' she agreed. 'Nathan did the same kind of thing, adopted Toby when both his parents were killed in a ferry disaster while they were on holiday. He was saved, and Nathan, who was his godfather, went out to get him, and as there were no close relatives to take him he adopted him and arrived back in Swallowbrook as a single father.'

'Hugo is fantastic with children. Nearly all parents with a sick child who come to the surgery ask to see Dr Lawrence. He would have made a wonderful father to any children they might have had, but it would seem that he is prepared to forego that because he loves Ruby so much, and you have to hand it to them, they are going to do the next best thing.'

He nodded sombrely. What *he* was thinking of doing could be described as the next best thing and time was pressing. He'd promised James that he would be in touch but it wasn't that simple. There was another side to it that he had to sort and he needed to do that first.

The following morning Ruby sought Laura out in her office, as she sometimes did, for a brief chat and the first thing she said was, 'When would you be free for us to return your hospitality, Laura? Either at the weekend or an evening during the week, either time would be all right for us.

'I know that the coming weekend is going to be stressful for you, having to oversee Libby's farewell party, so will leave it with you when you are able to come. Just say the word when you are free.'

As she was about to go back upstairs she hesitated in the doorway and asked, 'What did you think about me not being able to give Hugo the children that he would love to have?'

'I thought that you were two amazing people with

a love for each other that is strong and true,' she told her, 'and so did Gabriel. Ruby, you have only to look at Libby and Nathan with Toby to know that what you and Hugo are planning to do in the future for some parentless child or children will be a wonderful thing for all of you.'

'I needed to hear that,' she said. 'Sometimes it just gets to me that I can't give the man I love children of his and my blood because mine is tainted, but he won't hear of it when I tell him how sorry I am, and every now and then I need someone to say the things that you have just said to me. Thanks for that, Laura.'

Ruby was smiling as she went to join Hugo at the start of the weekly antenatal clinic that the two of them staffed, and Laura thought that to the rare woman with a problem like that of Ruby, the monitoring of someone else's foetus must be a bitter pill to swallow, but the young doctor who had just gone to do that very thing had an unselfishness that would carry her through whatever had to be done.

She was sure that if Ruby had asked the other doctors to be spared that part of her duties they would have understood, but with Hugo's love and her own acceptance of the blight that a hereditary gene had put upon her, she would cope.

The clinic beside the practice was taking shape from every angle. Soon it would be open and ready to take some of the burden off the main cancer unit at the hospital on the lakeside, and every time Laura gazed at its immaculate newness it brought a lump to her throat to know that someone would be doing the job that Gabriel excelled at within its walls, while he went fishing.

At the practice she was finalising the arrangements for the party and with that and her other normal duties the days seemed to be flying past.

All the surgery staff would be there to say farewell to the doctor who had spent all her working life looking after the health of Swallowbrook and its surrounding hamlets and was now about to take on the full-time role of motherhood.

There would be music and dancing on board, a buffet and a bar, and at some time during the evening elderly John Gallagher, who had been head of the practice when Libby had come straight from university to work there, and was now her father-in-law, would make the presentation that everyone had contributed to.

If Laura had been less busy she would have realised that Gabriel was preoccupied, and might have been surprised at him leaving the house one evening without explanation, but she'd reasoned that he was around the place all day with the children, so it wasn't surprising that he felt the need for a change of scene.

It would soon be a year to the day since she had appeared in his consulting room as a patient, and it would be an anniversary of pain and horror that would never go away until their lives were back on track.

But she'd given up on that, had accepted that second best was going to have to do. If she had to live with the knowledge that his days of cancer care were over it would be her punishment for wanting more from him than he'd had the time or energy to give.

He'd returned a couple of hours later looking calm enough, but hadn't lingered to talk. Instead, he'd just patted her cheek and gone straight to bed.

The night of the party on the boat was clear and starless with just a pale harvest moon in the sky, and as Laura watched Libby in the last stages of pregnancy greet her guests she was positioned nearby to make sure the arrangements she'd made were being carried out satisfactorily.

She'd gone ahead to be there from the start, leaving Gabriel and the children to follow, and as she watched the guests arriving she saw them walking along the landing stage towards her.

Sophie had on the new yellow dress as she held her friend Lily's hand, Josh was in long trousers and a smart short-sleeved shirt, and Gabriel was wearing a white dinner jacket, black trousers and bow-tie, and as she watched him approach Laura was aware of heads turning at the sight of the practice manager's husband.

Whether they were thinking the same as she was, that he would be the most attractive man there, or if he was of interest because it was said he'd been in prison, she didn't know, as some of the guests weren't the surgery staff who knew the story. They were relations and friends of Libby and Nathan.

Yet did she care what people thought? She was wearing the black dress that she'd bought to please him and knew he'd been right. The black *did* show off her golden fairness, and as he looked up at her from beneath the floodlights that were all around the boat it was there, the question that she sometimes saw in his eyes. *Do you still love me, Laura?* And she wondered how he could ever doubt it.

They didn't sleep together, admittedly, but Gabriel had been the one to reject *her* first, when she'd been longing to have him beside her again in the long night hours after he'd served his sentence, but instead he'd gone straight to the London house.

And even when he had come to Swallowbrook he had set a precedent that first night by sleeping in the spare room. Hurt and angry, she'd gone along with it and now *she* was the one who was choosing to sleep alone and wondering how long she could stand the loneliness of it.

The two of them talked more about surface things than what really mattered, yet she was there, wasn't she, ready and willing to accept a life of lesser closeness if he would only open up to her.

When they stepped onto the deck beside her Gabriel bent and kissed her meaningfully and when he put her away from him Laura saw a glint in the dark eyes looking down at her.

'That was for the benefit of those who have been sizing me up,' he said in a low voice as a waiter approached with a tray of drinks, and after passing glasses of fruit juice to the children he took champagne for himself when Laura indicated that she wasn't drinking while she was on duty.

The caterers were about to depart before the boat set sail and leaving Gabriel and the three children for a moment she went to thank them for their efforts. When she turned to rejoin them it seemed that Sophie, Josh and Sophie's friend Lily had already found Toby, and Ruby and Hugo had joined Gabriel, which left her free to make sure that all her other arrangements were up to the standard of the catering.

After the presentation had been made and most of the food eaten, Libby said, 'Laura, go and join your family and relax. There is nothing else that you need concern yourself about.'

Maybe not about the party, she thought, but her concerns about the future were many, though it wasn't the moment to be worrying about that, so she said, 'Yes, I will if you don't mind. Gabriel was with Ruby and Hugo, but I think they've met up with friends and he doesn't know many people here.'

Gabriel was leaning against the rail of the boat with arms folded when she found him, staring down thoughtfully at the foaming backwash that it was creating as it ploughed slowly through the water, and when she tucked her arm in his he straightened up and asked, 'Is that it, the finish of a job well done?'

'More or less,' she replied, and thought that Libby must surely be thinking along those lines as she said goodbye to the practice that she'd served so faithfully.

Looking around her, she asked, 'Where are the children?'

'They're on the lower deck, playing games with the other young ones on board,' he told her. He looked around him at the rest of the party guests. 'Now can I get you a drink?'

'Yes, please,' she said thankfully, and as she watched him stride off towards the bar thought achingly that her husband was a man amongst men, compassionate, caring, clever, and *for once in his life so unsure of himself that he couldn't or wouldn't talk to her about it.*

The magical sail across the long length of the lake and back was over. The party guests were making their way home, but the first stop for Laura and Gabriel was at the farm where Sophie's friend Lily lived, and once she had been safely delivered to her parents he drove them the short distance to Swallows Barn with Josh already asleep in the back seat of the car.

Scooping him up into his arms, Gabriel carried him inside and deposited him just as he was onto his bed and then drew the covers over him, and as Laura helped a tired Sophie to undress and then disappeared into her own room, silence descended on the house.

They were all tired except him, Gabriel thought, going out to sit in the moonlit garden. He felt restless and on edge as he thought of Laura sleeping above after a task completed to her satisfaction.

It was clear that she'd found the right sort of niche in the job at the practice and was able to see the results of her efforts the same as it had once been for him, and he couldn't go on much longer as the 'layabout' she'd described him as in a moment of frustration.

His life now was what he'd sometimes yearned for during the long and taxing days on the unit, yet its appeal was dwindling. He loved being with Laura and the children, but something had to give. He couldn't hold back any longer.

The energy he'd always had was back, the urge to heal and make well again was there once more, and so was Laura, who'd been hurt and ignored, and would be hurt again, beyond belief, if she was ever made to feel that she was the stumbling block that was keeping him from his patients.

A light footstep behind him and she was there, dressed in a crumpled nightdress, rubbing the sleep out of her eyes. When he gazed at her in surprise she said thickly, 'I went into your room. You weren't there and it all came back! The nights when I wandered around knowing that you were somewhere else, in a strange place, far away from us. So I had to come and find you, to make sure that you were actually here, that I wasn't dreaming.'

She was swaying with tiredness and was turning to go back to bed now that she'd satisfied herself that he was there, where she could see him.

'Of course I'm here, Laura. Where else would I be?' he said gently, and even as he said it a vision of the operating theatre where he'd spent so many hours came back to plague him.

He swept her up into his arms and she lay there

limply as he carried her up the stairs with the same gentleness that he'd shown to Josh earlier. After laying her carefully between the covers he sat beside her and held her hand until she was soundly asleep once more, and then went across the landing and opened his bedroom door wide, so that if she should awake again with the same feeling of dread she would be able to see him not far away.

His unexplained absence on the night when he'd left the house and not said where he was going had been because he'd had a phone call from Nathan during the day while Laura was at the practice. It had been about something they'd discussed a few times but hadn't yet brought to a conclusion, though not for the want of trying, and he had told Nathan that he would call round that evening.

When they'd finished talking, and he was leaving Nathan and Libby's extended cottage across the way from the surgery he'd said, 'I would be obliged if you didn't say anything about this to Laura in case nothing comes of it, Nathan. I've caused her enough distress already and don't want her to feel that I've messed up our lives once again if it turns out to be a letdown.'

As he'd gone striding off Nathan had thought that there went a man who had been to hell and back because of doing the job he excelled at to the extreme. He had paid a heavy price because of it, and there weren't many like him around.

Gabriel had come away from their chat feeling optimistic about the future, that if they gave him the go-ahead at the hearing he was going to be able to get it sorted soon in all their best interests.

But now, after seeing Laura's distress when she'd dreamt that she was back in the days of his imprisonment, he decided that tomorrow he would wait to see if she mentioned the bad dream.

It could have been that her mind had been on overdrive after the pressures of being responsible for the party arrangements. She'd been down by the lake most of the day and had been exhausted by the time they'd arrived home.

It was a long time before he fell into a restless sleep when he went up to bed, and his first thoughts on waking were of when she'd appeared in such distress and let down her guard about the bad times of when he'd been taken from them.

As he raised himself up off the pillows he saw that her door was open as he'd left it the night before in case she had a repetition of the bad dream, but the bed was empty and there was no sound of her in the *en suite*. Without dressing, he went down the stairs at speed and she was there, in the kitchen. The table was set, cereal dishes were laid out, and she was at the cooker, grilling bacon.

When she saw him she came across to where he was standing in the doorway and, reaching up, touched his face gently. 'I'm sorry about last night, Gabriel,' she said. 'I think I'd rather overdone it at the party and although I'd gone straight to sleep, my brain hadn't.'

'Has that sort of thing ever happened before?' he asked carefully.

'No! Last night was just a one-off, a bad dream. Why, what did you think it was?'

'I didn't know, but it did occur to me that it might be something else that I'm responsible for.'

'Don't say things like that!' she cried. 'All you ever did wrong was work too hard. If I could turn back the clock, I would. You aren't the only one to blame for what happened. Our lives will never be right again until we can put the past behind us.'

'Yes, I do know that,' he said gently, and thought that he was the one with the most past to put behind him. Would he ever forget the smells, the bars on the windows and the claustrophobic atmosphere of the place?

The bacon was beginning to sizzle and splutter. It took over the moment and nothing further was said.

On a continent far away Aaron Somerton was preparing to leave the place that had been his home for the last four years and it was a strange feeling to know that he would soon be back on English soil again.

He had been one of the doctors from the UK working at the hospital in an African township when Nathan Gallagher had arrived on a three-year contract, and when it had been up twelve months ago Aaron had been loath to see the other man go, as on meeting they'd discovered that they both came from the same county in England and had been brought up only miles apart.

It was the reason why Aaron had been keen to take

Nathan up on his suggestion that he take up temporary employment in the practice at Swallowbrook when he came back to the UK until he had sorted out his future.

The details of the accommodation he'd been sent had caused him to start counting the days and now there were not many left to cross off before he took a flight homewards.

As the two of them had chatted he'd been surprised to hear that Nathan was now married, had adopted a child, and was about to have a child of his own from his new wife, all in the space of a year.

Obviously his ex-colleague was not someone to hesitate when the moment was right, he thought, which wasn't exactly how he would describe himself, and wondered if all those of his kind who came to Africa to work had left behind some unfinished business.

It seemed strange on Monday morning for Libby's consulting room to be empty. Nathan had suggested to Ruby that she move into it as hers was rather small, but she'd told him that she was happy enough where she was, and when he'd reminded her that now she was the only woman doctor in the practice and that she would be getting the bulk of the patients of her own sex, she'd smiled and said, 'Lucky me,' and had meant it, even though there would be many pregnancies amongst them.

Her haemophilia nightmare had become bearable with Hugo surrounding her with his love and tender care and she was happier now than she'd ever been.

In her office in the basement Laura was receiving brief visits from surgery staff wanting to say their bit about how they'd enjoyed Saturday night, and she thought in a moment of quiet that the next happy event in the life of the head of the practice would be the birth of his child.

With sudden yearning the thought came that she and Gabriel could do with a 'happy event'. She would settle for a break in the sun somewhere, far away from painful memories, but they'd let the school's long summer holiday go by.

The next time the children were off would be the October half-term, so why not then? She was due some holiday leave from the practice, but Gabriel had one big commitment, his appearance before the hospital board. So it would be better for that to be over and done with and a holiday would be just the thing to take away the taste of it.

To her dismay, he didn't show much interest in the idea when she suggested it. His comment was a lukewarm 'Yes, possibly we could have a break, but shall we wait until nearer the time?'

He was taking into account that holidays meant being together non-stop, she decided. They would be much closer than in their daily lives and perhaps in the present state of their relationship he didn't want to rush that as he hadn't followed up her proposed nocturnal visit that had backfired when Sophie had been taken ill.

He had turned away to hide a smile at her suggestion. It was her birthday in the middle of October. He'd arranged for the four of them to go to one of the Greek islands for the week of the school half-term to celebrate the occasion, and was hoping that by then he would be able to offer Laura the peace of mind that he so much wanted to give her, which all fitted in with his lukewarm response.

CHAPTER EIGHT

IT WAS busy at the practice with a doctor short now that Libby had left.

Laura suggested to Nathan and Hugo that they take on a locum until Aaron Somerton arrived, but as it was only a few weeks until he put in an appearance they decided that it was hardly worth it, and that as the room that had always been Libby's was being decorated ready for his arrival it would be difficult to accommodate a locum.

Those were the problems of her working life, Laura thought, surmountable, possible to sort out. Her home life was a different thing. Every time she thought about the hearing all the new closeness that she and Gabriel had been achieving seemed to diminish, become distant, and she couldn't bear the thought of them going back to how they'd been before.

He hadn't been out in the evening again without explanation but she'd discovered from a casual comment by one of the practice nurses that she'd seen him at the local garage getting fuel one morning and she'd described him as looking 'scrumptious' in a dark suit, white shirt, and tie.

Thinking back, Laura recalled that when she'd arrived home that day Gabriel had been in jeans and a sweatshirt, mowing the lawns, and no comment had been forthcoming about where he'd been off to that morning.

They'd been used to telling each other everything before their breakdown of communications and had made every decision of importance together, but not any more. It wasn't surprising that he was not falling over himself to go on holiday with her. Closer they might be, yet the feeling of being on the fringe of what was happening in Gabriel's life was still there.

She would have been surprised to know that as he had driven out of the village on the appointment that he'd dressed so smartly for, he had been having similar thoughts. Hating to keep things from her but wary of telling her what he was planning in case it all fell apart.

While the children were playing with friends it had seemed that he'd also gone fishing on the day when the nurse had seen him. When Laura had gone into the kitchen to sort out the evening meal his catch had been there, gutted, cleaned and ready for cooking.

For a moment she'd thought that the nurse must have been wrong,

Yet who would mistake the man she was married to, especially in a smart suit, and if that *was* the case, where had he been going?

He'd been his usual self during the evening and the

same the next morning at breakfast, but the thought kept niggling at the back of her mind and was still there as she walked the short distance to the practice. They didn't sleep together, didn't talk all that much, he didn't want to holiday with her and went out on secret appointments. How much longer could she cope with this kind of life? she wondered. Roll on the day of the hearing.

There had been a fire at the cricket ground at the opposite end of the village from where the practice was situated. A storeroom where equipment was kept had gone up in flames from an electrical fault, to the dismay of the cricketers both old and young, especially the young, who flocked there on weeknights for practice and the opportunity of being with their own age group instead of hanging about on street corners.

Since the catastrophe various fundraising efforts had been held with a view to replacing what had been lost, and on a night soon to come the Swallowbrook Community Committee was holding a big barbeque on a field opposite the cricket ground as the final fundraising event. Most of the money had been raised and soon the cricketers would be back on the pitch with new equipment.

It was to take place on the Saturday night two weeks after Libby's farewell party and Gabriel was keen for them to go because he said that soon Josh and Toby would be there on summer nights with the young throng of hopefuls and maybe even Sophie, as it wasn't unheard of for the girls of the village to turn up for practice.

Laura agreed that whatever the future of the cricket team, the present was calling for their support and bought four tickets for the barbeque from the post office with the thought in mind that if she and Gabriel rarely spent time together with just the two of them, a family outing was always something to treasure.

There were sideshows at one end of the cricket ground with the barbeque positioned opposite, and already there were lots of folk there, mostly villagers with just a few strange faces amongst them.

When they came across Hugo and Ruby he had just won a cocoanut and on seeing his young wife eating candy floss Sophie asked if she could have some, and Gabriel went for it to a stall further down the field.

Laura chatted for a while to the newlyweds with the children playing nearby, and when they'd moved on she glanced in the direction that Gabriel had taken and saw him in conversation with the same nurse who had described him as 'scrumptious' when she'd seen him at the petrol pumps that day.

She was a captivating creature herself with long dark hair, hazel eyes with long lashes, totally beguiling, and whatever she was saying to Gabriel she certainly had his full attention. Yet he didn't linger, aware of Sophie waiting for the candy floss, and when he joined them again he said thoughtfully, 'That was a nurse from the practice.'

'Yes, I know,' she told him. 'What did she want?'

'She was asking if the new doctor at the practice was going to be me, and when I said no, that it was going to be this Somerton guy, I thought she was going to collapse. The colour just drained from her face. What do you think of that?'

'It seems very odd,' she replied. 'Her name is Julianne Marshall and if I remember rightly I have her address on file at the surgery as an apartment above the beauty salon on the main street of the village. Do you think she knows our new doc?'

'Maybe Somerton is from these parts and the name rang a bell,' he commented, and they left it at that and went to see what was happening on the cricket field.

When they arrived back at the house there was a message on the answering-machine to say that her uncle was spending what he described as a 'culture break' in London and would be coming to stay with them overnight the following day.

As she listened to the message from her only relative Laura was filled with a mixture of pleasure and dismay. Pleasure because she was fond of the elderly bachelor who had kept in touch ever since she'd lost both her parents when in her early twenties. Her dismay at the thought of him visiting was smaller than the pleasure, but was there nevertheless because of the situation between Gabriel and herself. He'd gone to live in Spain thinking that once they'd settled in the village it would be the end of their troubles, but her uncle was nobody's fool, *and there was the question of the sleeping arrangements.*

When she relayed the message to Gabriel he smiled. 'That is good. It will be great to see the old guy again, though I suppose you are concerned about where he's going to sleep as I'm using the spare room. Yes?'

'Yes, I am,' she said levelly. There was no way she wanted them to sleep together again under those sorts of circumstances.

'It won't be a problem, Laura,' he told her. 'With a sheet and an extra duvet in your room I'll be fine. Your uncle won't know what the arrangements are once the door is closed behind us. The farce will be for us alone to concern ourselves about.'

Fixing him with a steady blue gaze, she said, 'You always were good at finding the right word when you wanted to describe something, Gabriel, and you still are. A farce is a sham, an empty thing, and if that doesn't describe what our love life has become I can't think what does.' And without giving him the chance to reply, she went to check that the children were asleep before going to bed herself.

He made to follow her, wanting to hold her close and put an end to the thing that was keeping them apart, but what would he have to tell her? Nothing definite, that was for sure, and until there was he would have to wait until the time was right, and it wasn't now.

It was Saturday morning so they were all able to meet Gordon at the local railway station.

When he stepped out onto the platform Laura and Gabriel exchanged smiles. Dressed in a lightweight beige suit with a straw panama hat on his grizzled head, he was the picture of the elderly British ex-pat, and then Laura was hugging him, Gabriel shaking him by the hand, and the children, standing to one side, were warily observing the strange-looking visitor that they didn't see very often.

When they arrived at the house her uncle looked around him at the improvements she'd made. 'This place used to be just somewhere to eat and sleep when I had it. I can't believe it's the same house,' he said approvingly. 'It was always too big for me, a family like you folks was what it needed.' His glance still taking in the changes she'd made, he went on, 'I see that you've had it re-thatched and whoever did it made a better job of it than before.'

They had lunch on the patio and when Laura and her uncle were chatting afterwards Gordon said, 'I rang Nathan and his father while I was on the train to see if some of us could meet up somewhere tonight and took the liberty of asking them to come here, Laura. Is that all right?'

'Yes, of course. It is still just as much your house as it is ours,' she told him, with her glance on Gabriel who had gone to the bottom of the garden to get the children's ball out of thick bushes where it had just landed.

'Has the dust of the dreadful thing that happened to you both settled down?' he asked in a low voice.

'We're getting there,' she said lightly, and wished she was a better liar.

'That's good, though I do think you look a bit peaky,' he commented. His gaze transferred to Gabriel. 'And your man down there, how is he?'

She had a sudden urge to be truthful instead of doing a cover-up and told him, 'He has changed, compared to how he used to be, not with the children, he is lovely with them the same as he's always been, but Gabriel doesn't share things with me like he used to.

'He's waiting to go before the hospital board to see if they will agree to him still practising there, but even if they do I'm not sure that he will go back, and I feel so guilty because I was the one who triggered everything off that day. But please don't tell him that I've told you.'

He nodded. 'I promise I won't say a word. Give him time, Laura, that is what he needs.'

'Yes, but how much?' she said. 'He spends his days taking care of the children, going fishing, and is secretive about anywhere else he goes. It is Gabriel that I'm describing, yet it feels like a stranger.'

The evening was a happy one with those who had known each other a long time enjoying the company of old friends they could chat with about times gone by.

Libby and Nathan had come to Swallows Barn to meet up with Gordon once again. John Gallagher was there, eager to chat with someone who had been employed at the practice when he'd been in charge, and although Gordon had only known Hugo and Ruby briefly before he'd left, Laura had invited them because she was fond of Ruby, and her charming husband had been kind and helpful when she'd been moving into the house on her own when Gabriel hadn't been there for her and the children.

When the guests had gone Gordon said, 'I will be off first thing in the morning as I'm having afternoon tea with an old school friend, and have got a ticket for a concert in the evening. I've been doing the rounds of the shows while I've been in London and some sightseeing of special places. It has been exactly how I wanted it to be, a pleasant "culture break".

'I'm off back to Spain on Monday to tie up a few loose ends and shut up my house there for a while.' He observed them both calmly. 'I've been diagnosed with cancer of the prostate and want to be treated over here by you, Gabriel, if you will do that for me.'

There was a shocked silence for a few seconds as they took in what he'd just told them then Gabriel said, 'How long since you found out, Gordon?'

'The doctors over there have been monitoring my prostate count for some time and recently it has shot up quite alarmingly and the diagnosis is cancer.'

'I see, and, yes, it goes without saying that I will take you on as a patient,' Gabriel told him. 'It will be a privilege. Laura has perhaps told you that I haven't gone back to my London clinic, but there are ways and means in which I can treat you privately and be in contact with them at the same time with regard to your treatment if that would be all right with you?'

'And you must stay here with us until you are well again,' Laura said anxiously.

Gordon was smiling, the only one of the three of them who was.

'My answer to your offer, Gabriel, is, yes, please,' he said, 'and to yours, Laura, no, but thank you just the same. I have taken a rented apartment in London and will stay there during my treatment. I shall go back to Spain whenever possible as it's only a couple of hours' flight and will commute between the two countries.'

'Leave me the details of your medical people over there,' Gabriel told him, 'and I will get on to them to let me have your records and the results of any tests that you've already had sent to me immediately.'

The shock of what her uncle had told them left little room for thought regarding anything else and with Gabriel's sleeping arrangement as he had suggested and Laura lying wide-eyed and anxious in the bed, the night passed without any disturbances.

But not without much concern on their part for the kindly old man who had given them his house as a farewell gift when he'd gone to spend his retirement in a warmer climate, and now was having to come back to where there was someone he could depend on to provide him with the best possible treatment and care that he was going to need.

Was her uncle's illness going to be what Gabriel had

needed to take him back into cancer care? It was a shame if it was. It should have been of his own free will, but at least he had promised to be there for Gordon, as she'd known he would the moment he'd been told about the other man's problem, and it was a step in the right direction.

In the middle of Sunday morning they'd seen Gordon off on the local train that would take him to a major station where he could get a connection to London, and for once Laura and Gabriel were alone. Josh was at Toby's for the day, and Sophie had been invited to lunch at the home of Lily, the school friend that she'd brought along to the party on *The Lady of the Lake*.

'Why don't we go for a walk along the lakeside and have our lunch out, just the two of us?' Gabriel suggested as the train disappeared from sight. 'We've had no chance to discuss the bombshell that Gordon dropped on us last night, although we won't know anything constructive until I get the details from the Spanish side.'

'He seemed very calm about it, didn't he?' she commented. 'We were more alarmed than he was.' She was about to say more when an incredible thought struck her.

When Gabriel had gone down the village to get the Sunday papers while she'd been making breakfast, her uncle had gone to sit in the garden and while he had been there had made a call on his mobile.

She'd thought nothing of it at the time, but on looking back she remembered that he had been speaking to someone about renting accommodation in London. Could it be that their conversation the day before had made him decide to transfer his medical arrangements from Spain to London to get Gabriel back into cancer care, knowing that he would not refuse to treat him? And now, having blithely told them he'd got an apartment in the city, was about to back it up by finding one with all speed?

Gabriel hadn't noticed her hesitation. He was wondering what the count of Gordon's prostate would be when he received it from the other hospital. It would be a good guide to the seriousness of the cancer and the urgency of the treatment required, but he could do nothing until then, and as he and Laura had some time to themselves the next few hours were going to be *their* time and no one else's.

As they strolled along by the lake he took her hand in his and when they came to age-old rocks by the water's edge that would have been there ever since nature had created a lake of such a size beneath the towering fells, they climbed up onto them and sitting side by side took in the scene before them.

'I want us to live here for ever,' Laura said dreamily. 'And our children, *and* our grandchildren.'

He was smiling. 'I would say that is pushing it a bit. In this day and age offspring want to spread their wings, and the more they see in other places the less they want to live where they were brought up. I could see Josh maybe staying put, but not Sophie. She has too much get up and go for that.'

'She was a little lost soul when you weren't around,' she told him. 'I had to keep telling her that you were looking after sick people and she would accept that for a while and then begin asking where you were all over again.'

They were actually talking like normal people, naturally, freely, without constraint, and venturing further she asked, 'How do you feel about my uncle persuading you to go back to medicine for his sake?'

He wanted to tell her that he felt fine, that what Gordon had asked of him had made his blood run warm, his brain engage, that he would do all he could to cure him, or at the least lengthen his life, but that he had wanted his return to his profession to be more in keeping with what he'd been planning for weeks and still hadn't got the go-ahead for.

'I'm easy about it,' he said, 'and if we're going to have time for lunch before we collect the children, I think we'd better make a move.'

She'd spoilt it by mentioning his work, Laura thought as they scrambled down off the rocks. Why couldn't she have kept it light?

Yet why should she have to? She wasn't the one who had made it into something not to be discussed.

But Gabriel was right about their free time together being something not to be wasted and for the next couple of hours she was how she knew he wanted her to be, smiling and relaxed, and when Gordon's name came up again in conversation as they walked back into the village to collect Josh and Sophie after they'd had a leisurely lunch, the mention of him came from Gabriel.

'I will use the London house as my base while treating Gordon,' he said, 'and liaise with the hospital from there.'

'Yes, whatever is best,' she agreed without further comment.

He was observing her questioningly but didn't say anything further. There was no point until he knew where he was up to with the rest of his working life.

That evening there was a phone call from her uncle with the address and telephone number of an apartment not far from the hospital, and Laura was even more convinced that it had been arranged *after* rather than before she had confided her anxieties to him about Gabriel's reluctance to return to his profession.

If she was right in her surmise, it would seem that Gordon had been extremely quick thinking after she'd confided in him, and had seen a way of not only getting a man he greatly admired back to where he belonged but would also be benefiting himself by being treated by one of the top cancer specialists in the UK.

He was a crafty old love, she thought when he'd gone off the line. It would be the third time he had done something very special for them over recent months. He'd given them the house, recommended her for the job, and was doing his best to bring Gabriel back to where he belonged.

* * *

Nathan had arranged to have two weeks' leave when the baby arrived and in her role of practice manager Laura was concerned about staffing problems amongst the doctors. Ruby and Hugo were fine, no holidays due there. John Gallagher had said that in a real emergency he would be prepared to lend a hand but he might be a bit rusty, and then there was Aaron Somerton, Nathan's acquaintance from way back, due to get in touch any time to give her an arrival date.

But it was all going to be rather hit and miss until the little one had actually arrived, and then it would be all systems go, with September now well under way, October ready to step into its place, and the flu-jab season would be upon them.

On the home front Gabriel had received all the necessary information he required to be able to start treating Gordon's cancer and was now in control of the situation, with the sick man visiting him each week at the town house and then proceeding to the hospital not far away if any tests were required.

He had phoned James to tell him what he was involved in with Gordon, explaining that he was treating him as a private patient and was not expecting to create any waves at the hospital himself as all test results would be sent to him by computer.

There was only one situation where he might have to go there and it was if his patient should need surgery that he, Gabriel, would want to perform. If that should occur he wouldn't hesitate, would be over the threshold in a flash with the adrenaline pumping, but he wanted it to be an orderly, organised thing if he ever went back, not a sudden appearance in Theatre like a ghost from the past.

But Gordon's count *was* high. If the radiotherapy he had arranged for him to have at the hospital didn't have the desired effect, Gabriel would be back where he belonged, performing a prostatectomy with all his bad memories and heartaches put to one side as he did what came to him as naturally as breathing.

None of that had been part of his conversation with James. It had been just a courtesy call, and his friend had listened to what he had to say and wondered how Gabriel could endure being so near yet so far away from how it used to be.

But like Laura he'd thought it was a step in the right direction and knew there was no point in them discussing him returning to any other aspects of his work until the hearing had taken place.

Gabriel had just arrived home in the early evening from his second weekly appointment at the town house with Gordon when Nathan phoned to say that Libby was in labour and he was about to take her to the maternity unit at the hospital.

Laura had answered the call and she asked, 'What about Toby? Do you want us to have him, Nathan? Josh would be delighted.'

'No,' was the reply. 'But thanks for the offer. He's staying with my father until the baby is born, but I'm sure that he'll bring Toby round to play if you ask him. You know I'll be missing for the next two weeks, Laura?'

As she was replacing the receiver Gabriel appeared and on seeing her expression asked, 'What's wrong? You look serious. That wasn't James, was it, or your uncle? I only ieft him a few hours ago'

She shook her head. 'No, it was Nathan. It would seem that the baby is on the way. He's taking Laura into the maternity unit and Toby is with John Gallagher. Libby says that Grandfather Gallagher and Toby are big mates so that should work out well.'

'And so do I take it that your concerned expression is connected with staffing at the surgery?'

'Yes. It is,' she told him. 'Once we've had our meal I must get in touch with the new doctor, but first how did you find your patient?'

'Not bad. The waterworks aren't comfortable, of course. They never are in those kinds of cases, but if radiotherapy begins to have an effect soon, it might give Gordon some relief.'

The morning brought news that the Gallaghers had a daughter and a sister for Toby. The baby was to be called Elsie after Libby's mother and her arrival was the main topic of conversation at the practice, with Ruby joining in just as naturally as anyone else, with Hugo close by.

She would have had to face this sort of situation countless times, Laura thought, and would come across it many more. When they were ready to go ahead, adoption or fostering would hopefully fill the gap in their lives.

In the middle of the morning she had a reply from Aaron Somerton regarding her enquiry of the previous night as to when he could be expected to join the practice, and the answer was that it might be three weeks due to last-minute problems at the African hospital where he was based.

Not good news with regard to staffing arrangements at this end, she thought, as now the very thing he had been coming to do was upon them, with not only Libby no longer employed there but with Nathan also away now that the baby had arrived.

It occurred to her that maybe Gabriel would be willing to fill in for a couple of hours each morning and in the afternoon before he went to pick up the children from school.

It would be far from the kind of medicine he'd been involved in, but he would have seen hundreds of patients with hundreds of problems over the years, so wasn't likely to be fazed by what he came across at the Swallowbrook Medical Practice.

The only problem was that he didn't know she was thinking along those lines, and there was his commitment to Gordon, which meant him spending a day in London each week. But four days of his presence would be better than none, and if what the doctor who would be taking Libby's place had said was correct, it would only be for three weeks that she would be asking Gabriel to help out at the practice.

There would have been no necessity to involve him if the original arrangements had been carried out, but the baby had arrived a little earlier than expected and Aaron Somerton wasn't going to be there to fill the gap yet.

CHAPTER NINE

SHE was going to mention the idea to Gabriel before she said anything to Hugo and Ruby, who were holding the fort, and his reaction to the suggestion made her feel that she'd done a wise thing in consulting him first.

When she put the question to him that evening he said, 'How do you know that the other doctors would want me to muscle in on them? I would imagine that Hugo and Ruby are very capable.'

'Yes, they are,' she agreed, 'and, no, I don't know what they will think of the idea. I wanted to suggest it to you first as staffing arrangements *are* my responsibility.'

'Don't you think the patients are going to be wary of being treated by someone with a reputation like mine?' he said quizzically. 'When I was down on the river bank the other day there were two guys fishing nearby and they kept checking that their catch was still where they'd laid it. They must have known I'd been inside and thought it was for thieving. I imagine they would have run a mile if they'd known the real reason.'

'Do you have to be so flippant about it?' she choked.

'Anyone knowing the truth of what happened would never pass judgement on you.'

'Possibly not, but the judiciary system did, if you recall.'

'Of course *I recall*,' she said indignantly. 'I can't believe you might think that I don't.'

'I'm sorry, Laura,' he said contritely, and reaching out for her he held her close. 'You are the last person I should be whingeing at. Yes, of course I'll fill in at the practice if you want me to. Just tell me what you want me to do.'

She was still in his arms and wanting to stay there, but he put her away from him gently and said, 'I've waited long enough and can wait a little longer.'

Her blood, which had been warming at the closeness of him, cooled, and as if his thoughts were already back to basics he said, 'When do you want me to start?'

'In the morning, if you will. The sooner, the better.'

'Right, I'll go straight to the surgery when I've dropped Sophie and Josh off at the school and will work through the lunch hour to make up for having to pick them up at half past three.'

'We could have lunch together in my office if you like,' she suggested.

He was smiling. 'Let's see how it goes first. If I receive a general boycott from the patients I might be back home filling the dishwasher and going around with the vac by lunchtime.'

'You are doing it again,' she protested.

'What?'

'Making it sound as if you care about the opinions of others when you don't.'

'It's true, I don't. The only person whose opinion matters is yours, and I know that it has hit a few lows over the last twelve months.'

'I've accepted all of what is past,' she told him. 'What I can't accept is that you know there are people out there who need all the help they can get and yet you are frittering your time away as if they don't exist.'

'You mean as the local layabout who is doing you out of the school walk? Are you sure those aren't the kinds of reasons why you want to get me in harness at the surgery, and has it occurred to you that your uncle might have ditched his arrangements for treatment in Spain to get me back in touch with my London roots, even though I am only too happy to do what I can for him?'

'Yes. I have to confess that it has,' she told him, 'though I wasn't sure.'

'And you didn't think to pass on your thoughts about it?'

'What would have been the point? I knew that you would want to treat him, whatever the ploy he had adopted, and with regard to me asking you to help out at the practice, it was for a few reasons. One was the shortage of staff, another was that you might enjoy the change from fishing, and I wanted us to be together during my working hours.'

'But not during the night?' he couldn't resist commenting. Even though it was the opposite of what he'd said earlier when she'd been in his arms, and he got the answer he expected.

'No, not then,' she said in a low voice, and went to call the children in from play.

Ruby and Hugo were delighted to know that Gabriel was going to fill in one of the gaps at the practice when Laura phoned to tell them later that evening, and when he put in an appearance the following morning there was none of the aversion he'd expected from the patients.

There was plenty of curiosity and quite a bit of interest in knowing that a big-wig from London in a smart suit was there to listen to what some of them had to say about their health problems and prescribe whatever medication he thought was necessary.

Hugo told him laughingly, 'They'll be coming to consult you from miles around when the news gets out that you're the new temp at the surgery. If they haven't got anything wrong with them, they'll invent something.'

Gabriel went down to Laura's office in the lunch hour and when he was framed in the doorway with sandwiches and two mugs of tea she saw that he was smiling. When she asked what sort of a morning it had been he said, 'It was better than fishing,' and for the first time in weeks she felt light-hearted.

'Why don't *you* go to meet the children?' he suggested when the lunch hour was over and he was ready to go back to the activity up above. 'That way I can work straight through until the surgery closes. I will be more help to Hugo and Ruby that way.'

She was only too happy to agree. For one thing she would get to see Sophie and Josh earlier than when she was there until the surgery closed for the night, and for another because Gabriel had slotted into the surgery type of routine as if he'd never left it, and that could only be good.

For it to be *excellent* it would have to be the same kind of thing on a much bigger scale, and how that was going to come to pass she didn't know.

As she waited for the children to come pouring out of school amongst the throng of primary and junior pupils Laura felt as if she was lit up like a beacon because bringing Gabriel into the practice, if only for a short time, had turned out to be the right thing to do, and it had been such a long time since she'd done anything that wasn't wrong where the two of them were concerned.

When Aaron had heard from the practice manager in Swallowbrook wanting to know how long it would be before he joined them there, he had been loath to inform her that he would be delayed. He was a man who when he made an arrangement liked to keep to it, but that wasn't always possible under the circumstances that prevailed at the hospital where he worked.

Two of the doctors were ill from another of the gastric bugs that always seemed to be lurking in the dry heat of the country that had been his home for the last four years, and like every other problem of that nature it was threatening to assume epidemic proportions, so he'd had no choice but to delay his arrival in the UK until he could leave with an easy conscience.

He'd been happy enough there, had achieved a sort of uneasy contentment, but from the moment he had decided to go home he had been longing for the day when he was back where he belonged, so when he'd replied to the message from Swallowbrook it had been with regret that he'd explained about the delay.

It was working well, Laura thought at the end of Gabriel's first week as locum at the practice. When Libby and Nathan called in with Toby and their newborn they were impressed to find him dealing with patients in one of the spare consulting rooms. 'This is great!' Nathan exclaimed. 'Did Gabriel need much persuading?'

'He wasn't sure if it was a good idea when I first suggested it,' she told him with the memory of his comments about the reaction of patients to his past, 'but it is working out well from everyone's point of view.' *Especially mine.*

They were having lunch together each day in her office, and she was picking the children up from school instead of having to wait until the evening to be with them, and if it wasn't exactly how she longed for Gabriel's expertise to be put to use, between them she and Gordon had found ways to rekindle his dedication to healing.

The truth of it, if she only knew, was that they had nothing to congratulate themselves about. Gabriel's dedication to his calling was alive and well in the form of an aching void inside him that would never go away until he was back where he belonged, with those whose lives were under the threat of cancer.

Gabriel had his heart's delight family-wise in Swallowbrook and would never want to change that, but the ache inside him was stronger than it had ever been and he regretted ever telling Laura that he was going to give up medicine.

As Nathan and Libby were leaving the practice with baby Elsie, so was the patient that Gabriel had been seeing, and he came out to congratulate them on the birth of their daughter,

While Laura and Libby were chatting he managed to have a quick word with Nathan and asked him urgently, 'How much longer?'

'There is a meeting next week,' was the reply. 'You will know definitely by then, and, Gabriel, they are crazy if they don't agree to what you want.'

'Hmm,' he murmured doubtfully. 'I wish I was that sure. It's Laura's birthday the week before half-term and I do need to know before then.'

'The vicar came to see me today as soon as he heard I was helping out at the surgery,' Gabriel said when he arrived home after six o'clock that evening. 'He has had good news about the throat problem and wanted to share it with me. It would seem that the radiotherapy is working and the tumour is shrinking.'

'He is a great guy. Has had no moans or groans since

he was diagnosed, just wants to get his voice back so that he can communicate with his people once more.'

There was a lift to his voice, a new purpose in his manner, and Laura prayed that it would continue. Though how could it? He was going to be working at the surgery for just three weeks if Aaron arrived when he'd said he would, and immediately after that Gabriel would be driving to London for the hearing, and if it didn't go down well, what then? Would he go back to fishing?

He'd been observing her expression and said levelly, 'Don't start crossing bridges that you don't have to, Laura. We've got used to living one day at a time, so why not keep on doing so?'

'Because that isn't how I want it to be,' she protested, 'and it isn't how you should want it to be either.'

'Sometimes we have no choice,' he told her, with the thought in mind that if the local health authority would get a move on he might be able to contradict what he'd just said and give Laura something that she really wanted for her birthday.

In the meantime, tomorrow was his day for seeing Gordon at the town house, where he would be going over the results of tests he'd arranged for him to have over the last few days.

Blood tests and a bone scan had so far indicated that the cancer didn't appear to have spread to any other organs, which was good news, and though it was too early to expect any results from radiotherapy, he was hoping that if a full recovery wasn't possible he might at least be able to halt the spread of it and create a situation where it was kept under control for the rest of his elderly patient's life.

Gabriel was off early in the morning before any of them were up and when Laura went into the spare room and saw that the bed covers were in a tangle as if he'd had a restless night. She wondered just how much longer they would be able to endure the crazy game they were playing with their emotions and desires.

The flame was still burning, the desire just as strong, so why weren't they doing something about it?

Later that week she saw Gabriel chatting to the builder whose firm was responsible for the completion of the clinic building next to the surgery and when he joined her for lunch at midday she asked, 'Did the builder say how long it will be before the clinic will be open and working?'

'Yes, he expects it to be finished by the end of the month,' he told her. 'The guy said that there is going to be a special opening ceremony with the mayor doing the honours and all the local big-wigs present who have contributed to the cost, which I imagine has been enormous.

'I'd had a quick look around the place before you saw me talking to him and it will be fantastic when it's finished, with all the latest equipment, attractive waiting areas, a café and snack bar, and countless toilets and kitchen facilities. The environment will hopefully make patients' treatment easier to endure.'

They hadn't discussed it further as a medical rep had an appointment with her and had just arrived, but later in the afternoon she had a few moments to spare and spent them gazing across at the new building that was going to help improve cancer care in the area, while Gabriel seemed to be content to let his contribution towards it go to pot.

Baby Elsie was to be christened on the Sunday of that week with Ruby and Hugo as two of the godparents and Libby's friend Melissa from Manchester making it a total of three.

'How is the vicar going to manage that?' Gabriel said immediately when Laura told him about the christening.

'He's going to use a hand mike.'

He wasn't impressed. 'Why the rush? Some people don't have their children christened until they're walking and talking.'

'The reason is because Libby's father is coming up from Somerset for the christening. He is a sick man with severe heart problems and doesn't know how long he might have,' she explained.

'Fair enough, then,' he agreed. 'As long as the vicar doesn't over-tax his voice.'

Gabriel was on edge and knew it. He was going to tell Laura on her birthday about the holiday he'd arranged on the Greek island for the four of them, and there would be no problem about that. It was somewhere she'd always wanted to visit and all the arrangements were made.

The half-term break from school would commence a week after her birthday and he had arranged for them to fly to Greece on the Monday at the start of it. By the time they were ready to go Nathan would be back at the surgery, and hopefully Aaron would have put in an appearance, so all ends would be neatly tied up.

He intended to burden her with gifts on her special day, the holiday being the first, with others to follow, but first, before that, there was the hearing, and a phone call that he was waiting for. With regard to that he had hoped that Nathan might have some news for him at the christening.

He had, and it wasn't what he wanted to hear. The phone call was going to be delayed due to someone's illness. A meeting had been postponed and would take place the following week. So he gave his full attention to the simple yet moving service of baptism in the village church.

Later that evening when the children were asleep Laura asked, 'What was wrong at the christening? You were very sombre. Were you wishing that *we* had a tiny newborn to present for baptism?'

He laughed but it was a hollow sound. 'Our present circumstances don't exactly lend themselves to that sort of longings,' he said dryly, 'and for it to happen any other way I would have to be a contortionist.'

He was right. It had been a foolish question, she thought, turning away. Amongst the things that were not right in their marriage, *and top of the list*, was that they hadn't made love since he had been released.

She longed to lie with him and let the desire that had always been so strong between them wipe away the hurts and misunderstandings, but even that had gone all wrong. They weren't in tune any more, and until they were the future would always be a blur.

The days of the following week were dragging for Gabriel, and for Laura her pleasure at having him working in the surgery was dimmed after their downbeat conversation in the wake of the christening.

The two things should be separate, she told herself, their home life and Gabriel's career. However far apart they might have grown, nothing would diminish her delight if he ever changed his mind and went back to what he had been doing before she'd brought his neglect of her into focus.

One thing was for certain, she was expecting her birthday to be a low-key affair. He wouldn't have forgotten, but compared to years past it would have little to commend it with their lives in such a mess. She would just have to smile and make sure she didn't give away the hurt that she carried around with her all the time.

On Friday morning the phone message he'd been waiting for came through. After seeing the children to school, he called back at the house to see if there had been any calls. The phone rang while he was there and the words that came over the line were what he wanted to hear.

All that remained now was the hearing scheduled for Friday of the following week, the day before Laura's birthday. He strode out briskly towards the surgery where he was going to spend the day with the ailing folk of the lakeland valley that he'd fallen in love with. It wouldn't be the first time he'd given the sick the benefit of his expertise, and if the phone call he'd just received was anything to go by, it wouldn't be the last.

When he breezed into her office with only seconds to spare before the surgery opened its doors Laura saw that something had pleased him and was grateful for it, whatever it might be, if it was going to get Gabriel through the week in a reasonably happy frame of mind.

For her own part it was like a knife in her heart every time she thought about what lay ahead of him. The only good thing was that whatever the verdict might be from the hospital board it would give some degree of closure to the unhappiest time of their lives.

As the days went by Gabriel's good humour persisted and she began to wonder if it was due to him not being bothered either way what the verdict would be because he intended opting out of medicine no matter what, and if that should be the case it would mean that in spite of her hating the idea of him giving up, he was still going to do it.

A break in the tension came in the form of an invitation to supper at Ruby and Hugo's.

Their house, Lakes Rise, which Hugo had bought off his sister when she'd gone to live abroad, wasn't far from their own and as Laura, Gabriel and the children walked the short distance between their two houses they had to pass kennels, and as soon as Sophie and Josh saw the dogs of all shapes and sizes it was inevitable that they should want one. They were especially taken with a golden Labrador called Max.

'What do you think?' Gabriel asked Laura, and was surprised to see her shake her head. It was rare that either of them denied their young ones anything, unless they deemed it totally unsuitable, and for some reason she wasn't in favour of the idea.

So with some persuasion and a few maybes they managed to get the children to leave the dogs behind and continued on their way to Lakes Rise.

'Why don't you want the children to have a dog?' Gabriel asked Laura in a low voice, but got no reply, and as minutes later they arrived at their destination the discussion had to be shelved, and it wasn't brought up again until the children were in bed.

'If you get the all-clear from the hospital board on Friday and we have to move back to London, the city isn't the place for a dog,' she said when he asked once more what her objection was, 'And I don't want the children upset by having a pet that they can't take with them.'

He was observing her in angry astonishment. 'What makes you think we will be returning to London?' he demanded. 'Do you honestly think I would drag you all back there to fall in with my wishes? I love this place as much as you do and no way are we going to leave it because of my career, no matter what the outcome of the hearing.'

'I'm sorry,' she told him, 'but you can't blame me for thinking that one day we may have to go back to the town house in the square and the big city hospital again.'

'Not at all!' he said levelly. 'No way are we going back there to live, Laura, you have my promise on that. So maybe we can give some thought to a pet for the children in a few weeks' time.'

CHAPTER TEN

WITH a robe over her nightdress Laura was on the front step waiting to wave him off into an autumn dawn on Friday morning and he was still smiling, his good humour having returned after they'd sorted out the business of the dog. Suddenly exasperated, she said, 'I'm glad that you're so happy about all of this. Can it be that you already know the verdict of the hearing, is that why?'

'No, of course not. How could I?' he protested, and held her close for a moment. 'Are you going to wait up for me, Laura? It could be late as I intend paying your uncle a brief visit after the hearing.'

'Yes, of course I shall wait up, and will you please stop being so chirpy about today's ordeal?'

'I'll try,' he promised, and within seconds he was off, heading for the motorway and a decision that a few weeks ago he would have been dreading, but the fates had been kinder to him in the last few days than of late, and if they wouldn't let him carry on as before in London, all would not be lost.

* * *

James was waiting for him at the entrance to the boardroom when he arrived and as they shook hands his friend said formally, 'They will be ready to see you in a few moments. We are waiting for a couple of latecomers and then will commence.' In a more normal tone he added, for Gabriel's ears only, 'You know how much I want you back here, don't you, Gabriel? Have you got any plans for if you get the all-clear?'

'Er, yes,' he told him, 'but you may not want to hear them.'

'Sounds ominous,'

'Not entirely, but we aren't at that point in negotiations yet, are we?

The hearing was going as he'd expected. Some of the elderly diehards were dubious about him being allowed back, but the number of those who knew his strengths was far greater and soon Gabriel was asked to leave the room while a decision was made.

It didn't take long and when he was called back in James was smiling and soon congratulations were being showered upon him. When everything had quietened down Gabriel told him his plans and because James knew the pain and heartache that his friend and his wife had endured over recent months, he had no fault to find with what Gabriel was suggesting.

The two of them had a late lunch together and then Gabriel went to call on his elderly patient, and Laura's uncle was delighted to hear that he would once more be doing the work that he excelled in.

'Don't say anything to Laura before I get the chance to tell her myself, will you?' he asked him as he was about to set off for home.

'It is her birthday tomorrow and I'm hoping she will feel it is the best one ever when she sees and hears what I have for her.'

Laura was asleep, curled up on the sofa, when he let himself into the house at gone ten o'clock in the evening. He'd made no noise, but almost as if she sensed his presence she awoke the moment he entered the room, and as she raised herself into a sitting position the question was there. 'Gabriel! How did it go?'

'It went well,' he said softly, perching down beside her and taking her hand in his. 'I can go back to what I was doing before any time I want.'

'And do you want?' she breathed.

'Yes, I do.'

She reached up and cupped his face in her hands. 'I'm so glad, Gabriel, so very happy for you, and in spite of what you said when we were discussing a puppy for the children, if London is where you need to be, we will go back there.'

He shook his head. 'No, Laura. I meant what I said. Here in Swallowbrook is where we are going to stay. London is a fabulous city, but we are all happy here, and it would be cruel to uproot the children again.'

'So are you intending staying in the town house during the week and coming here to us at the weekends?' she asked as the bubble began to burst, 'because if you are, it will be like taking a step backwards and I don't want that to happen.'

'No, I'm not intending anything of the sort,' he said reassuringly.

'So how, then?' she asked. 'You surely can't be thinking of commuting every day!'

'No, of course not, but there is always a way and I will find it.' He already had, he thought, and tomorrow Laura was going to know what it was.

'It's your birthday tomorrow,' he reminded her, 'and I don't want there to be any clouds in your sky, so are you going to trust me on this one?'

'Yes,' she said weakly, with the feeling that there was no way that Gabriel could combine working in London with her and the children in Swallowbrook, without the stress being worse than it had been before. Was he so much on cloud nine at being reinstated that he wasn't seeing the difficulties of what he was planning?

He was reading her mind, eager to tell her his plans to stop her from fretting, but her special day was only hours away, and he said, 'Tomorrow is your birthday and there have to be no clouds in your sky, so why don't you pop up to bed and get your beauty sleep while I make myself a drink, and tomorrow I'll tell you all about what went on when I was in front of the firing squad.'

She smiled. 'It would seem that they were out of bullets.'

'Yeah, they must have been,' he agreed, adding as

she began to climb the stairs, 'Would you like your breakfast in bed on your birthday?'

She shook her head. 'No, Gabriel. I want it with you and the children. I want us all always to be together…' she raised her eyes heavenwards '…until our young birds fly the nest.' As she slowly climbed the stairs, Laura thought she couldn't have explained it much clearer than that.

The day of her birthday had dawned and the children were beside her bed the moment she opened her eyes with the presents and cards that they'd made, and with one cuddling up on each side of her she opened their childish offerings and expressed her genuine delight at the thought that had gone into them.

There had been no sign of Gabriel so far and when hunger overcame excitement and the children went downstairs she threw on a robe and went to see where he was.

He was in the kitchen and Sophie and Josh were eating their breakfast in front of the television in the sitting room when she appeared, still tousled from sleep.

'Happy birthday, Laura,' he said, kissing her lightly on the cheek, and handed her an envelope.

As she opened it slowly she saw that it wasn't a card. Inside were flight tickets, a paid-up booking form and a brochure of an hotel beside a golden beach on an island that she'd always wanted to visit. As he watched her surprise become delight she said softly, 'Is this why you weren't interested when I suggested we go abroad, Gabriel?'

'Yes, I'm afraid so.' He smiled. 'I already had it sorted and you took me by surprise when you came up with the suggestion, so I had to play it down, otherwise it would have meant telling you and spoiling the surprise.'

She went up to him and held him close for a precious moment. 'How could I have thought that my birthday was going to be a non-event?' she choked.

As he looked down on to her he said, 'I have something else for you, Laura, but I want to give it to you when we're alone. Do you mind waiting?'

'No, of course not,' she said dreamily, with the thought of the holiday he had planned making her feel warm and cherished.

They'd had a lovely day, the four of them, a picnic lunch on the lakeside down by the marina, a sail in the afternoon and an early evening meal at the hotel before they went home to Swallows Barn. As Laura tucked the children in later she reminded them joyfully that they had just one more week of school and then at half-term they would be off to sun, sea and sand on a beautiful island.

When they were asleep she took off the jeans and the top she'd worn that day and changed into a dress of soft apricot silk that Gabriel had always liked to see her in, before going downstairs to where he was waiting for her.

There was stillness all around them as she went to

join him in the sitting room and when she had settled herself across from him she noticed that there were no gift-wrapped boxes or bags to be seen, and wondered what it could be that he had for her.

'You look very beautiful,' he said gravely. 'I hope that what I have for you will match the occasion.'

'What is it?' she asked with a sudden feeling of confusion.

'It is something rare and comes under the heading of "peace of mind". When I've told you what it is I hope you will understand and see it that way too.'

'What is it?' she asked again, feeling suspended in space and unable to get a footing on anything solid.

'I want you to answer me a question first,' was his reply.

'All right, then, go ahead.'

'Do you still want me to go back to oncology?'

'You know I do, Gabriel,' she cried. 'There is nothing I want more. It was my fault that you gave it up in the first place.'

'It was not your fault and I beg you not to ever say that again,' he told her. 'Getting back to what I have to tell you, I've been asked to take over the running of the new clinic when it opens.'

Her eyes were wide with wonder. She'd been able to see the clinic as it took shape from her office window on a lower level and had imagined Gabriel finding the fulfilment that he was being denied there. But her thoughts hadn't gone any further than the odd moment of wishful thinking because she knew that his heart belonged to a big hospital in London, well worn, well used, that he must surely yearn to see again.

'Just like that, without any ifs and buts and whys and wherefores about your past?'

'Yes, that describes it,' he said calmly, 'but I have had Nathan on my side, determined that I should get the job, and he has a lot of pull in the area's health arrangements.

'I've had a few interviews towards that end and only heard that the position was mine a few days ago. I've kept it to myself until I'd been to London because if they'd banned me I would have wanted to know if that made any difference to the job here, even though I'd been assured that it wouldn't.'

If he'd expected delight, it was slow in coming.

'But what about London and the hospital there… and James?' she cried. 'What if you grow bored with small-town medicine?'

He was smiling. 'You are incredible. I thought you would be over the moon to know that I'm going to be working in Swallowbrook. No more late nights, no more being overworked.'

'I am! Have no doubts regarding that. It will be wonderful, marvellous,' she told him with shining eyes. 'How long have you known about this?'

'I was approached some weeks ago and have caused a delay because I wanted the appointment to be on my terms and I only heard a few days ago that I had the agreement of the governing body.'

'And what are your terms?' she asked tremulously.

'That I work in London two days of every week, and for the rest am based in the clinic at Swallowbrook. I intend to spend most of my time in Theatre in both places as surgery is my main occupation, and in the case of the clinic, where there will be no facilities for it, I will do my consultations there and use those of the new hospital on the lakeside when I operate.

'I've arranged with James that I will do each Tuesday and Wednesday at his end, which will fit in with me seeing your uncle, and I will only be away from you for just the one night.

'What do you think? I hope I've got it right for everyone *and you most of all.*'

Her cheeks were wet with tears. 'You *have* got it right for everyone, and I love you so much for it, Gabriel, but is it going to be right for you? What about you?'

'I've got you, haven't I? What more do I need?' he said gently.

The tears were still flowing as he produced the box that held the eternity ring and he wiped them away gently before telling her, 'I had got this to give you on our wedding anniversary, but if you remember your job got in the way and I was introduced to the feeling of having made a meal for someone who didn't appear, as you must have done many times in the past, so the ring stayed in its box, but not any more.

'There will never be a moment that is more right to slip it on to your finger than this, but read what it says inside before I do that.' And he placed it on her open palm and waited.

'"*True love never dies*",' she said softly, holding the gold band with its circlet of diamonds up to the light, then she held out her hand and as he slipped the beautiful ring onto her finger it was as if their world had righted itself at last.

'Do you think our love got lost somewhere along the way?' he asked as he held her close.

She shook her head. 'No, Gabriel. Underneath all the misery and heartache we never stopped loving each other because ours is of the kind described in the engraving and it does last for ever.'

Lifting her into his arms, he carried her up the stairs and into the master bedroom, and when he laid her on top of the covers she gazed up at him and it was there, the need they had always created in each other. It wasn't dead, it had just been sleeping.

Later, after they had made love with passion and tenderness, like wanderers coming home after a long journey, Gabriel raised himself onto one elbow and looking down at her said softly, 'Tonight has blotted out the pains of the past, Laura, and the only thing we have to concern ourselves about now is the future, the fantastic, wonderful future.'

Reaching up, she brought his face level with hers and as their glances locked it was there in their eyes, the promise of what was to come in the days ahead, *and all of it was good.*

EPILOGUE

It was the opening day of the clinic and they were all there in the foyer. The mayor and his associates, the representatives of the area health authority, the doctors from the practice and Gabriel, looking tanned and relaxed after their Greek idyll.

Seated on the front row of chairs that had been set out to accommodate guests, Laura was remembering how he had given her the precious gift of not only what he'd described as 'peace of mind' but also a rekindling of their love.

If ever she had any doubts about that she need only take off the beautiful ring he had given her and read once again the message inside it.

'True love never dies' had been the words of the engraving and she was wrapped around with the wonderful truth of them.

It was done. The mayor had said his piece and declared that the clinic was now open and functioning, and that refreshments were available at the back of the entrance hall.

As Laura looked around her at the immaculate newness of the place and compared it with the well-used facilities of the London hospital that Gabriel hadn't forgotten during the months of his absence, she was happy that he hadn't cast aside the old in preference of the new.

When he appeared beside her and took her hand in his it was there again, the feeling that all was right with their world and that after many long months this time it was here to stay.

* * * * *

CELEBRITY IN BRAXTON FALLS

BY

JUDY CAMPBELL

First published in Great Britain 2012
by Mills & Boon, an imprint of Harlequin (UK) Limited.
Harlequin (UK) Limited, Eton House, 18-24 Paradise Road,
Richmond, Surrey TW9 1SR

ISBN: 978 0 263 89789 0

Harlequin (UK) policy is to use papers that are natural, renewable and recyclable products and made from wood grown in sustainable forests. The logging and manufacturing process conform to the legal environmental regulations of the country of origin.

Printed and bound in Spain
by Blackprint CPI, Barcelona

Dear Reader

The idea for this story came from reading about a family feud and how it affected the other people involved. I wondered how it might impinge on the lives of two people in love if they were caught up in a feud—could it ruin their future? Or would they be able to overcome all obstacles and find future happiness together?

I set the story in the beautiful countryside of the Peak District, although Braxton Falls is an imaginary village. I hope I've brought a flavour of the area to the story, and the sense of community that binds a small place together in adversity.

I so enjoyed writing this story—I hope you will find pleasure in reading it.

Best wishes

Judy

Judy Campbell is from Cheshire. As a teenager she spent a great year at high school in Oregon, USA, as an exchange student. She has worked in a variety of jobs, including teaching young children, being a secretary and running a small family business. Her husband comes from a medical family, and one of their three grown-up children is a GP. Any spare time—when she's not writing romantic fiction—is spent playing golf, especially in the Highlands of Scotland.

CHAPTER ONE

'GOLDEN sands fringed by waving palms, an azure sea and balmy days that you will love…'

The photograph of an idyllic beach scene underneath the caption in the brochure looked impossibly alluring—Kerry Latimer could almost feel the texture of the warm sand between her toes, imagine the limpid water lapping against her body, the sun sparkling on the waves, palm trees rustling in the light wind…

'Too right I'd love it,' she muttered wryly, then tore the brochure firmly in two, crushing it into a ball and flinging it sadly into the waste-paper basket. 'A shame I won't be going to the golden sands and azure sea after all…'

She looked bleakly through the surgery window, made blurry by the lashing rain, and at the dark sky outside, with the glowering shadows on the hills in the distance. During the past few days there had been a continuous torrential downpour, and the river flowing through the village was ominously high—a world away from dreamy islands in the middle of the Caribbean and their sunny climes. If only Frank had been more careful. If only he'd slowed down a bit, she would be almost there by now.

The horribly expensive pale coral silk dress hanging in its clear plastic cover on the wall of the surgery caught her eye—at this very moment she ought to have been on a plane, tossing back champagne as she winged her way to her cousin's wedding in Tobago, looking forward to wearing the dress later that week as one of her cousin's bridesmaids. Now, of course, after what had happened, she was stuck at work in Braxton Falls for the foreseeable future, covering for Frank, any hope of jetting off to beautiful sun-kissed beaches absolutely scuppered.

'Just my luck that my first holiday after a year's hard grind should be hijacked.' Kerry sighed—there was nothing she could do about the situation but grit her teeth and bear it, as her mother used to say.

She picked up the phone on her desk, and stabbed out a number. 'Hello?' she said as it was answered. 'Is that Denovan O'Mara? This is Kerry Latimer. I'm a colleague of your brother's at The Larches Medical Centre. I'm afraid that I've some bad news about him…' She took a deep breath and said gently, 'I'm very sorry to tell you that Frank was in a car accident last night and was seriously injured.'

There was a second's silence—Kerry imagined the shock Denovan would feel as he received the information about his half-brother, and she waited for the appalled intake of breath at the news, the concerned enquiry about his condition.

The reply sounded exasperated rather than anxious. 'The stupid fool—what the hell was he doing?'

Kerry stared at the phone, rather taken aback—it seemed a callous response to such awful news. 'We think Frank touched the accelerator instead of the brake—it's an automatic car—and he went through the garage door and out of the back wall of the garage down a steep incline, hitting a tree.'

A derisive short laugh. 'I don't suppose I'm all that surprised—it's typical of him. I always knew Frank was an accident waiting to happen—he's impatient and reckless. Were any other people injured?'

'No,' she answered coldly. 'No one else was involved.'

'Well, that's a blessing—he's an awful driver.' Privately Kerry agreed with Denovan—Frank always seemed to be taking corners too fast and scraping his car, or denting his bumpers when he reversed.

'So where is he now?' asked Denovan briskly.

'He's in the local hospital at the moment, but will probably be transferred to Derby for further detailed trauma scans. He has serious injuries to his head and a very bruised back. He's stable but in an induced coma. I thought I should let you know as I believe you're his only relative.'

'I see. Well, I suppose I'll have to come up then, although it's highly inconvenient. I could really do without this.'

'Excuse me?' What was this man like, and how self-centred could you be, weighing inconvenience with seeing a desperately ill brother? Kerry felt a slow burn of anger. If anyone should feel aggrieved, it was she, Kerry Latimer—obliged to cancel her holiday at the last minute, and then having to hold the fort at a two-handed medical practice for the foreseeable future.

Denovan's voice sounded tetchy. 'I'm in negotiations for a new contract and it could be rather tricky to leave at the moment.' Then he added unenthusiastically, 'But I will come up, of course.'

'If you think you can spare the time,' said Kerry sarcastically. 'He is very poorly, you know.'

'I'm sure he is. Sounds as if he'll be out of commission for a while—that won't make your job any easier, I guess,' he conceded. 'I'll be up when I've finished the programme this morning. I should be in Braxton later this afternoon.'

'I'm sure he'll be delighted to see you when he comes round.'

There was a short mirthless laugh at the other end of the line. 'You think?'

'Of course he will!' said Kerry rather indignantly. 'I assume you'll stay at his house?'

'I'll stay in the local hotel—what's it called? The Pear Tree?'

'Do you want me to book you a room?'

The voice softened. 'That's kind of you. One night will do. And it was good of you to let me know about Frank, I appreciate it. I'll see you when I arrive.'

The phone clicked and Kerry leaned back in her chair, frowning, and tapped a pencil against her teeth. She wasn't quite sure what to make of Denovan O'Mara—known to a huge following of adoring fans as 'TV's Dr Medic', helped in no small part by his good looks and knowledgeable, kindly manner.

Kerry grimaced—she felt she'd seen the real Denovan O'Mara a few seconds ago, and it revealed the flipside to his smooth public image—an impatient, irritable and arrogant side. And talk about unsympathetic. If he was as unfeeling as he seemed to be with his brother's plight, what was his bedside manner like with patients?

She'd never actually met Denovan face-to-face, just seen him occasionally on some morning breakfast show, giving his opinion and advice on the latest medical news story or answering viewers' concerns—every inch the glamorous and dreamy TV celebrity doctor with trademark tousled dark hair and piercing blue eyes. His strong, aquiline features regularly appeared on magazine covers, his advice was given in many newspaper articles and, in fact, he seemed to be always in the public eye, but from the conversation she'd just had with him, Kerry wasn't sure she was in a hurry to meet him personally.

'Talk about arrogant and selfish,' Kerry muttered as she sorted out the mail left on her desk. 'The guy only seems to think of the inconvenience he's been caused, with not an ounce of sympathy for Frank.'

It was Denovan, the younger of the two brothers, who had the celebrity looks. Frank was a good, reliable doctor and Kerry had a high opinion of his work, although he had a short fuse, even worse now he was divorced—and perhaps in that respect there was a similarity between the two men! Anyway, Kerry could put up with Frank's occasional moods because she loved working in beautiful Braxton Falls.

The brothers certainly didn't appear to be close. As far as she knew, Denovan had never been up to Braxton since their father had died six years ago, and Frank rarely spoke of him. Now she came to think of it, the few times she had heard Frank mention his brother, it had been in slightly mocking tones, implying that Denovan thought highly of himself and his celebrity role and was rather a womaniser, never seen with the same girl twice. Having just spoken to Denovan, she thought Frank might have had a point!

Kerry flicked a look at her watch and guiltily started up her computer, clicking on to the patients she had listed for that morning. No good musing about the brothers' relationship with each other—it was nothing to do with her. The list was a full one, reflecting the fact that she'd got some of Frank's patients too—it was going to be a hard slog over the next few weeks, trying to cope by herself without help.

But, boy, was she in need of a holiday. She'd looked forward to being her cousin's bridesmaid for months, and with the wedding set in such an exotic location it had been extra thrilling. It had been something to take her mind off the emotional roller-coaster she'd experienced over the past year. She closed her eyes for a second and swallowed hard, trying to blank out of her mind the heartache and loneliness she'd endured after the shock of Andy's death—at times she wondered if she'd ever get over it. In a world that seemed to be filled with couples it was hard to force herself as a single woman to go out and socialise, and consequently her social life was pretty non-existent. She was getting used to single meals heated up in the microwave. That was why this holiday was going to be such a momentous thing, supposedly kick-starting her to a more positive future. She put all the medical magazines that had arrived to one side and quickly shuffled through the printed emails that had come through with blood-test results and hospital appointments, forcing her mind on to other things. But the incipient headache that had been threatening for some time came on more persistently and she swallowed two painkillers before putting her printouts neatly in her in-tray.

There was a tap on the door, and Daphne Clark, one of the receptionists, came in with a cup of coffee.

'I thought you might need this,' she said. 'After all the excitement last night and getting Frank into hospital you must be exhausted. Have you heard how he is?'

'He may be moved some time today to Derby for further tests, but I can tell you that it'll be a long time before he can get back to work again. I'm on the look-out for a locum urgently, though I doubt I'll get one.' Kerry's voice was gloomy. 'The man that was going to replace me when I was away rang up only yesterday to say he couldn't take the job on after all.'

Daphne shook her head sympathetically as she

handed her the coffee. 'It's such a terrible shame about your holiday.'

'If only he'd waited to have this damn accident when I was safely in Tobago!' Kerry said, then she grinned ruefully. 'Oh, no. Forget I said that! Of course I'm very sorry for poor old Frank. He's in a bad way and he certainly didn't mean to crash his car. I guess it was at the end of a long day and he wasn't concentrating.'

'Could you not have gone anyway on a later flight perhaps and asked the medical centre in Laystone to take over?'

'I don't know if they could have taken it on at such short notice, and anyway,' she admitted candidly, 'I couldn't possibly have left Frank, knowing how ill he is.' Kerry took a gulp of the coffee and smiled, raising the cup in salute. 'Now, this is doing me more good than anything could—a large injection of caffeine is just what I needed. And talking of holidays, you might go and put that bridesmaid's dress in its box because every time I see it I want to cry! Oh, and by the way, would you please book a room for Frank's brother at the Pear Tree? He's coming up this afternoon to see Frank.'

Daphne's round face beamed. 'Not the gorgeous Dr Medic? Certainly I will—I shall ask him to give me an autograph for my mother—she's potty about him. Watches every single programme he's on and says he makes her feel better just looking and listening to him.'

Kerry raised an eyebrow. 'He didn't sound all that charming to me. More annoyed that he had to make time to come up here. I think he's a crusty self-centred old bachelor!'

'Don't say that,' protested Daphne, as she walked out. 'I may have been married for seventeen years and have three children, but I can still dream about impossibly handsome men and romance, can't I?'

She unhooked the bridesmaid's dress from the wall and folded it carefully over her arm. 'By the way, Liz Ferris wants you to go and see old Nellie Styles if you can. She had a another fall yesterday and Liz feels she needs an assessment prior to getting some carers in. Of course Nellie won't have it—she told Liz that she wouldn't allow any more community nurses in, she could manage fine by herself and she wasn't having any of those meals on wheels either!'

Kerry laughed. Nellie Styles was a feisty and wilful old lady, but she couldn't help admiring her. 'I'll go at lunchtime,' she promised. 'Then hopefully I'll be back to greet Denovan O'Mara—but I'm not looking forward to it particularly. I have a feeling he and I might not hit it off!'

Inside Nellie Styles's cottage it was very cold, and there was a general air of neglect about the place. The little home she took such pride in had deteriorated, thought Kerry sadly. A few months ago it had been spotless, every surface gleaming and the brasses round the fireplace twinkling. Now there were bundles of local papers and magazines littering the floor. The many photographs of Nellie's scattered family were filmed with dust and there were dead flies on the windowsills and plates of uneaten food on the table in the living room. It was a picture of decline Kerry had seen before in some of her elderly infirm patients whose relations lived too far away to help. She would have to persuade Nellie somehow that the time had come to accept help.

The old lady was standing precariously by the door to her kitchen, clinging to the back of a bookcase. She had an old blanket wrapped round her shoulders and she looked pinched and cold. She turned round as Kerry entered, a frown crossing her face when she saw who it was.

'I thought that nurse said Dr O'Mara was coming today,' she said grumpily.

'I'm afraid Dr O'Mara's been in an accident and injured himself rather badly. I don't think he'll be back for a while.'

Nellie pursed her lips. 'The way he screeches through the village in that car of his it's a miracle he hasn't come to grief before.'

The old lady turned back to her chair and staggered slightly as she let go of her support. Kerry went swiftly over to her and guided her gently back to her seat.

'It's a bit cold in here, Nellie, you haven't got your fire on,' she said, bending down and switching on the electric fire in the grate. 'How are you feeling?'

'Not bad…not bad. Just a bit chilled, like, but what can you expect with this weather? I've not seen so much rain for many years.'

Kerry nodded—she'd had to cross parts of the road

near Nellie's that were awash with huge puddles, and even from here she could hear the river gushing as it flowed along the main village road.

'Perhaps it'll stop raining soon, it did look a little lighter over the hills,' she said brightly. 'Now, Nellie, have you had anything to eat or drink today?'

Nellie looked evasive. 'I was just about to get myself a little something.'

'A bowl of soup might warm you up—I can easily heat some in a saucepan—and before you say anything, it isn't too much trouble.'

Kerry smiled at the old lady persuasively and was rewarded by a flicker of interest in her eyes. 'Well, just to please you, like, a little bit in a cup would be grand.'

In a few minutes thin hands were clasped round the warm cup and Nellie was sipping the soup eagerly, a little colour returning to her pale cheeks. 'That's very nice, Doctor, but I could have got it myself, you know.'

'I know you could, Nellie, but I want you to have a little rest for a while. I don't think you've ever recovered your strength from that last infection.'

Nellie's eyes flashed rebelliously. 'I'm not going back into that hospital, whatever you say!'

Kerry patted her hand. 'I don't want you to, but I do want to get you some help, just for the time being. Someone who can bring you a little food every day and perhaps do your washing, build you up a little—otherwise you're going to end up in hospital anyway.'

Nellie's frail old face looked fiercely at Kerry for a minute, then slowly her expression changed to one of resignation and she nodded her head slowly. 'Perhaps I am a bit run-down. If you could organise something, then—just temporary, mind!'

She must be feeling pretty awful to capitulate like that, thought Kerry. It was never easy to admit, after years of independence, that the time had come to be cared for.

'I'll see to it,' promised Kerry. 'In the meantime, Liz Ferris will be popping in to see that you're OK.'

'That Liz Ferris,' grumbled Nellie. 'She's always getting on at me to put more fires on and get more food in. She must think I'm made of money!'

'Now, now, Nellie—she's only doing it for your own good, you know. We're all very fond of you and want you to get stronger.'

Nellie looked slightly mollified. 'I know, lass, I know.' She took another sip of soup and then looked up at Kerry inquisitively. 'So what will you do now without Dr O'Mara?'

'Oh, I'm sure I can get someone to fill in fairly soon,' said Kerry, with more assurance than she felt. She'd already been in touch with several agencies in the area with no luck.

'I knew Frank O'Mara when he was a little boy—him and his brother. I used to do some cooking for them,' said Nellie, taking another sip of soup. 'Ee, they were chalk and cheese, those lads. And wild—always at each other's throats! Of course,' the old lady reminisced, 'that father of theirs was hard on them, and after he lost his first wife and his second wife left them all so sudden, like—well, they were left to their own devices and they were right tearaways!'

'I hope they've got over their differences now. His brother's coming up this afternoon to see Dr Frank,' said Kerry.

Nellie gave a cackle of laughter. 'Well, you may get fireworks between them—their father was a difficult, womanising man—perhaps they've taken after him! I always wondered if that was why Denovan's mother left—she was only young herself. But it was a cruel thing, if you ask me, to leave a young lad like that. You'll have to act as referee between them, my dear!'

That's the last thing I'm going to do, thought Kerry as she left the cottage. *I shall stay well clear of both of them.* She had enough on her plate without keeping the peace between two grown men! She had to admit, however, that the unexpected revelation Nellie had given about the O'Mara boys' childhood was rather intriguing. It sounded as if their childhood had not been a happy one.

She drove back to the surgery. The rain still beating down remorselessly—she wasn't surprised that the small car park was covered in huge puddles. A red sports car had taken the only dry slot near the staff spaces, so that Kerry had to park awkwardly against a wall and squeeze out of her door, putting her feet into a small pothole filled with water. She opened the boot and took out a large file and her medical bag, holding them in both arms as she picked her way over the flooded car park, the rain lashing down onto her and soaking her hair and clothes.

She squelched crossly into the building, hoping she could dry her feet out before the late afternoon surgery. Surely the day couldn't get any worse! No happy holiday, just continual rain and cold and the prospect of weeks of hard work. Burdened by the things she was carrying, she opened the office door by pushing it with her back and going in backwards.

'Some stupid idiot's put their car in the only dry space,' she complained to the office at large. 'My feet are absolutely soaked.'

She dropped her files and bag on a chair and then a deep voice behind her made her whirl round.

'Ah—I'm sorry about that. It's my car taking the space. I'm afraid I didn't realise it was the only dry spot.'

A tall man with tousled dark hair who had been lounging against the side of the desk unravelled himself and stood up. His gaze swept slowly over Kerry's drenched figure and the dripping tendrils of hair plastered against her face, down to the soggy remnants of her shoes. Beside him, a small boy of about four years old, with a snub nose and round wire-rimmed glasses, sat on the desk, drumming his heels against the drawers.

'You're certainly very wet,' he murmured.

Tell me something I don't know, thought Kerry caustically, but she managed to disguise her irritation.

'You must be Denovan, Frank's brother,' she observed. 'I didn't think you'd be as early as this.' She looked at the small boy, now making little indentations with a pencil on the top of the desk. 'And this is?'

'This is Archie, my son,' explained Denovan. 'I had to bring him up with me as his nursery school closes in the afternoon and his childminder isn't well.' He smiled down at the child, and suddenly his stern face was softer, gentler. 'I couldn't leave you behind, could I, sweetheart?'

There was no mistaking the resemblance between the two—Archie was a miniature version of the man. She'd never heard Frank mention that Denovan had a child, or indeed of him having a partner. What an odd family they were. Kerry wondered where Archie's mother was—perhaps she had a high-powered job that meant she wasn't around in the evening?

Denovan O'Mara was taller and broader than she'd thought he'd be—in fact, the television screen didn't do him justice. He was one hot guy, over six feet of impressive bodywork and a strong no-nonsense face—firm lips, incredibly blue bright eyes. He was impeccably dressed in a dark blue suit with a crisply knotted tie. No wonder he'd fitted so easily into celebrity status. Central casting couldn't have done better!

She caught an alarming glimpse of her own appearance in the mirror over the basin—hair hanging like rats' tails over her face, slightly blurred eye make-up… for some reason it irked her that she looked such a wreck in front of Denovan O'Mara and his smooth appearance.

She opened a drawer in the desk and took out a small

towel, drying her face and hands vigorously. 'You must have set off quite early from London,' she said.

'I came straight from work this morning—I told you I'd come as soon as I could,' he said. 'I've only a very limited amount of time here, but I thought I'd pop into your surgery first to tell you I'd arrived.' He shook her hand in a firm grip, his vivid blue eyes holding hers.

'You'll be pleased to hear that they've stabilised Frank—although he's still in ICU,' Kerry informed him, then added with slight emphasis to ensure that Denovan realised just how ill Frank was, 'I think it was pretty touch-and-go last night.'

He nodded. 'Sounds as if he was lucky to get out alive. But he's a strong man—he'll pull through, no doubt,' he said in an offhand way. His glance swept over her keenly, noting the dark shadows under her eyes, the strain showing on her face. 'This can't be easy for you,' he observed. 'I suppose you're trying to organise a locum and a hundred other things as well? You look a little bushed.'

For a 'little bushed' read a 'complete wreck', she thought wryly, blinking in some surprise at his understanding of the situation. She nodded briefly—there was something about his sympathetic tone that undermined her previous impression of a self-centred man. No wonder he held thousands of women viewers under his spell—not only looks, but reasonably charming when he wanted to be, as well. In fact, she could see that some women would find his type of looks quite sexy! But again, Frank knew his brother better than she did and she could quite believe his remarks that Denovan had an inflated idea of his own importance.

The small boy put his face close to his father's. 'I'm hungry,' he pronounced. 'I need a biscuit!'

'You wait until we get to the pub where we're going to stay then you can have lots to eat,' his father promised.

Archie pulled his father's ear. 'I can't wait.' He raised his voice. 'I'm very hungry!'

'I don't know if Daphne's rung up the Pear Tree yet—your room probably won't be ready,' said Kerry.

'I've had bad news on that front.' Daphne came into the room, catching the end of the sentence. 'The drains can't cope with the extra water at the bottom of the hill and the pub's completely flooded—they've had to close it and there's nowhere else to stay for miles.'

'Oh, no!' Kerry looked in dismay first at Daphne and then at Denovan and Archie. 'If the pub's flooded, what about all the other buildings down there?' And even more urgently, she thought worriedly, where was this man and his little boy going to stay?

'I'm *really* hungry, Daddy,' growled Archie, looking angrily at his father. 'Please can I have a biscuit, quickly? You promised before!'

Kerry couldn't help smiling at the little boy. She could imagine where he got his impatience from! 'Daphne, you've met Frank's brother already, I think?'

Daphne dimpled at Denovan, clearly smitten. 'Only a few minutes ago. Look, why don't I give Archie something nice to eat from the kitchen?' She held out her hand to Archie. 'You come with me, pet.'

Archie slid down from the desk and ran across the room to Daphne.

Denovan smiled wryly. 'Looks like he's got a friend there. It's a nuisance about the hotel. I guess I'll have to drive back to London after I've seen Frank this evening.'

Kerry had a spare room in her little cottage. It was filled with junk, but it did have a bed in it, and it would only be for one night after all. It was a nuisance, but for Archie's sake she would have to offer the arrogant Denovan and his son a room for the night.

'You're very welcome to stay with me,' she said, without much enthusiasm. 'I've a sleeping bag that Archie could have, and…' she looked doubtfully at Denovan's large frame '…a single bed in my spare room—it might not be very comfortable.'

There was a surprising sweetness in the smile that lifted his stern face. It made him seem younger, more approachable.

'That's very kind. I don't really feel like making the journey back tonight.' His periwinkle eyes smiled engagingly at her. They were quite startling, those eyes of his. 'I'm sorry to impose on you. I feel I've put you out enough, but I promise we'll be very quiet guests.'

'No, that's fine, it's no trouble.'

'Well, we'll be out of your hair tomorrow anyway, but I'm very grateful to have somewhere to sleep tonight!'

'That's OK,' she said brusquely. She delved in her bag and brought out her house keys, tossing them to him. 'You might as well go there now and get settled. There's food in the fridge for you and Archie. The house is at the top of the hill beyond the surgery—you can't miss it, it's the only one with a blue door.'

Denovan jingled the keys in his hand before he turned to go, with a slightly apologetic expression on his face. 'Actually, I have another very big favour to ask you. I'll go and see Frank this evening—but an ICU isn't the place for a little boy, and I was planning to ask one of the hotel staff to watch him for me, but that plan will obviously need to change. So, if you're not doing anything tonight, could I possibly leave Archie with you for an hour?'

Not doing anything tonight? Kerry almost laughed. She only had about a hundred things on her to-do list from the fallout of Frank's accident, like sorting out the paperwork she should have done last night, trying yet again to get some cover for her colleague, catching up on the seriously ill patients on his list. It seemed an endless catalogue of things. But Denovan had to see his brother and Archie had to be looked after.

She hid her sigh behind a smile. 'No problem—I'll be back after surgery at about six-thirty.'

'I'm very grateful. I just want to satisfy myself they're doing the best they can for him. Then I really have to get back to London early tomorrow. Archie needs to get back to his nursery school.'

'Of course.'

'I don't know when I can get back here again, it rather depends on my other commitments. As I said before, Frank's accident couldn't have come at a worse time.'

Kerry thought of poor Frank lying so very injured in the local hospital, and raised her eyebrows. Denovan watched her expression.

'You look very disapproving,' he remarked, a sudden coolness in his tone. 'I do have an incredibly busy life, and it's been a nightmare trying to rearrange things today, but I managed it.'

Bully for you, thought Kerry scornfully, but she said lightly, 'I guess I'm just a little surprised that you couldn't have found time to come at the weekend perhaps. I'd have thought…'

The blue eyes turned flinty. 'You'd have thought what exactly?' he enquired frostily. 'With the deepest respect, you have no right to presume anything about my arrangements.'

Talk about pompous! Kerry's cheeks burned angrily. 'I don't presume anything—and it hasn't been easy for me either, as a matter of fact, but if he was my brother—'

'But he's not!' cut in Denovan harshly.

Kerry stared at him incredulously, astounded by his rudeness. Extraordinary how touchy and defensive he was about visiting his brother, it was as if she'd lit a blue touch paper! She felt she'd glimpsed the real Denovan O'Mara again, arrogant and self-centred, and all of a sudden the atmosphere in the room had dropped several degrees.

Denovan stared at the floor for a second, taking a deep breath as if trying to keep his anger under control, then he shook his head apologetically and looked slightly shamefaced.

'Look, I'm sorry. I didn't mean to fly off the handle. It was completely uncalled for, especially when you've been so kind.'

Hah! thought Kerry cynically. Now she was seeing his charming TV persona once more.

'I guess it's been a hell of a long day,' Denovan continued. 'I just wish Frank could learn not to take liberties with his blasted car.'

Amen to that, agreed Kerry. Frank wasn't aware of the upset he'd caused her over the past twenty-four hours!

'Perhaps he's learned his lesson,' observed Kerry tersely. 'However, I'm sure when he sees you, it will do him a lot of good.'

Denovan shrugged. 'Actually, it could have quite the opposite effect. The last time I saw or spoke to Frank was over six years ago, and that wasn't exactly a happy occasion.' He said it lightly, but that only seemed to emphasise the gravity of their differences.

He turned and left the room, striding quickly down the corridor and attempting to gather his thoughts. God, he was a fool. Why had he flown off the handle when Kerry had queried his commitment to his brother? All she had done was express sympathy and offer hospitality to himself and Archie—and he'd repaid her by being incredibly rude.

The truth was, he admitted to himself, he had a terrible fear that coming back and seeing Frank would raise all kinds of ghosts that he'd tried to bury over the years—and perhaps there was some guilt that he had never attempted to build bridges with his brother.

Of course, Kerry knew nothing of the terrible legacy of betrayal and disgust he felt for Frank, and the bitterness that had grown up between the two men. He clenched his fists angrily. Hell, he didn't owe his brother any sympathy at all after what he'd done to ruin the family. He took a deep breath and went to collect his little boy from the kitchen.

Kerry sat down and stared after him in astonishment. What earth-shattering event could have caused a six-year rift between the two brothers? And whatever it was, did it justify Denovan's rudeness?

CHAPTER TWO

ARCHIE settled happily in front of the television while his father went to see Frank in the local hospital, which was about five miles away across the valley in the larger town of Laystone. Denovan said he would probably stay an hour and find out what the prognosis on Frank was.

Kerry put on the kettle and started to make a quick supper for herself and Archie. She flicked a look at the little boy, endearingly quaint with his round glasses perched on the end of his snub nose, his jaws moving rhythmically as he devoured a little bowl of raisins. He seemed an adaptable child—obviously well used to adjusting to new people and situations.

'Would you like some pasta?' she enquired.

He didn't take his eyes from the screen. 'No, I don't like pasta, thank you.'

'What about some baked beans, then?' Kerry rooted around in a cupboard looking for suitable food.

'No, I don't like baked beans, thank you.'

'Then what do you like?'

Archie dragged himself away from watching the flickering screen. 'I like chips and burgers and ice cream and crisps and chocolate,' he said firmly.

Kerry's lips twitched in amusement—evidently his parents didn't bother about healthy diets!

'Is that what you're allowed at home?'

Archie fixed Kerry with his bright blue eyes and nodded vigorously. 'Yes. Daddy says I can have what I want.'

'Right, well, I'll see what I can find,' she promised, wondering where Mummy fitted into the picture.

A few minutes later Kerry collapsed on the sofa next to Archie and tucked into her pasta, giving the little boy some ice cream she'd found at the bottom of the freezer, and both of them sat in silence, one absorbed in the television, Kerry starting to look through her mail and flicking through the newspaper she hadn't had time to read that day.

The room was warm and she fought against drifting off to sleep—it had been a hectic twenty-four hours, and she was feeling the effects of cramming a lot of things into a short time with little sleep. Archie leant cosily against her like a little hot-water bottle and she looked down at the top of his head. He was such a lovable little boy, even if his father was the arrogant Dr Denovan O'Mara!

She sighed softly. A year ago her future had seemed to be mapped out—a wedding, a loving husband, hopefully followed by children like Archie… Then all that had been taken away from her brutally and swiftly, and the children and family life she longed for were nothing but a faded dream.

She was vaguely aware of the sound of the front

door opening just as she closed her eyes in a troubled doze. Denovan walked into the room then stopped suddenly when he saw his son and Kerry relaxed together on the sofa. Archie had his head against her shoulder, and Kerry had one arm round him, her freshly washed dark cloud of hair tumbling over the cushion she was leaning against, mouth slightly open as she dozed. He smiled wistfully at the picture they presented—it twisted his heart to see Archie nestled up against Kerry, for it seemed to highlight the lack of a motherly figure in his precious son's life.

He sighed and pushed that thought to the back of his mind then leant forward and touched Kerry lightly on her shoulder. 'Sorry to disturb you when you both seem so comfortable,' he said.

Startled, Kerry sat bolt upright on the sofa and stared at him in surprise. 'You've hardly been gone any time!' she exclaimed.

'I haven't been able to get to the hospital,' Denovan explained drily. 'The wind's brought down several big trees by the riverbank and the bridge has collapsed—there's no way over the river now, so getting anywhere out of the village at the moment is impossible. It won't take much for the river to burst its banks completely.'

'What?' Kerry gently put Archie to one side and stood up, staring in disbelief at Denovan. 'The village is cut off altogether? So what's happening down by the river now?'

He shook his head. 'People are working like mad, putting sandbags or anything else round their properties to keep the water out. But the most immediate problem is that a woman's trapped under part of the bridge wall that's collapsed.' His face was grave. 'I'm sorry to say I'll have to drag you away. We're both needed urgently, and this woman needs medical help. There's no way an ambulance can get through at the moment. There are people trying to free her, but she's bound to have injuries—we should be there.'

The day she'd thought could get no worse had reached rock bottom, thought Kerry wryly. A disaster in the village and no backup from essential services. Kerry hauled on her cagoule and pushed her feet into some wellingtons—she flicked a look at Denovan's stalwart figure and suddenly she was extremely grateful to have him with her to help, pompous and arrogant man though he was.

'We'd better take my car,' she said. 'It's a small estate so we could get her up to the surgery in that if necessary. We keep some equipment there for the Mountain Rescue Team—a stretcher, a collapsible splint, blankets and a neck collar, that sort of thing. We can call in and get them.'

'A good idea,' said Denovan. 'It's very cold out there.'

Kerry noticed the little boy looking solemnly at them both. 'We'll drop Archie off at Daphne's—she's only a door or two away and I know she won't mind.' She bent down and smiled at him. 'You know that nice lady who gave you biscuits and hot milk this afternoon? We're taking you to stay with her for an hour or two while your daddy and I go and help a poorly lady.'

Archie's mischievous blue eyes gleamed. 'Will she give me some more biscuits?'

'I dare say she will.' Kerry smiled. 'Come on, let's go!'

A small crowd had gathered round the bridge where the river started to run through the village. Car headlights were trained on the dramatic scene where the woman lay trapped, with her legs pinioned underneath the collapsed stones. The lashing rain glinted on a million drops in the beams of the light, and the river looked very full; it was obvious that the bridge had been swept away.

Kerry's eyes widened in horror as the enormity of the situation hit her. 'Oh, my God,' she breathed, scrambling out of the car. 'How on earth will we get her out without equipment?'

Denovan opened the car tailgate and lifted out the blankets. 'We'll do it somehow,' he said confidently. 'You'd be surprised what a few strong men can do.' He gave her a quick grin of encouragement. 'You keep the lady calm and assess her condition and I'll help these men to lift that rubble.'

Kerry turned to a woman on the edge of the little crowd. 'Have you any idea who's under all that rubble?' she asked.

'She's Sirie Patel. She runs the Post Office and shop on the corner, poor woman. She never stops working—if it wasn't for her, we wouldn't have a village shop.'

Kerry pushed her way through to the stricken woman, forcing herself into professional mode and forgetting her own shock that it was her friend Sirie who was hurt. She didn't deserve this, giving so much of her life to the community, allowing those who were hard up to pay her 'next time', lending a ready ear to listen to the woes of any of her customers. It wasn't fair.

In her next life, thought Kerry grimly as she packed the blankets as best she could around Sirie in the howling wind and stinging rain, she would come back as something less stressful than a GP trying to calm a terrified woman trapped under a bridge wall with water gushing over her. Perhaps she'd have a career as a lion tamer or a high-flying trapeze artist!

She pushed a folded blanket gently behind Sirie's head, all the time talking to her, reassuring her that she was being looked after. Kerry knew the psychological importance of making sure the victim was aware that she wasn't alone but in safe and capable hands.

'It's all right, Sirie, love, we're here to help you now,' shouted Kerry above the noise of the rushing river. 'Try and stay calm. Here, hold my hand and grip it tightly. If you keep as still as possible, there's going to be no danger.'

Oh, how she hoped that was true! The river was so very close and fast, the roar of it filling their ears. She had a horrible vision that if Sirie were to slip into it when they released her, she could be swept down into the torrent. It was a steep hill, and even though it was raining and dark, the ribbon of lights along the road at the bottom of the valley could be seen clearly, twinkling many feet below.

Kerry looked across at Denovan lying on his stomach close to Sirie as he tried to see where her legs were trapped, and if the two large slabs of stone were actually compressing the limbs. She admitted to herself that she hadn't expected a man like Denovan to hurl himself into the situation as he had—to be so hands-on. He'd surprised her, but after the way he'd lost his cool with her earlier, she wasn't about to become his biggest fan. However, she admitted grudgingly, she was very grateful that he was there, and revealing himself to be so competent.

He scrambled up and crouched near to Kerry, his eyes looking searchingly at the victim's face. 'How is Sirie?' he asked. 'Bearing up?'

'Very shocked. She's in considerable pain, and her pulse is quite thready—of course I don't know what her sats are or her BP. I've morphine in my bag so perhaps you'd dig it out. Any sign of outside help yet?'

'I've rung for an air ambulance, seeing nothing else can get through here at the moment,' said Denovan, rummaging through Kerry's bag to find the morphine. 'The reception was incredibly bad, but I think they've got the gist of it. It sounded like a ten-minute ETA.'

Sirie's grip on Kerry's hand was fierce. 'Will they be long getting me out?' she whispered, screwing her eyes up. 'I don't know how long I can stand this…'

'It's all right, Sirie, you're going to feel more comfortable very soon. Dr O'Mara's just going to inject you with something that'll make you feel much easier.' Sirie's eyes fluttered open. 'What about my girls?' she whispered. 'I've got to pick them up from their Brownie meeting.'

'Don't worry. We'll make sure that they're looked after. One of the mothers will take them to her house,' Kerry assured her. Thank heavens for a small, close-knit community, she thought. They did look out for each other here.

Denovan tested the syringe he was holding, then smiled down at Sirie. 'Hang in there. Ten mils of this magic stuff will help you to relax. In fact, you'll feel on top of the world, as if you've had two double whiskies…'

Sirie's face flickered into a frail, brave smile. 'I'm teetotal, Doctor,' she whispered. 'I never touch the stuff!'

'Well, now you're about to find out what you're missing,' he joked. He turned to Kerry, his voice low enough so that Sirie couldn't hear him but audible to Kerry above the noise of the voices of the men and the howling wind. 'We're nearly there now. Keep your fingers crossed.'

Kerry bit her lip, watching the last stones being inched away from Sirie's legs, praying that the muscles in the legs wouldn't be badly crushed. Whatever damage Sirie had suffered, it was imperative that she was hospitalised as soon as possible.

She watched the men grunting and groaning as they tried to lever the stones up without slipping in the thick mud around the site. Denovan and two other men had placed the stretcher on the ground as near to the bridge as possible and were waiting to pull the victim out as soon as they dared. It was a tense few minutes and Kerry kept up a low flow of conversation with Sirie, distracting her from the shouting and noise of falling rubble that was going on around her.

At last, with infinite care, Sirie was lifted away from the broken bridge and placed as gently as possibly on the stretcher. Kerry and Denovan bent over her to examine the damage that had been done to her legs. One lay awkwardly, bent at a strange angle with multiple contusions and a large gash down the shin bone.

'We might have guessed Sirie wouldn't get away without any injury,' said Denovan, straightening up. 'That left leg's almost certainly broken, from the way it's positioned. It's taken the brunt of the fallen wall, but I don't see a protruding bone, so hopefully it's not a compound fracture.'

Kerry squeezed Sirie's hand comfortingly, and Sirie's large, scared eyes looked from one doctor to the other. 'Am I going to have to have an operation?' she asked in a quavery voice.

'Until you've had X-rays we won't know for sure. First thing we need to get you to hospital.' Denovan squatted down next to the frightened woman and smiled kindly at her. 'You've been absolutely great—really brave. Just hang on a little longer.'

Kerry was amazed at how sensitive Denovan could be, what a contrast to the impatient doctor of an hour or two ago. He seemed to have another, softer side to him that he'd hidden well when she'd first met him—perhaps he was just very good at acting!

He was looking at the raging river a few feet away from them. 'Perhaps we'll move Sirie nearer the car first and then strap her leg.'

Kerry followed his glance and swallowed hard. Was it her imagination, or did the water seem higher than it had been? It looked as if the river would burst its banks any second and completely cover the road.

'OK, Doc, but let's do it before the whole damn things goes,' urged one of the men. 'Hopefully the helicopter will be here soon. It'll land on the field at the top of the village.' They slid the stretcher into the back of the estate car, although it wouldn't go in completely, and Kerry bound the affected leg above the site of the fracture to the splint—just securing it enough to stop it from being bounced around. Four men, including Denovan, supported the stretcher as Kerry drove very slowly back through the village to The Larches. As she left the scene, she heard a sudden commotion behind her—a roar of water, the cracking of trees.

'What's happening back there?' she shouted, keeping her eyes glued ahead of her.

'The river's burst its banks—we got Sirie out just in time,' yelled one of the men.

Oh, the relief when the little entourage eventually reached the medical centre—three stalwart figures in familiar orange and green emergency suits were racing down the road to meet them.

'We've managed to land in the field at the top of

the road,' panted one of the paramedics. 'You did well to get this lady out when you did. I believe the river's completely out of control now. We'll just do an assessment of the victim before we move her any farther—get a take on her oxygen levels, BP, etc.'

Kerry leant against the car and watched Sirie being monitored by the medics. If the men in the village hadn't managed to free her so quickly, there might have been a tragic end to the story, she thought with a shudder. She glanced across at Denovan, who was talking to one of the paramedics and watching as they assessed Sirie's condition.

'Can you get word through to the other emergency services that the village needs help?' he asked one of the paramedics. 'My mobile's not getting through to anyone at the moment and someone's just told me some power lines are down.'

Sirie was eventually taken away, wrapped in a foil heat blanket to keep her body temperature up, and soon the clatter of the helicopter's rotor blades were heard as it rose in the air and headed off across the valley. Kerry brushed a weary hand of relief over her eyes—what a way to finish the last twenty-four hours! Adrenaline had been pumping through her for the last hour, but suddenly the drama was over and she felt drained of all her energy.

'Tired?' asked Denovan, his eyes looking critically at her exhausted-looking face.

'A little,' she admitted, then added with sudden candour, 'Actually, I feel I could go to sleep on a clothesline for three days after all that's happened. I'm going to leave the car here, I think, as I thought I heard something important give a horrible crack as we set off with Sirie, but I'll look at it in the morning.'

'You need a hot drink,' he ordered, mock-severely. 'And perhaps something a little stronger, if you've got anything in. Come on, I'll walk you to your house before I pick up Archie.'

'You've no need to,' protested Kerry firmly. 'It's late. You go and get Archie now.' She wasn't about to get too chummy with an unpredictable man like Denovan just because he'd helped out so much that evening. She was still smarting at the conversation she'd had with him earlier.

'Your house is on the way to Daphne's so I might as well see you back first,' he said easily.

They went up the hill together silently, heads down against the wind. In the dark it was hard to see the path, and although Kerry moved cautiously, the pothole she stepped into took her by surprise. Suddenly she sensed the ground coming towards her face and flailed her arms to keep her balance and stop her smashing against the asphalt of the path.

In an instant Denovan's arms were round her waist, pulling her towards him. 'Steady does it,' he murmured.

She gasped in surprise, momentarily winded, and for a second she clung on to him, dazed at the speed of it all, braced against his rocklike frame. Feeling the rough texture of his chin stubble rasping against the softness of her face, and the cold damp clothes he was wearing pressed against hers somehow seemed embarrassingly intimate with someone she didn't know—but nevertheless she leaned into him, prolonging the contact, relaxing as she savoured that sensation of protection, the physical strength of him. And unexpectedly for an extraordinary moment she felt the unmistakeable flicker of physical attraction for Denovan O'Mara, a man she'd instinctively disliked since she'd spoken to him on the phone that morning.

A poignant memory of being in another man's arms floated into her mind, and in her imagination she was close to Andy again, so close that she could feel the thump of his heart against hers, enclosed in the warmth and safety of the man she'd loved so much only twelve months ago. But how long ago that seemed now, another life away…

Then the wind blew cold against her face and she was back in the present, and to her embarrassment tears welled up in her eyes. Her grief for Andy was still very near the surface, and she felt a funny little shiver of guilt, as if she'd betrayed his memory. She stepped back from Denovan hastily, almost shoving him away from her, and gave a nervous laugh.

'I'm so clumsy…'

'It's pitch dark—no wonder you lost your footing. Are you OK?' he asked, his hand taking her arm in an iron grip again. 'We don't want another casualty, do we?'

He looked down into her eyes, his own glinting with amusement, rivulets of water running down his face, his teeth white in the shadows, the lean planes of his muddied scratched face showing up every so often in the headlights of the cars coming up the hill and away from the flooding.

There was no doubt about it—he was a very attractive man. Kerry's heart did a stealthy double beat and the treacherous flicker of attraction flashed through her again, and to her shame in her imagination she pictured herself kissing this man, feeling his firm mouth on hers, his cheek against hers. Then she looked away, sick at heart. How could she fancy another man so quickly? It was Andy she wanted, missed so desperately, and no one could fill the gap he'd left. What on earth was she thinking of—allowing herself to imagine anything intimate with a man she didn't even like?

'I'm absolutely fine,' she said distantly. 'Just lost my footing for a second.'

'Lucky I'm here, then, isn't it?' he murmured, his hand still holding her arm as they went into the warm little cottage.

He flicked on the light switch. 'A miracle,' he remarked. 'The power's still on.' He looked at Kerry's white face and said sternly, 'You need some sleep. Get up to your bedroom, and I'll bring you a hot drink when you're actually in bed.'

Denovan looked pretty tired, as well. His face was covered with mud, as was his hitherto immaculately tailored suit—the trousers were ripped and the sleeves of the jacket almost torn away from their seams. But it was his hands that Kerry noticed with horror—torn, bleeding, the nails jagged—they had been badly damaged in the race to free Sirie.

'Oh, Denovan, your poor hands!' She forgot that she disliked the man and without thinking took his hands in hers and looked down at them in distress. 'You've got to get these cleaned as they're very badly cut. There's disinfectant in the bathroom cupboards.'

He pulled them gently away from her. 'Don't worry, Doctor, they'll be OK. It's just a few surface abrasions.'

Kerry bit her lip. Why had she done something so personal as holding his hand? It implied a degree of intimacy with him that she certainly didn't feel.

He said briskly, 'Now, I'm going to make you some hot cocoa with a nip of whisky in it. It'll do you a world of good.'

Kerry didn't argue, too tired to dwell on her embarrassment at holding his hands, but stumbled into her room, not even bothering to pull off her clothes. She collapsed onto the heavenly soft bed in her filthy clothes, and as soon as her head hit the pillow her eyes closed, and she never heard Denovan come upstairs with a mug of cocoa.

Denovan put the mug on the side table and smiled down at her wryly. No wonder the woman was exhausted—she'd had a lot to cope with since the night before. For a few seconds he looked at her recumbent slim figure, her tangled dark hair spread across the pillow, long eyelashes sweeping over her high cheekbones. Those delicate looks belied the toughness she'd shown tonight in the raging storm, he reflected.

He grinned, forgetting for a moment how tired he was. It was hard to believe that a few minutes ago he'd held this beautiful woman in his arms, felt her soft body pressed to his—and very nice it had been, too! And hadn't it reminded him very forcibly that despite the so-called glamorous social whirl he was supposed to enjoy, he'd led a pretty monastic life over the past few years despite his years in the limelight and being featured with nearly every glamorous young woman in London? Since Archie's mother had left he was wary of being linked to any one woman. And anyway, he had to be very choosy—whoever he took up with had to be very, very special, someone who would cherish his little boy as much as he did. And, he thought sadly, show more affection for Archie than his own mother ever had.

He supposed that someone like Kerry would have a boyfriend. Obviously she wasn't married, but she was an attractive and successful woman. Fleetingly he wondered how she could work with a bastard like his brother—but he guessed that Kerry was pretty feisty and she wouldn't suffer fools gladly. Or perhaps it was more likely, Denovan thought cynically, that his brother had hidden his true character from her. After all, that was Frank's stock in trade—pretending to be something he wasn't.

Gently he placed the duvet over her and turned to go out of the room, nearly falling over a large suitcase with a folded dress draped on top of it by the door. He bent down to look at the labels and raised his eyebrows. It looked like Kerry was, or had been, going on holiday—Frank's stupid accident had obviously meant that she'd had to forfeit that. No wonder she'd been a bit tetchy with him. Her plans had been ruined and instead of a fairy-tale holiday she was back at work for a long stint if Frank's injuries were as serious as they thought they were.

He went down to the little kitchen and stretched before flopping down in a chair, his elbows on the table, and closed his eyes for a second. Although he felt exhausted, he had decisions to make before he returned to London. His contract with the television company was ending, but the company wanted him to front another programme about the general health of the population, and he was wondering whether he really wanted to take on more work. Wondering, in fact, if he actually wanted to do any more television work at all.

On the face of it, his life had all seemed so glamorous and exciting, working in a place with a buzz to it, mingling with the good and the great, knowing that he had a certain cachet amongst his colleagues. But the truth was he was bored with answering people's queries and giving his opinion on hypothetical questions—and the boredom was beginning to show. He was easily irritated, becoming autocratic if someone didn't agree with him, used to having his own way.

Tonight had made him realise that he was becoming further and further removed from the practical care of the patients he'd loved treating. He'd just been thrown into a situation a few hours ago where he'd used the skills he'd been taught at medical school and as a result he felt alive, stimulated, his body humming with the unaccustomed rush of adrenaline. It had been so rewarding to help in Sirie's rescue, working in a team and establishing a relationship with the victim, persuading her to put her trust in himself and Kerry. It had been worthwhile—and how long had it been since he'd felt like that at the end of a day's work? A few years ago he'd have given anything to achieve what he had done in the media world, but suddenly it was beginning to seem a very hollow world.

He rose restlessly from his chair, went to the back door and opened it. The wind had died down and it had stopped raining, and there was a sweet country-fresh smell from the fields. He took a deep gulp of the crisp air into his lungs; he'd forgotten how much he'd loved Braxton Falls, the little valleys and the rolling hills. It had been the best part of his childhood, growing up in the countryside. He hadn't realised how much he'd missed it since he'd left six years ago after falling out so spectacularly with Frank. His father had wanted them both to take over the practice when he retired—but Denovan had known that working with his half-brother was an impossibility. After what had happened, they could never live near each other again, and so he'd ended up in London and his life had taken a very different direction from anything he'd imagined.

He closed the door and turned back abruptly into the room. He would have to go and collect Archie from Daphne's house, and then tomorrow start thinking seriously about his future, because it wasn't just his future that was affected but his dear little son's—and he was the most important thing of all.

CHAPTER THREE

SHE couldn't understand where the voices were coming from… Kerry stirred restlessly as she slowly awoke and a child's high little voice floated upstairs, singing 'Humpty Dumpty', penetrating her sleepy brain. And then there was a burst of giggling, a clattering of kitchen noises, and someone running a tap.

She squinted across at her bedside clock, then as it came into focus gave a yelp of horror—it was nine o'clock and she should have been at work an hour ago! She saw the still-full mug of cold cocoa on the table and everything came flooding back—Frank's accident, the drama last night, and the bursting of the riverbank. So many things had happened yesterday. She'd almost forgotten that Denovan and his son were staying with her.

Denovan O'Mara. She rolled on her back and closed her eyes and like the rerun of a film a picture floated into her mind of her falling forward and being swept up in his arms. She could still feel the shiver of attraction that had flickered through her body and how it had shaken her. Oh, sure, he was the kind of drop-dead gorgeous male that most girls would die for—but not her. She had fallen in love with Andy, sweet, gentle, self-effacing and kind. She'd never been attracted to Denovan's assured, smooth type—especially when it was mixed with arrogance!

OK, she'd been grateful for his undoubted skill last night, and he'd certainly thrown himself into the rescue. He'd actually been rather heroic, she admitted, battling against the weather as he'd helped to dismantle the fallen wall, directing the team of men, putting himself at risk when he'd helped to lift Sirie over the mud near the raging river. And perhaps it was her admiration for his contribution last night that had made her act in such an odd way—yes, that had to be it. And anyway, and most importantly, Denovan O'Mara was obviously a family man with a child—however attractive, he was off-limits!

She swung her legs over the bed and started to peel off her filthy clothes from the night before. She drew back the curtains and looked down the street, amazed that, instead of rain, sunlight bathed the village in a golden light and the hills beyond had a backdrop of blue skies. It was hard to believe that there'd been a raging storm that night. Still, the road was covered with thick mud and she could see knots of people making their way up the hill from the flooded road below. Abandoned cars were strewn haphazardly on pavements and across the road. She was profoundly glad that Denovan and his son were only staying for the one night and would be going today—she had enough problems to worry about without catering for two guests.

A quick shower and a change of clothes and Kerry made her way downstairs, a delicious smell of fresh coffee permeating the little cottage. It reminded her that it had been a long, long time since she'd had anything to eat or drink and a cup of hot coffee would revive her more than anything else. Straight afterwards she'd ring the surgery and tell them she'd be along directly. She imagined the bulging roomful of patients waiting to see her, and sighed. How the hell would she ever get through them all?

In the kitchen Denovan was on his mobile phone, his back to her, and Archie was sitting at the kitchen table, consuming a pile of toast. He gazed at Kerry and smiled.

'Here's that lady again,' he informed his father. 'She's got out of bed now.'

Kerry pulled the coffee pot towards her and poured out a large mug of coffee. 'Hello, Archie, did you have a good sleep?'

The little boy nodded solemnly. 'But Daddy didn't. He kept falling out of that bed. It's too small for him.'

Denovan snapped his mobile shut and turned round with a grin. 'Hey, I was very grateful for that bed, young man.' He looked at Kerry. 'You went out like a light—I'm not surprised.'

The ruined suit had gone and now he was wearing jeans and an old fisherman's jersey, and although his hair had been washed, as it had dried it had sprung up in a tousled way over his forehead—he looked very casual and it suited him. Kerry pinched a piece of toast from Archie's plate.

'What's been happening? What about the village—I suppose they've managed to open up the road?'

Denovan shook his head. 'No bridge, no road, some power lines down—and a lot of houses with flooding. No way out or into the village, and now I was just hearing there may be a problem with the helicopter. By the way, I went down to the surgery and told them you'd be a little late.' His eyes twinkled. 'I think you're in for a busy morning.'

'I can imagine,' remarked Kerry wryly. 'How about your brother? Have you managed to contact the hospital?'

'Still stable—and Sirie Patel is having surgery this morning on her leg. There is evidence of crush syndrome, I'm afraid. Her kidney function seems impaired with all the toxins in her blood—but hopefully they've got it under control.'

So much had happened—so much to do. 'I'll get going, then,' said Kerry briskly. 'No good sitting around here.'

'I wondered can I be of any help?' suggested Denovan slightly tentatively. 'I don't want to step on anyone's toes, but if we could find some childcare for Archie for an hour or two, I could see some of your patients for you until they manage to open up the road.'

Kerry looked at him sardonically, and couldn't help enquiring rather pertly, 'I thought you had to get back to London—that it was very inconvenient to stay on?'

Touché, thought Denovan wryly. He deserved that dart of sarcasm! 'I won't be able to leave Braxton, with the roads as they are, and even if they do manage to get a helicopter through I doubt if I'll be a priority. I might as well make myself useful.'

Kerry's face softened—she'd be stupid to pass by the offer of help from someone she'd seen to be competent. 'You're sure? I have to admit it would be a great help. And perhaps by lunchtime they'll have repaired the bridge. And as for Archie—there's a little nursery school in the church hall just across the road. I'm sure in an emergency they'd look after him.'

They'd probably fall over themselves to look after the famous Denovan O'Mara's son, Kerry reflected with a little private grin to herself.

To Kerry's amazement, the church hall was milling with people, children ran round excitedly and some of the older men and women were sitting on benches by the wall looking disorientated and a little lost. A trestle table had been set up along one side of the room, where several women, including Daphne, were filling mugs with tea and coffee.

'What on earth's going on?' Kerry asked her.

'Everyone from down near the bridge has had to be evacuated. Some of these people came up here early in the morning to sleep because the water got so high in their houses. It's complete bedlam,' said Daphne.

'I suppose Freda's in charge at the surgery, then?' said Kerry resignedly.

Freda Knight was their trainee receptionist. She'd

only recently left school but her grip on the job was precarious, as most of her life was lived vicariously through the pages of the gossip magazines and the celebrities in them, and she seemed to have little interest in the running of the surgery. Kerry wondered if Freda would be able to concentrate at all when she realised that Denovan O'Mara was going to be helping out!

'I'll be over very soon,' promised Daphne. 'We just felt we had to give some of these elderly folk something hot to drink.'

Kerry looked around the crowded room. 'I don't suppose the nursery school is operating today, then,' she said. 'Denovan's offered to help out with this morning's list and we were hoping we could leave Archie with them for an hour or so until he goes back later today.'

Daphne looked quizzically at Denovan. 'Unless your car has wings, I don't think you'll be going anywhere fast—they say the bridge will take days to repair. The army's down there now, but it's not looking good.'

'It doesn't matter.' He shrugged. 'They'll get someone else to step in and hold the fort for me no doubt. It's just Archie I'm concerned about.'

'I tell you what,' suggested Daphne. 'My three boys are in the hall right now and Archie got to know them last night. I know they'd be pleased to look after him for you. Larry's fifteen and reasonably sensible. School's been cancelled for today at least, so they can take him home and play with him. If they need you, you're only at the medical centre, which is practically opposite our house.'

Archie was already beaming up at his father. 'Jack's got a great big train with signals,' he said. 'He'll let me play with that!'

Daphne laughed. 'You've certainly got an easy son to deal with,' she said. 'You don't know how lucky you are.'

Denovan smiled and for a fleeting second his eyes met Kerry's. 'As long as he hasn't inherited the O'Mara temper—I wouldn't wish that on anyone!'

In the waiting room the patients looked tired and shocked after a terrible night of confusion. There was a low murmur of hushed conversation as they went over the awful events of the night. Many of their homes would have been ruined with the flooding and most of them would have had no sleep. Kerry wasn't surprised that some of them looked bruised and battered. She called out a cheery 'Hello, everyone—we'll see you as soon as we can,' and there was no disguising the lightening of the atmosphere and a general undercurrent of excitement as they recognised 'Dr Medic'. He might well be killed in the rush to see him, reflected Kerry with amusement.

'This is Dr Frank O'Mara's brother,' she explained to the room. 'As some of you may know, Dr Frank's had a bad accident and his brother, Dr Denovan, has kindly volunteered to help this morning. I take it most of you have seen him on the telly so I hardly need to introduce you to him!'

Freda was staring over the counter at them as they

came into the office, her expression a picture of incredulity.

'You are him, aren't you—that Dr Medic?' were her first words to Denovan.

He grinned good-humouredly. 'I'm Denovan O'Mara,' he agreed. 'I'm just helping out a bit.'

Kerry stepped in hastily—she had an idea Freda would waste precious time questioning Denovan about life in the media and probably ask for his autograph for herself and her friends if she had the chance!

'It looks like chaos in the waiting room,' Kerry said. 'Are these patients all booked in?'

Freda rolled her eyes dramatically. 'I've no idea as none of the computers are working. I think last night had something to do with it. What patients shall I send through first?'

'The very young and the elderly should get priority—but if you see anyone obviously injured, send them first. If you're not sure, ask me.' Kerry flicked a look back at the waiting room and the strained faces of the patients. 'I wouldn't normally ever do this,' she declared, 'but these people look shocked. When Daphne appears can you give everyone a small cup of coffee? There's a pack of polystyrene cups in the cupboard. I think a bit of TLC is in order and they're going to have to wait for much longer than usual.'

She and Denovan went through to Frank's consulting room and Denovan sat down at the desk and whirled round in the chair with a grin.

'I never thought I'd be doing Frank's job,' he remarked. 'If he knew, he'd probably be furious—I'm the last person he'd want to be filling in for him.'

Kerry frowned. 'He ought to be grateful to you for helping. I know I am. I'm afraid you're going to be thrown in at the deep end, but if you need to ask anything you'll just have to knock on the door as the computers are down. I think it'll be a very haphazard list—some people won't have been able to make it over the bridge to see us, and we'll have others who've come at the last minute.'

Denovan nodded. 'I'll do my best,' he said as Kerry left. He pressed the button to activate the screen in the waiting room to call in the first patient. A burly middle-aged man limped very slowly and awkwardly into the room, his mouth a grim line of pain. Denovan indicated the chair on the other side of the desk.

'Do sit down,' he said.

The man shook his head and grimaced. 'If I do, I'll never get up, Doc. My back's gone—it feels really bad. I've done something to it and I can hardly move.'

He clung onto the back of the chair and Denovan looked at the man's face, noting his pallid complexion and the slight sheen of perspiration on his forehead—he was in great pain and it was obviously more than a muscle strain.

'I think we've met before, haven't we?' Denovan asked the man as he went round to examine his back.

The man nodded. 'I was with that lot helping last night to get Sirie Patel free and then I helped to stabilise the stretcher as we got her up to the surgery in Dr Latimer's car. My name's Gerry Cummings.'

'Of course, that's it! You did a great job there, Gerry—everyone did. We wouldn't have got Sirie out before the river burst its banks unless we'd had a team like yours.' Denovan rubbed his hands together to warm them. 'Let me just feel the area,' he said, pulling Gerry's shirt up. He ran his fingers lightly down the spine and looked at the alignment of the man's back, although it was hard to assess as poor Gerry was locked in a stooped position.

'I'm going to give you some painkillers—quite strong ones,' Denovan said, going back to his desk and starting to write out a prescription. 'They'll also help the muscles relax as they're in spasm at the moment and that's causing some of the pain. But more importantly, when they get a helicopter down here I want you to be taken off to have an X-ray as soon as possible. You may have dislodged a disc when you were heaving all that stone about.'

He handed Gerry the prescription and the man looked worriedly back at him. 'Do you think it's serious? My wife's expecting and she's due any time now. I'm supposed to look after our little girl while she has the baby.'

Denovan shook his head. 'I'll be honest with you. I don't think you'll be up to looking after a child at the moment. Can a neighbour help out? And another thing, if your wife's due to deliver a baby imminently I think she should be on the helicopter, too—just to be on the safe side!'

Gerry Cummings looked in dismay at Denovan. 'She won't fly,' he said dolefully. 'I don't think I'll get her on a helicopter for love or money!'

'Perhaps I can have a word with her?' suggested Denovan. 'And I'm going to find out the latest news on the helicopter and get you booked on. Do you have a mobile? Give me the number and I'll contact you.' He watched as Gerry started to inch his way painfully to the door. 'If you can get hold of a walking stick, that should help support you,' he suggested.

Gerry managed a wry chuckle. 'Perhaps I can borrow my father's Zimmer frame...'

The morning was filled with people like Gerry—many of them traumatised by what they'd gone through, worried out of their minds about the condition of their homes and the welfare of their children or elderly relatives. One couple, who had a shoe shop in the village, had battled all night to try and save their stock, to no avail, and the man had a deep gash on his arm where a metal box had fallen on him.

'I'm the third generation in the business—my grandfather and father built it up from nothing—and I can't bear the thought that this might be the finish of it,' said Peter Whittaker, looking mournfully at Denovan as the doctor swabbed his wound with disinfectant and held the skin together with steri-tabs.

'It's awful for you,' said Denovan sympathetically. 'I take it you're insured?'

Peter nodded. 'Oh, yes, we're insured for the loss of stock and putting in new fitments. But we're just starting our busy season when all the walkers come in for boots and trainers and that sort of thing. If the shop's not up and running we stand to lose a hell of a lot, and I dare say it will take months to sort things out.'

His wife, Donna, put a comforting hand on her husband's arm. 'We'll get my brothers to come and help us clean up. You'll be surprised how quickly we'll get it up and running again.'

They smiled at each other and Peter patted her hand. 'Of course, love—no good looking on the bleak side, is it?'

Denovan watched them go out rather wistfully. They were a lovely couple, obviously totally supportive of each other and not much older than him. They didn't lead a glamorous life and they probably worked a darned sight harder than the wealthy people he mingled with, but they were happy with each other and with their lives. He envied them.

He went over to the window and pulled aside the blinds. The room looked over the back of the medical centre towards the countryside and the patchwork of fields across to the hills. What would it be like to live in a place like this again? Very different from the sophisticated bustle and excitement of London, he guessed. But he had been brought up here and although his childhood had not been a happy one, a part of him longed for the open spaces and beauty of the countryside. He'd at least had freedom to run where he wanted and he'd been part of a small community that knew everyone, in contrast to the anonymity of a big city.

He turned away abruptly from the view and let the blinds go with a snap. It was no good theorising about a life here—he didn't want to live or work anywhere near his half-brother anyway.

A tap at the door and Kerry came in. 'I think we're nearly through. How are you getting on?'

'I enjoyed it,' he said honestly. 'They've certainly all been through the mill, these people. There's one man who urgently needs an X-ray as he's injured his back badly, and I think his pregnant wife should be airlifted out as well.'

'I've been told a helicopter's on its way. I've treated an elderly man with a bad chest, and I'd be happier if he was out of here. We'd better contact these people and tell them to get to the field.'

Denovan looked at his watch. 'I'll go and relieve Daphne's sons from looking after Archie. I can't expect them to look after him all day. And then I'll go down and see how the bridge repair is going on.'

'I'll come down, too—I want to see the damage to the village, so I'll probably see you there when you've got Archie.'

In the cold light of day the damage to some of the houses looked catastrophic, and part of the road had become like a river, water swirling down the high street and onto the playing fields of the local school like a vast lake. In an odd way, it looked rather beautiful, with the sunlight making the water sparkle, and there was warmth in the air—it was hard to believe there'd been torrential rain a few hours before.

People were wading about in some of the houses, trying to salvage possessions, hauling them up the stairs to another storey, and in the homes higher up the hill, where the water had receded slightly, attempting to brush the water away.

In the little square a man with a microphone and wearing fisherman's waders, with a camera trained on him, was interviewing someone. Trust the media to get a camera into the place somehow, when no one else could get in or out! Kerry recognised the man being interviewed as the local MP. Tall, white-haired and imposing, Sir Vernon Hood was generally regarded as being good at his job, but there was an arrogance about him that revealed he was very aware of his position. Kerry reflected that she hadn't seen him for some time. At one time he'd been present at all the local functions, glad-handing everyone. Cynically she thought that he'd probably appeared just to show his concern over the disaster in Braxton now that it was headline news. She flicked a look at him as she turned away and the thought struck her that he looked much older than the last time she'd seen him—perhaps it was the shock of seeing what the flood had done to the place.

She went up to a woman she knew as a patient, who was leaning against her doorstep looking bleakly into her house. The woman shook her head in a despairing way. 'It's the smell and the mud…it's just horrible. We'll never get it right again.'

She dabbed at her eyes and Kerry hugged her. 'It will be OK eventually, Mary. They've got marvellous machines now that can dry places out and pumps that will get rid of this water. I believe the army's bringing equipment over the river to help everyone.'

Mary gave her a tremulous smile. 'At least we can have the place redecorated—we've been meaning to do it for months!' She jerked her head across at Sir Vernon Hood, still talking to the interviewer. 'I hope his nibs will do more than talk a lot of hot air like he usually does and get things moving! He promised us flood defences years ago but I haven't seen anything yet.'

Kerry made her way slowly back up the hill, wondering how long it would take to get things back to normal, and thinking wryly that it would be more difficult than ever to get a locum doctor to help out over the next few weeks.

'Things are pretty bad, aren't they?'

She looked up, startled out of her reverie, to see Denovan's tall figure standing in front of her. She nodded. 'Worse than I thought—the only good thing is that the sun's shining and it's stopped raining.' She looked at him, puzzled. 'Where's Archie? I thought you were collecting him?'

He smiled. 'Those boys of Daphne's are real gems. They've taken him to the field behind their house and are having a picnic. Archie's loving it. He doesn't get to do that kind of thing in London much.' He looked at his watch. 'I don't know about you, but I'm starving. I see that little café near the village hall is doing a brisk trade, but they might squeeze us in—what about a coffee and something to eat?'

There was hardly any room but they managed to squeeze into a corner of the shop, side by side, legs squashed together under a tiny table that would just about accommodate two people. She was aware that people were staring at them—or rather at Denovan! The whole village knew who she was and she could imagine their curiosity wondering why a celebrity doctor should be in their little village with her.

She flicked a look at Denovan's profile. No wonder he'd got that job on TV. Up close she acknowledged that he was startlingly good-looking—firm lips, mesmerising blue eyes, the kind of eyes that when they looked into hers made her feel rather unsettled. And suddenly being quite so near him, feeling his muscular body next to hers, brought back the embarrassment Kerry had felt the night before. If she was any closer, she'd be sitting on his knee!

She took a deep breath and edged away slightly, trying to put some distance between them. Even if she was interested in Denovan O'Mara—which she definitely wasn't—she had to remember that this man was spoken for. The mother of his child had to be somewhere in the background of his life.

The light was dim in the café, the conversation around them a dull murmur, and Kerry leant back with her head against the wall and tried to put Denovan's disturbing proximity out of her mind. The young girl who came to serve them did a double-take when Denovan gave his order, pausing with her pencil hovering in the air before writing anything down.

'Oh, wow, you're that doctor person on TV aren't you?' She grinned cheekily at him. 'You look better than you do on that programme.'

'I'll take that as a compliment,' remarked Denovan wryly. 'Now, please would you bring us two coffees and two big plates of your best fish and chips?'

Kerry looked at him curiously when the girl had disappeared. 'Don't you find it a nuisance, everyone always recognising you?'

Denovan shrugged. 'You get used to it and I suppose it means that people are at least keen on watching the wretched programme.'

'*Wretched* programme?' enquired Kerry in surprise. 'Don't you enjoy what you do?'

He hesitated for a moment then said candidly, 'Perhaps not as much as I did. Of course London is a great place, but coming back here I can remember some of the good things about Braxton that I enjoyed as a little boy—the fresh air, fishing in the river and the beautiful surroundings.'

'You didn't want to be a GP here then, like your father and brother?'

He reached across the table and poured out two glasses of water, a guarded look on his face, but he said lightly, 'Better not to have too many O'Maras in one place.'

Kerry sighed. 'I imagine you have a glamorous life in London anyway, meeting lots of important people.'

Depends what you mean by glamorous, Denovan thought to himself. It was getting closer to make-your-mind-up day as far as his job in London was concerned as he had to let the powers that be know what he was going to do very soon. Did he like the job enough to go along with a new contract? Or if he decided to move on to pastures new, where would he go? He glanced at Kerry. She was the kind of colleague he'd like to work with, both reliable and feisty. Pity she was in the one place he could probably never live in again.

He grinned at her. 'I'm too busy to immerse myself too much in London's social whirl. Besides, the excitement begins to pall after a while.'

'And was Archie born there?'

'No. Archie was born in New Zealand. I came back to England a few months after his birth.'

Kerry flicked perceptive a look at him—she felt there were many things unsaid behind those brief remarks. *Ah, well, everyone has a past,* she thought. *I'm not the only one with ghosts in the background,* but some devil inside her made her want to know more. She looked down at the table cloth and rearranged the cutlery slightly.

'And is Archie's mother in the media as well?'

'Archie's mother?'

Kerry looked up at him, startled by the harshness in his tone. 'I'm sorry. I don't want to pry.'

'Archie's mother is a free spirit,' Denovan said

shortly. 'She joined some hippy community in Cornwall after we came back to England, and I don't think she thinks of Archie from one day to the next!' He took a deep gulp of water from his glass and an expression of deep sadness flitted across his face. 'Archie probably hardly remembers her at all.' And suddenly Kerry saw before her not the polished, glamorous, smooth celebrity, Denovan O'Mara, aka Dr Medic, but a father who loved his child very much and who suffered the same anxieties and worries as any man would, trying to protect that child from harm.

'I'm sorry,' she began inadequately.

'It wasn't Lorna's fault. She'd always made it clear that she never wanted a child.' His forlorn words hovered in the air, giving away a glimpse of his private life. 'I was the one to blame. I thought she would change her mind, but I was wrong.'

'You can't blame yourself surely?'

'Oh, but I do,' he said simply. 'One can't force people into being what they're not, and Lorna will never be maternal.' A wry grin twisted his mouth. 'And it could be I'm just too damn difficult to live with. It taught me one thing—commitment's a very serious step. Don't make it lightly! It'll be some time—if ever—before I contemplate settling down!'

Kerry nodded, but felt an odd flicker of disappointment. She wasn't surprised Denovan was wary of starting another relationship after his experience, but perhaps she'd been secretly hoping that he'd have changed his mind.

'And now…' He changed the subject abruptly. 'Enough about me. I believe you were all set to go on holiday until Frank messed it up?'

'How did you find that out?'

'I nearly fell over the suitcase in your bedroom when I brought your cocoa up last night.'

She shrugged. 'It's true. I should be lounging on a beach under a hot sun in Tobago today, preparing to be my cousin's bridesmaid on Friday.'

'That's too bad…perhaps another time?'

She laughed. 'I've no more cousins getting married!'

'You'll have to wait until it's your turn to get married, then.'

Kerry ignored the little knife that twisted in her chest. 'Maybe one day,' she said lightly.

'Come, now,' he said teasingly, giving her a penetrating look. 'I can't believe you don't have some adoring guy in the background.'

'No adoring guys, not even in the far distance.'

Then the waitress appeared with a huge tray of food, which she put on the table in front of them. 'Here you are, folks, fish and chips for two. Enjoy!'

Denovan grinned. 'Just what the doctor ordered. Let's tuck in.'

CHAPTER FOUR

'THERE'S a message from Laystone Hospital for Denovan to ring them,' said Daphne, when he and Kerry returned to the surgery after their lunch. 'At least the telephone lines have been repaired.'

While Denovan was ringing them back, Daphne gave Kerry a list of the home visits that had been requested that day.

'Looks like the army has done a great job with putting a temporary bridge up. I think you'll be able to get to most of these people now,' Daphne said. 'One of them is little Tilly Thompson up at Hill Farm—her chest is very bad. The call's just come in and her mother sounded very worried.'

'I'll go right away.' Kerry grabbed her bag and turned to Denovan, who had just finished his phone call. 'You'll be able to get back to London sooner than you thought. The road's open again.'

'Yes,' he said briskly. 'I should make it OK today, but I'll go and see Frank first. They've done a craniotomy to drain the bleed in his brain, and it seems he's holding his own. Then, of course, I'll get back as soon as possible as there's no point in hanging around here.'

'Of course not.' agreed Kerry, but there was something a little hollow about her agreement.

It wasn't only his help she would miss, Kerry admitted, but the man himself. She'd been prepared to dislike Denovan O'Mara, both from his manner when she'd first spoken to him about Frank and from what she'd heard about him from his half-brother. Funny how much her views had changed in twenty-four hours, she admitted. Denovan wasn't as bad as she'd thought he'd be. In fact, under the tough exterior there had been glimpses of a rather fun guy. And in the café just a few minutes ago she'd seen a loving father behind the glamorous celebrity image he projected. Even if she'd sworn lifelong celibacy, she couldn't help noticing that he was drop-dead gorgeous and exuded sex appeal!

She felt almost ashamed to confess even to herself that she'd felt the old thrill of attraction sitting next to a sexy-looking man, conscious of a vague feeling of disloyalty to Andy's memory. Then she bit her lip. She had to accept that Andy wasn't here now but Denovan was, and the fact that it was the first time she'd felt a frisson of magnetism for anyone since Andy had died showed that she was beginning to feel more human again. She told herself sternly that this was just a normal reaction to a good-looking man, because of course Denovan meant nothing at all to her. And she could mean nothing to him—he'd practically said that permanent relationships were not for him any more.

All the same, I don't want him to go, she thought, and then with a burst of honest introspection she acknowledged that it wasn't just because of his help at work but because she wanted to get to know more about Denovan O'Mara the man.

She said lightly, 'Give Frank our love. I imagine you're taking Archie with you to the hospital, then?'

'Don't worry about that,' interposed Daphne, who was sorting out prescriptions. 'You can't drag Archie to the hospital. The boys will be happy to look after him for another hour or two. I'll phone Larry on his mobile.'

'Those boys of yours are real stars,' said Denovan fervently. 'They deserve some decent remuneration. I'll pick Archie up on the way back from the hospital, but I'm so very grateful to them.' Denovan unleashed one of his sudden, sweet smiles, then turned to Kerry, holding out his hand. 'I'll be off when I've picked up Archie, so I'll probably not see you until I come back up to see Frank again.'

His clear blue gaze locked on to her face almost as if he was trying to memorise it.

'Keep well,' he said softly. 'I'll be in touch with you about Frank's progress.'

His mobile rang and Kerry went out to her car, leaving Denovan conducting an animated conversation with the person at the other end of the line. He followed Kerry with his eyes as he talked—she was such a bright, feisty woman, and knock-down gorgeous too. She'd never admit that she'd find it hard to cope and he admired her for that. He just wished he could get to know her better. He sighed and tried to concentrate on what the person at the other end of the line was saying.

That would probably be the last she'd see of the hot-shot celebrity doctor for a long time, Kerry reflected ruefully as she crossed the car park and got into her car. Then she shrugged rather irritably, cross with herself for thinking so much about Denovan. Putting the car into gear, she set off for Hill Farm out in the countryside.

The Thompsons lived on an isolated farm on a hill-side outside Laystone. Bathed in sunlight today, it was picture perfect—the stone farmhouse, its outline soft-ened by ivy, sheep grazing in the patchwork of stone-walled fields, and the fresh green of the trees. Still, Kerry guessed it was a hard life for Laura Thompson, the mother of two young children.

Laura's face was tearstained as she answered the door to Kerry's knock, a round-eyed little boy cling-ing to her skirt.

'I'm so sorry to bring you all the way out here, Doctor,' she said in a choked voice. 'I'm just at my wit's end with Tilly…she sounds awful. I didn't know what to do for the best.'

'Don't worry, Laura, that's our job. If you're worried about your little girl, you did the right thing.'

How often Kerry had had to reassure parents that they weren't making a fuss when their children were ill! Although sometimes, she admitted, it was the other way round, with people ringing up for a visit when there was nothing wrong with them at all.

Laura led the way to the large kitchen, the little boy pattering along beside her, but even from down the corridor Kerry could hear the stertorous, gasping sound of a child fighting for breath.

'We brought her cot down here because it's warmer,' explained Laura. 'And I've got all the pans and kettles I can manage boiling as I remembered a steamy atmosphere is a good thing for bad chests.'

'Absolutely right,' agreed Kerry. 'Anything to try and open up her airways a bit.'

Tilly was sitting in the middle of her cot, a picture of misery, half crying, her plump little face red and blotched, every intake of breath an enormous effort, and it was obvious that she had a high temperature. Kerry's heart went out to the child.

'Hello, darling, you do look poorly, poor little thing—but we'll soon get you better. Mum, would you put her on your knee please, while I have a listen to her chest?'

Laura looked more composed, the relief of having a professional to assess her little daughter giving her more confidence. She lifted the child out of the cot and cuddled her as she sat down on a kitchen chair, rocking her backwards and forwards.

'It's all right, pet, just let Dr Latimer listen to your chest through this funny little tube.'

Kerry closed her eyes, concentrating on the sounds in Tilly's lungs she could hear through the earpieces of her stethoscope. She bit her lip. Tilly's heart was galloping, her chest full of wheezes and whistling noises. It was getting increasingly harder for the little girl to get air into her lungs and they needed to get her to hospital as quickly as possible.

She hooked the stethoscope round her neck. 'Where's your husband, Laura? Can he look after your little boy while we take Tilly to hospital in my car? It's all right,' she said quickly and reassuringly as Laura's face began to crumple again. 'What Tilly needs is some oxygen, possibly some nebulised adrenaline or cortisone—that should help her enormously. I don't want you to worry.' Kerry gave a short laugh. 'That's a silly thing to say, isn't it? You can't help worrying, but I assure you this croup is very common in young children with a viral condition and hospitals are well used to treating it.'

Laura gulped back her tears. 'I'll call Bill on his mobile. He's out in the field at the moment, mending a wall. He can be here in a minute to look after Ben.'

Kerry took out her own mobile and punched in the numbers for Laystone Hospital. 'Fast Track Admission Department, please. It's Dr Latimer here. I need a paediatrician and anaesthetist on standby for an eighteen-month-old girl in acute respiratory distress. I'm bringing her in now.'

She looked at Laura's stricken face as the terrified mother heard the words 'anaesthetist' and gripped her shoulder reassuringly. 'Don't be alarmed, it's just a sensible precaution to have everyone we might need available.'

'I know, I know,' said Laura miserably. 'I've got to pull myself together.'

'You're doing brilliantly. You look after the little one and I'll get us there.'

Thank goodness the roads were passable, thought Kerry as she navigated the twists and turns of the country road that led from Braxton to Laystone. She went carefully, not daring to risk an accident. Having a child sure was a roller-coaster of emotions, she thought wryly, and she had no doubt that she would have been just as overwrought as Laura if it had been her daughter she was taking to hospital.

Tilly had been safely installed with an oxygen tent over her cot and Laura had been assured by the paediatrician that the little girl would be very much better within the hour, but that they would keep her in for twenty-four hours to monitor her. Tilly had fallen into a restless sleep, but Laura refused to leave her child's side, and the nurse went to get her a cup of tea, offering to get one for Kerry, as well.

'No, thanks. While I'm here I think I'd better go and see how Dr O'Mara is. It's a good opportunity to do it while I can.'

Laura put her hand on Kerry's arm. 'Thank you,' she said in a choked voice. 'I don't know what I'd have done if you hadn't been there.'

'Glad to have been of help,' smiled Kerry. 'I'll be in touch with you tomorrow to see how things are. I'm sure Tilly will be back to her bouncing self very soon.'

A small glow of pleasure and satisfaction fluttered through Kerry as she made her way down the maze of corridors to the high-dependency unit, where Frank had been taken to be monitored. There was a lot of stress in her work, but sometimes when she felt she had made a difference to the outcome of a situation it all became worthwhile. Then her thoughts drifted back to the myriad things she had to do that afternoon…more visits, and then loads of paperwork, the results of blood tests and hospital reports to catch up on when she got back to the surgery. Normally she could have coped for a week or two, she supposed, but with the added complication of the flooding and the extra problems that had arisen because of that, there was more pressure than usual.

Then, as sometimes happened unexpectedly, her darling Andy's voice came back to her, calm, quiet but firm. *'You'll be all right, we can get through anything together.'* That's how he'd been whenever she'd been worried, or something had gone wrong—a quiet tower of strength. She stopped for a minute and took a deep breath to calm herself. He wouldn't have wanted her to go to pieces just because life was going to be hectic, he would have told her to plough on and get on with things regardless. She straightened her shoulders and pressed the bell by the door of the high-dependency unit to gain admittance.

'Dr O'Mara's doing very well,' the sister in charge of the unit told her reassuringly. 'Breathing well on his own. His brother, Dr Medic…I mean Dr O'Mara…is just with him at the moment.' She smiled rather archly. 'It was quite a surprise to realise who he was.'

Another female who'd fallen for Denovan's charm, thought Kerry with amusement. She hadn't realised that Denovan would still be at the hospital. Perhaps she wouldn't have come to see Frank today if she'd known. She hated saying goodbye twice, but she went through to the bay where Frank was lying with his eyes closed, hooked to various bits of monitoring equipment—tubes supplying salts and glucose to replace vital bodily fluids, machines measuring his blood-oxygen and blood-pressure levels. Kerry stood quietly for a moment, listening to the faint ticks of the machines and watching the blips dancing across the lines of the monitors. She didn't like to interrupt Denovan's time with his brother.

Denovan was looking down at Frank and from where Kerry stood, his unguarded expression seemed quite detached: he might have displayed more emotion for a patient he'd never met before than what he was showing to his brother, Kerry reflected wryly. With a little shiver of disbelief she felt it was almost as if he hated Frank. Just what had happened between the two men that made them so at odds with each other? She found it hard to understand Denovan's attitude because although she'd never been very close to Frank socially, he seemed a reasonable and competent colleague who worked hard and seemed popular with the patients—she got on with him well. What was there to hate about him?

'Hello, Denovan,' Kerry said softly. 'How are things?'

He looked across at her in surprise. 'I didn't know

you were coming to the hospital!' he exclaimed, coming over to her.

'I had to bring a young patient in unexpectedly and while I had the chance I thought I'd just come and see how Frank was doing.'

'He seems to be holding his own after yesterday's craniotomy and, as you can see, he's breathing by himself.' Denovan sighed. 'Poor blighter. I wish…' His voice faded away and Kerry looked at him questioningly.

'What do you wish?'

He said bluntly, 'I wish I could feel more sympathy for him, I suppose.' He looked at Kerry's shocked face and smiled faintly. 'I'm afraid we've never got on—and for various reasons we became at daggers drawn.' He shrugged. 'I guess we're just too different in character. Incompatible.'

'You should make it up with him. Brothers shouldn't have disagreements surely?'

'Depends what they disagree about, doesn't it?' he replied tersely. There was a moment's awkward silence then he flicked a look at his watch and with a change of tone said, 'I'm glad I've seen you. I'd like to talk to you about something. Let's go into the corridor for a minute.'

Kerry followed him out of the room and looked at him enquiringly.

'I've been thinking about how you're going to manage over the next few weeks,' he said. 'Are you sure you can't get some help? You can see that Frank's going to be a long time recuperating.'

Kerry shrugged. 'It sounds so heartless to think of my problems at the moment when Frank has the biggest problem, but the fact is there's a huge shortage of locums around here. Anyway,' she said brusquely, 'it's no good worrying, I'll manage OK. I'll just have to, won't I?'

She tilted her chin determinedly and her petite figure braced itself as if preparing for a rough ride in the future.

Denovan grinned at her. 'You've got the resolve to do anything, I'm sure, but there are only so many hours in a day.' He paused, looking down at his feet, jingling some change in his pockets, then said rather awkwardly, 'I've been speaking to my agent today and she seemed quite amenable about deferring the signing of my new contract. She says I don't have to make my mind up immediately. If you want, I could stay on for, say, two weeks and help you out over the worst.'

Kerry stared at him, open-mouthed. 'But…but I thought you had to get back urgently for work?'

'I've told you—they are prepared to give me breathing space and I'm happy to take it. I could do with a break myself.'

She smiled wryly. 'It wouldn't be much of a break, helping in the practice, would it?'

'Believe me, I'd look forward to being a bit hands-on and not just giving advice and opinions on theoretical case histories. Don't you know that a change is as good as a rest?' His blue eyes rested on hers. 'I think we've proved over the past twenty-four hours that we can work rather well together.'

She said diffidently, 'Are…are you sure about this? And what about Archie?'

'Where there's a will there's a way—there's always the nursery in the village. I could bribe them to take him for two weeks, I think.'

Kerry took a deep breath, a mixture of emotions churning up inside her. Did she want to work with someone who seemed so at odds with his brother, her colleague? Could it lead to complications when Frank came back to work?

Denovan regarded her closely and frowned. 'You have a problem with me working here?'

'You and your brother don't get on—he could be annoyed with me for accepting your help,' Kerry replied honestly.

'I'll be working with you, not him. I'm sure he'll be relieved that someone's filling in for him, whoever it is.'

'I suppose…'

'Look, if he objects, I'll go back to London.' Denovan grinned at her, his eyes twinkling. 'At the moment he's not going to know anyway as he's out for the count, isn't he?'

Kerry tried to look disapproving then laughed. 'Don't be so cruel! OK, you're right—I do need someone, and you're the only person who's offered so, yes, I'm grateful to you if you're sure you're able to spare me the time. To be honest, it's a load off my mind.'

She felt overwhelming relief that the short-term worry of sorting things out was going to be shared and if she was honest, wasn't there another emotion crackling away as well? A kind of suppressed excitement at working with Denovan!

'Then it suits both of us—I get to do something useful, and you get a little support.' He looked slightly embarrassed. 'There's only one slight drawback for you, though not for Archie and I, but can we stay with you for a night or two until the pub reopens or I find somewhere else?'

'Of course. Though you're probably not getting much sleep in that small bed.'

'I never find difficulty in falling asleep.' He grinned. 'Tell you what, I'll get a take-away and a bottle of wine for this evening to seal the arrangement!'

Denovan watched her walk away and smiled wryly. He'd only told a few little white lies regarding his agent. He'd had to use all his powers of persuasion to get her to agree that it would be good for him to defer signing a new contract with the TV company for a week or two. The fact was that over the last two days he'd realised how much Braxton Falls meant to him, even though his childhood had some bleak memories. Now he was up here he wanted to spend a little more time in the place, allow Archie to breathe the fresh air of the country—the little lad barely knew what a live cow looked like!

And then, of course, there was Kerry. He folded his arms and stared unseeingly out of the window in the corridor. Had she been part of the pull to stay in Braxton too?

Over the years since Lorna had disappeared he'd been out with several women, many of them blind dates set up by friends dying to marry him off. Some of his dates had been good fun and attractive—and most of them had been very keen to prolong their friendship. Too keen. Many of them had been excited to be with someone who was in the public eye—he was never sure if they were more attracted by the thrill of going out with a so-called 'celebrity' than their liking of him, but there was no thrill of the chase, just coy allusions to happy married life and future plans. Most of the girls were pleasant with Archie, a few ignored or even resented his little son, but naturally they couldn't feel for him as he did as a father.

But Kerry, well, she was different. Feisty when she wanted to be, not too cloying with Archie—just natural. He could tell she'd be someone he'd like to work with. And there was something else, too—a flicker of that special attraction he'd found so elusive with other women. He didn't think she was the type to care whether he was well known or not. The truth was, she was gorgeous and he wanted to get to know her better, to know what made her tick. That certainly didn't mean that he wanted a permanent relationship, his young son came before any romantic commitment, but surely a brief encounter was allowed? Forty-eight hours seemed too soon to say goodbye!

A slight smile played over Denovan's lips. It was

a paradox that two days ago he'd hated the thought of coming back to Braxton Falls and all the memories it held for him, but all of a sudden the picture had changed. The place was imbued with an exciting and interesting aura—and mostly due to Kerry Latimer!

The afternoon passed by in a haze for Kerry. A few hours ago she'd been worried out of her mind about how she would cope and now, even if it was only for a short time, she had some respite from the problem. And not just that, of all people it was Denovan O'Mara who would be working with her! She was feeling pleased because he was a good, competent doctor, she told herself sternly, and not because she felt this peculiar kind of excitement when he was near her. He wasn't even the type of man she went for—he wasn't quiet, diffident or unassuming, like Andy. He was full of macho confidence, probably opinionated and well aware of his own abilities and used to fawning adulation, as well! But the main thing was, she told herself, he would be a reliable colleague.

There wasn't much room in her little cottage for quiet reflection with an energetic little boy to be bathed and put to bed. Kerry was refreshing her make-up in her bedroom and could hear roars of laughter from the bathroom and then a lively game of tag being played up and down the stairs. Denovan and Archie had a great relationship.

She looked at her reflection in the mirror—thick glossy dark hair held back from her face by two combs, and wide hazel eyes that looked back at her with a sparkle of excitement in them. It was odd that she felt this animated about having a take-away and a bottle of wine. Of course it wasn't a date but, as Denovan had said, it was a sort of celebration, and she'd had so little to celebrate over the past year that that was excitement indeed.

It was cosy in the little sitting room with the curtains drawn, and there was even a small log fire burning in the grate, which Denovan had insisted on lighting. He looked far too big for the room, thought Kerry with amusement, his head almost brushing the ceiling, and when he sat down his long legs seemed to stretch right over the carpet. He handed her a glass of red wine.

'Cheers!' He grinned at her, sipped the wine and grimaced slightly. 'Not the best vintage, but it's the top of the range at the corner shop—where, by the way, I learned from Sirie's husband that she's doing really well and should be home fairly soon.'

'That's great. It seems ages since we had all that drama. Can you believe that it was only about forty-eight hours ago? So much has happened.'

'I know. And even after all the destruction, there's been an amazing community spirit here in Braxton. It's one of the attractions about the place, that and the beauty of the countryside.'

'Do you miss it?' asked Kerry, looking at his wistful expression.

He gave a short laugh and tossed back his wine in two gulps. 'It's been years since I lived here and, to tell the truth it wasn't the happiest of childhoods, but when I see the hills and the dales I realise that part of it will never leave me.' He smiled at her. 'I take it you intend to stay here?'

'I hope so—I love it.'

'Just happy times here, then?' He looked at her with a grin, refilling his glass after he'd emptied it so quickly.

Just happy times? To her horror Kerry felt the familiar prickle of tears well up in her eyes when she was reminded of what might have been, and a deep flush of embarrassment spread over her cheeks. She tried to smile, cover up the awkward pause, then swallowed hard. 'Not…not always, of course.'

The periwinkle-blue eyes missed nothing and he frowned. 'Hey,' he said softly, 'I've put my foot in it, haven't I? I'm so sorry. Did something happen?'

Kerry looked down at her hands and started to pleat, very precisely, the cream shirt she was wearing. 'It's nothing,' she mumbled. She didn't want to dwell on her past—she had to come to terms with it.

'Oh, come on, now,' he said gently, pulling back a tendril of hair from her forehead, his glance sweeping over her face, 'We're going to work together—I have to know some things about you. Tell me what went wrong.'

She would never have thought the tough, arrogant Dr O'Mara could be this sympathetic, this kindly, and why shouldn't she tell him the truth? It was common knowledge in the village that she'd been about to get married, and that suddenly it had all ended—the excitement of organising everything, the wonderful future they were going to have together—all gone in the space of a few seconds.

'There was someone,' she began haltingly, then ground to a halt, struggling to find the words to describe what had happened.

Denovan waited, watching her expression as she tried to compose herself. 'I get the picture,' he said gently. 'Something happened between you and someone you loved?'

Kerry gave a twisted little smile. 'You could say that. A year ago Andy Robinson and I were going to get married—Andy was a climber and also part of the mountain rescue team.' It was pointless going into the detail of the story, she thought, just deal with the facts. 'He was killed trying to help a couple who'd got into difficulties. It's hard to come to terms with.'

The words sounded completely inadequate, but their very simplicity added to the horror of the story, thought Denovan with a shiver of shock.

'I'm so very sorry,' he said softly, putting his hand over hers.

Kerry dashed the tears from her eyes and shook her head. 'I'm sorry, this is ridiculous.'

'Of course it's not. You must have been devastated.'

He put his arm round her shoulders and hugged her to him. It was just a kind gesture, she knew, something that anyone might do, but there was such comfort in it and strangely she felt soothed—even though Denovan was a man she hardly knew. Telling him about Andy seemed to have acted like balm on the open wound of grief. How odd that someone she had been wary of only a short time ago could help her in this way.

'Look,' he said softly. 'Ghastly things happen, things that you think you'll never get over—but life goes on, and somehow you learn to live with what happened.'

'That sounds as if it comes from the heart,' murmured Kerry, looking at his face and its fleetingly sad expression in the flickering firelight. 'I…I suppose you mean Archie's mother leaving you?' she questioned with hesitation.

He shook his head. 'No—I wasn't referring to that. To be honest, it was a relief when Lorna and I parted—we were totally incompatible and things were pretty difficult between us. I was only desperately sad for Archie. It's very tough that he should never know his mother, because I know only too well from my own experience…' He stopped in mid-sentence, then said gently, 'But we weren't talking about me—you were telling me about Andy. I'm so, so sorry. You've had a lot to cope with, and now you've got to deal with all this bother of my brother having an accident.'

'Your brother was very kind when Andy died—easy to talk to.'

'I'm glad, but having to cope now on your own at work must be doubly difficult, especially with the floods.' His smile was kind and his finger went under her chin and gently turned her face towards his. 'Not many people could cope like you have.'

'I can deal with it. Please don't worry,' she said rather breathlessly.

She was aware that somehow the atmosphere between them had changed, become more personal, intimate. She was confused by her own conflicting emotions and the proximity of Denovan. Every nerve in her body was aware of how dangerously close she was to him. She was sure that something—she couldn't articulate just what it was—was about to happen and her heart bounded uncomfortably into overdrive.

'Seems we've learnt quite a bit about each other in the past twenty-four hours, haven't we?'

'Yes. I suppose so.'

'And one of the things I've learnt about you, Kerry, is that you're one feisty woman.'

His arm was still around her, holding her against him, and he leant forward and brushed her forehead with his lips. She didn't draw back. Rather she allowed herself to imagine the sweetness of his mouth on hers—because wasn't this secretly what she had been longing for, perhaps even needing? She closed her eyes, willing him to kiss her on her lips, for his arms to pull her towards him. After all these empty months of grieving for Andy it was as if every erogenous nerve in her body had been galvanised. She allowed herself to lean against this man she hardly knew and it felt natural and right and wonderful.

In the back of her mind a little voice whispered, *You're mad—you've only known this guy for two days!* Whatever Denovan said, they were still almost strangers. She didn't know his background or what sadness he referred to in his past, and he'd only brushed his lips across her forehead, but in that moment she'd realised that she had been attracted to him from the first moment she'd seen him. She pressed her lips to his cheek, responding to his feather-light kiss with eagerness, giving in to the clamour of her own longing. A kind of dizzy freedom from the sadness and constraints of the past year swept through her, and she couldn't help her response—an almost compulsive need to make love to this man she'd only known for a short time.

Then suddenly there was the sound of the wooden door being opened and banging against the wall behind them.

Denovan gently drew back from her and turned round to see who was there.

'Daddy…Daddy, I want a drink and I can't get to sleep.'

Archie's forlorn little figure stood in the doorway, clutching a teddy, illuminated by the light from the hallway. Denovan gave Kerry a half-shrug of apology before leaping up from the sofa and going towards his son, catching him up in his arms.

'Hello, sweetheart, of course you can have a drink. How about another story? You'll soon drop off then.'

'What were you and that lady doing?' asked Archie in his clear little voice.

Denovan laughed. 'Just getting to know each other,' he said lightly.

He took the little boy upstairs and Kerry watched him go with wistful thoughtfulness. What a fool she was if she believed that Andy's place could be taken by a man like Denovan—he had other things to think about, like his little boy. And, of course, Archie would always come first in his life. Any romantic interest would be put on the back burner because Denovan's priority would naturally be his child. And hadn't Denovan made it clear that he wasn't on the lookout for a partner?

Kerry stood up and touched her lips. Even in that brief contact against his cheek, they tingled with the memory. She shook her head in confusion—his friendly gesture of comfort had allowed her to think for a moment that she and Denovan had some kind of future, and how deluded and stupid was that? No good falling for a man who wasn't interested in romance before he went back to London and his glamorous life. If she didn't want another broken heart, she'd better keep well away from Dr Medic and regard him strictly as a colleague for the next two weeks.

CHAPTER FIVE

How quickly the two weeks had gone. Kerry had really been grateful to Denovan for his support because the surgery had been working at top capacity—one person would have found it impossible to cope. The floods had taken their toll on the villagers mentally and physically. It was surprising how many accidents had happened with people trying to salvage goods from houses ruined temporarily with flood water—putting their feet through rotten floorboards or cutting themselves on broken glass. Liz Ferris, Denovan or herself had spent nearly every afternoon patching people up with bandages or stitches.

And now, thank goodness, it was lunchtime on Friday and, whatever happened, Kerry was going to have a rest over the weekend, although she rather dreaded the next week when Denovan left Braxton.

She flicked a glance at him as she munched on a sandwich in the office. He was standing in front of the computer, his tall body half bent towards it as he ran through the hospital referral emails on the computer, his dark hair endearingly rumpled and a little too long over his collar. She reflected rather wistfully that there'd been no more intimate moments alone with Denovan during these hectic two weeks, although she was intensely aware of his presence when he was in the room with her. But she'd been very firm with herself—no hint of flirtation with him, being businesslike and brisk at work and spending many an evening staying late at the surgery. She wasn't going to embarrass him again.

How stupid she'd been to come on so strongly to that casual comforting hug he'd given her two weeks ago—and how embarrassing it had been to see him the next morning at breakfast-time. He'd just been a ship passing in the night, and was only going to be with her for two short weeks. For heaven's sake, he must have thought she was completely sex-starved! And he wouldn't have been far from the truth, she thought wryly.

She recalled how Archie had been sitting in the little kitchen, eating some cereal, when she'd come down the morning after, and Denovan had been squeezed behind the table, drinking a cup of coffee.

'Would you like some of my great coffee?' he'd asked with a smile, holding up the coffee jug. His blue eyes had seemed to hold hers like a magnet. 'I hope you've recovered from the events of yesterday!'

Kerry hadn't been sure if he was making some coy allusion to what had happened between them the previous night, but she'd refused to react to it. It had meant nothing to him, and she was going to treat it the same way—however difficult it was. She'd ignored the last part of his sentence.

'It's OK, thanks. I'll just go straight across to the surgery if you don't mind,' she'd said lightly. 'There's some paperwork I must get down to, and I want to know what's happened to one of my elderly patients with an acute chest infection—he was taken by helicopter to hospital when the bridge collapsed. Daphne will give you a list of your patients when you've got Archie settled.'

She'd practically run out of the house, only pausing to grab a jacket from the row of hooks by the front door. She wouldn't give him any cause to be frightened of her!

They hadn't been alone much since then—Archie had had two little friends for a sleep over during that time, Denovan had been over several times to see his brother in hospital, now making good progress and in a general ward, and there had been two night home visits, which they'd taken in turns to do. Sometimes she'd seen Denovan looking at her rather intently and once he'd put a hand on her shoulder as he'd bent over to show her something on the computer and a thrill of excitement had zipped through her body as if she'd touched two electric terminals, but mostly she'd managed to keep her distance.

Kerry sighed and threw her half-eaten sandwich into the bin. Denovan would be gone next week so she could relax. She started to look idly through one of the many medical journals that arrived every day and Denovan stood up from the computer and stretched to relieve his back. His gaze flickered over to Kerry and unconsciously he clenched his fists in his pockets. She looked incredibly efficient and sexy in that neat white collared blouse with her thick hair in a neat pleat at the back of her head and a leather belt emphasising her small waist. Why the hell hadn't he made more of an effort to get to know her better, to be alone with her? He was even staying in the same tiny cottage with her, for heaven's sake, and yet for some reason it had never seemed the right time to get closer.

With a certain grim humour he reflected that in London he wouldn't have had this trouble—women seemed almost too willing to encourage him. Perhaps the answer was, he told himself flatly, that Kerry Latimer wasn't at all interested in him. And yet two weeks ago he'd have sworn that she'd responded with more than a little eagerness to his brief kiss, although the next day she'd certainly been brusque enough with him at breakfast-time. When he'd offered her coffee, she'd refused and practically run out of the house.

'Was that a brush-off, Archie?' he'd murmured to his little son as he'd poured himself another cup of coffee. Perhaps she'd been trying to tell him something—possibly that he should step back a few paces and not assume that his affectionate gesture the night before had meant anything at all to her.

And yet just the briefest touch of her lips on his face had set an astonishing longing burning inside him. Lorna leaving him and their little son so abruptly had left him embittered. He had been very careful since then not to get involved too much with any woman, however attractive she was. Now he acknowledged, almost with surprise, that if Archie hadn't appeared at the very moment he'd kissed Kerry that night, he might have thrown caution to the winds.

And now two weeks had passed and it was as if they'd only just met, that brief kiss the only memory he had of something more intimate between them. He smiled grimly to himself. The truth was that he found Kerry the most irresistible and breathtaking woman he'd ever met, and his heart had melted when he'd seen her tears at the mention of her fiancé. Perhaps he'd been grossly insensitive, coming on to a woman whose heart had been broken by the death of her fiancé—a tragedy that she'd obviously not got over. How crass was that? He scowled unseeingly into space. Had he ruined any relationship he might have had with Kerry, even if it wasn't going to be lifelong commitment?

And yet…and yet he was sure that there had been something electric between them. He could swear that he hadn't been deluding himself when he'd thought she had responded to his kiss with something a little more than acquiescence. He closed his eyes for a moment and recalled the soft feel of her full lips on his mouth, the moulding of her body against his hard frame. How sweet it had been and how long ago since he had felt that magnetic attraction with any girl! But the way she'd rushed out of the house that morning had shown that she had been embarrassed by him—probably thought he'd taken advantage of her. Perhaps he ought to have apologised. What a waste of two weeks it had been!

The only thing vaguely positive, he supposed wryly, was that he and Frank were at least communicating in a stilted way with each other.

'Daddy. Daddy! Here I am. We can go to the shops now. Daddy, you're not listening.'

Archie's indignant face swam into focus in front of Denovan and he started guiltily. He'd entirely forgotten that he was taking Archie in his lunch hour to buy some provisions for a picnic they were going on the next day.

'Oh, OK, Archie, I'm ready. We'll just go down to the corner shop and I'll drop you back for your last afternoon at the nursery.'

Freda and Daphne were gazing dolefully at the computer. 'The blasted thing's going round in circles,' Daphne informed Kerry. 'It keeps telling me I've made an illegal move. I've tried to ring the helpline but I can't get through. I guess it's something to do with the electrics and the flood.'

Kerry dumped her bag on the table in the office and sighed. 'Do we have any idea who's on the list?'

'Not really, we'll just have to take people as they come. Oh, and there's the baby clinic and I'm afraid Liz rang in to say she's got a stomach bug, so she can't do it.'

Kerry closed her eyes and groaned. Could anything else go wrong? 'That's all I need! Perhaps you could ask Denovan to do that clinic, then? He'll be in soon, he's just taken Archie to the shop in his lunch hour to get some picnic food.'

'We're going to miss him, that's for sure,' said Daphne. 'He's been such a great help for you.'

'And he's so cool,' sighed Freda. 'All my friends tried to make appointments to see him.'

'Not unless they were ill, I hope,' retorted Kerry tartly. 'No wonder we were so busy if all your friends were turning up in perfect health! Would you pass me those files, Freda, please?'

Freda handed her a sheaf of files and prattled on unconcernedly. 'Apparently Dr O'Mara's got so many women in London after him that he's hardly ever seen with the same woman twice!'

Kerry couldn't help laughing. 'I don't know where you get your information from.'

'Oh, he's in all my favourite celebrity magazines,' Freda informed her eagerly. 'Look, there's a gorgeous photo of him on the front cover of this one, and a great article inside about him and who he's been out with.' She thrust the magazine into Kerry's hands. 'Why don't you look at it when you've got a minute?'

Kerry's eyes met Daphne's amused expression. 'Honestly, Freda, you'd believe any old trash you're told about celebrities. Now, Daphne, would you ask the two-thirty patient to come in? We might as well start the ball rolling. I haven't time to pore over magazine articles!'

As she walked into her consulting room Kerry reflected wryly that Freda's gossip magazine was probably only too true—someone like Denovan in the public eye, invited to every media event in London, could have his pick of females and doubtless enjoyed every minute. What man wouldn't? She flicked an idle glance at the magazine cover. Freda was right, Denovan did look gorgeous and, despite her scorn of Freda's reading material, she knew she'd be looking at the article later on!

Kerry recognised Sir Vernon Hood MP as soon as he came through the door and recalled seeing him the day before being interviewed again by the media. Once more she thought how much he'd aged. He certainly didn't look his usual debonair self. He seemed thin, careworn, his eyes rather sunken and his usually upright figure stooped and frail. What had happened to the man? He was no longer the urbane figure who stood out in public meetings, appeared on television in Parliamentary debates, or opened fetes so charmingly.

He sank down into the chair opposite Kerry. 'How can I help you?' she asked pleasantly.

He leant forward, put his hands over his face and in a muffled voice muttered, 'I don't know…I don't know how to explain…'

There was something pathetic about this man and that was all the more extraordinary because he was a man who normally exuded confidence.

'I can try and help you,' Kerry said gently, 'if you tell me what's wrong.'

He looked up at her miserably. 'It…it's very personal…' he began.

'Look, that's what I'm here for. To try and sort out personal problems, physical or otherwise. You've managed to get yourself here, so you might as well tell me.

There isn't much I haven't seen,' she said persuasively. 'Do you feel ill?'

Sir Vernon shook his head and said slowly, 'I'm a damn fool. I've jeopardised my life and my family's happiness. I've ruined everything.'

Kerry waited silently, giving the man a chance to talk. What seismic event had occurred to make the man look so defeated and diminished, almost haggard—such a far cry from the self-assured member of parliament striding through the village greeting people, perhaps, it had to be said, a little too much aware of his own importance and impressed by his own opinions? She knew that he had a glamorous, supportive wife and three young children who went to local schools. He seemed to have the perfect life.

At last he raised his head and began haltingly. 'I've been in London for some time—I wasn't expecting to come back for a week or two. Then this flood occurred and of course I had to be here.'

Kerry nodded, not wanting to interrupt his flow. He looked beyond her, as if embarrassed to meet her eyes. 'The thing is, I should have been here when the waters started rising, before the river burst its banks and the bridge collapsed, but I didn't know that things were taking a turn for the worse.'

Kerry looked at him in surprise. 'You didn't?'

'No. I wasn't in the House of Commons, I was…er… busy elsewhere. My agent had tried to get hold of me but I'd lost my mobile so I wasn't getting any messages.'

'You didn't hear it on the news, or see it in the newspapers? We had journalists sniffing around for a few days before the flood. It's big news nowadays.'

For the first time his eyes met hers and after a second's pause he sighed and said in a flat voice, 'You might as well know the truth, I didn't know because, Dr Latimer, I was stoned out of my mind.'

There was a short silence and Kerry wondered for a second if she'd heard correctly. Sir Vernon Hood, respectable pillar of society, who served on numerous committees, a *druggie*?

He looked at her bleakly and shrugged. 'It's true, I'm a drug addict. When I should have been sitting in the House I was snorting cocaine in a hotel. I'm the lowest of the low.'

Kerry took a deep breath, trying not to let her inner astonishment show in her facial expression.

'How did you get into your addiction?'

A bitter laugh. 'The old story. I fell for a young pretty woman who flattered me. London can be boring on your own at night, Dr Latimer. Somehow, through her I got inveigled into trying the damn stuff. I was very tired and the drugs seemed to perk me up—that and the odd glass of wine. It didn't take long to get a hold but now she's blackmailing me.'

There was a certain self-pity in his voice, and Kerry's sympathy dissipated. Why should she feel sorry for this man born to privilege with every advantage in life? He'd betrayed his wife and family just because he'd been bored in London and had needed a little excitement. No wonder he'd not been in evidence lately. He'd been having a sordid affair, and now that his comfortable life looked as if it might implode, he was terrified of the consequences.

He looked at her narrowly, as if guessing her true thoughts. 'You want to know why I've come to you, I suppose.' He leant forward, looking at her pleadingly. 'You've got to help me get free of these drugs. If Claudia spills the beans, the press will be down on me like a ton of bricks. At least if I'm clean I can say I've conquered the problem. I want to feel as if I'm in control of my life again.'

'It won't be easy. You've got to have a real resolve and help and support from those around you. Motivation is the key thing. Does your wife know about this?'

'I...I told her last night. I had to, because I'm frightened that if the hacks did get hold of the story they'd come to the house, and I wouldn't be able to keep it under wraps.' For the first time he looked ashamed. 'She'a a good woman. She's said she'll stand by me—whatever happens.'

'You're lucky to have that support.'

He grimaced. 'I guess I could be the next big story now—splashed across every tabloid in Britain. "MP in cocaine ring". That would be my career done for.' His voice faded away, then he looked at Kerry almost defiantly. 'So, what can you do for me?'

'I can refer you to the drug centre in Laystone, which will use a combination of medication and counselling to help your recovery.'

'Why can't you do it? You're my GP. I don't want to

go anywhere else—anywhere I might be recognised. Good God, if I'm seen going into a drug centre, the whole world's going to know.'

'We don't provide those sorts of facilities here Sir Vernon. The centre is a place dedicated to the rehabilitation of drug addicts and we've found that because they specialise in the problem and devote all their time to it, there's more chance of success.'

'So you're not going to give me any treatment?'

'I can't—not at the surgery—only at Laystone. It's part of the hospital in a new wing…'

'I know where it is all right. I opened the place not five years ago! I didn't realise that it had completely taken over the GPs' responsibility for treating drug addiction.'

'Do you want me to refer you? It really would be a good idea after you've made the first move by coming for help. That's very commendable. You will have dark days with withdrawal symptoms, but the centre will give you treatment for that.'

The MP sighed. 'Then you'd better refer me. I'll have to hope people will think I'm going on some government business if they see me.'

Kerry printed out a referral letter and handed it to him. 'I wish you luck, Sir Vernon. I'm sure you can break your addiction with their help. You've made a brave start by admitting you need to change your lifestyle.'

He nodded and went out slowly. It was tragic that the man had almost ruined his life and that of his family.

What a fall from grace! The flood had had an impact on people's lives in many different ways—if Vernon Hood hadn't had to come back so quickly to Braxton Falls, he might have been able to wriggle out of his difficulty somehow in London before the affair became public knowledge. But she suspected that he would have been found out sooner or later and the dignified front he presented to the public would have crumbled.

After the surprising revelations from Sir Vernon, the afternoon became busier and busier. Never had Kerry welcomed the end of the day with as much enthusiasm as this. Although the computers were once more up and running, the results of the floods had thrown up a multitude of problems—she had a long meeting with the public health department over the worries of sewage from overflowing drains, and with Social Services about moving elderly and infirm patients out of houses that were no longer habitable. So much had to be squeezed into a short time and her brain felt so full of decisions to be made it was jumbled up like the ingredients in a food mixer.

With a sigh of relief she said goodbye to her final patient of the day and stood up to stretch her stiff back, then picked up her handbag. The magazine Freda had lent her had been pushed into it, and she pulled it out. Denovan's photo stared back at her from the cover—blue eyes gazed gravely towards the camera, set in a clean-cut face, dark hair slightly tousled over his brow. A slight smile played on his lips, preventing him from looking too severe, but he didn't look too cheesy. Every girl's dream man, she thought wryly.

She flicked through the pages to the article about him—she might deem the mag a load of rubbish, but she certainly was going to read it! A montage of photos spread across the centrefold page showed Denovan in a variety of settings: in front of camera during a programme, with his arm slung round various glamorous-looking women at nightclubs, concerts and even film premiers. The largest picture had him looking into the eyes of a statuesque blonde who was leaning towards him in a provocative pose, glossy hair tumbling over her shoulders and a low-cut dress showing plenty of cleavage. In all of them he looked assured and perfectly at home in the sophisticated world he lived in.

'Hot Spot of the Week,' proclaimed the headline. *'Our hottest guy this week is dishy TV doctor Denovan O'Mara, who has everyone guessing who his latest love is! He remains cagey, saying that marriage isn't for him—we guess he's having too good a time, but rumour has it that his taste is for someone in the showbiz world called Suzy de Forno, featured in our main photograph. But when he's out of the public eye, the hot doc's priority is his little boy, Archie. Separated from Archie's mum, we say Denovan O'Mara's the most eligible bachelor in town!'*

Kerry threw the magazine irritably into a drawer. Even if she had been having a pleasurable fantasy about a liaison with Denovan, he was out of her league altogether. There were far too many reasons not to fall for the man! How could she hope to compete with someone like Suzy de Forno? Perhaps Frank's assessment of his brother as a womaniser had been right.

She went to the window and stared moodily at the little village below. Gloomily she supposed she was one of thousands of women who'd shown a marked interest in Denovan O'Mara—one only had to look at the photos in the magazine!

He was a man who had another life she knew nothing about—as Freda had said, a life filled with adulation, not only from viewers but from the women in his social circle. He wasn't likely to be excited by a woman in a little country place like Braxton Falls who had leapt on him at the least encouragement.

She had to get out into the fresh air, Kerry decided firmly, clear her head and have a good walk, away from the stuffy atmosphere of the surgery. She would have a brisk stroll when she'd dumped her things in the house and changed her clothes, and perhaps the change of scenery would put the darned man out of her mind. With a sigh of relief she turned off the computer, shoved some papers into a drawer and said goodbye to everyone in the office.

Kerry took a deep breath of the brisk, cool, evening air as she set out along the side of the hill beyond her house. The patchwork of fields below her still had large lakes of flood water spread over them, giving a different look to the countryside she was used to, but the evenings were getting lighter now, and the sky was a rosy pink over the hills against a pale blue sky. How could she live anywhere else? She pitied anyone who didn't have this countryside to refresh themselves in, these wonderful walks up and down the little hills and valleys. Gradually the stresses of the day seemed to fade and even the thought of Denovan returning to London was something she would get used to, she supposed. It was ridiculous to fall for the first gorgeous guy she'd met since Andy had died. Denovan wasn't available, full stop! And anyway, hadn't he said that although he loved it in Braxton, he could never live here because of the past?

Her stride lengthened as she reached the little copse that grew above the village, the leaves of the oaks and ashes beginning to uncurl and the hedges showing a haze of green as spring began to take a magical hold on the countryside. She began to think of the things she would do in the summer—play more tennis and go riding. There were stables in the next village, and there was nothing more exhilarating than cantering along the hillside on a fine evening.

Vaguely she heard footsteps some way behind her, then they came closer and she turned round, and with a jolt of surprise saw Denovan running along the path and behind him Archie's little figure was scampering as fast as he could to keep up with his father. Damn, she thought irritably, just when I thought I'd got Denovan O'Mara out of my head!

He drew up beside her, and she tried not to stare at his tall, rangy figure dressed in faded khaki shorts.

Why did he have to be so attractive? The trouble was, men with his looks were thin on the ground in Braxton Falls.

'My goodness, you're a fast walker!' observed Denovan, his eyes sweeping over her slight figure. 'We saw you setting off as I brought Archie back from nursery and I thought that some exercise on an evening like this would be a great idea.'

'Please don't let me stop you, then,' Kerry said politely, the hairs on the back of her neck prickling under his scrutiny. 'I'm just having a quick stroll myself.'

Denovan grinned. 'We've run enough, haven't we, Archie? We'll just walk along with you, if that's OK.'

Kerry wanted to say that, no, it wasn't OK, that she'd come out to free her mind from work and concerns about him and not to find herself an inch away from the man and his splendid physique.

'If you want to, of course.' She looked down at Archie. 'And how was your last day at nursery, Archie? Did they have a good party for you?'

The little boy frowned. 'It was good, but I sat next to a girl who took my colouring pencils. I didn't like her.' He kicked a stone on the path. 'Luca's my friend—he's in London. I want to see him.'

Denovan's patted Archie on his head. 'You'll be seeing him next week when we go back.'

'Why can't he come here? It's good here. Larry's getting a puppy and he said I could play with it!'

'We can't stay here for ever. We've got to get back to the flat.'

Archie's earnest round face looked up at his father. 'Could we have a puppy in London?' Archie watched Denovan's negative expression and suddenly beamed at his father. 'I've got a great idea—we could buy a house here and I could have Luca to stay and get a puppy and a kitten and some chickens!'

'And what about my job, young man? How am I going to earn money to keep all these animals?'

Archie looked puzzled, then his face cleared. 'Kerry has a job' He turned his little face up to Kerry, his round glasses making him look grave. 'You'd help him, wouldn't you?'

Kerry gave an embarrassed laugh. 'Your daddy already has a job on television—he can't be in two places at once! Besides, what about all the exciting things you do in London? Like playing in the park with your friends?'

Archie pursed his lips as if considering the idea. 'I do like the park…' His attention was suddenly taken by two rabbits chasing each other along the path. He gave a whoop of delight, and ran after them. 'Come back, rabbits…come back here!'

Denovan watched the little boy's flying figure proudly. 'He's certainly smitten with Braxton. This weekend I'm going to take him to a few of my childhood haunts—there's a little cave up in the hills with a waterfall that I used to love, and of course the miniature railway has opened up again at Laystone. He'll find that great fun.' He looked at Kerry. 'I don't suppose you'd fancy coming with us?'

'You're very kind but I'm afraid I haven't really time,' said Kerry quickly. 'I've got a tremendous amount to do...so if you don't mind...'

Was he being kind to her, including her in their activities because he assumed she didn't do much at the weekends? Or, thought Kerry cynically, pitching a line to her like the lothario he seemed to be, according to the magazine? Perhaps that wasn't fair to him, but she wasn't going to be drawn into his life any more than she had to be. She'd had a shock two weeks ago when she'd realised just how much she was attracted to Denovan, and the more she saw of him, the more attractive he seemed. She wasn't going to make a fool of herself again with a doctor who seemed to be the toast of London!

She flicked a glance at him—the casual outfit he was wearing definitely emphasised his athletic physique. She looked away again quickly.

'Oh, come on—it will only be for the afternoon and that gives you loads of time to catch up on things surely? Don't you think you deserve a bit of time off after the two weeks you've had?' He smiled at her persuasively, putting his hands on her shoulders, turning her to face him. 'I know Archie would love you to come and so would I, of course. After all, it is our last weekend here,' he added as a sort of casual afterthought, his blue eyes looking down at her compellingly.

Kerry hesitated, a feeling like an electric shock whipping through her body at the touch of his hands, and tried to avoid his eyes. If only he wouldn't come so close to her. It made every sensible thought fly out of her head. She drew back from that magnetic aura that seemed to surround him and pulled a leaf from a hedge, rubbing it nervously between her fingers.

'I'm not sure.'

Denovan gave her a shrewd look and spread his hands out, almost in supplication. 'Look, I'm sorry. Perhaps I got off on the wrong foot two weeks ago when I hugged you. I suppose I just wanted you to know how sorry I was for your loss—it won't happen again.'

Kerry looked at him in surprise, then forced a smile. 'Oh, that?' she said loftily, raising an eyebrow with a pretty good imitation of casual indifference. 'Don't worry, I knew you were just being very kind and understanding as you could see I was upset about Andrew. Of course I never assumed that you meant anything by it.'

Denovan thought wryly that he supposed it was a relief that his brief kiss had meant nothing to her at all, except as a gesture of kindness. He must have imagined Kerry's spark of response, the way he'd thought she'd pressed her soft body against him, and then her brush-off at breakfast-time. And what a fool he'd be to start a relationship anyway. He'd learned his lesson—too often he'd been duped by women in his life. Bitter experience had left him with little faith in women and love. And yet there was something about Kerry that he trusted, something about her that made him want to be in her company. Surely he could do that and not be compromised? 'Well, then,' he said jovially, pushing negative thoughts to the back of his mind, 'there's no reason for you not to come with us, is there, just for an afternoon of fun and exploration?'

How easy it had been to lie to him, reflected Kerry. He obviously hadn't noticed her over-eager response that night to his kiss! But now Denovan had made it clear that he had only been trying to comfort her and she was unlikely to be thrown into any intimate sort of situation with him, it was hard to refuse. It was just going to be a pleasant afternoon, a kind of farewell after the two weeks he'd worked at Braxton. Denovan was right, it had been a gruelling, tense fortnight and a little outing would be invigorating.

'OK, then,' she said brightly. 'Just for the afternoon, of course. It would be lovely.'

A boyish grin lit up Denovan's face, his eyes crinkling. 'Terrific! I know we'll have a good time. Don't forget to wear your walking boots tomorrow,' he added. 'It's quite a long way from the little railway to the waterfall—I shall be taking some drinks to help us on our way!'

'And I'll bring some snack food for a little picnic, as well. I know what Archie likes—biscuits and crisps.'

Denovan laughed. 'Yes, you can't go wrong with salt, fat and sugar with Archie.'

And even though she knew that Denovan was off-limits where romance was concerned, Kerry felt a thrill of excitement at spending an afternoon with him and his little boy. Suddenly the weekend had a purpose, and the promise of companionship and fun.

CHAPTER SIX

'DADDY, this is great! Can I get on that train now? I want to go in the front near the driver, I want to see him drive the train, I want…'

Archie bounced up and down in front of Denovan and Kerry, his cheeks pink, and eyes sparkling with excitement behind their owlish glasses. It was just the day for an outing, thought Kerry—warm sun, jolly crowds, and the pleasure of taking out a little boy to enjoy himself in a country theme park.

'OK, Archie,' said Denovan, laughing at the little boy's elation. 'Give the train a chance to stop at the platform.' He looked round at the little mock station and nodded in a satisfied way. 'This is just how it was when I was young,' he remarked. 'Actually, it's better than it was then, because I think they've made more of the scenery. They used to have a part that went through a wild wood with animated tigers and lions in it. I wonder if they've still got that?'

Kerry flicked an amused glance at him. He was nearly as excited as his son!

'Brings back happy memories, does it?' she asked.

'My mother used to bring me here when I was little—I thought it was heaven!'

The briefest shadow crossed his face, then he put a hand out to prevent Archie from running towards the miniature train as it came to a halt and disgorged its small passengers with their parents. It had several open carriages, and the little boy grabbed Denovan's and Kerry's hands.

'Come on,' he urged, pulling them with him. 'Let's get in now at the front.'

The driver turned round and smiled at them. 'Does the young man want to sit with me?' he asked. 'It's first come, first served, and it means he can ring the bell. Mum and Dad will have to sit behind us, I'm afraid, as there's only room for one beside me!'

Denovan eyes twinkled at Kerry. 'There you are, Mum! That's your role for the day.'

'I'll try and keep you both in order, then.' She smiled, a faint blush of embarrassment on her cheeks.

A look of bliss suffused Archie's face as he scrambled up beside the driver, and sat proudly very upright, holding on to the bell until told to pull it. He turned round and beamed at his father, informing him, 'I'm going to start it off!'

'That's made his day.' Denovan grinned. He turned to Kerry. 'Come on, you'll have to get in beside me. I can't wait to go down memory lane!'

Kerry squashed in, jammed tight against Denovan's muscular thighs. The small carriage hadn't really been constructed with men the size of Denovan in mind.

She pushed herself into a corner as much as she could, pulling her legs to one side and trying to relax against the rather uncomfortable wooden slats of the seat, determined to try and keep her distance. Denovan had made it clear that this was to be a social outing, an afternoon for fun and entertaining Archie, and if she was too near the man she was sure her thoughts wouldn't just be about Archie!

The afternoon was turning out to be great fun, she acknowledged. The sun was shining, everyone looked happy—the flooding down the valley and all the devastation temporarily forgotten. She couldn't remember the last time she'd had the pleasure of going out and doing something different at the weekend. She gave a happy little wave to Archie as he turned round to look at them both.

Denovan looked covertly at Kerry's profile, with its tip-tilted nose and her cloud of dark glossy hair held back by two combs at the side, a blush of excitement on her cheeks. She looked so natural, so gorgeous! It was just as well that Archie was with them—if he'd been alone with her he didn't know if he could have kept his resolution to retain their relationship on a strictly friendly basis! He was intensely aware of her nearness, the fresh smell of her light perfume tantalising him, stirring far too many feelings that had lain dormant for a long, long time.

He flicked a look at the little crowd of people getting on the train with them—did they see a happy family unit of three, as the driver had? A daddy and a mummy and a happy little boy?

A forlorn sense of what might have been in his life suddenly surged through him. If only Lorna and he had made a go of it and she had taken to motherhood, Archie would indeed have been part of a family unit, instead of having to make do with a father who generally didn't have enough time to take him on outings, or various childminders who were kind to him but were merely doing a professional job. A rerun, he thought sadly, of his own life.

The bell clanged suddenly and Archie shouted excitedly, 'We're going! Off we go!'

Kerry turned to Denovan and laughed, her cheeks dimpling. 'I feel as if I'm going on a real adventure.'

And he laughed back at her, both of them caught up in the happiness of a little boy. Denovan put his arm casually round the back of the cramped seat and tried to stretch his legs, shifting in his seat and coincidentally getting even closer to Kerry.

'It seems much smaller in this carriage than it did when I was five,' he observed. 'Ah, we're coming to a tunnel now. I remember this.' He grinned, pointing to the arch. 'But I don't remember that notice over the top of it—"The Tunnel of Love to the Land of Enchantment".'

The little train gave a shrill blast of its whistle as it drew into the tunnel, and Archie shouted in the darkness. 'I pulled that whistle! I pulled that whistle!'

Then the driver's voice came over a loudspeaker.

'Gentlemen, as you saw, this is the tunnel of love—it's imperative to show the girl of your dreams how much you admire her!'

Kerry giggled rather nervously. It was all rather intimate and in the gloom of the tunnel she felt even more aware of just how close Denovan was to her. His arm was only touching her back lightly, but she was very conscious of that slight contact, and a treacherous frisson of attraction flickered through her body like a pulsating wave. She knew that he had turned his head towards her, she could feel his warm breath on her cheek, smell the faintly astringent scent of his aftershave. If only, she thought wistfully, he was just an ordinary guy and someone not in the public eye, who didn't appear to have a string of girlfriends—then perhaps she would have shifted slightly nearer to him, given him a little encouragement. But she was darned if she was going to join the throng of women who were apparently drooling over him in London.

Just how long was this tunnel? Every second in that suddenly private little world seemed to heighten the atmosphere between them, but perhaps Denovan didn't feel it, and it was only her fevered imagination that allowed her to imagine his lips on hers and his arms around her?

He gave a low chuckle and murmured, 'These are the most uncomfortable seats I've sat in for a long time.'

'Yes, aren't they?' agreed Kerry rather breathlessly.

Then suddenly they were in the daylight once more and Kerry blinked in the bright sun and Denovan put on dark sunglasses so that she couldn't see his blue eyes. When the train drew into the little station at the end of the ride, there was a crowd of children waiting to get on, and as Archie scrambled down from the driver's cab, he gave a shout of delight.

'There's Larry and the other boys and Daphne. Hi! I've been helping to drive this train. I blew the whistle! Can I go on again with them, Daddy?'

'We're going to the waterfall now, Archie. It's quite far away so we've got to get going before it gets cold.'

Archie's bright little face dropped. 'I want to stay here with the boys,' he muttered. 'I don't want to go to the waterfall today.'

'Let him stay with us,' suggested Larry. 'We'll look after him, won't we, Mum?'

'I can't let you do that,' protested Denovan. 'You've been looking after him for the past few days. Enough's enough!'

Daphne laughed. 'For goodness' sake, Denovan, we love having Archie and he seems to have a civilising effect on my lads. We actually came over to ask him to come with us anyway, but you'd gone out when we called round.'

Kerry bit her lip—the afternoon wasn't going quite as she'd planned. It was meant to be an outing for Archie now suddenly the stage seemed to be set for just her and Denovan to spend the next two hours totally alone.

'But we ought to stay here with Archie. After all, he doesn't see much of you during the week and we're having such fun,' she remarked hopefully.

'*I* don't mind,' said Archie brightly, adding reassuringly, 'Daphne will look after me!'

Daphne laughed and looked at the two doctors' faces. 'This is the first time in days I've seen you two looking at all rested and relaxed with some colour in your cheeks. The past two weeks have been a nightmare for you. You go and have an hour or two to yourselves. A good walk would do you good. Really, I insist!'

Archie looked pleadingly at Denovan. 'Go on, Daddy—let me stay with them!'

Denovan shook his head helplessly. 'Well, if you're absolutely sure…' He took out his wallet. 'But this I insist. I want you all to have a huge cream tea at the café here when you've done all the rides and slides you want. I'll see you back at the village. Can you fit him in your car?'

Archie gave a whoop of delight and hugged his father round his knees. 'Thank you, thank you, Daddy,' he shouted.

'It's Daphne and her boys you ought to be thanking, not me.' He turned to Kerry. 'Right you are, then. We'll set off for the waterfall—it should only take us about forty minutes from here if we walk briskly.'

One thing was clear, reflected Kerry, breathing hard as she tackled the steep hill up to the waterfall, she had to get fitter! It was embarrassing to trail behind Denovan as he strode briskly out across the path through the fields that bordered the adventure park. Of course, she hadn't done any proper exercise for a long time and it was showing in her feeble attempts to keep up with him. When Andy had been alive they'd delighted in going on long hikes over the moors, and without him she'd definitely been using the car too much, because somehow walking by herself had led to too much introspection and loneliness.

'I hope I'm not tiring you out,' remarked Denovan, his amused eyes watching her as she scrambled up towards him, her cheeks pink with exertion. 'At least it's getting your cardiac rate up.'

'Don't be ridiculous. I'm not a bit tired,' she retorted, taking a deep breath and trying not to gasp too much. It had become very humid, and surreptitiously she wiped her forehead with a hanky and ran a tongue over her dry lips. She pulled out her water bottle from her pocket and took a grateful swig. 'Just keeping myself hydrated,' she said defiantly. 'I'm in great shape, actually.'

'You certainly are.' he murmured, then bit his lip. Why was he flirting with her? Hadn't he decided that flirtation wasn't on the agenda?

Kerry looked at him sharply and decided to change the subject. 'So where is this waterfall? I think I can hear it.'

'Just round this corner—and then perhaps we can have a pit stop for some food.'

'Not on my account,' Kerry said loftily. 'I can certainly go on for ages yet.'

Denovan grinned sardonically. 'I'm sure you can. However, it's a good place to sit as there's a lovely view, and it will give us fuel for the next little trek.'

They turned the corner, and suddenly there was the

waterfall, tumbling over a high rock in the hill, a never-ending torrent of water, sparkling silver in the sunlight as it plunged down into the river below in a cascade of boiling white foam.

Kerry stopped short and gazed up at it, mesmerised. 'Wow!' she gasped. 'And I never even knew this was where the falls were.'

'How long have you worked in the area, then?' Denovan asked. 'This is where Braxton Falls gets its name from, of course.'

'Goodness—quite a few years, but although I used to walk with Andy at the weekends, we'd go further afield because he was a warden in his spare time in another part of the Peak National Park. We didn't make it up here.'

'And he was a member of the mountain rescue team? A busy guy, I reckon. You must miss him very much.'

Kerry paused for a minute without replying, and frowned, trying to put her feelings into words. She realised with surprise that Andy's loss wasn't tearing at her heartstrings as much as it had even a few days ago, and she seemed to be able to talk about him without her eyes filling with tears any more.

'Of course I miss him. But I have to admit I think of him now with more happiness at the memory than sadness at the loss. Perhaps time is helping to heal things a bit.'

And there was something else that helped, Kerry reflected, trying to be honest with herself—she'd learned she wasn't immune any more to an attractive man. It was Denovan who was helping to heal the scars of living life without grief for Andy's death overshadowing it. Two weeks ago she'd still been in mourning for Andy but suddenly she was looking forward and not back to the past. Was it because a drop-dead gorgeous male had come into her orbit, even if he was off-limits? She flicked a glance at Denovan sitting near her on the grass, all too aware that they were alone together in this beautiful place with nothing to distract them but each other.

Denovan sighed and took off his rucksack, slinging it to the ground before he sat down. If only he could let go of the past, like Kerry had. Returning to Braxton Falls had brought too many painful memories back: he loved the place, but he had so many unresolved issues with his half-brother still weighing him down that it would be difficult to make a new life here. He smiled wryly to himself as he pulled a small bottle of wine from the rucksack. When he'd come up to Derbyshire three days ago the thought of moving back here had never entered his head, but now it didn't seem all that preposterous. Perhaps one day it might happen. He shrugged and opened the wine, pouring measures into two plastic cups and handing Kerry one of them.

'Cheers! I think we deserve to relax after such a gruelling time over the last weeks.'

She raised a cup in his direction. 'And thank you for staying to help me out. I don't know how I would have coped if you hadn't been here. You were a star!'

His eyes locked with hers for an instant. 'I assure you it was a real pleasure.'

Kerry sat down rather self-consciously near him—but not too near. She took a gulp of wine and looked around, trying to concentrate on something other than Denovan and his disturbing presence. It was so lovely—the background sound of the waterfall, the warmth of the sun on her face, and high above a buzzard wheeling around lazily as it quartered the sky looking for prey.

Denovan's rangy body lay half-upright, long legs stretched out before him, his strong profile and tousled hair in relief against the green of the trees. He sipped his wine and smiled across at her. Perfect setting and a perfect man, Kerry reflected. So much for concentrating on something else and pushing him out of her mind.

'Penny for them. What are you thinking about?' he murmured.

'Oh, nothing really. Just thinking how lovely it is here. I feel as if I've come on holiday.'

'It's not quite Tobago, I'm afraid—I guess the wedding's taken place by now?'

'That's right. I spoke to Rachel just before the ceremony. She was very excited.'

It seemed a lifetime ago that she'd been packing excitedly to go to her cousin's wedding—and to her surprise she didn't have any pangs at all about not being there. She looked again at the tumbling, sparkling cascade of water.

'Actually, I think this is probably more beautiful than anywhere abroad,' she mused.

Denovan sat up and took another swig of wine. 'Glad it measures up OK. I've always loved this place. Mum and I would come when I was a kid with a picnic in the holidays.'

'Just you two? Did your brother never come?' Somehow she couldn't stop probing—longing to know more about this man, his background and what made him tick.

Denovan shrugged. 'My father wasn't very interested in walking or views, and Frank…well, Frank was a lot older than me, and he and I didn't get on anyway…'

'Even when you were young?'

'Even then,' he remarked sadly. 'I suppose he regarded my mother as a usurper, coming into his life after he'd lost his mother. My father had remarried my mother very quickly and then I appeared—and perhaps that was a mistake.' His expression hardened. 'We never had what I'd call an idyllic family.'

Suddenly Kerry remembered the words of Nellie Styles, the old lady she'd visited before the flooding. She had mentioned the boys' animosity towards each other…and something else, but she couldn't remember quite what it was.

'It's a shame you've never made it up with Frank. He always seems quite laid back and he and I get on well. He's a good doctor.'

Denovan frowned. 'I'm sure he's a good doctor, but you don't know him as intimately as I do,' he said tersely. 'You make it sound as if we'd had a minor spat but I can assure you it runs more deeply than a childhood difference, because in fact…' He stopped in mid-sentence and looked at her guardedly.

'Because what?' she prompted.

He shook his head. 'Nothing. It's too complicated.'

Kerry bit her lip. She should have avoided the subject of his brother. 'Look, I'm sorry. It's nothing to do with me, I know. I suppose I just wanted to know more about your family. Frank never talks about the past at all.'

'I'm not surprised Frank keeps his past to himself—it doesn't make good listening, I'm afraid.' Denovan's voice was bitter. 'You wouldn't believe me if I told you the whole story anyway.'

'It's your past, not mine, Denovan. There's no need to tell me,' she said gently, but she burned with curiosity to know the truth of the rift between the brothers, to know more about Denovan's mysterious other life, which he so obviously wanted to keep to himself.

'Let's forget about him,' said Denovan in a lighter tone. He leant over and topped up Kerry's cup with more wine. 'You'd better finish this—after all, I'm driving back in an hour or two so I'd best stick to one glass.'

Kerry felt delightfully relaxed after some alcohol racing through her on an empty stomach. The stress of the past week seemed to evaporate as she rolled over on her back on the mossy grass and looked up at the canopy of trees over the little plateau they were on.

'Oh,' she murmured, 'this is heaven. I could just go to sleep right here in the sun.'

The smile left Denovan's lips as he looked at Kerry's slender body lying so close to him. Slender but quite curvaceous, he thought gravely. She wasn't skinny with hip bones that stuck out, but had the kind of body it would be wonderful to feel against his—soft, warm, yielding. Her eyes were closed, her lips slightly parted and the urge to taste those soft lips was suddenly overwhelmingly tempting.

He sighed. The last person he should be fancying was his brother's colleague—how complicated would that be? It was extraordinary that he should even be working with Kerry with the bad history between him and Frank. Yet two weeks ago he had been in London and couldn't have imagined himself sitting on a grassy bank by Braxton Falls with a gorgeous girl like Kerry whom he'd only just met! He leaned nearer Kerry, still holding the paper cup in his hand, feasting on the softness of her skin, the way her cloud of dark hair framed her face.

A sudden babble of voices made Denovan look up as a party of hikers appeared, walking briskly down from the side of the waterfall. They gave him a friendly wave and disappeared down the valley path. He waved back at them, forgetting he was holding a cupful of wine in his hand.

'Eek! What was that?' Kerry gave a scream and sat bolt upright, brushing a stream of cold wine from her face.

'Hell…sorry… I waved with the wrong hand at those walkers! Oh, damnation, it's all over your T-shirt…' He made to dab the spill on her chest with a handkerchief he'd pulled out of his pocket. 'Let me dry it…'

She snatched the handkerchief and said quickly, 'It's OK. I can do that myself, thank you very much!'

There was laughter dancing in his eyes as he murmured, 'A pity...'

Kerry flicked a stern look at him before catching his eye and suddenly dissolving into giggles, and he laughed too as he watched her. Then gradually their laughter died away and they were staring at each other as if both had realised something momentous had occurred in those few moments. There was an almost palpable silence, the atmosphere electric with anticipation. Kerry began to breathe a little faster, her heart thumping uncomfortably in her chest. She was so close to him that she could see the thick lashes round those sexy, humorous eyes and the slight late-day stubble on his chin. Another second, she thought, and something was going to happen. Something she might regret.

Denovan broke the silence and leaned towards her, whispering, 'Kerry, you must know...'

With a great effort of will Kerry sprang to her feet and gave a forced laugh. 'Any more of that wine left?' she croaked. 'Or have you spilt it all?'

He got up slowly and raised a sardonic eyebrow. 'I might be able to find a few drops,' he remarked, his eyes still holding hers.

Denovan poured what was left into her plastic cup, and she turned away from him and sauntered casually away to lean against a tree, pretending to look at the view across the valley with her back to the falls, trying to calm her heart, which was beating like a demented drum against her ribs. There was no way anything could happen between them—Denovan was returning to London next week. She had to remember that. She could sense that he was very near her and she turned round brightly.

'We really ought to take this opportunity to have a discussion about the practice,' she said rather wildly, her voice breathless. 'I don't know if you've any more patient notes to load into the computer before you go?'

'Forget about the practice,' he said tersely. He put his hands on her shoulders, and looked into her hazel eyes. 'Kerry,' he said softly. 'What are you frightened of?'

She swallowed nervously. 'I don't know what you mean…' she faltered. She looked at her watch—her not-so-adroit change of subject hadn't worked. 'Perhaps we ought to be getting back. We've seen the falls and they're very beautiful, but it's going to take quite a while to walk back to the car.'

'We have plenty of time, and you haven't answered my question—what are you frightened of?' His grave face looked down at her and it was difficult to avoid his compelling gaze. 'You see,' he continued softly, 'I'm sure you wanted to kiss me then, just as much as I wanted to kiss you. Aren't I right? I know there was something electric between us a moment ago.'

Kerry took a deep breath, and said coolly, 'Denovan, don't be ridiculous. For goodness' sake, you've only been here a few days—I don't really know you at all. You're imagining things.'

He smiled and shook his head. 'I don't think so, Kerry—I know when there's a spark...'

Kerry felt a flash of irritation—he was so sure, so confident in his assumption that she was attracted to him, unable to think for a moment that she might *not* wish to kiss him!

'For goodness' sake, Denovan,' she snapped. 'I was sceptical when your brother told me you were a womaniser—now I believe him!'

Denovan stepped back from her and said quietly, 'You think that, do you? You believe what Frank said, although you've admitted you don't know me very well?'

Kerry looked at him scornfully. 'Oh, I don't have to go by just what Frank said. You just have to look in most of the celebrity magazines to see you're featured with a bevy of beauties.'

Denovan's lips twitched and then he gave a roar of laughter. 'So that's it? Oh, Kerry, if you believe them, you'll believe anything!'

Kerry looked at him, rather nonplussed. 'What about Suzy de Forno, then?' she demanded, folding her arms. 'One magazine said you were practically engaged to her. And if you are, what are you doing making a pass at me?'

His blue eyes danced as he regarded her pugnacious figure. 'Suzy de Forno and I barely know each other—and I happen to know that she's actually engaged to a very nice guy who works in marketing.' He stepped towards her and, putting his arm round her waist, pulled her close to him, one hand tracing a delicate path across her jaw and down her neck. And Kerry felt her body respond instantly to that butterfly touch, and, angry with herself for being so pliant, she stiffened her body and turned her head away.

'A magazine photo doesn't mean anything, Kerry—you can make up any old caption for it,' he said. 'Those are just make-believe stories, but this is reality. Believe me, there's no one in my life at the moment and hasn't been for a long, long time. So I ask you again, what are you afraid of, sweetheart? After all, I was only going to give you a gentlemanly peck. Something just like this…'

And he leaned forward and brushed her lips with his. 'There!' he exclaimed. 'That wasn't so frightening, was it?'

His deep blue eyes danced at her and she found herself melting and trying to suppress a giggle. Denovan O'Mara might not want a lifelong commitment, but how wonderful it was to be desired by a drop-dead gorgeous guy after such a long time without anybody to love. And if he was free, why should she be afraid to let herself go a little with him?

Before she could reply, he leant towards her again, kissing her on her warm, soft, pliant mouth, not briefly as before but long and hard and passionately, and she didn't resist. His arms imprisoned her against the tree trunk and slowly her arms curved round his neck and pulled him against her. His mouth fluttered down to the little hollow in her neck, his hands caressing the soft swell of her breasts, and every nerve in her body tingled with anticipation, her limbs as pliant as jelly. This wasn't just a casual embrace—this was deliberate, exciting and mind-blowing!

Somewhere in the deep recesses of her mind she wondered if she was being a complete fool to allow… no, enjoy this man she'd known so briefly to make love to her—the man who not long ago she'd thought had been tough, unsympathetic, and who was leaving in two days' time. But she'd been lonely for too long and he was the first man since Andy who had made her pulse race. She sighed and gave in to the completely erotic pleasure of his touch on her body, his hard, demanding frame against hers, and she melted against him, never wanting this heaven to stop. She'd tried to resist him, but now she'd given in, and any problems there might be in the way of a relationship disappeared like gossamer in the wind.

CHAPTER SEVEN

THE sudden crack of thunder almost directly over their heads and a flash of lightning to the side of them was unexpected and terrifying. Kerry was still entwined in Denovan's arms, both of them blissfully relaxed, totally unprepared for the rapid darkening of the skies and the ominous drops of rain that started to fall.

She flinched and screamed, clutching Denovan. 'What's happened?'

Denovan hugged her to him and mumbled, 'It's OK, it's just a thunderstorm.'

'What do you mean, just a thunderstorm? We could get killed! We're under a tree, for heaven's sake!' She wriggled from him, stood up and grabbed her rucksack.

The drops of rain changed in an instant to a deluge, hitting them both with such force that in a few seconds they were completely soaked, as wet as if they'd been swimming.

Denovan took her hand and shouted over the noise of the storm, 'Perhaps you're right—we'd better take shelter. We'll go behind the waterfall. There's a cave there—we'll be safe until the storm blows over. Hang on to me!'

He bent down and scooped up his rucksack and Kerry clung to him as inch by inch they managed to negotiate the slippery rocks on a ledge behind the cascade of water, all the time aware of the nearness of the lightning forking the ground too close to them for comfort, and the deafening crash of the thunder overhead. By the time they made the safety of the cave, their clothes were clinging to them and water was streaming down their bodies.

Denovan pushed back his dripping hair from his face and laughed, leaning against the wall of the cave. 'That's what happens when I kiss a girl,' he remarked with a smug grin. 'She feels as if she's been struck by a thunderbolt!'

Kerry wrinkled her nose at him and shook her head mock sternly—but it was only too true she admitted, still dizzy from his kisses a few minutes before. It had happened as suddenly as the thunderstorm—one minute they'd just been talking then, as if a switch had been thrown, the atmosphere between them had become charged, pulsating, and if this sudden storm hadn't burst on them, who knows what would have happened?

She looked down in comical dismay at her dripping trousers and T-shirt. 'Our clothes are wringing!'

'Perhaps we'd better take them off, then,' Denovan murmured, pulling off his shirt and throwing it over a rock in the corner of the cave. He turned towards her with dancing eyes. 'We don't want to catch pneumonia, do we?'

'Don't be ridiculous. Anyway, how are we going to

dry them?' Kerry's voice was husky, trying not to look at his impressively muscled chest. 'We can't walk home with nothing on!'

'It'll stop raining in a minute and we can squeeze them and hang them out for half an hour. I bet the sun will come out. And we both have cagoules in our rucksacks.'

'And what are we going to do for the next half-hour? I'm freezing!' she said, then bit her lip. She'd walked straight into that one as it was quite obvious that Denovan had plenty of ideas on that front!

He grinned wickedly at her and put his hands round her waist. 'I can think of plenty of things to warm us up,' he murmured, sliding his hands onto the bare flesh beneath her T-shirt. 'We were rudely interrupted a few minutes ago, just as we were getting to know each other better.'

Kerry laughed, but stepped back firmly and peered out through the cascade of water. The rain had almost stopped and just as suddenly as the storm had come it was moving away and blue sky and sunlight appeared in its wake. Perhaps it had been a blessing in disguise that the storm had come when it had—now she'd had time to pull herself together she realised what a fool she'd have been to have given in to the temptation that was Denovan. He was a temporary fixture, someone who'd admitted he wanted no ties, and probably looked on their liaison as a pleasurable interlude while he was in the area.

'We need to get going,' she said brusquely. 'I don't

care how wet we are, it's not raining now. We have to pick up the car from the little railway and then you have to collect Archie.'

Denovan took her hand in his. 'Don't tell me this hasn't changed things,' he said softly.

Kerry's voice was as brisk as she could make it. 'It can't change things. You're going on Monday, for heaven's sake. You've another life…a wonderful job in London, and you don't want to work here. Better that we don't make too much of our…little liaison.'

The past few passionate minutes couldn't possibly have meant as much to Denovan as it had to her—perhaps in the circles in which he moved in London it was a normal occurrence. Sudden desolation filled her heart—she couldn't allow herself to hope that theirs would be a permanent love affair when he was going back so soon to his other life. The whole thing was fraught with difficulties. And after all it had just been a passionate kiss, nothing more!

'We must get back,' she repeated. 'Get into some dry clothes before we go and get Archie.'

Denovan took her arm and pulled her to him roughly. 'What the hell are you talking about—do you call what we just did "a little liaison"? We can't go back to where we were before—not…not after the past few minutes. I tell you, Kerry, that meant more to me than a "little liaison".'

Kerry shook her head. 'But your home and work is in London with Archie, and mine is here in Braxton. When

Frank's better he'll be coming back to work here—how can we have a future?'

And all that was true, reflected Denovan. He was at the pinnacle of his job in London—that was why they were offering him another contract, something he had to decide about very soon. Most importantly, Archie needed stability, and at the moment Archie had a lovely childminder and a nursery school he enjoyed. Then he looked down at Kerry, at the curve of her cheek, the soft fullness of her lips and the remembrance of the passion between them a few minutes ago. Women like her came along very rarely. He had to think of something to keep them together.

'I'm not giving up on us before we've hardly started,' he said softly. 'Look, I'm going back to London on Tuesday, but I'll be coming back here to see you as soon as I can.' He held her against him, stroking her hair. 'I mean it, Kerry, you won't be able to keep me away. Let's take it one glorious step at a time and enjoy ourselves.'

Those were the sort of reassuring comments that just put off the evil day of decision—and how would that leave her? reflected Kerry rather bleakly. She was falling for a man who wasn't really available. It had probably been spur-of-the-moment passion on his side anyway. During the past weeks they'd each kept their distance, and suddenly in the space of an hour they'd started something passionate. And now there was no time left for them to get together alone. How could they build a solid foundation for their relationship after such a brief encounter? Then she flicked a look at Denovan's strong, sweet profile in the darkness of the cave and any sensible ideas of backing off from a relationship melted. At the moment, she decided, she'd go along with his suggestion. What had he said? One step at a time?

He hugged her to him again, and she knew when he held her close to him that there was no turning back for her. What had started that afternoon as a light-hearted kiss had become something that meant much more to her than that.

Denovan took her hand and squeezed it. 'Back to reality again, then. We'd better do something to make ourselves presentable.'

It had been a wonderful weekend and they'd had a happy Sunday with Archie, Kerry cooking a huge breakfast for them and in the afternoon going to show the little boy a farm with newborn lambs that he helped to feed. Afterwards he'd ridden on one of the little Shetland ponies the farmer kept.

Archie had been so excited and happy, clinging to both Denovan's and Kerry's hands, dragging them over to see the donkey that lived in the field with the ponies, roaring with laughter as a goose chased a duck for bread he'd thrown into the pond.

'I want to stay here for ever and ever,' he'd declared when they were leaving. 'This is my favourite place!'

'We'll come back very soon, I promise,' Denovan had said, and he'd smiled across at Kerry.

Kerry had smiled back, but she'd wondered if he'd be able to keep his promise.

'You look so much better than the end of last week!' exclaimed Daphne as she poured Kerry and Denovan a cup of coffee after they'd done the surgery on Monday morning. 'You were both dead on your feet on Friday afternoon—your outing on Saturday must have done you a lot of good.'

Kerry could feel Denovan's eyes boring into her back as he said enthusiastically. 'It certainly did, Daphne. I can't think when I've enjoyed a weekend more. And once again, thank you for looking after Archie, he didn't stop talking about the great time he had with you. I'm very grateful to you.'

'He's a dear little boy.' Daphne smiled. 'Didn't you find that walk up to the waterfall very exhausting? And you had to walk back soaking wet because of the rain. I can hardly manage to do anything energetic after I've climbed up!'

'Oh, we kept going quite well,' said Denovan, his voice smooth.

Kerry felt an urgent desire to giggle and she looked away from Denovan's dancing eyes. 'We did get pretty wet, but we sheltered in the cave for a while, so we were fine, thanks,' she said.

'Absolutely fine,' agreed Denovan solemnly, as he stirred two large spoonfuls of sugar into his coffee. 'It gave us a chance to discuss quite a few things.'

'That's good,' said Daphne comfortably. 'It's as well to know everything you can about the practice, even though you're only here until tomorrow.'

'I certainly think I know much more about things now.'

His steady glance held Kerry's for an intimate second, and her pulse rate bounded into rapid mode, as if he'd pressed an accelerator. Two days ago her relationship with Denovan had changed dramatically—it was no good pretending that they were just colleagues any more. Her passionate embrace with him still ran vividly through her mind, every moment precious and memorable. She'd known him for only a couple of weeks and now she couldn't get the man out of her mind!

Her emotions were like a see-saw, one minute filled with excited happiness and then, when she considered the episode more soberly, her excitement evaporated. She mustn't think of that afternoon as a prelude to a long-lasting relationship, she told herself sternly. Denovan would be gone to his other life in London tomorrow and soon she would probably be a fading memory for him.

Freda had been answering the phone, which seemed to ring continually as it usually did after the weekend. She swivelled round in her chair. 'There's an urgent call here—Nellie Styles's daughter, Betty, has just rung. She's up staying with her mother and when she came back from the shops she found Nellie on the floor, unable to move. The ambulance has got stuck in some deep mud in the valley on the way up and can't make it. Betty sounds distraught.'

'Oh, no, poor Nellie. I was hoping she'd improve now we had more help for her. I'll go at once,' said Kerry, pushing thoughts of Denovan firmly out of her head. She picked up her medical bag and turned to Denovan.

'She was the old lady I told you about who knew you as a small boy,' she explained.

'I remember her well. She used to cook for us all when we needed some help after my mother...well, that is, when we needed some help,' he amended. Then he added lightly, 'I'd like to see her again.'

Kerry flicked a look at her watch. 'If you can spare the time now, it might be a good idea if you could come with me. I'll need help to get Nellie off the floor if I have to take her to hospital myself in my car and I'd appreciate your input anyway.'

They walked briskly to Kerry's car and she continued to fill him in on Nellie's medical history.

'It might be a TIA. She's had a history of them over the past few months, although she's never had a true stroke.'

'How is her health otherwise?'

'She's very frail—she's recently been in hospital for a urinary tract infection. She's also very determined. She was adamant she wouldn't go into hospital last time I saw her, but it may have to come to that.'

Nellie's daughter was standing at the door of the little house as they drove up, her hands clasped in agitation, looking anxiously up and down the road. It was obvious she'd been crying, and her face cleared in relief as they came in.

'Oh, thank goodness you're here,' she choked. 'I haven't known what to do. Poor Mum. When I came back from the shop, she couldn't seem to get the words out right and was just lying in a heap on the floor near the kitchen. I can't move her—she's a deadweight.'

She followed the two doctors into the house, twisting her hands together, her face distorted by worry. 'I'm sorry to be so jittery. It's just that Mum's always been such a strong character and it's horrible to see her laid so low.'

Kerry squeezed Betty's shoulder comfortingly, knowing the terrible panic and helplessness that Betty would feel. 'I know, Betty. You've had a terrible shock, but the main thing is you've got help quickly.' She turned to Denovan. 'This is my colleague, Dr O'Mara, who's been filling in for his brother for us. I thought it was a good idea to bring him along, too. Now, let's see how Nellie is, and perhaps you can answer some questions for us…' Her voice was brisk and no-nonsense, trying to bring things back to normality, to keep Betty composed in front of her mother.

Betty had put a pillow under Nellie's head and draped a blanket over her. Kerry bent down beside Nellie and smiled into the old lady's pale, frightened eyes.

'Hello, Nellie, how did you manage to fall, then? Did you trip or just feel very dizzy?'

'Dizzy,' said Nellie after a few moments of working her mouth. 'I'm OK,' she said after another pause, finding difficulty in forming words. Then she clutched Kerry's hand and looked at her imploringly. 'Don't… Not hospital…'

'Let's just see how you are, Nellie. Look, I've brought

someone with me that you knew from a long time ago—do you remember him?'

Denovan squatted down beside her. 'I was only a lad when you came to cook for my father and Frank and me. I loved your hot scones with the home-made jam you made!'

Nellie stared up at him, and gradually a smile appeared on her lined face. 'Denovan…young tearaway!' She lifted her frail hand and clutched his arm. 'Eh… good…good boy!'

Kerry slipped a cuff round the old lady's arm and began to take her blood pressure. 'Fancy you recognising him after all these years—that's a pretty good effort!'

Nellie actually chuckled, a mischievous sparkle returning to her eyes. 'Still…very handsome!'

'You'll be making him big-headed,' remarked Kerry with a grin, unwinding the cuff. 'BP's a bit low—one hundred and five over seventy,' she murmured to Denovan. She looked up at Betty standing rigidly with her hands to her mouth. 'Does your mother's speech sound any better than when you first came back?'

Betty brushed a tear from her eye and nodded. 'Yes…much better. At least she's saying something—she couldn't say anything before, although she was trying to. Is she going to be all right, Doctor?'

'Hopefully she'll be feeling better very soon. Why don't you go and put on the kettle and we'll have a nice cup of tea?'

Oh, the wonderful calming effects of making tea

and drinking it when there was a crisis! Betty trotted off with alacrity, already feeling more in command of herself by doing something constructive.

'What do you think, Denovan?' asked Kerry.

'Nellie's speech has obviously been affected, but it's not very marked dysphasia. I think it's transient and she's getting it back,' he said thoughtfully. 'Her limb movement seems OK. I guess you're right and she's had a slight TIA. Let's see what her swallowing reflex is like and then perhaps give her an aspirin to dissolve any clot.'

'Fine. Can we get her in a sitting position first?'

Denovan pushed a chair behind Nellie and between them they managed to prop her up against the seat of the chair with a cushion behind her back. The colour had come back into the old lady's cheeks and she looked at the two doctors in a resigned way.

'So…am I going to live?' she said slowly.

'Of course you are! Just take a sip of water for us.'

'Water?' said Nellie with spirit. 'I want some tea and a biscuit!'

It was obvious that Nellie was improving rapidly and Kerry laughed. 'Have the water first, Nellie—we just want to make sure you can swallow it properly. We don't want you choking!'

Betty returned with a tray of tea and biscuits, looking in a frightened way at her mother as if expecting her to expire any moment. She put the tray down and Kerry got up from Nellie's side and drew Betty slightly away from the patient.

'It's all right, Betty,' she said reassuringly. 'We think your mother's had what we call a TIA or transient ischaemic attack, which is when an artery supplying blood to the brain becomes temporarily blocked.'

'How do you know that's what it is?'

'We can't know absolutely until tests are done,' said Denovan gently. 'But all your mother's symptoms point to that—a very sudden attack of dizziness and disturbance of speech, which starts to come back fairly soon. But we're going to take Nellie to hospital for a check-up.'

'I told you I don't want to go to hospital!' Nellie's voice had surprising strength in it—she'd obviously picked up the word 'hospital'.

'Come on, Nellie, it's unlikely you'll be in overnight, but we've got to make sure we know what's going on.' Denovan turned his most persuasive and sweet smile on her and Nellie subsided with a sigh.

'You doctors, all bullies…' she murmured.

There was a knock at the front door and two burly men in paramedic uniform appeared.

'Hello, there! Sorry we're late. We had to get a farmer to pull us out of the mud at the bottom there. There's still so much mud about. Now, how's the patient?'

Kerry quickly filled him in on Nellie's history, relieved that she wouldn't have to take her to hospital herself. It was much better to be transported by an ambulance with all the equipment in it to help Nellie—oxygen, monitoring of her blood and her reactions.

'I'm sure you want to go with your mother, Betty,'

said Kerry. 'Why don't you get together her night things and toiletries…just in case she has to stay in?'

Nellie didn't hear her last remark as she was too busy trying to tell the paramedics that she was absolutely fine and it was ridiculous that she was going near a hospital.

'You do as you're told,' Denovan instructed her, mock severely. 'That's what you used to tell me when I was young.'

Nellie smiled at him as she was taken out in a wheelchair to the ambulance. 'Cheeky thing,' she mumbled. 'You got a girl yet, young man? About time you did…' She grinned wickedly and pointed to Kerry. 'You won't find a prettier lass around than Dr Latimer…get on with it, lad!'

This time her speech came out as clear as a bell and Denovan flicked a mischievous glance at Kerry. 'I'll work on that advice, Nellie!' He grinned.

'Mum!' said Betty in shocked tones. 'You mustn't say that!'

Then Nellie and Betty went off in the ambulance, and Denovan put his arm round Kerry as they watched the vehicle disappear down the road.

'Still happy?' he asked, looking down at her with that sweet smile and hugging her against him.

'Whoa!' She laughed. 'We need to be a bit discreet, Denovan, especially in a small place like this. People will be talking!'

'Who cares? Does it matter that we're rather fond of each other?'

'Let's not broadcast the fact, that's all,' she said

lightly. 'You'll be gone tomorrow and who knows? You may decide to take up that new contract for television work.'

He looked at her gravely. 'Suppose I did—suppose the terms were so incredible that it would be difficult to refuse? Why don't you think about working in London? You'd easily get a job, and we could be together.'

It was a tempting thought, and rather exciting. She'd be able to go out with Denovan properly then, with no small community following their every move or a disapproving Frank nearby. She'd be a completely free agent. She almost laughed at the thought—how mad was that, to hare off to an unknown future in the hope that after one passionate kiss her relationship with Denovan might be permanent?

Kerry looked down the little main street of Braxton. It still looked a muddy mess, and many houses still stood empty even a couple of weeks after the flood. So much still to be done, so many lives disrupted, businesses ruined. Whatever her dilemmas, thought Kerry resolutely, the village people were going through a crisis with worries much worse than hers, and she would do her level best to help them.

She shook her head. 'No, Denovan, I can't do that. I love Braxton and the people here. They've been so kind to me, especially since Andy died. I'm going to do all I can to help them and try and repay some of their kindness—they deserve that at least. I feel I belong here. Do you understand?'

He hugged her to him. 'You're right—why should I

suggest you leave this beautiful part of the world because of me? And what did I say before? I'm not going to give up on you, Kerry. And I'm taking you out tonight. It'll be somewhere special so I've asked Daphne to babysit. And it won't be a "farewell" dinner, just a taste of things to come, I hope!'

And she laughed up at him, her heart leaping with the prospect of a romantic evening with Denovan—and yet her happiness was mixed with a flickering doubt that he might seem to have a better future in London than in Braxton Falls.

CHAPTER EIGHT

KERRY looked doubtfully at her reflection in the mirror. Was the coral silk dress she'd bought for her cousin's wedding a little over the top for a meal out in the country? She adjusted the straps slightly—perhaps it revealed more cleavage than she remembered, but she knew the vibrant colour suited her, and she wanted to look every bit as glamorous as the women Denovan was used to dating in London, didn't she? Why shouldn't she pull all the stops out for the first proper date she'd been on for over a year with a gorgeous guy she might not see again?

She gave a little twirl, liking the feel of the fluted skirt as it rippled out around her legs, and a little shiver of excitement whipped through her—for once she had something to dress up for! She bent nearer the mirror to check on her make-up and added a touch of blusher to her cheeks and a quick spray of perfume on her wrists.

In the mirror her eyes looked large, sparkling with excitement and something else—perhaps anticipation? She was only too aware that a man like Denovan wasn't going to be satisfied with a passionate kiss at the end of the evening—after what had happened two days ago they both knew that there was a sexual tension between them that could only lead one way. Would she go along with that? She wanted to, of course. More than anything in the whole world she longed to be made love to by Denovan—and probably, she reminded herself, so did many, many other women! Was she going to allow that to happen knowing that this might be the first and last time he took her out?

She frowned into the mirror as if her reflection would give her the answer. Should she go with the flow and enjoy her time with Denovan while it lasted, or was she risking her heart falling for a playboy doctor? Then just as she started to put in her favourite pair of drop earrings, the doorbell rang.

'Who can that be? Whoever it is I hope they don't take too long about it,' Kerry muttered crossly.

Denovan had taken Archie round to Daphne's house as the little boy had pleaded to stay with them the night so he could play with their trains, and Denovan was due back any minute to take her out to the restaurant. With an impatient sigh she ran down the stairs and went to answer the door, hoping it wasn't a medical emergency—one of the drawbacks about living in the centre of the village was that she was far too accessible! She opened the front door then stared with incredulity at the frail figure on the door step.

'F-Frank!' she stuttered. 'What on earth are you doing here? I thought they were going to keep you in for a few more days?'

He shook his head. 'I feel much better and I'm sick of lounging about in the hospital so I decided to take a taxi home and it's waiting for me now, but I wanted to see you first. I'm only staying for a minute.' His eyes travelled over her glamorous dress. 'Wow!' he said appreciatively. 'You look wonderful. What's the occasion?'

'Don't stand on the doorstep, Frank, for goodness' sake. Come in.' Kerry stood to one side and he stepped past her into the little living room.

Frank sat down on one of the chairs. 'You haven't answered me. Is there something special on?'

'I've been asked out to dinner, so I thought I'd wear the dress I was going to wear at the wedding in Tobago.'

'Oh, Kerry, I'm sorry about that. Because of my accident you had to cancel, didn't you?'

'It's not important—the main thing is that you're back on the road to recovery.' She looked at him sternly. 'You're not thinking of working yet, I hope?'

'That's what I needed to speak to you about,' Frank said. 'I realise I must give it a little while longer to work full time yet, but you can't carry the burden all yourself.'

'I can manage…'

'Denovan's going back tomorrow, isn't he? I imagine you'll miss his help. Has he managed to slot in OK?'

'We've worked well together—and the patients like him very much.'

'Oh, yes,' said Frank lightly, and with a smile to soften his words, 'I can imagine he's gone down a storm with our female patients. Denovan always has a host of groupies following him, like bees round a honey pot really.' He laughed. 'I believe he's quite a ladies' man. I expect that's one of the reasons he's become such a celebrity.'

It was true, thought Kerry wryly. Denovan was gorgeous, and it was no good assuming that he'd lead the life of a monk when he returned to London.

'Everyone likes him, Frank, not just the women!'

'You've not been tempted yourself, then?' asked Frank with a teasing grin.

Kerry hoped the blush that she felt rising in her face wasn't too apparent—obviously Frank was just trying to rib her, but she wasn't going to admit to him that she had feelings for Denovan, too!

She ignored his remark and said briskly, 'Actually, it's been a great relief to have someone here to help out. Now, how about a cup of tea? And what about your house? If you'd told me you were coming home I'd have stocked up your fridge for you and put the heating on.'

'That's kind of you, but I managed to get in touch with my cleaner and she's got the house ready. I really came round to put a suggestion to you. How about if I were to come in for two hours every day?'

'Don't be silly, Frank, it's only two weeks since your operation…'

Frank held up his hand. 'Hear me out, Kerry. I need something to do. I can't bear lolling about the house all day without a purpose. At least I'll be able to sort out the paperwork, see the occasional patient perhaps—nothing too taxing. And I really do feel so much better.'

'I think it's most unwise…'

There were sounds of footsteps outside and then the front door opened and Denovan came in. He stopped short when he saw Frank, his smile fading from his face, but his voice was reasonably civil when he spoke.

'So you're back! I certainly didn't expect you to be discharged yet,' he observed.

'Oh, I'm well on the road to recovery—back to normal. I'm not spending any more time in hospital so I discharged myself,' said Frank equably.

'Don't you think that's rather foolish?' exclaimed Denovan bluntly. 'Your head's had a hell of a battering.'

Frank laughed. 'I know what I'm doing, Denovan. Anyway, I believe you're leaving tomorrow? Back to being a celebrity hot-shot doc, I suppose? I dare say you've missed all the attention you get in London in a little place like Braxton.'

Although his tone was light and inoffensive, Kerry looked at Denovan, wondering if he would rise to his brother's teasing. Denovan's face darkened, his fists bunched hard in his pockets.

'What do you mean by that, Frank?' he growled. 'I haven't missed London. I've enjoyed my time here—but I can tell it's time to go back now you're on the scene.'

'Don't go back on my account, dear brother,' said Frank smoothly. 'I believe you've done an excellent job here. Charmed everyone as usual!'

Denovan's eyes glinted dangerously. 'Don't patronise me, please!'

'I'm not!' protested Frank. 'I'm very grateful to you for helping out.'

Kerry looked from one man to the other. Although Frank had been very pleasant to all intents and purposes, she could feel the tension between them, especially from Denovan. Suddenly the atmosphere seemed to crackle with hostility and to Kerry's eyes it looked as if the brothers were almost enjoying sparring with each other, winding each other up.

She stepped forward and said lightly, 'Now, Denovan, I'm sure Frank wasn't patronising you.'

Denovan whipped round. 'Please don't enter into it,' he snapped. 'I know very well what Frank's implying.'

Kerry stared at him, her mouth open. The charming Denovan had disappeared and in his place was the dour, taciturn man she'd first spoken to on the phone after Frank's accident.

She shrugged. 'I just don't understand why you're at daggers drawn with your brother—and I don't want to know. I just think it's a pity that you can't forgive and forget whatever it was that happened between you.'

'I can never forget what he did,' snarled Denovan.

Frank's benign expression changed, and his eyes became cold. 'Always harking back, aren't you? But, then, you always were a mummy's boy!' he said mockingly. 'To be honest, your mother was no better than she should have been…'

There was a stunned silence, except for Kerry's horrified intake of breath.

'How dare you say that?' said Denovan, his voice

dangerously quiet. 'My mother made mistakes, sure, but she was unhappy.'

'You always blame me, Denovan—I'm no saint, but it's about time you stopped accusing me of ruining your life. Get over it, for God's sake!'

The two men glared angrily at each other, their fists clenched, and Denovan stepped forward as if to punch his brother. Any minute now, thought Kerry, they'd be literally at each other's throats! She put her hand up as she stepped between them and looked at them severely.

'Will you two listen to yourselves? Stop hurting each other like this! You should be utterly ashamed, both of you, behaving like street kids. It's appalling.'

Denovan shrugged and stepped back, and Kerry took a deep breath.

'Frank didn't come to rile you, Denovan—he merely came to say he'd do a few hours a week to help out until he's stronger. It's not what I'd advise, but he knows all the implications as much as we do—and if he really wants to, I'm grateful. And now I'll go and make some tea.'

Frank stood up. 'Not for me, thanks, Kerry. My taxi's waiting.' His gaze flickered over Denovan's tall figure, dressed in an open-necked white shirt and jacket and lightweight trousers, and he added with a tight smile, 'And you're obviously the person taking Kerry out to dinner now. Where are you off to?'

'The Farmer's Plough,' said Denovan dourly.

Frank looked from him to Kerry and raised an eyebrow, then nodded slowly. 'Ah…I see. Very upmarket.

Well…have a good evening. I'll speak to you tomorrow, Kerry.'

He gave a brief nod to Denovan and went out.

There was a short silence then Kerry observed angrily, 'You acted like a schoolboy—can't you try and behave together? I know you feel he's done you a great wrong, but—'

'You know nothing about the situation between us,' rasped Denovan, his eyes bright with anger.

'Maybe I don't,' retorted Kerry, 'but at least remember Frank's been seriously ill.'

That familiar closed look came over Denovan's face and he replied stonily, 'And he's a fool to discharge himself so early.'

'Well, I suppose he knows how he feels—and he was good enough to offer to help me out a bit.'

Denovan raised an eyebrow. 'If he thinks he can help, he damn well ought to. He's put you to a lot of inconvenience.'

Kerry sighed—there seemed no way he could be reconciled with his brother, and she didn't want to spoil an evening she'd been looking forward to so much by bickering. *Oh, dear,* she thought crossly, *we've started off the evening on the wrong foot.* She looked at Denovan's thunderous face and wondered how they were going to get through the next two hours in a pleasant manner.

'Look,' she said crisply, her eyes sparking angrily across at him, 'if you'd rather not go out tonight after all, that's fine by me—but I certainly don't want to sit in front of an angry man for the rest of the evening. I know you brothers have some sort of issue between you, and you may not think it's any of my business, but frankly it affects me inasmuch as it makes you disgracefully bad-tempered!'

Denovan scowled. 'So you think it's all my fault, do you? I'm to blame, despite Frank making the most crass remarks?'

'Yes,' conceded Kerry. 'What he said about your mother was very hurtful. But he's been ill—you don't try and hit a man who's just come out of hospital, for heaven's sake,' she snapped. 'Besides, he's always been perfectly pleasant to me—I can't imagine why you rile each other so. Even when I first rang you up to tell you about his accident, you were incredibly unsympathetic.'

'Then perhaps I should tell you,' growled Denovan. 'Stop you jumping to the most unfair conclusions.'

Kerry looked at him icily. 'Perhaps you should. At the moment it all seems so childish and completely inexplicable, scoring points off each other like juveniles.'

They stared at each other angrily, a brief silence between them, and Kerry bit her lip, suddenly wondering how it had come to this—two people who'd exchanged the most passionate kisses two days before now shouting at each other so angrily. Denovan brushed a hand through his hair in exasperation, leaving it standing in rough spikes over his head.

'Oh, hell,' he muttered, 'it all happened a long time ago now.'

'What did?'

He was silent for a second or two, looking down at

the floor as if psyching himself up to tell her, then he looked at Kerry directly and said bluntly, 'If you really want to know why Frank and I fell out, I'll tell you. Many years ago, your precious Frank seduced my young, vulnerable mother. My father found out and, ashamed and terrified, she fled from home. I never saw her again.' His voice was harsh. 'There! Does that convince you that I have some reason to dislike my dear half-brother?'

For a moment or two Kerry could find no words in response as she gazed at Denovan in horror. Eventually she stammered, '*F-Frank? Frank* seduced your mother? How do you know?'

'After my father's death I was going through his papers and I found his journal—it was all written down meticulously there.'

Kerry looked at him mutely, devastated for the young Denovan, never seeing his mother again, and learning about her infidelity with his half-brother.

Denovan watched her expression and sighed. 'Oh, I didn't know at the time it happened, of course—I was ten years old and was told that my parents had split up because my mother had had to leave. You can imagine how that rocked my world. I was a very sad young boy during my school days. I did have one letter from my mother saying that she would come back one day, but that never happened…'

His voice drifted away, his sad words hanging in the air, poignant, tragic. Kerry shook her head, hardly able to believe what she was hearing. She looked compassionately at his sad face, half-shadowed in the small room. 'Oh, Denovan,' she said softly. 'I'm so sorry.'

'Do you really want to hear this sob story?' Denovan said wearily. 'It doesn't show my family in a very good light, I'm afraid.'

'But you must tell me,' said Kerry, putting a hand on his arm. 'It'll help me understand why you and Frank seem to be at each other's throats.'

He sighed and started to pace the floor. 'Very well… My mother was very young when she had me—barely twenty years old—and it was soon obvious that the marriage was a disaster. She had been my father's receptionist and I suppose she saw marriage to the village GP as a step up in her humdrum life. After my father's first wife died I guess he was lonely, and although I suppose he loved my mother in his way, they didn't have a happy marriage.'

'Oh, my,' breathed Kerry, dumbfounded by the story. She sat down on the sofa abruptly. 'It's the most tragic story.'

'My unhappy mother was looking for comfort and perhaps she thought she'd found it with Frank. OK, she was a bit older than he was, but her confidence had been shattered by my father. Frank started an affair with her, then dumped her when our father found out.' Denovan's expression was stony. 'It's no good crying about it. I don't think I've ever told anyone before… it all seemed so sordid, something to keep to oneself. It's something I try and forget, but when I see Frank, it brings it all back.'

Kerry shook her head and said gently, 'Where Frank's concerned, it's still very raw. Perhaps it helps to talk about it.'

'Maybe you're right.'

'I suppose Frank's nose was pushed severely out of joint when you came along—he'd lost his own mother and he resented the new baby and woman in his father's life,' suggested Kerry.

'Perhaps,' admitted Denovan. 'But we never got on—the incident with my mother was just a climax to our bad feeling for each other.' He leaned back against the wall and folded his arms, looking down at Kerry sardonically.

'So there you have it,' he said matter-of-factly. 'The saga of the O'Mara family. When I discovered the truth in Dad's journal years later, I confronted Frank and I'm afraid the resulting row left scars between us that have never healed and probably never will. You see, I had to stand up for my mother whatever the circumstances.'

'I…I don't know what to say,' said Kerry at last. 'The Frank I know as a colleague is easy to work with and works hard himself. I feel sorry that both of you had an unhappy past, but you were young then and surely you aren't going to let this hatred you both feel for each other destroy the rest of your lives?'

'It's so hard to brush it aside, Kerry, but perhaps one day we'll manage to bury our differences. I guess Frank and I've been at each other's throats so long that we don't realise the impact it has on everyone else—we've got used to it.'

'So no chance of you coming back to Braxton Falls, then?' she said lightly.

He hesitated for a moment, fiddling with his watch strap. 'I love Braxton, but it would be difficult—you can see that, can't you?'

Then he put his hands on Kerry's shoulders, looking down at her with those amazing blue eyes of his that made thinking of anything else but his electric presence impossible.

'Look, sweetheart,' he said softly, 'let's start the evening again, shall we? I'm sorry about what happened with Frank and I just now. I don't want to think about him at the moment. You're a much more interesting subject to me right now. I want to concentrate on you. You look absolutely delectable and if I wasn't so hungry I'd suggest we didn't bother with any food tonight. Please don't let's spoil our last night together.'

Their last night together. It sounded so final, something over before it had hardly begun. She couldn't let Denovan leave on a sour note, thought Kerry—she wanted their last meeting to be a happy one. Even the light touch of his hands on her shoulders sent a tremor through her body, and the tension between them melted away. She stood up and took Denovan's arm, smiling up at him.

'Let's get going, then,' she said. 'I'm starving.'

The Farmer's Plough was only a five-minute walk away from Kerry's cottage. It stood at the top of a hill overlooking the village and the pretty valley with its patchwork of fields, an old barn converted into a restaurant. Oak beams criss-crossed the high ceiling and there were cosy tables in intimate little alcoves around the walls, while bigger tables occupied the centre of the room. Soft golden lights on the tables gave the whole place a warm and cosy feel, and in one corner a pianist played softly by a small dance floor.

'This is lovely, Denovan,' murmured Kerry, looking round the room with pleasure, suddenly feeling her mood lifting. 'Who told you about it?'

He grinned. 'I asked Daphne where she thought I could take you for a farewell meal. She said this was the best place in the area, though it's not long been open.'

They were led to one of the little alcoves, where a waiter pulled out chairs for them and with a flourish placed napkins on their laps.

'I feel this is our own private little room.' Kerry smiled.

Denovan looked at her covertly as she studied the menu. In the glow from the table lamp Kerry's soft skin looked peachy cream, and the curve of her full breasts under the neckline of her dress was tantalising. She looked a knock-out in that sexy dress! He took a deep breath and tried to concentrate on choosing some food for himself. This time next week he'd be in London, plunging back into life in the fast lane, possibly back on a new television show with a juicy contract to go with it. How different from the past two weeks in the idyllic countryside of Braxton, working alongside one of the most beautiful women he'd ever met. He remembered how reluctant he'd been to come back—and how surprisingly happy he'd been while he'd been working in Braxton. He was going to miss Kerry very much—it wouldn't be easy, adjusting to life without her.

He had ordered champagne and the waiter poured it into their two glasses. Denovan raised his glass. 'To the future,' he said with a smile. 'It's been a great two weeks, especially this last weekend!'

'To the future,' agreed Kerry, but a shiver of sadness flickered through her. 'I hope it all works out for you in London—and I really want to thank you for your help over the past two weeks. I couldn't have managed without you.'

'I was glad to help.' He paused for a second, holding his wine glass up to the light and letting the bubbles swirl round, then smiled at her again. 'Actually, I should be thanking you. I've enjoyed being back in general practice, even if there has been a lot of water around!'

Kerry felt her heart turn over. When he smiled so engagingly he looked so gorgeous. His eyes danced and held hers, sending a familiar flash of response through her body. It wasn't fair, she thought mournfully, that a man she liked so much should be vanishing from her life when she was just getting to know him. And now she knew the story behind the two brothers' antipathy towards each other, she supposed there was no chance that Denovan would want to come back to Braxton. She would miss him so much—and also little Archie, with his mischievous ways. How quiet her world would seem without them.

In the background the piano was playing a rather dreamy, romantic tune and their eyes locked over the table. Were they thinking the same thing? Kerry wondered. Was this evening to be a prelude to something more permanent or, as she suspected, the finale to something that had only just started? Would this be their first and last date? Denovan watched the grave expression on her face, and as if he'd read her thoughts stood up and held out his hand. 'Cheer up, Kerry,' he murmured. 'You've got to work for your supper. Let's have a dance.'

He pulled her closely to him and put his face to hers—and she forgot about being gloomy, because her body was pressed to the hard wall of his chest. It was heavenly to feel the beat of his heart against hers, the slight roughness of his chin against her cheek, his hand firmly in the small of her back, as they swayed silently together to the gentle rhythm of the music.

But even through the longing of desire as they danced, Kerry decided firmly that this was as far as it should go. Frank's words about Denovan being known as a ladies' man stuck in her mind, so although every nerve in her body was responding like a light switch to his fizzing sexiness, on no account was she going to finish the evening by going to bed with Denovan, only to be just another conquest in his busy social life when he left for London!

It was a cool night, but the sky was clear and like a velvet cloth sparkling with myriad stars. It had been a lovely evening after all, and it had passed very quickly—too quickly, thought Kerry ruefully. She couldn't stop thinking as the evening progressed that it was Denovan's last night, and there was only an hour or two left with just the two of them together.

They held hands as they sauntered down the hill and past the little shops, some of them still boarded up after the floods.

'It doesn't seem that it was such a short time ago that we rescued Sirie from the fallen bridge,' Denovan commented. 'So much has happened since then.'

It was hard to believe that then she hadn't known Denovan at all, reflected Kerry, whereas now she knew so much about his sad background and the circumstances that had torn his family apart. No wonder he was wary of having a serious commitment after his experience with the women in his life—he'd been let down too many times.

Denovan slipped his arm round her shoulders and smiled down at her as they went up the path to the cottage. 'How about a nightcap before we go up?' he suggested.

Kerry swallowed hard—this was where she would be very firm and say a brisk goodnight then march up to bed, she thought. She turned the key in the front door without answering, and he bent down and kissed the nape of her neck.

They stepped through the door and Denovan pulled her towards him before she could get to the safety of the stairs.

'How lovely that for once we're alone,' he murmured.

'With no one to interrupt us.' He put his hands on her hair and pulled out the pins that held it in its chignon so that it tumbled in disarray round her shoulders. 'Ah,' he said in satisfaction. 'I've been longing to do that all evening.'

Kerry put up a hand to push her hair back. 'You…you shouldn't have done that,' she said reprovingly.

Denovan laughed. 'Why not? You look sensational with your hair down.'

Then he held her at arm's length for a few seconds, his eyes sweeping over her. 'Oh, Kerry,' he said huskily, 'you are utterly beautiful. We've had so short a time together.'

She wanted to cry out, *Then stay here! Stay with me—forget London!* But she couldn't bring herself to do it.

He bent his head and his lips touched hers softly at first, then more passionately, moving down her neck with the softest of butterfly kisses. A heady, disorientated feeling swept through Kerry—her good resolutions seemed to be dissolving rapidly.

It was crazy. Denovan was leaving Braxton and might never return, and however much she longed to be desired and loved again, she mustn't give in. It would be too easy at this moment to capitulate completely.

'I've got a busy day tomorrow—I must get a good night's sleep,' she said breathlessly, pulling away from him.

He dropped his arms to his sides and nodded. 'Of

course…and I've got an early start, so perhaps we'd better turn in.'

Their eyes met and held in the silence of the room, and then, as she'd known he would, he moved towards her again and put his arms round her, and suddenly she didn't care if he wasn't looking for commitment and that he was going back to London the next day. She wanted him now and to hell with the consequences.

'I've been wanting to do this all evening,' whispered Denovan. 'I know we only have such a short time…' His voice trailed off as he nuzzled into her neck, then gently he pulled her down onto the floor.

'I thought we were going to have an early night?' teased Kerry.

'Change of plan,' he said with a grin.

Then gently he peeled the straps of the coral dress from her shoulders—and she did nothing to stop him, just watched as he tossed his jacket to one side and tore off his shirt. He propped himself up on his arms, looking down at her with his startling blue eyes dark with desire.

'I truly didn't think the evening would end like this,' he whispered. 'But it sort of seems a fitting way to say *adieu*.'

'A perfect way,' breathed Kerry.

She stretched her limbs under him, luxuriating in his strong-muscled frame on hers, every nerve in her body seeming to tingle with anticipation. Had she ever felt this powerful explosion of passion with Andy? Unfair, unfair to judge. She couldn't think of that. She was with

Denovan now, so skilled at arousing her to a fever-pitch of desire, his hands exploring her most secret places, his own craving for her only too obvious.

He drew her to him and said throatily, 'My beautiful, fiery Kerry—how wonderful is this?'

And afterwards, as he held her in his arms, she felt a marvellous sense of release, of letting the past go. From now on she'd look to the future—and surely, after what had just happened, it had to include Denovan. This couldn't be the end of the story, could it?

As if in answer to her unspoken question, he brushed away the strands of hair that had fallen across her forehead, and looked deep into her eyes. 'Don't let this be goodbye,' he murmured. 'Let's just say it's a work in progress!'

CHAPTER NINE

How quiet the cottage seemed! And no toy cars lying about, ready to send her flying when she stepped on them, no shirts festooning the rail in the bathroom, only one coffee cup on the drainer by the sink in the kitchen. Kerry looked mournfully around at the empty room. Denovan and Archie had left the day before for London, and she felt a horrible void of loneliness.

It was only two nights since the momentous revelations about the brothers' past had been disclosed. It had been a bad start to an evening she'd been so excited about, and then miraculously it had improved beyond all imagination! In her mind's eye she recalled the way Denovan had looked at her in the restaurant, the way he'd held her when they'd danced, but most of all the end of the evening when they'd made such passionate and wild love.

Had she made the biggest mistake in her life, making love to a man who'd said he didn't want a permanent relationship? Too late, she thought wryly. She had done and now she couldn't help wondering if she was joining a long line of his ex-girlfriends.

She'd had a phone call from Denovan when he'd arrived in London to say that he'd been offered a big contract to appear daily on a talk show where he'd be required to interview people and comment on health issues. He was excited about the prospect because it seemed to involve more than his previous work—and the salary was huge! He begged Kerry to come and see him the following weekend.

'I'm so sorry, Denovan, I'm busy this weekend and my mother may come up some time. She wants to tell me about my cousin's wedding.'

'Pity. I thought we could celebrate my new job—if I finally decide to accept it,' he said.

Gloomily Kerry wondered if she would feel like celebrating something that would anchor him even more firmly in London. And next Saturday would be her birthday. Somehow celebrating that by herself didn't seem any fun at all.

She sipped her breakfast coffee, now grown cold, and gazed unseeingly across the kitchen. She felt in limbo, not sure of Denovan's feelings for her and yet certain that when they were together they clicked like two pieces in a jigsaw. Then gradually the clock on the wall swam into focus, and to her horror revealed that it was nearly eight o'clock! Her first patient would be in at eight-thirty. She grabbed her coat and bag and ran out of the house to the surgery.

'So how was your evening at the Farmer's Plough?' Frank O'Mara had come into her room as she was reading through the emails on her computer before she started her working day. 'Did it live up to expectations?'

'Yes, oh, yes, it was lovely, thank you.'

Kerry tried to sound composed, but the mention of her night with Denovan made her heartbeat rocket. Of course it hadn't been just lovely—it had been sensational, and far beyond her expectations.

Frank sat on the side of the desk, watching her face. 'Denovan always knew how to give a girl a good time,' he remarked blandly. 'I suppose he'll be coming back to see you in Braxton?'

'I've no idea, Frank.' Kerry's voice was cold—she was a little irritated by Frank's frequent allusions to Denovan's prowess with women. 'I believe he may be offered a very good job on one of the TV channels so he probably won't have time.'

'Perhaps you'll go and see him?'

'What? Oh, I don't know. There's lots to do here at the moment.'

Frank nodded, smiling. 'Oh, well, back to business as usual.' He stood up from the desk and said briskly, 'Right, I think we should look into getting a permanent part-time partner—we're going to need someone else even when I come back full time, what with the new housing estate up the road pushing up the patient numbers. I'd like a meeting at the end of next week to discuss that and other matters if that's OK with you?'

'Of course. It's about time we reviewed things. I haven't had time for the administration aspect of the practice lately.'

Kerry was glad he'd got off the subject of Denovan and on to the concerns of the practice. She felt on easier ground when she was talking to Frank about work and not her private life. They'd always had a cordial business relationship, but except for drinks with the rest of the staff at Christmas or New Year didn't see each other socially. He was much older than her and had been married until an acrimonious divorce a year ago. Frank turned at the door before he left the room. 'By the way,' he said casually, 'if you're free this weekend, I'd like to take you out for dinner—just a little thank-you for all you've done for me while I've been in hospital.'

Kerry looked at him, startled, and for some reason a little uncomfortable at the thought of an evening by herself with Frank. It may have been many years ago when he was a young man that the incident between him and Denovan's mother had occurred, and it probably hadn't been all his fault, nevertheless, Denovan felt Frank had ruined his life—she'd feel a little awkward going out to dinner with his half-brother.

'Oh, really, Frank, there's no need to entertain me. As long as you're feeling better, that's reward enough. And actually my mother's coming over on Sunday with some friends.'

'What about Saturday night, then?' Frank persisted, then put his hand up as if to pre-empt anything Kerry might say. 'Please! I'd like to—it's only a small thanks for carrying on so gallantly when I was fool enough to injure myself.'

Kerry sighed inwardly. For some reason she felt

flat, not in the mood for going out—especially not with Frank.

He looked at her assessingly as if trying to read her thoughts, then said lightly, 'I hope you're not prejudiced against me. Whatever Denovan said, I don't seduce young women, you know. It really wasn't as Denovan told it!'

Kerry's face reddened slightly. 'That's nothing to do with it,' she remarked, crossing her fingers behind her back at the white lie.

'Well, then?'

Kerry thought of the long succession of weekends that stretched out before her, blank and horribly empty. Perhaps after all it might be a good idea to go out for the evening with Frank—he was only trying to show how grateful he was. And just because he'd asked her out for a meal it hardly meant a lifelong commitment!

She sighed. 'Well, thanks, then, Frank. I'll look forward to that.'

Frank gave a little nod of satisfaction and went out.

Kerry pushed all thoughts of both O'Mara brothers out of her head, and settled down to the everyday life of a country GP.

The woman sitting opposite Kerry was slim, well dressed and very attractive—the kind of woman who carried herself with poise and confidence, who sat on committees and volunteered for charities. Only she wasn't poised at the moment. She twisted a handkerchief round in her hands perpetually, her face seemed pinched and her eyes were red, as if she'd been crying.

Kerry thought she could take an educated guess as to why Lady Bethany Hood was in such a state—it had only been a few days ago that her husband, Sir Vernon, had come in to confess that he was a drug user and to ask Kerry's help to kick the habit. He'd told her he'd already confessed all to his wife.

'What's the matter, Lady Hood?' she said gently. 'I very rarely see you in the surgery.'

'Please call me Bethany.' The woman put a hand up to a stray lock of hair over her forehead and brushed it back nervously. 'Oh, dear, I don't know really why I came. I doubt there's anything anyone can do anyway…'

'Why don't you try me?' suggested Kerry. She pushed a box of tissues over the desk towards the distraught woman, who now had tears pouring down her face.

'You…you're not going to believe this. I couldn't believe it at first…'

Her voice trailed off and she looked at the floor as if looking for the words to convey her distress. Kerry waited patiently. It was no good hurrying someone on in these circumstances.

Then Bethany took a deep breath and said shakily, 'It's my husband…you probably know he's the MP for this area? Recently he seems to have changed. He used to have quite a sunny disposition, but now he seems moody and taciturn. I'd thought it was pressure of work—he's home so seldom and seems to be on so many committees. Then he…he told me out of the blue that he's been taking drugs…he's addicted to them!' Bethany dabbed at her eyes with the tissue. 'I feel as horrified as though he'd threatened me with a gun, and completely bewildered…'

She stopped talking for a second and looked perceptively at Kerry. 'I guess he's already been to see you, hasn't he?' Then she sighed. 'Don't answer that—it's patient confidentiality, isn't it? I suppose I must be thankful that he realised he had to get professional help.'

'At least he has told you—that must have taken some courage.'

Bethany looked at Kerry sceptically. 'Courage, you think? More like he's just frightened I'll find out from someone else…the papers perhaps! The fact is, Doctor…' her sad eyes met Kerry '…I've put up with a lot over the years one way or the other, but I never dreamed that he'd resort to drugs. I love him. Don't ask me why, but I do, despite everything, and I'm not going to let my marriage break up without a fight. I want to know if it's possible for this rehab to work and how I can help him.'

Vernon Hood didn't know how lucky he was to have such a strong wife, reflected Kerry. 'I think with your support he'll do well,' she said. 'He'll have bad days and good days, and you'll have to ride those out. Make sure he goes to the centre—they'll need to do regular blood tests to check that he's keeping his side of the bargain.'

Bethany nodded and said bitterly, 'I can't understand him—a man who has everything fooling around with things I'd be shocked that my teenage son would take, let alone a mature man.' Her voice hardened. 'He says he's going to rehab and he'll never take them again but I don't know that I believe him.'

Kerry leaned back in her chair, thoughtfully drumming her pencil on the desk. 'You know, Bethany, this might be a good time to get your husband more involved in local issues. What could be better at this time than when everyone's trying to get back to normal after the flood? It might take his mind off his problem. I'm thinking perhaps of a fundraising event for people who've been very badly affected.'

Bethany said slowly, 'Could be a good idea. You mean like a garden party or something? I suppose we could have it in our garden—invite the whole village to come, and have cake stalls, things like that!'

'Absolutely. People need something to bring them together after the trauma Braxton's suffered. And if you need an extra pair of hands, I'll be willing to help.'

Bethany gave a watery smile. 'You know, this is perhaps the focus that could help Vernon and I get together again. He's not been involved in many local issues recently…' Her voice trailed off, then she stood up resolutely and said, 'I feel so much better. Thank you so much for listening to me.'

'Any time you need me, I'm here. As I said, you will go through bad patches, but please don't struggle on thinking no one can give you any help.'

Bethany looked quite different as she left the room, walking with quite a spring in her step, obviously motivated to cope with her husband and start a new project. *Let's hope my advice works,* thought Kerry wryly.

The Pear and Partridge was the local pub and had been badly affected by the flood, but had now reopened again. Frank and Kerry had to fight their way through a jolly crowd of people round the bar to one of the tables at the end of the room.

'I'm sorry this isn't in quite the same league as the Farmer's Plough,' apologised Frank. 'The trouble is, I can't drive for a while, and the Farmer's Plough was booked up.'

'This is fine, Frank. Don't worry.'

They sat down and Frank smiled at her. 'I'd like to have taken you somewhere more special—I know it's your birthday today.' He reached in his pocket, brought out a slim, gift-wrapped parcel and passed it over the table to her. 'Just a little thought and a sort of thank-you for all your work,' he murmured.

Kerry gazed at it in surprise. 'You shouldn't have done this, Frank.'

He watched as she undid it and pulled out a beautiful silk scarf in soft rainbow colours. 'That's lovely, Frank…very kind.' Her voice trailed off, slightly embarrassed.

He leaned forward over the table. 'I thought it would suit your colouring. And I'm so glad you could come out tonight—it gives us a chance to get to know each other properly. I guess we've been leading different lives.'

'I suppose so,' replied Kerry, rather uneasily. She

didn't know if it was necessary to know each other 'properly' in order to work together—things seemed to be moving on to a more personal footing than she wanted.

She looked at him brightly. 'Anyway, it's a good chance to discuss our thoughts on getting some help in the practice—Liz Ferris is keen for us to get another practice nurse.'

The waiter poured some wine into Frank's glass and he took a sip, nodding his approval of it. 'Oh, I don't think we want to talk shop tonight, do we?' he said easily. 'I'd rather talk about you and how you've been faring this year since poor Andrew's death. I feel I've rather left you to get on with your life since he died. It must have been so difficult for you.'

Why was Frank suddenly bringing this subject up? Kerry didn't want to talk to him about Andy—she knew she'd moved on from that tragedy.

'I've put that behind me, Frank,' she said firmly, taking a long drink of wine.

'Good, good. That's a great step forward. A new life ahead of you!' He smiled broadly at her, a smile that sat strangely with his austere features. 'Now, what would you like to eat?'

'A steak would be nice, with a salad.'

While Frank waved the waiter over, Kerry's mind drifted back to the evening she'd spent with Denovan only a few nights ago and the fizzing electric tension there'd been between them, the way they'd kissed so passionately and then the unbelievably wonderful ending when they'd done much more than kiss. Like the re-winding of a film, she recalled every passionate frame, stamped for ever in her mind—so very different from this mundane evening with Frank.

Frank's voice intruded on her thoughts. 'So, have you heard from Denovan recently?' he asked casually.

'Oh, yes. He's told me he's contemplating taking this new job—quite a good offer, I think.'

Frank nodded, a wry smile on his face. 'Denovan was always born to do well,' he said quietly.

Kerry looked at him in surprise—there was almost a hint of pride in Frank's voice. Perhaps underneath the veiled criticisms and anger with each other, there was a kind of love between them after all.

Kerry took a sip of wine and looked at Frank over the rim of her glass. She took a chance to speak bluntly. 'It can't have been easy, having a young brother and a stepmother suddenly break into your world, Frank. You must have felt very isolated.'

He nodded. 'Yes, that about sums it up. We both have hot tempers, I guess—but I'll be honest. I wish we were closer, and I'm glad and surprised Denovan came up when I was in hospital.' He looked slightly shamefacedly at Kerry. 'We were out of order, quarrelling in front of you the other day, but we find it difficult to communicate.'

'So I've noticed,' said Kerry with a grin.

He smiled back at her, the atmosphere lightening somewhat. 'Changing the subject, I wanted to know if you've ever been to the Opera House in Buxton?'

'Oh, yes, it's absolutely lovely.'

'They've got a very good programme this summer. I wonder if you'd like to come to one of their concerts—I think you'd enjoy it.'

Frank seemed to be making a pass at her, Kerry thought in astonishment. There had never ever been any inkling of that before his accident. She looked across at him appraisingly and saw a lonely, middle-aged and rather sad man, weakened through illness, with no other family except Denovan, and probably suddenly aware how time was passing. How could she get out of any future dates without offending him? She didn't mind being his friend, but she didn't want to encourage him in any other kind of relationship.

'I'm sure I'd love it,' she said vaguely, then tried to change the subject. 'I'm looking forward to seeing my mother tomorrow—I haven't seen her for ages. I thought I'd take her over to Dovedale and Hardwick Hall.'

To her relief their conversation turned to the other delights of Derbyshire and Kerry began to relax.

He'd made it! Driving through London on a Saturday evening had been a nightmare, but once he'd got onto the motorway it had been reasonably free of traffic. Denovan hummed to himself happily as he drew up on the road outside Kerry's cottage. The light was on in the living room, although the curtains were drawn. It was her birthday and he'd been determined to surprise her. He pictured her face as he appeared at the door. He'd learned by chance from Freda that it was Kerry's birthday, when she'd shown him a card she'd got for Kerry that she thought was particularly hilarious. When Kerry had said she couldn't come to London, he'd known he had to see her anyway. Archie had been very happy to stay with his childminder for the night.

Until now he'd come to the conclusion that he would never find anyone he'd love—hadn't really cared whether he did or not. Somehow relationships with women didn't seem to work with him and anyway, with Archie to think of, she had to be an ultra-special person who loved children, and would love Archie especially.

And then he'd met Kerry! During the last few days away from her it had hit him like a thunderbolt that he'd found that special person. He grinned happily. Kerry was perfect—fun, beautiful, kind, and their lovemaking had been wonderful. He wondered if she'd missed him as much as he'd missed her. He couldn't wait to see her—to tell her that he loved her and that he wasn't going to sign that contract after all.

He unclipped his safety belt and was about to open the car door when he noticed two figures strolling up to the front door of the cottage. In the light streaming through the fan light of the door he could see that one of them was Kerry, and the other, to his surprise, was Frank.

'What's she doing with him?' he asked himself. Then he thought that it had to be something to do with work—probably they'd had a meeting at the surgery with the other staff. He would wait to get out of the car until

Frank had gone—he didn't particularly want to see him so soon after their last acrimonious encounter.

He wound down his window to see them more clearly and their voices floated over to him.

Kerry was saying, 'It's been a lovely evening, the food was delicious—and thank you for the lovely present. You really didn't need to buy me anything.'

'It was my pleasure,' Frank replied. 'I've enjoyed every minute of it. I hope we can do it again very soon. Perhaps Buxton Opera House next time?'

Frank leant forward and brushed Kerry's cheek with his lips, and Denovan watched with disbelief and a feeling of angry bewilderment. They obviously hadn't had a meeting regarding work—it had been just the two of them, out for dinner!

Denovan ran a distracted hand through his hair. She knew the background of how things were between him and Frank—how could she, only days later, allow the man to kiss her, arrange future outings? Only two nights ago he and Kerry had been in each other's arms, making passionate love in that very cottage. Surely she was aware that he thought she was very special, that they were more than just good friends?

Denovan stared transfixed at the tableau of the two of them smiling at each other, at Frank patting her cheek before he turned away, and a crashing disappointment overtook him. Denovan had been under the illusion for the past few days that he and Kerry were special to each other, and that there was no one else in her life. It was almost like a betrayal, he reflected bitterly.

Now he knew just why she was so busy that she couldn't come to London this weekend—she was busy dating his brother while he was out of the way! It hadn't taken her long to fasten on to Frank, he thought savagely. Now he came to think of it, she'd often seemed sympathetic towards his brother. Perhaps Frank had always been in her sights, and now he was back from hospital, available, and the coast was clear.

Frank was walking away down the street now. Denovan watched him disappear and stared at the closed door of the cottage. Well, he wasn't going to be cast away like an old glove—off with the old, on with the new! He wanted an explanation—he'd come all the way from London and he wasn't going to creep back without knowing precisely what Kerry was up to!

He leapt out of the car and slammed the door shut, then strode angrily towards the cottage. The light was still on in the lounge and he rapped on the front door. A few seconds later Kerry opened it and a look of amazed delight spread over her face.

'Denovan! What on earth are you doing here?'

For a second he hesitated, stunned again by her beauty, the happy look of welcome on her face, then he pushed past her into the little room. He wasn't going to have a row with her on the doorstep. He whipped round to look at her, his face a grim mask.

'I know now why you were too busy to see me this weekend,' he grated. 'While the cat's away, the mice play! Why didn't you tell me you were involved with Frank, of all people? Why did you lead me on?'

CHAPTER TEN

THERE was deathly silence, except for the ticking of the clock in the kitchen and Denovan's words ringing in the air.

Kerry's welcoming expression changed to one of incredulity. She was speechless for a moment, then she gathered herself together.

'Lead you on?' she said, her horrified eyes wide with disbelief. She shook her head helplessly. 'I don't know what you're talking about,' she said at last.

The blue eyes flashed at her. 'Do me a favour, Kerry—in future tell me the truth!'

Kerry looked at Denovan's thunderous face. Suddenly he'd become the man she'd first encountered over the phone only three weeks ago—arrogant and surly, his charm and charisma put firmly on the back burner. She wasn't about to take that from anybody.

'Don't insult me, Denovan. I've never lied to you!'

'You told me you couldn't come to London because your mother was coming to see you—you never mentioned that the real reason was because you were seeing

Frank. You might have told me that you and he were more than colleagues.'

'I didn't mention it because it isn't true! He kindly asked me out to thank me for all the hard work I've put in while he's been in hospital. And please don't dare come and tell me who I can see and can't see. As far as I'm aware, I'm a free agent.'

His eyes locked with hers stonily. 'So our little liaison the other night meant very little to you, then? I was just a ship passing through the night, a bit of fun, was I?'

'This is utterly ridiculous,' she snapped, treacherous tears of fury and frustration welling up in her eyes. She loved this man, she wanted him like crazy, but not like this, accusing her of betraying him, of treating their lovemaking so lightly.

She drew herself up to her full height and looked at Denovan scornfully. 'I don't have to defend myself. I'd like to know why I can't go out with my practice partner if I want. It's absolutely no one else's business… he's purely a colleague.'

'It didn't look that way. I thought you never went out with him socially?'

'I don't—this is the first time I've had dinner with him. As I said, he was grateful to me. I don't have to apologise to you or anyone for spending an evening with Frank.'

'Don't be fooled by him, Kerry—he's a con man.'

Kerry almost stamped her foot on the floor. 'Oh, for heaven's sake, Denovan, change the record! I'm sick of you both denigrating each other.' She looked at him coldly and pointed to the open door. 'Please leave. If you think I'm untrustworthy, perhaps we'd better call a halt to our friendship.'

Denovan glowered at her. 'Don't worry, Kerry—I know when I'm not wanted. I thought we had something good going between us. Obviously I was wrong.'

This was so unutterably stupid. 'I too thought we had something very special…' Kerry's voice faltered.

'If you'd thought anything of me at all, you wouldn't have gone out with the one man who helped to ruin my life. Why choose Frank, of all people?'

He strode out, and Kerry went to the doorway, her blood boiling with disbelief and anger.

'You can't let the past go, can you?' she shouted as his retreating back. 'This isn't about me and you. This is about you and Frank and what went wrong in the past!'

She watched as he turned to look at her briefly before he got into the car and accelerated away in a spray of pebbles. The hot tears that streamed down her cheeks weren't just tears of anger but of sadness that everything seemed to have gone wrong between them.

It had started to pour with rain, but Denovan hardly noticed as he whipped through the dark countryside.

'What have I done?' he groaned, his hands gripping the steering wheel until the knuckles were white. The image of Kerry's slender figure in the doorway and the heart-rending expression on her face stamped themselves on his mind. 'What a fool I've been…' Cold reality hit him forcefully, sickeningly. 'Kerry's right. I've allowed what happened between Frank and me to ruin any future I might have had with her.'

A lorry blared its horn at him as he rounded a corner in the middle of the road and the vehicle behind flashed its lights. He was in no fit state to drive—he knew that. He drove into a layby and parked the car, then put his arms on the wheel and rested his forehead on them. No doubt about it, Kerry and he were finished, and it was all his fault. How could he have said all those horrible things to her, accusing her of betraying him, telling lies? He loved her, dammit, probably had done almost since the first day they'd met. And now it was all over, his ungovernable, unreasonable behaviour putting an end to any dream he had of marrying the most wonderful woman he'd ever met. No woman would put up with the way he'd treated Kerry.

And why did he hate his brother so? It had been years ago that his mother had left, and after all Frank had still been a teenager. Sadly he reflected that both he and his brother had suffered tragedies, both without mothers and a father who hadn't had the time or the patience to look after them or give them the love and security they needed. He, Denovan, had to learn to forgive and forget. He was poisoning his own life, and had allowed jealousy to destroy any love Kerry might have felt for him.

He gazed bleakly ahead of him through the lashing rain on the windscreen. Sadly he thought that if he wasn't careful he'd be so wrapped up in his own troubles that it would affect his son. He had to pull himself together and restart his life in London, accept the contract and be damn glad he had such a good job. Until three weeks ago he'd not had a thought of leaving

London, and now he'd got to get back to that mind set and pick up where he left off.

Wearily he started the car again and started the long drive back to London.

Somehow Kerry got through the next week, plastering a smile on her face to mask her sadness. She presumed that Denovan had gone straight back to London, because he was certainly nowhere to be seen in Braxton the next day. She felt numb and bewildered that he should imagine she had betrayed him by going out with Frank—and it was so unfair, because she hadn't wanted to go out with Frank anyway!

She decided halfway through the week that she would write to Denovan—emails were too glib somehow. She would explain that she'd had no idea that Frank would look on their evening together as a prelude to other outings: and she would tell Denovan that she could understand why he was upset that she had gone out with his brother, but the evening had meant nothing to her. And finally she resolved that, foolish or not, she would tell Denovan that she loved him—put her cards on the table. Yes, he could be totally unreasonable and he could be arrogant and overbearing, but he could be so tender, so loving and such fun—she wasn't going to let him go out of her life without a fight!

She switched on the television to watch the news as she settled down with paper and pen to compose something she hoped would build bridges between Denovan and herself.

Drumming her pen on the table as she pondered what to write, Kerry vaguely caught the news headlines—a fire in the Midlands, strikes in Europe, a woman who'd received a bravery award… Then a presenter introduced someone who was taking up some important new job. A tall, dark, impossibly good-looking man with startling blue eyes stood by her side. Kerry drew in a breath of shock, dropping her pen in astonishment as a shot of Denovan, debonair and smiling, appeared on the screen!

An excited presenter thrust a microphone under his nose. 'I believe you're the new star who's going to front the new daily magazine programme on health matters?' she stated enthusiastically.

'That's right—we'll be covering concerns that people have over every aspect of health, with advice and information from agencies all over the world. We want to present it from all sorts of places—hospitals, villages in Africa, surgeries in South America—and we're going to make people aware not only of the latest technology but also the old-fashioned remedies that have proved successful.'

'It sounds as if it will be very interesting.'

'I'm sure it will. I'm looking forward to doing it immensely. I'll be travelling all over the world.'

The presenter asked him other questions, but Kerry hardly heard them. She was transfixed, staring at Denovan's image. He looked thinner, slightly drawn, perhaps a bit tired, but he was still the drop-dead gorgeous man who'd made love to her only a few days ago. The man she couldn't get out of her head—or her heart.

Then he gave that familiar heart-stopping smile into the camera, and his figure faded from the screen and a sports item took over. For a few seconds Kerry stared numbly at the screen without seeing anything on it, then slowly she got up and switched off the television.

So Denovan had finally decided to stay in London, to take on this wonderful contract—not that she blamed him for that, but somehow it was so very final. He had said before that he would let her know of his plans—it looked like he wasn't going to bother, and where would he find time for her in his new life? He'd looked cheerful and positive, clearly not suffering as she was.

Kerry snatched up the half-written letter and tore it into shreds. He was starting his life again without her—so she would do the same without him!

The Hoods' garden was a lovely one, with herbaceous borders curving round spacious green lawns that swept down to a small copse. It was late spring, and there was a haze of light green over the hedges and trees, the sun stronger now as it rose higher in the sky.

A bustling crowd filled the lawn, children shrieking with excitement as they bounced on a bouncy castle, and a little roundabout in a corner of the garden was attracting lots of small visitors. In ten days Vernon and Bethany Hood had mobilised an army of volunteers to help raise money for victims of the floods, and there were cake stalls, trestle tables groaning with second-hand books, and a section filled with donated plants to be sold.

There was an air of jollity about the place, a renewed sense of optimism after the tragedy of the flooding, and it seemed the only person who wasn't happy, reflected Kerry gloomily, was her! She fixed a smile on her face as she helped to serve coffee and tea, but inside she felt as churned up as colours in a kaleidoscope—for the whole week she'd been unable to stop thinking of the terrible night when Denovan had appeared and accused her of betraying him. It was so unjust! She hadn't wanted to go out with Frank particularly, but why should she stay in like a nun, just because Denovan wasn't around?

Her future with Denovan had seemed so vague. He'd given her no promises. Surely if he'd really loved her, he'd have told her so? When he'd returned to London with Archie, she'd known that he was contemplating taking this new job, and that perhaps their little love affair wouldn't last as far as he was concerned. But there'd always been hope that he wouldn't drop her completely, and might eventually realise how much she meant to him. Now that hope seemed to have been dashed completely.

Now she'd made up her mind—she was going to get a job somewhere else. Working with Frank and the perpetual reminder of Denovan, by association, was too much for her. She owed the people of Braxton a lot, but they would get someone else who would come to love the area as much as she did, and work with more enthusiasm than she could bring to the village now. She needed a fresh start, something to engage her mind that would obliterate any thoughts of Denovan. She had already contacted an agency that was recruiting doctors for jobs in Australia. She hadn't told Frank yet—she would give him time to get back on his feet—but she had mentioned it to Daphne one morning before anyone else had come in. Daphne had gazed at Kerry in disbelief then she'd given a sudden hoot of realisation.

'Aha! It's Denovan, isn't it? You and he are getting together? I knew all along he was mad about you—he never stopped looking at you when you were in the room. I thought there was something going on! I suppose you're going to join him in London, then?'

Kerry had managed to mumble, 'No, I'm not going to London. The job is in Australia.'

'What? Australia?' Daphne had gasped. 'Wow! What a place to settle down together!'

'Not…not together, Daphne, I'm afraid. By myself.'

Daphne had frowned. 'But why go so far away? I thought you loved it here. Oh, you will be missed. You're the best doctor we've ever had! No one else listens like you do. Why on earth are you going there?' Her round, kindly face had been filled with concern, then she'd looked perceptively at Kerry's pale face and said slowly, 'What's going on, lovey? There's more to this than wanting a new job, isn't there?'

Kerry had shaken her head wordlessly, but her anguished face had given her away.

'Oh, Lord, it is Denovan O'Mara, isn't it? What's happened? I was positive you and he were falling in love.'

Kerry had swallowed a lump in her throat and said in a small voice, 'I thought we'd got something going too, Daphne, but whatever it was, it's over now, and although I love him, he definitely doesn't need me, so… I don't know, I feel I need to start again.'

'Oh, you poor love.' Daphne put her arm round Kerry and hugged her. 'He must be mad not to see that you were meant for each other. But please, Kerry, please don't do anything in a hurry. It's only been a few days since Denovan left. Give it time before you make such a drastic decision.'

But the decision had been made—she'd set the ball rolling before she could change her mind, and now she gazed abstractedly across the garden, vaguely watching everyone milling around the stalls, their happy chatter a background to her sad thoughts.

'Any chance of a coffee, Dr Latimer?'

Kerry jumped out of her reverie to see Vernon Hood standing in front of her. He looked slightly embarrassed, bunching his hands in his pockets, a wary look on his face as if he was uncertain what sort of reception he was going to get from her.

'Certainly you can have some coffee,' said Kerry, smiling at him. 'You and your wife have done a marvellous job here—it's just what the village needed to cheer them up!'

He took the cup of coffee from her and put in a spoonful of sugar, stirring it in thoughtfully.

'I took your advice,' he said in a low voice. 'I'm finding it difficult, but I have stuck to the plan.' He glanced across to his wife, who was selling sweets at the sweet stall. 'Bethany's been marvellous. She told me she'd been to see you. I just wanted to thank you for suggesting this, it's given us something to do together.'

A child came running up, shouting to Vernon, 'Come on, Daddy, come on! Come and guess how many sweets are in the jar. If you get it right, we win it!'

Kerry smiled at Vernon. 'Looks like you have plenty to keep you occupied. And I must say you've done a fantastic job getting all this organised.'

She watched the little girl drag her father off to the sweet stall, and Vernon putting his arm round his wife when he got there. Perhaps he would manage to get drug-free after all and get his life back together again. She smiled to herself, the first feelings of optimism starting to stir inside her. If Vernon Hood could get his life back together, so could she! Roll on, Australia!

The stalls were being dismantled now, the bunting unhooked from the trees, and the crowds were beginning to disperse. Kerry lugged a large sack with used polystyrene cups and plates back to the bins by the house where the volunteers were clearing away.

'Kerry! Kerry! Hello!'

The voice was a child's and had a rather familiar ring to it. Kerry put the sack down and turned round. She could hardly believe her eyes as she watched Archie O'Mara scampering across the lawn towards her, his little face wreathed in a happy grin, a large football in his arms.

'Look what I've won,' he panted, looking at her gleefully through his round metal-rimmed glasses. 'I scored a goal in the net—you get a football if you do that.'

'Archie! How lovely to see you. I thought you were in London.'

'We had to come back for something important, so I'm staying with Larry and Daphne.'

'Did…did they bring you here today?'

'No, Daddy did!'

Kerry looked around the garden, her heart pounding like a drum against her ribs. Was Denovan here—was she about to bump into him?

'Where is he now?' Her voice sounded rather breathless.

'Somewhere over there,' shouted Archie carelessly, throwing the ball in the air and kicking it hard down the lawn.

Kerry looked in the direction he'd indicated, and there, standing under the trees and looking at her, was Denovan. As she watched, he started to walk towards her with a sense of purpose, his eyes never leaving her face, steady, unblinking, an unreadable expression in their clear blue depths.

Why was he coming towards her? What could he possibly have to say to her that hadn't been said before? Kerry's mouth went dry and she felt a prickling sensation at the back of her neck.

He stood in front of her, and Kerry looked up at him wordlessly, her eyes drinking in every aspect of him—his athletic figure, his strong, mobile face and firm lips.

He was just as she'd been dreaming about him every night since he'd left.

'Why are you going to Australia?' he asked very quietly. 'I didn't know that was in the pipeline.'

She stared at him and said stupidly, ignoring his question, 'Why are you back here? I thought you were about to start this amazing new job?'

'Possibly.'

Kerry frowned. 'I don't understand. And how do you know that I'm going to Australia? I haven't told anyone except for… Daphne! Did she tell you?'

A glimmer of smile touched his lips. 'She mentioned it,' he admitted. 'When do you go?'

'I don't know yet.'

'So it's not been finalised yet?'

'There's a lot of paperwork to do.' She bit her lip. 'You didn't answer my question. I asked why you'd come back—Archie said it's for something important?'

'It is important, but I'd rather not discuss it here. Do you mind if we take a walk around the field at the back of the garden?'

'Surely, Denovan, we've nothing left to say to each other?'

He took her arm. 'Oh, yes, we do,' he said firmly, guiding her to the gate that led to the field.

They were alone, just the wind whispering through the trees and a lark somewhere high above them singing his soaring song. Kerry's heart hammered against her ribs, a million unanswered questions jumbling in her mind.

'What's this all about, Denovan, this very important thing you want to tell me? We're not friends now—remember?'

He put his hands on her shoulders and looked intently into her eyes. 'You have every reason not to be my friend any more,' he said huskily. 'I've been such a damn fool. You see, I realised I'd blown our relationship sky high—messed up with you completely. I thought it was the end between us. Then I got a phone call...'

'A phone call?' echoed Kerry. She frowned up at him. 'What about?'

'It was from Daphne, and she put it bluntly—she wanted to know what on earth I'd been saying to you. And then she told me something rather amazing.'

'Amazing?' Kerry began to sound like an echo chamber, repeating everything that Denovan said.

'She said that after all that had happened she got the impression you might still be rather...fond of me?' Denovan's eyes never left Kerry's face. 'I want to know—is she right?'

Kerry started to tremble, a sudden little chink of happiness pushing its way into her sadness. 'What gave her that impression?' Her voice was shaky.

'She said you were very sad that we'd parted, and that you'd told her you'd thought we had something special together.' He smiled wryly. 'She said I was a fool—and she was right. Then she told me you were going to Australia—and it hit me like a bombshell. I suddenly realised I couldn't bear it—couldn't bear having you so far away from me.'

'Daphne seems to have told you a lot of things,' said Kerry with some asperity, but inside her the little chink of happiness had become a huge beam, flooding through her, bubbles of euphoria threatening to burst out in a big shout of delight! She opened her mouth to speak again, but he put a finger on her lips.

'Let me have my say, please, Kerry. I know I've hurt you, thrown many insults at you. I don't deserve it, but I want to know—can you ever forgive me for being so boorish, saying you'd betrayed me, told me lies?' Then he added softly, putting his finger under her chin and lifting her face towards his, 'Please, my darling Kerry, give me another chance. I love you so very much—and I want you to be the centre of my world and Archie's. I want us to be together for ever.'

His hands on her shoulders tightened, and he pulled her towards him, looking down into her eyes. 'And if you won't give me another chance,' he added firmly, 'I won't take no for an answer anyway. Archie and I will follow you anywhere you go until you say yes!'

And the big bubble of joy burst inside Kerry and she threw back her head and laughed. 'Then I'll have to forgive you, won't I?' she gulped, brushing away the happy tears that poured down her cheeks.

She wound her arms round Denovan's neck and smiled at him. 'And tell me, where is our world going to be?' she asked. 'London?'

He shook his head. 'I think it's about time I made it up with my brother, don't you? I'm coming back to

Braxton Falls, back to my roots, and I'll apply for the job of new partner—if Frank will have me!'

'I think Frank would like you to be friends,' said Kerry. 'Despite everything, I think there's a bond there you haven't realised.'

Denovan grinned. 'I'll tell him that I'm very grateful to him—after all, if he hadn't crashed his car and gone to hospital, I might never have met you! I owe him everything.'

There was a loud bang and a football came hurtling over the hedge, followed by a small boy scrambling through the gate. Archie looked crossly at his father and Kerry.

'Where have you two been?' he demanded. 'I've been looking all over the place for you.'

Denovan crouched by his little son and put his arm round his waist. 'I've got a bit of news for you,' he said. 'We're going to move from London and live here with Kerry—what do you think of that?'

Archie looked solemnly at his father. 'For ever? Near Larry and Daphne?'

'Yes.'

The little boy turned a somersault and laughed. 'That's cool, that is!' Then he looked up at them impishly. 'I'm very hungry—can we have a pizza?'

So they all went hand in hand to get a pizza.

EPILOGUE

THE sand was warm between Kerry's toes, and it stretched white and gleaming in a curve round the bay, where the waving palms rustled and the light wind made her filmy white kaftan billow out like a cloud about her. Beyond her the sea sparkled with myriad diamond drops in the hot sun, and under an awning in front of her she could see Denovan turning to watch her as she walked towards him on their wedding day.

By Denovan's side was Frank—how glad she was that he had consented to be best man. After all that had gone on between the two brothers, this was sweet indeed. And by her side, holding her hand and jumping up and down excitedly, was Archie, wearing stripy cotton shorts and a little straw hat. Sitting on chairs under the trees were her mother and sister, her mother dabbing tears of happiness from her eyes.

This was the island she'd thought she'd never get to, the dream she'd thought she'd lost when Frank had been injured. It was hard to believe that now, only a few weeks later, her life had turned round and she was miraculously marrying Denovan O'Mara in a place where 'golden sands fringed by waving palms and an azure sea' surrounded her.

Denovan took Kerry's hand as she came beside him and held it tightly. He didn't speak aloud, but she knew when his deep blue eyes held hers so tenderly that he loved her. And that was all she needed to know.

* * * * *

A sneaky peek at next month...

Medical Romance™

CAPTIVATING MEDICAL DRAMA—WITH HEART

My wish list for next month's titles...

In stores from 6th July 2012:

- ❑ Sydney Harbour Hospital: Marco's Temptation – Fiona McArthur
- & Waking Up With His Runaway Bride – Louisa George
- ❑ The Legendary Playboy Surgeon
- & Falling for Her Impossible Boss – Alison Roberts
- ❑ Letting Go With Dr Rodriguez – Fiona Lowe
- & Dr Tall, Dark...and Dangerous? – Lynne Marshall

Available at WHSmith, Tesco, Asda, Eason, Amazon and Apple

Just can't wait?

Visit us Online

You can buy our books online a month before they hit the shops! **www.millsandboon.co.uk**

0612/

Book of the Month

MILLS & BOON

We love this book because...

Alison Roberts' Heartbreakers of St Patrick's Hospital duet should come with a health warning —*dishy doctors: heart palpitations likely!* No one is immune to Dr Connor Matthews and neurosurgeon Oliver Dawson's irresistible charms!

On sale 6th July

isit us
Online

Find out more at
www.millsandboon.co.uk/BOTM

0612/BOTM

Join the Mills & Boon Book Club

Subscribe to **Medical** today for 3, 6 or 12 months and you could **save over £40!**

We'll also treat you to these fabulous extras:

- **FREE L'Occitane gift set worth £10**
- **FREE home delivery**
- **Books up to 2 months ahead of the shops**
- **Bonus books, exclusive offers... and much more!**

Subscribe now at

www.millsandboon.co.uk/subscribeme

Visit us Online

Save over £40 – find out more at
www.millsandboon.co.uk/subscribeme

SUBS/OFFER/M